A city-
Cudmo
active ch____ ___ and a ___y daft dog.__
ate, with an MSc in Human Resources, _____ ___
many years working in multinational companies and
can't believe she is lucky enough now to have a job that
involves daydreaming about love and handsome men!
You can visit Katrina at katrinacudmore.com.

Though her name is frequently on bestseller lists, **Allison
Leigh**'s high point as a writer is hearing from readers
that they laughed, cried or lost sleep while reading her
books. She credits her family with great patience for the
time she's parked at her computer, and for blessing her
with the kind of love she wants her readers to share with
the characters living in the pages of her books. Contact
her at allisonleigh.com.

Also by Katrina Cudmore

Swept into the Rich Man's World
The Best Man's Guarded Heart
Her First-Date Honeymoon
Their Baby Surprise
Tempted by the Greek Tycoon

Also by Allison Leigh

Show Me a Hero
Yuletide Baby Bargain
A Child Under His Tree
The BFF Bride
One Night in Weaver...
A Weaver Christmas Gift
A Weaver Beginning
A Weaver Vow
Fortune's Homecoming
Wild West Fortune

Discover more at millsandboon.co.uk

CHRISTMAS WITH THE DUKE

KATRINA CUDMORE

THE RANCHER'S CHRISTMAS PROMISE

ALLISON LEIGH

MILLS & BOON

First Published in Great Britain 2018
by Mills & Boon, an imprint of HarperCollinsPublishers,
1 London Bridge Street, London, SE1 9GF

Christmas With the Duke © 2018 Katrina Cudmore
The Rancher's Christmas Promise © 2018 Allison Lee Johnson

ISBN: 978-0-263-26535-4

1018

MIX
Paper from
responsible sources
FSC C007454

This book is produced from independently certified FSC™
paper to ensure responsible forest management.

For more information visit: www.harpercollins.co.uk/green

Printed and bound in Spain
by CPI, Barcelona

CHRISTMAS WITH THE DUKE

KATRINA CUDMORE

To Ava, my modern girl full of wit,
intelligence, acceptance and ambition.

The world is yours to conquer.

CHAPTER ONE

'GOOD GIRL, CIARA, just another foot to go and you'll be there.'

Despite her shaking legs, Ciara Harris could not help but grin to herself at her boss's good-natured encouragement. Sean was the head gardener at Loughmore Castle and, having known Ciara since she was a teenager, at times still treated her as one despite the fact that she was now thirty years of age.

Her smile soon faded, however, when she made the fatal mistake of looking down from her twenty-foot-high perch up on the stepladder. The Connemara marble floor of the Great Hall swam up and then back down in a sickening vortex.

She grasped the stepladder's metal rail for dear life and cast an unhappy eye over the reason she was twenty feet up in the air. The fine-boned angel, dressed in gold silk, her cheeks painted with a dash of pink blush, calmly considered Ciara back, as though wondering why she was making such a fuss.

Standing with Sean at the base of the stepladder, looking way too amused for her own good, Libby the head chef at Loughmore called up to Ciara. 'Sometime in the next year would be helpful, Ciara. I've five layers of Christmas cake to ice and a ton of petit fours to make for tomorrow night's lighting ceremony,'

Ciara scowled down at Libby, who had one foot casually propped on the bottom rung of the ladder, with a glass of mulled wine in one hand and a mince pie in the other, and muttered through clenched teeth, 'I nominate *you* to climb up here next Christmas.'

'Oh, no, the pleasure will be all yours until a new member of staff is recruited,' Libby called back, with a tad too much relish.

Given the amused expressions of all thirty or so of the other Loughmore staff, who had come into the hall to watch the final finish to the tree decoration and, more to the point, rush to the buffet table, to partake in the refreshments Libby's team had organised, Ciara guessed they shared Libby's entertainment at Ciara's terror.

'Gird your loins...' That was what her granddad had used to say to her as she'd buried herself beneath her blankets as a teenager, when he'd called her before dawn in order to polish the vast marble floor she was now suspended over. To this day she still had no idea what that expression really meant, but she knew it had been his way of telling her just to get on with it.

Ciara's mum was definitely cut from the same cloth as her grandad. As a child, whenever Ciara had grumbled about a playground slight or wished she had a sister to play with, or a dad who would come to watch her play football like all the other dads, her mum would say, 'Don't overthink things, Ciara. Accept that life is unfair, put a smile on your face and just get on with it.'

Which she now needed to do.

Tentatively she moved on to the next step, inhaling deeply of the pine-scented air, before humming a Christmas classic in the hope of channelling some of the festive spirit.

Every Christmas Sean cut down a Noble Fir from Loughmore Wood. It was always huge—it had to be to suit its new home, the Great Hall at Loughmore Castle, which lived up to its title by having a forty-foot vaulted timber ceiling. But this year Sean had surpassed himself by cutting down a stunning blue needle perfectly symmetrical twenty-four-foot specimen.

It had taken the gardening crew of five an entire day to transport it, install it and hang two thousand lights and the endless baubles the Benson family had collected over the years from the tree's branches.

Sean had rather cleverly waited until the last moment to announce that it was a castle tradition that the newest employee always had the honour of placing the delicate porcelain angel.

For a few moments Ciara had actually bought that story. But then she had spotted the mischief twinkling in Sean's eyes, and the elbowing amongst her fellow gardeners. Honour, indeed. More like the short straw. Obviously no one else wanted the task—especially when Libby's mince pies were on offer.

She had tried to protest that technically she *wasn't* the newest employee, given she had worked in Loughmore as a cleaner during her school summer holidays. But her protest had fallen on deaf ears in the buffet table raid.

Anyway, as the only female member of staff on the gardening team, and a conservation and heritage horticulturalist to boot, Ciara knew that, apart from Sean, the rest of the gardening team were sceptical about her role and her ideas.

Only yesterday there had been a stand-off between her and one of the others, who had wanted to cut some holly for decorating the castle. Ciara had tried to explain to him just how important the holly and its berries were for the birds and small animals, both as a source for food and shelter, but her colleague had shaken his head and muttered, 'You're pure cracked, Ciara...' before walking away.

So, ignoring the screaming alarm bells in her brain, she had grabbed hold of the angel and begun the climb. It was only when she'd been halfway up the stepladder that the voice of reason in her head had finally broken through her indignation at her co-workers and pointed out that she was terrified of heights.

But now, determined to continue on, aided by the combination of singing and her refusal to look down, she soon reached the top of the tree. Gingerly she leant into the branches, trying her best to ignore the pine needles stabbing against her bare forearms.

The ladder wobbled ever so slightly. Below her she heard a few gasps.

'Steady now…take it easy,' Sean called up.

Ciara leant in even further, keen to get the job over and done with. Inching forward, she managed to place the angel on the top branch, using her fingertips to straighten it when she slouched to the left.

Below her, applause rang out.

She'd done it!

Her elation lasted all of five seconds—until it dawned on her that she now had to climb back down.

Gripping the rails, she began her descent, her feet blindly searching for each tread beneath her.

The Christmas tree was positioned in front of the Great Hall's vast Pugin fireplace and a gold over-mantel mirror. A few steps down from the top, in a gap between the branches, Ciara grimaced when she caught her reflection in the mirror. Pine needles were scattered in her hair and a smear of dirt stained the collar of her denim shirt.

And then she saw him.

Standing at the heavy wooden entrance door to the castle. Silhouetted by the late-afternoon burnished gold sky.

Staring up at her.

She faltered mid-step, her heart dropping to her steel-toecap boots and then catapulting back up into her chest.

Was it really him? After all these years?

Below her the idle chatter of the other staff died away. Ten seconds later all hell broke loose.

'Your Grace! I had no idea... I understood from the estate office you were to remain at Bainsworth until the twenty-ninth, as is tradition.' Stephen, the head butler at Loughmore, was barely able to keep the panic from his voice.

Ciara just about managed to find the next step on the ladder before turning to face the scene unfolding below her.

All the crowd had shifted away from the tree to stand a respectful distance from him... Tom Benson... Eleventh Duke of Bainsworth. Under one arm he was carrying a scruffy-looking terrier, who was panting and wriggling in his eagerness to be let down.

The Duke had spent his childhood summers here in Loughmore, adored and indulged by all the staff. But he had not visited the castle for the past twelve years. The newer staff had never met him before, and even those who knew him seemed uncertain of how to greet him or even who they were dealing with.

For the briefest second he glanced up at her, those silver eyes giving nothing away. Ciara gripped the ladder rail even tighter, feeling completely off-balance. He still had the ability to make the world more vivid, more exhilarating, just by being in the same room.

He had changed. At eighteen he had been boyishly handsome, with brown hair deliberately too long and a restless energy that had never seen him stand still. Now his short hair only hinted at previous curls, and all that restless energy seemed to have been turned inwards, transforming him into a silent observer.

The intelligence in his eyes was sharper, his tall and lean athletic build more defined. The smoothness of his eighteen-year-old skin was gone, replaced by the hint of a five o'clock shadow and faint lines at the corners of his eyes.

His grey wool overcoat, gleaming black brogues and the dark suit underneath were in keeping not only with his title but also with his position as the owner of a chain of globally renowned restaurants that bore his name—Tom's.

The last time she had seen him he had been wearing faded jeans and a crumpled polo shirt. He had caught the last flight from London to Dublin one late September night. Ciara flinched at the memory of that night and how they had argued. Across the hall she saw his shoulders stiffen even more, as though he was remembering that night too.

He flicked his gaze away from her and lowered his dog to the ground. It ambled away to sniff at a nearby pot plant. Then the Duke walked towards Stephen.

Both men shook hands before Tom…no, the Duke, as she needed to remember to call him now, said, 'My schedule changed and allowed me the opportunity to travel early. My mother, the Duchess, and my sisters want to spend Christmas here in Loughmore…' He paused before adding, 'Away from Bainsworth Hall.'

Uneasy silence descended as everyone reflected on the reason why that would be the case.

Then, clearing his throat, Stephen said, 'On behalf of myself and all the staff here at Loughmore, condolences on the death of your father.'

With a stiff nod of his head the Duke acknowledged Stephen's words. Then yet more awkward silence followed as everyone waited for the Duke to speak. To acknowledge their condolences or to explain why he was here earlier than expected. Perhaps even to explain why he hadn't visited Loughmore in years, or why it had taken him five months since his father's death to visit.

But instead he caught everyone unawares as he moved forward and began to introduce himself to the rest of the staff.

Libby was the first in line. She blushed and smiled and thrust a plate of gingerbread Santas in the Duke's direction. He declined her offer with a polite shake of his head.

Maggie, the head of Housekeeping, was next in line. Maggie had used to fondly scold the Duke as a teenager, for the endless mess he'd created around the castle—especially when he had friends to stay. Now she looked as though she wanted to hug him, as she had each summer when he'd arrived back from Eton. But the Duke held his hand out to her and formally they shook hands.

Forgotten by all and sundry—Sean and Libby having long neglected their promise to hold the ladder steady—Ciara had no option but to climb down on her own. Her already wobbly legs now felt truly un-coordinated. Her heart was unhelpfully lurching about her chest and the single looping question in her brain was slowly driving her to distraction—what on earth was she going to say to him when they came face to face?

When she was nervous her default setting was to joke and make light of the situation. Sometimes it worked, and defused the tension, but at other times it fell flat and she ended up looking like a complete fool. It was something she was trying to control, but it was hard to change a habit of a lifetime.

But maybe she was overthinking this. In all likelihood she was just a forgotten memory from his teenage years.

Long-buried memories accompanied each of her steps downward. Watching him cook in her gran's tiny cottage kitchen, where his inventiveness as a chef had turned from a hobby into an all-consuming passion. Kissing him under the bridge at the far end of the lake, with the confined space, dim light and the trickle of water amplifying their laughter and chatter.

She remembered how Tom would climb to the top of the Japanese cedar in the Arboretum and dare her to join him… But even watching him forty feet off the ground had left her feeling giddy, and she would barely climb ten feet before giving up. And the way he would block out the sun when he leant over her as they'd lain in a mossy hollow they had found at the centre of Loughmore Wood, the affection shining from his eyes confounding her.

He had convinced her that the hollow had been created by a meteor. And it was there that her passion for native Irish plant species had begun. Later she would train to be a horticulturist, driven by the desire to preserve those plants and to conserve the historical importance of gardens such as Loughmore for future generations. Lying on that soft green blanket of moss, her hand in his, she had seen up close for the first time the intricate and delicate beauty of those often rare plants. Her gaze would shift from him to the breathtaking wonder of willowherb and Black Medick, and the world had been full of wonder and possibility and maybes.

But then reality would dawn and she would have to return to work. Dressed in her cleaning uniform, she would nod politely in his direction whenever they passed in the corridors of the castle, and he would do likewise in return. She'd tried to pretend to herself that she didn't care, but deep down the easy distance he was always so capable of had made her wonder at the truth of their relationship.

Lost in thought, she clambered down the ladder—but her lack of concentration caught up with her when she was less than six feet from the bottom. Her foot moved to connect with the next step down, but she must have overreached because suddenly she was feeling nothing but open air. With a yelp, she clung desperately to the ladder. But in slow motion she felt her whole body fall backwards, and then she was flying through the air.

Her only thoughts were of the hard marble floor about to greet her and the ignominy of her situation.

Talk about making a holy show of yourself.

But instead of feeling her bones crunching against a hard surface she fell into a solid grip.

Winded, she threw her head back in confusion to come really close to those silver eyes.

'You're still a terrible climber, I see.' His voice was a low rumble.

She tried to leap out of his arms, but they tightened around her. And she had to bite back the crazy temptation to say, *Welcome home, Tom, you've been missed.*

Cursing under his breath, Tom pulled the wriggling Ciara closer, trying to ignore the energy surge flooding his body at having her hip pressed against his stomach, her tumble of auburn hair softly tickling his wrist.

Other staff were starting to crowd around them, fussing over Ciara. He needed to make sure she was okay. He needed some space to think.

He shifted around and caught a horrified-looking Stephen's eye. 'Please bring tea to the morning room.'

He moved quickly away, Ciara still in his arms. Past the tapestries and family portraits lining the wide corridor. Not looking down. Trying to remember that he had come to Loughmore with one single purpose.

Boarding his private plane earlier that day, at the City of London airport, he had been determined to approach the next week logically. Even though he had done a double-take when he had seen Ciara's name as he'd glanced through the names of personnel employed at Loughmore that the estate office at Bainsworth Hall had sent through, he had remained determined that he was taking the right decision in returning to Loughmore and making the announcement that had to be made.

But as he had wound his way from the outskirts of Dublin city and into County Wicklow, the Garden of Ireland, past familiar landmarks—the rolling Wicklow mountains, the hidden lakes, the silent narrow roads with towering trees and road signs for ancient monuments, the Christmas lights threaded across the narrow main street of Avoca Village, the doors of the brightly painted terraced cottages wearing Christmas wreaths—something had shifted in him.

And when he had come to the brow of Broom Hill and Loughmore Castle had appeared below him in the valley he had pulled his rental car to the side of the road and climbed out. Standing on the edge of a ditch, in the fading light of a winter afternoon, he had buttoned his coat against the sharp breeze carried all the way in from the distant Irish Sea with bittersweet memories confounding him.

Loughmore Castle hadn't changed. It still sat proudly in the valley, its medieval tower standing pencil-sharp against the blue winter sky, the Victorian addition flanking it to the west, the Georgian courtyard to the rear. To the front of the castle sat Loughmore Lake, where Tom had learnt to sail and had had his first experimental kiss in the shadows of the boat house, with Hatta Coleridge-Hall.

To this day, his mother still dropped not so subtle hints that Hatta would make a good duchess.

It hadn't been until Ciara, though, that he had understood what a kiss should *really* be.

To the rear of the castle, beyond the walled garden and orchards, lay Loughmore Wood. The place where he and Ciara used to escape to, to talk and poke fun at each other at first and then, over the long weeks of that final summer together, to make love.

Standing there on the edge of that ditch, with the icy breeze whistling around him, he had winced at all those wonderful and sad and painful memories and he had known more than ever that he had come to the right decision on the future of Loughmore. It was time he put the ghosts of his past in Loughmore behind him for once and for all.

And as he had driven through the imposing limestone arched entrance to the estate, and along the three-quarter-mile entrance avenue past the wide open fields, where deer were sheltering under oak and chestnut trees, he had been pulled back to his excitement as a child, when he had travelled to Loughmore each summer, relishing the freedom he'd got there, away from the ever-present sense of failure that had marked his schooldays.

His younger sisters, Kitty and Fran, had brought friends for company, and on occasions, to satisfy his parents' insistence that he 'socialise and network', Tom had too, but in truth he had wanted nothing more but to immerse himself in castle life. He had driven tractors, helped bring in the hay and milked the cows. He had spent hours with Jack Casey, the Yard Manager at Loughmore's stables, learning about horses, and even more hours in the kitchen with Jack's wife Mary, at first devouring her home baking and then, to his own surprise, cooking and baking himself under her guidance.

She had grown nervous about his visits, politely asking what his father would say, but he had charmed his way around her resistance. In time he had learned of his father's attitude to his passion for cooking but back then it had been his secret.

And then, one summer, Jack and Mary's granddaughter Ciara Harris had blown into the estate—like a turbocharged breath of fresh air. Funny, outspoken, often unknowingly irreverent, she had questioned everything.

And for the first time he had seen that his life could be different...

A fire was lit in the morning room, where table lamps cast faint shadows over the pale pink embossed wallpaper. Before the fire on a Persian rug was a footstool, still bearing the business and scientific journals and periodicals his father had insisted were to be ordered for all three of the estate's main properties—Bainsworth Hall, the two-thousand-acre main seat of the family in Sussex, Loughmore Castle, and Glencorr, the family hunting lodge in Scotland.

He lowered Ciara on to the sofa in front of the fire and stood back. Too late he remembered the time he had found her in here cleaning, and had dragged her giggling in protest to the sofa and kissed her until they were both breathless, hot with the intoxicating frustration of unfulfilled desire.

He shook away the memory and tried to focus on the woman before him—not the girl he had once known 'Are you injured in any way?'

Immediately she stood and moved away from him, stepping behind the arm of the sofa as though that would shield her from him. She folded her arms and gave a wry shrug. 'Just my pride.'

For long moments they regarded each other, the crack and hiss of burning wood the only sound in the room.

Ciara tucked a lock of her long red hair behind her ear and rubbed her cheek. She rolled back on one heel. as though fighting the urge to move even further away. She regarded him warily and then, in a low voice, asked, 'How have you been?'

She'd always used to do this to him. Disarm him with the simplest of questions that left him floundering for an answer. How did you sum up twelve years?

'Good. And you?'

She tilted her head, the deep auburn tones of her hair

shining in the light of a nearby Tiffany lamp and answered, 'Yeah, good too.'

A discreet knock sounded on the door to the room. Stephen entered, carrying a tray bearing a silver tea service and china cups. Storm bounded into the room behind him and jumped up on Ciara, his paws clawing at the denim of her black jeans.

He called to Storm, but the terrier ignored him as Ciara bent over and patted him, murmuring, 'Hello, cutie.'

Stephen placed the tea service on a side table, along with some delicate triangular sandwiches and some mince pies, before awkwardly considering Ciara. Then, clearing his throat to gain her attention, because she was still chatting with Storm, he said, 'If you are feeling better, Ciara, there is tea ready in the staff kitchen.'

Ciara straightened. Glanced in Tom's direction and then went to leave with Stephen.

Tom gritted his teeth. 'Stay and have tea here.'

Stephen did a poor job at hiding his surprise at Tom's words but, gathering up Tom's overcoat, simply asked, 'Would you like me to take your dog away, sir?'

'He's called Storm—and, no, he can stay here with me.'

After Stephen had left, Ciara motioned towards the door. 'I should go.'

'Why?'

'Staff don't have tea with the Duke.'

'I'm not my parents. I don't give a fig about what's the *done thing* or protocol. Now, have some tea and stop arguing with me.'

She looked as though she *was* going to argue with him, but then with a resigned shrug she went to the side table and poured tea into two cups, adding milk to one. Turning, she brought one of the jade-rimmed cups, with the family crest printed inside, to him.

Black tea—just as he had always drunk it. Was she even conscious that she'd remembered?

He gestured for her to take a seat on the sofa facing the fire, and took a seat himself on an occasional chair facing the bay window overlooking the lake.

Ciara watched as Storm settled on his feet, his belly lying as usual on Tom's shoes.

'Why did you call him Storm?'

'I didn't. He belonged to my ex-girlfriend. When she decided to return home to Japan I adopted him.'

Ciara said nothing in response. Instead she sipped her tea quickly.

Tom watched her, still thrown by seeing her after so many years.

They had once been so close. Ciara had been the first person ever to ask what his dreams were, who had seen beyond his title and the expected path that had been mapped out for him from the moment he was born. It was Ciara who had encouraged him to follow his passion for cooking—who had challenged him to write to some of London's top restaurants seeking an apprenticeship. She had been the first person to believe in him. The first person who had helped him see who he *was* rather than who he was supposed to be.

But she was also the first person to have broken his heart; in truth the only ever person to do so. After Ciara he had been more circumspect in his relationships.

He could not go on reliving the painful memories of that time. It was time for closure.

Placing his teacup on a small walnut console table, he said, 'I understand your grandparents have retired?'

His question elicited a smile from her. 'Yes, they've moved back to County Galway. They bought a house in Renvyle—close to the beach. They love it there, but they miss Loughmore. Grandad especially misses the horses, and both miss the other staff. After working here for over fifty years leaving wasn't an easy decision for them.'

Years ago Tom would have understood why her grandparents missed Loughmore. He had once loved it more than any other place on this earth. But what had happened between him and Ciara had ruined his love affair with the castle. Now it represented guilt and shame and pain.

But did the fact that Ciara was working here mean that she had been able to bury the past? Was she unaffected by those memories?

'Is that why you're working here now—did you miss it?'

Ciara gave a non-committal shrug. 'I trained as a conservation and heritage horticulturist. Knowing how many rare Irish plant species there are at Loughmore, I applied for the gardening role that was advertised here during the spring of this year. You remember Sean? The head gardener?' When Tom nodded she continued. 'In the interview I told Sean about my interest in identifying and conserving the rare and threatened plants that are here. Thankfully he was interested in the project, and he also asked me to lead a programme to reintroduce heritage plants back onto the estate.'

'All those days in the woods…' Too late he realised his words.

Ciara flinched and looked into the fire, shifting her feet, clad in heavy boots, further beneath the sofa, as though she was trying to hide them.

In their last summer together, when they were both eighteen, their relationship had become much more than just friendship and flirting. It had started with a kiss in Loughmore Wood, as they had lain staring at the stars one July night. That summer had been wild and intoxicating. And special. They had made love several times. The first time for them both.

As the summer had drawn to an end, and he'd had to

leave for his apprenticeship at one of London's Michelin-starred restaurants, Ciara for her horticultural course in Dublin, they had promised to stay in touch. See each other over term-breaks. It had been much too early to talk about a future together, but Tom had silently envisaged a time when they would be together for ever.

And then one day in late September, as he'd dashed from his apartment into the rain, late for work, he had crashed into Ciara as he'd rounded the corner of his street. Delighted, but thrown at seeing her standing on Kentish Town Road as the bus he needed to catch sailed by, he had simply stared at her when she'd told him she was pregnant.

He hadn't been able to take it in. He had muttered something about them working it out and that he had to get to work—that his head chef took pleasure in firing apprentices for being late. He'd given her the keys to his apartment. Promised to call her during his break.

Only hours later had he come to his senses. He had ignored the head chef's threats to fire him for leaving early and, despite the cost, had taken a taxi home. His father had refused to support him in his bid to become a chef, telling him it was 'beneath a Benson.' He had even threatened disinheritance. Tom hadn't known how he was going to support Ciara and a baby. But he'd known he would find a way.

His father's stance on Tom's career had summed up their relationship—he had never trusted Tom to make his own decisions, and dug his heels in when Tom went against his wishes. He'd pushed him further and further away, his disappointment and anger at Tom clear—so much so that since Tom had commenced his training they had rarely spoken to one another.

When he'd got to his apartment it had been empty. His frantic calls to Ciara had gone unanswered, so he had called a friend who'd got him to Heathrow within the hour. Just in time to catch the last flight to Dublin.

He'd gone to her mum's address. But the house had been empty. He'd waited on the doorstep and at one in the morning a taxi had pulled up. Ciara, pale and drawn, had emerged first, followed by her stony-faced mum. Ciara had refused to speak to him and both women had gone into the house, the front door slamming behind them.

An hour later the door had swung open again and her mother had whispered furiously, 'She'll talk to you for five minutes. No longer. This is to be the last time you ever see her. My daughter deserves someone better than *you*.'

He had tried to hold Ciara. To say he was sorry. But she had quietly told him she had miscarried and then asked him to leave.

When he had refused to go her expression had turned to one of contempt. And icily she had told him of her regret at sleeping with him. That she had made a stupid mistake she'd regret for ever.

He had returned to London, and despite the humiliation and guilt burning in his stomach at her rejection, at how he had failed her, he had called her several times a week for months. But she had never answered his calls.

Now, he looked up as Ciara stood, her fingertips working against a smear of dirt on her collar. 'I need to go and help with cleaning up after the tree installation.' She paused and bit her lip, and then, tilting her chin, asked, 'Can I meet with you tomorrow?'

'Why?'

'I'd like you to understand what we're trying to achieve with both the conservation and the heritage programmes I have introduced.' Her chin tilted back even further, and a hint of colour appeared in her cheeks. 'To continue with the programme next year we'll need a larger budget.'

He stood and walked towards the marble fireplace. The fire was burning out. He had planned on briefing the senior management at Loughmore first. But, given their history, and the way he had messed up everything all those years ago, the least Ciara deserved was his honesty.

Placing his hands behind his back, he squared his shoulders, turned back to her and said, 'I'm putting Loughmore up for sale.'

CHAPTER TWO

FOR A BRIEF second Ciara hoped Tom was teasing her. Like he'd always used to do.

He had spent one whole summer trying to convince her that the entire dairy herd at Loughmore talked to him. Whenever they passed the grazing cows on their way to the woods he would stop and chat to them over the still-to-ripen blackcurrant laden hedges, relaying back to her what they were saying.

'Blue says it's going to rain later, but Nelly says Blue is talking rubbish. What's that, Nelly…? Ciara's looking beautiful today? Can't say I'd noticed it myself.'

At which point Ciara would give him a friendly thump on the arm and start pedalling her bike away, trying not to laugh, happiness bubbling in her chest at his words and at the way he would softly gaze at her when he said she looked beautiful.

But now there was no softness or laughter in his eyes.

She stepped towards him, murmurs of panic breaking through her disbelief. 'Sell Loughmore? Are you serious?'

He looked away from her and out towards the formal terraced gardens of Loughmore, rolling his neck from side to side. 'With my work commitments I rarely get the chance to come here. It doesn't make sense to hold on to the castle and estate.'

His voice was impassive, as though selling Loughmore was nothing other than yet another business deal to him.

Ciara moved away to the tea tray, staggered by just how devastated she felt by his casualness, by how little the castle meant to him. Her teacup rattled as she poured more tea. She could not let him see how upset she felt.

Loughmore was everything to her. Embraced not only by her grandparents, but also the rest of the staff, it had been a refuge from her lonely childhood in Dublin. It was where she had fallen in love for the first time...with the man so offhandedly telling her now he was selling it. The man she had lost her virginity to. The man who had created a baby with her, here on the grounds he was so indifferently about to sell.

Anger and deep upset fought for supremacy in her chest. She inhaled time and time again. Trying to calm down. Eventually she managed to say, 'Loughmore has been in your family for ever...you can't sell it.'

He glanced at her unhappily before walking towards the log basket at the side of the fireplace. 'There's no point in retaining a property that's never used.'

Seeing he was about to take some firewood and add it to the now-dying fire, she dashed forward and took hold of the log in his hand. 'I'll take care of the fire,' she said tersely.

She pulled at the log but he refused to let go. 'I'm perfectly capable of looking after it,' he said.

Ciara tried again to drag the log towards herself. 'It's not expected of you. I should have seen to it.'

With a heavy sigh Tom prised the log out of her grip, muttering, 'To hell with what's "expected".'

Bending, he lifted another log from the basket before walking back to the fire.

'I don't have the same old-fashioned expectations of my staff as my father did.' Throwing the logs onto the fire, sending a shower of sparks rising upward, he added, 'I thought you'd know that.'

Standing upright, he pulled off his suit jacket and threw it on the back of a nearby chair. His tie soon followed. Then he eyed her silently, his mouth set angrily, his shoulders squared, his hands propped on his hips.

They'd used to have stand-offs like this before. But back then Tom hadn't been quite so resolute. There was a harder edge to him now.

Ciara rolled back on her feet. She was unsure how to play this. He was the Duke now. She had to respect his position. But the anger and hurt inside her had her saying curtly, 'Those logs are smothering the fire—you need to set them at a more upright angle.'

Tom scowled at her. 'I didn't say I would do a good job of it, though, did I?'

And then for the briefest moment his mouth twitched.

Her heart took flight in her chest.

Oh, Lord, he was always irresistible when he smiled. His eyes would become magnetic in their silver sparkle and his wide-mouthed grin would swallow up everything that was wrong and horrible in the world.

But today the hint of that smile was nanosecond-brief before he turned back to the fire.

Ciara leant against the warm marble mantelpiece as he adjusted the logs with a fire iron. 'You're going to cause consternation amongst the staff if you change the way things are done around here.'

Hunkered down before the fire, he turned to her, those silver eyes holding hers. Softly he said, 'I'm selling Lough-more, Ciara.'

She winced at his words, but even more so at the heat that seeped through her body at the memory of how he'd used to whisper softly into her ear, telling her how much she meant to him. She'd used to laugh off what he said, calling him a chancer, terrified of believing him.

She moved away, taking care to skirt the antique Persian rug and cringing at her clumpy footsteps on the oak floorboards, thanks to her heavy work boots. She stood at the window on the opposite side of the room overlooking the walled garden. She had spent all summer working in there, reintroducing specimens that had been removed during an ill-judged replanting over forty years ago. What on earth would happen to the castle and its unique gardens and grounds if new owners took over?

Surely his mother and sisters weren't in agreement with him selling? They spent every summer and New Year here, and from what Ciara could tell they adored it. His mother was a remote and formal figure, who kept her interactions with staff to a minimum, but her affection and loyalty for Loughmore was clear in the way both she and the late Duke had carried out a thorough tour of every single part of the property each time they returned, making instructions on improvements and repairs to be made.

'What do your family think?'

'I haven't told them yet. I'll do so in the New Year.' He paused and frowned. Cleared his throat. 'A hotel consortium has signalled its interest in acquiring Loughmore.'

'Loughmore turned into a *hotel*! They'll change the castle beyond recognition. I've seen similar developments all over Ireland. They'll add on modern conference centres... build new homes and golf courses on the grounds. They'll wreck the place. Would you be happy to see Loughmore changed so utterly?'

'Things can't stay the same for ever—I'm sure whoever buys it will be sympathetic to its history.'

'I wouldn't be so certain. And have you thought about the staff? Loughmore and working for your family means *everything* to them.'

Tom gave an exasperated flick of his hand. 'That's why I'm here—I want to give them as much notice as I can. And I'll do my best to ensure they are all employed by the new owners'

'Working in Loughmore isn't just a job for the staff, though, it's a way of life. Many of them come from families that have worked on the estate for generations. They *love* Loughmore—they're immensely proud to work for your family.'

He considered her unhappily for long seconds and then gave a terse shake of his head. 'I'm holding a meeting with the senior staff tomorrow morning and I will brief all the other staff after that. The hotel group is keen for the sale to go ahead as soon as possible.'

'Can't it wait until after Christmas?'

'No. It's better the staff have as much notice as possible.' Moving towards the door he said, 'I have some work to do. I need to get my laptop from the car.'

'Stephen will have had it carried in already.' Pushing in front of him she added, 'Let me go and find out where he's put it—I suspect the library.'

She reached for the doorknob and pulled the door open an inch. But suddenly Tom was behind her, closing it with a push of his open palm.

For long seconds she stood with her back to him. He was wearing an aftershave she didn't recognise. But she did recognise the chain of reactions he caused whenever he came close—the thrill in her stomach, the inability to breathe, the heat that whipped through every cell in her body.

'Why are you acting like this?'

She jerked at his soft voice. Willed herself not to lean back into him.

Slowly she turned around. She breathed deeply against

the impulse to reach out and run her thumb against his evening shadow…and then along the hard lines of his lips.

'Acting like what?'

His head tilted. 'As if you have to run after me…do every small task that I can do for myself.'

She hesitated, but then the question spilled out of her. 'Selling Loughmore…has it anything to do with what happened between us?'

He stepped back a bare inch, but it was enough to allow her to breathe.

His mouth tensed. 'Why would it?'

Twelve years ago, after the initial shock of discovering she was pregnant had worn off, she had naively hoped she and Tom would somehow cope. She had known it wouldn't be easy—they were both only eighteen, after all, with their own dreams and ambitions to follow. But her biggest mistake in her desperation to believe everything would be okay had been foolishly ignoring the fact that they were from different worlds, with families who didn't approve of what they believed was nothing more than a friendship.

Know your place, Ciara. Don't be getting any notions.

That had been her gran's constant refrain. It had used to drive her crazy—but no more so than the way she'd been treated by Tom's family, who didn't even seem to realise she existed as she went about her cleaning duties throughout the castle. She was a staff member, and she had been warned time and time again never to speak to a member of the family unless spoken to, and to leave a room if any of them entered.

When Tom had invited her to some social events in the castle, his parents' disapproval had been obvious. As had his sisters' awkward embarrassment at having a member of staff in their midst. Their friendship had caused raised eyebrows not only in their families but also in the wider community.

One evening, at a recital that had been held in the castle, she had overheard two of the Duchess's friends talking.

"What does she think she's up to? Have you heard that accent of hers? As if a *Benson* would have anything to do with a working-class girl from Dublin."

No one but her mother had ever found out that they'd become more than friends. They had agreed to keep their relationship a secret. At first Ciara had been happy with that, but in their final weeks together, as they'd grown ever closer, the secrecy and lying had felt all wrong. It had felt as though she was living two separate lives—as though they were doing something shameful and what they had was nothing but a lie.

That day she had told him about the pregnancy she had flown home to Dublin early, unable to face any further humiliation. The sharp drawn-out pain in her stomach had started over the Irish Sea.

The moment she'd walked in the door of her mum's terraced house in Coolock her mum had instantly known something was wrong. She had taken her to the Rotunda Hospital, holding her hand for the entire taxi journey.

The fact that her mum had held her hand had freaked Ciara out—her mum wasn't given to demonstrative acts, and Ciara had known then that her baby was in serious trouble.

Later, after a young male doctor with sad eyes had gently told her she had miscarried, she had told her mum who the father was. Her mum had paled, called her a 'big eejit' and then turned away to stare out of the hospital window, before returning to her side and admitting her own relationship with Tom's father when she was Ciara's age.

Her mum had stumbled over her words, and the difficulty of confiding her secrets had been obvious in the anger in her eyes, the tension in her mouth. She'd only found out that Tom's father was marrying Lady Selena

Phillips when it had been announced in the newspapers. She had called him at Bainsworth Hall. He'd eventually returned her call, incredulous that she hadn't realised they could never *possibly* have a future together, and telling her it was his duty to marry well.

Less than a year later Ciara's mum had married herself, after a rebound romance with a man who had subsequently walked out on them when Ciara was only a year old. Ciara's grandparents had disapproved of the marriage, and until she was a teenager there had been no contact between her mum and her grandparents.

Her childhood had been lonely. Her mum had worked long hours and Ciara had spent most evenings on her own. When her mum had come home, she'd always been too tired to talk, or to play with Ciara.

Her mum's confession that night in the hospital had been the first and only time her mum had opened up to her—allowed Ciara even a glimpse into her emotions. The default position in the Harris household was to be glib and pretend all was okay, to bury emotion beneath laughter and avoidance.

Now Ciara regarded Tom and wondered how he felt about everything that had happened all those years ago. A trace of humiliation still burnt brightly in her stomach, but mostly she just felt sad for the foolish and naive eighteen-year-olds they'd been then.

'You haven't been to Loughmore in twelve years.'

He blinked at her words. 'I've been busy.'

There was much she regretted about her relationship with Tom, but nothing more so than the way she had lashed out at him when he had come to her bedroom that night, pale and apologetic. It would be so easy not to talk about what had happened, but Ciara couldn't wish away just how close they once had been…those two naive eighteen-year-olds who had hurt one another so badly.

'That night in my mum's house… I was angry.'

A slash of red coloured his cheeks. 'You had a right to be.'

Ciara's heart squeezed tightly at the prideful tilt of Tom's head that did little to hide the emotion playing out in his eyes.

For the first time ever, when she and Tom had become lovers, she had let her guard down and ignored the Harris family motto of 'everything is fine'. She had told him her inner secrets, her loneliness and her guilt that her dad had left because of her, despite there being no evidence to back up that belief.

Tom had tried to persuade her to accept that she shouldn't feel responsible, but it still sat inside her—that feeling of being insignificant that came with having a father who had walked away from her for ever.

She had even embarrassingly admitted that she wanted to create a family of her own, with at least five children. Tom had teased her over that…but she had fallen even deeper in love with him when he'd said that she'd be the best mother ever. She had opened her heart to him. She had been stupid. Because doing so had only made his rejection—which she should have known was coming—a thousand times worse.

It was a mistake she'd never make again.

She looked at him now, sadness and regret bubbling in her throat. 'We should have just remained friends.'

His eyes held hers for what felt like for ever.

Eventually he nodded and said gently, 'Perhaps you're right.'

Overwhelmed by how emotional she felt, she stepped around him and collected his cup and saucer, placed them on the tea tray with her own, buying some thinking time in the process.

She liked her new life in Loughmore. Yes, she was

occasionally caught unawares by a memory of Tom that rooted her to the spot. But she had long ago accepted that she needed to forge a life for herself. And through years of study and work in various conservation centres and heritage gardens, both in Ireland and Scotland, she had built a life she was proud of.

The conservation and heritage programmes she had started here in Loughmore needed to be continued. Loughmore itself needed to be saved from developers. And if that meant she needed to spend time with Tom, persuading him not to sell, then no matter how uncomfortable and awkward it would be she would do it—to save Loughmore.

She adjusted the tray in her hands and said, 'Don't tell the staff yet—let them enjoy Christmas.'

'I have to return to London on the first of January. I want to be here and available to talk through any concerns they may have.'

'Then plan on coming back in the New Year. You're only in London—it's not far to travel.'

He gave an unenthusiastic shrug and said, 'Perhaps.'

Her heart sank. He clearly wanted to spend as little time as possible in Loughmore. But, forcing herself to smile, she said, 'You never know—you might change your mind about selling over Christmas.'

His eyes narrowed. 'I have a buyer lined up. That's not going to happen.'

Ciara nodded. She needed to get Operation Save Loughmore underway immediately.

'The staff have organised a charity event in memory of your dad tomorrow night. Two hundred and fifty guests will be attending the turning on of the Christmas lights, with a choral concert and dancing later. I assume you'll attend?'

'I had forgotten it was taking place,' he answered, uninterested.

'But you'll come?'

'My father wasn't the easiest of men—it's a generous gesture by the staff.'

It was true. His father had terrified most of the staff in Loughmore. But at least he would never have dreamed of selling it.

Adjusting the tray in her hands, Ciara moved to the door, which Tom opened to allow her to exit. Just as she was about to step out into the hallway she stopped and said, 'He was tough, but he commanded respect. He was loyal to Loughmore.'

Tom's mouth tightened. 'And I'm not?'

Ciara shrugged and said, 'I'm sure you have your reasons,' before walking away.

The following evening Tom half listened to the back-and-forth one-upmanship of the two opposing politicians who had collared him once the guests had moved from the tree-lighting ceremony and choral concert in the Great Hall into the ballroom for dancing. Several times he had tried to break away, but both men seemed determined to impress on him why he should consider becoming a supporter of their political party.

Not for the first time that night his gaze wandered once again over the invited guests in search of Ciara.

He took a slug of his Irish whiskey when he saw her still out on the dance floor with a guy he'd privately nicknamed Mr Brite, given his dazzling white smile. Wearing a knee-length red lace dress and towering heels, with her tumbling red locks worn loose and her sinful brown eyes full of laughter, she and Mr Brite twirled around the dancefloor.

Ciara looked like a fantasy Christmas present for every hot-blooded man. And she was a woman on a mission. It had taken him only a few hours today to cotton on to her plan.

After a lavish breakfast from Libby, Stephen had politely insisted he give Tom a tour of the castle, pointing out the renovations that had taken place in recent years and reminding him of the historical importance of the castle not only to County Wicklow but to the whole of Ireland.

Stephen had conveniently ended the tour in the courtyard, where Liam Geary, Loughmore's estate manager, had just happened to be standing by his estate vehicle chatting with Ciara. Before he'd known it Tom had been in the passenger seat, and Liam had taken him for a tour of the land, recounting his plans for extending the dairy herd and the possibility of introducing buffalo on to the estate.

On their way back to the castle they'd 'happened' to bump into Ciara again, this time chatting with her boss Sean at the start of the garden's Palm Walk.

'Wait until you see the orchard, sir,' Sean had said with great excitement. 'We've expanded it greatly and we supply farmers' markets nationwide. This year, thanks to Ciara's knowledge, we've planted new apple and plum saplings— they're old varieties that would have once grown here in Loughmore.'

Sean had then taken him on an extensive tour of the walled garden, the lakeside gardens and the orchards, breathlessly talking about his plans to extend the market garden.

His tour had ended at the glasshouses, where Ciara herself had taken him on a tour of the heritage plants she was cultivating.

He knew he had been cool with her throughout the tour—her jibe about his loyalty to Loughmore the previous evening had still been fresh in his mind. For a brief moment, when she'd said it, he'd wanted to tell her the truth. About how his father had left the estate in debt through poor financial investments. How selling Loughmore would significantly rebalance the books.

Tom had only learnt of the debts after his father's death. At first he had been angry—especially when he'd realised that his father had left it to *him* to inform his mother of the situation. Later he had felt nothing other than regret. A father and son should have had a better relationship. One with trust and mutual respect.

In the aftermath of his father's death Tom's resolve to value and cherish his own children, if he was ever to have them, had become all the more resolute.

Now, beside him, the politicians had moved on to a heated debate about land tax, and both became indignant when Tom interrupted to point out that their policies sounded remarkably similar and equally non-progressive.

Out on the dance floor Ciara turned to study him, before leaning towards Mr Brite and whispering something into his ear. Mr Brite turned and studied him too, before saying something to Ciara which, even in the low lights of the ballroom, Tom could see had made her blush.

Tom took another long slug of his whiskey, but the smooth tones of the ten-year-old blend were doing little to improve his mood.

With narrowed eyes he watched Ciara leave the dance floor and head in his direction. What was she up to now?

Beside him, the two politicians miraculously grew silent as Ciara approached them. Giving them her widest beam, she said, 'I'm sorry to break up your conversation, but the Duke promised me a dance earlier.'

Placing her hand on his elbow, she tugged him towards the dance floor. At first he resisted—but then he considered his options. The company of two self-important politicians or Ciara? She was the lesser of two evils. But only marginally.

He went with her, but at the edge of the dance floor he pulled her to a stop. 'Hold on—I believe we have a number of problems here.'

Ciara tilted her head and waited for him to explain.

'First off, I *didn't* promise you a dance.'

'You looked as though you needed rescuing.'

He'd give her that. 'Secondly, I don't think your previous dance partner will be too impressed with losing you.'

Ciara raised an eyebrow and pointed to the far end of the ballroom, where Mr Brite was surrounded by a group of women of varying ages, who were clapping along to his extravagant dance moves.

'Vince McNamara is the doctor in Loughmore now. His husband Danny is away skiing at the moment. He'll happily dance with anyone who admires his moves.'

'Which brings us to our third problem. You might not remember, but I can't dance.'

Amusement danced in her eyes. 'Oh, I remember, all right. But you need to get into the Christmas spirit.'

With that she dragged him out on to the dance floor. He shuffled along as she shimmied before him and the crowd around them bopped along to the band's rock 'n' roll rendition of another Christmas classic.

She gestured to him to take off his jacket, but he shook his head. Instead he leant towards her and said in a low voice, so only she could hear, 'I'm not going to change my mind about selling Loughmore.'

She shrugged and continued dancing, and then she leant towards him. 'So you said yesterday.'

She smelt of roses and vanilla. He tried to ignore the way her hips swayed along to the beat of the music. 'I'm on to you, you know.'

'What do you mean?'

'Libby's cooking, my tours of the castle and grounds today, then hot port and carols outside the front door at five. You're not going to change my mind.'

'They were all just coincidences.'

On the stage, the band segued into another song. This time it was much slower, and around them couples formed.

Ciara looked towards the stage with a frustrated frown and then gave him a bright smile, 'Well, I guess that's you off the hook.'

He should let her go. He knew he should. But all of a sudden he wanted to play her at her own game. As she moved to pass him he placed a hand on her waist and twisted her around, his other hand reaching for hers.

She tried to step away but he pulled her back.

She gave him a tight smile. 'I'm not sure this is appropriate. Us dancing together will have raised some eyebrows—slow dancing will set the cat amongst the pigeons.'

'You started it. Now, tell me what you've said to the rest of the staff.'

Blinking rapidly, Ciara protested, 'I've said nothing.'

He shifted nearer, stared her in the eye. 'Ciara…'

The two glasses of champagne she had drunk earlier were to blame. Ten minutes ago asking Tom to dance had seemed like an inspired idea. She wanted him to *enjoy* his Christmas in Loughmore, and he sure hadn't looked happy having his ear chewed off by two local politicians. But now that they were slow dancing that 'inspired idea' was quickly morphing into the worst decision she had taken in a very long time.

His hand enclosing hers was too familiar, too heart-stoppingly reassuring…too strong a reminder of how he'd used to touch her. His arm on her waist—heavy, in charge—was sending jittery shudders down the length of her legs. Pretending to be relaxed, to be unaffected by him, was already tearing her apart.

But what choice did she have? She had to save Loughmore. As her mum had always said, she needed to stop overthinking and just get on with it—preferably with a cheery smile on her face.

She craned her neck and met his gaze for a brief second, before shifting her eyes to the safety of the fine navy wool of his suit jacket. 'Okay… I'll admit I've said we need to make a special effort to make you feel welcome and part of the castle.'

She felt his muscles tense beneath the palm resting on his shoulder. In a low voice, much too close to her ear, he said, 'My life is elsewhere.'

Despite the hollow sensation that cracked in her chest at his words, she forced herself to keep her voice casual when she said, 'I think you'll regret selling Loughmore… Don't you want to pass it on to your heirs?'

His eyes duelled with hers while his hand on her waist shifted slightly, so their hips were now only inches apart. 'Who said there will *be* any?'

She raised an eyebrow. 'I bet you're beating back wannabe duchesses with a stick.'

A grin hovered on his lips. 'There *are* a few.'

'Bet your mum has a shortlist.'

All titled, beautiful, and with the right social graces, Ciara would wager.

Tom shrugged in response.

They moved around the dance floor, Tom awkwardly leading the way. His inability to keep to the beat of the music was rather endearing.

'Are you in a relationship?'

She looked up in surprise at his question. 'Not at the moment.'

'But you have been?'

It felt wrong to be talking like this with him. 'Kind of.'

'Meaning?'

'I've moved around a lot with my work. It doesn't lend itself to serious relationships. How about you?'

'I've had a few…but they haven't worked out. Now I'm too busy juggling my restaurants and the estate to find the time to sleep, never mind date.'

Her heart banged hard and furiously at the thought of him being with someone else. Even worse, a part of her wanted to know about every single relationship he had had. Had they been serious? Why had they broken up?

She bit the inside of her lip, and mentally gave herself a ticking-off. Why on earth would she do that to herself? She had to focus on saving Loughmore. Forget about the past.

'Loughmore will be a great summer home when you do eventually marry and have children. Remember how much you loved coming here?'

He shook his head but a smile glittered in his eyes. 'You're as persistent as ever, aren't you?'

He said it with such fondness that for a moment she forgot he was her boss, a member of the British aristocracy, the man who had once broken her heart.

His arm shifted on her waist and something darker, earthier entered his eyes.

She knew she should break her gaze away, but she couldn't. His eyes were so hypnotic, full of intelligence, integrity and pride, but also a beguiling undercurrent of sensual suggestion.

A charge of dark, dangerous desire rippled in the air between them.

He pulled her closer. She didn't resist.

'Tom—why didn't you *tell* us you were coming to Loughmore?'

Ciara jumped at the excited squeal behind her, and Tom's arms floated away from her.

Turning, she had to step out of the way as a blonde-haired woman dressed in black trousers and a silver blouse, with a long grey cashmere coat draped over her shoulders, moved in to hug and air-kiss Tom.

Then, waving in the direction of the outside terrace, beyond the row of French windows that formed one wall of the ballroom, the woman added, 'Tania and Jacob are outside, catching up with Becky Johnson. They'll be back in a sec. It's freezing out there, but they're huddled under an outdoor heater, eating the toasted marshmallows on offer from the outside caterers. What fun! How fab to see you! We dined at Tom's in Barcelona last month—the food was to *die* for. Clever you!'

Ciara went to leave, but Tom called to her. 'Ciara! Let me introduce you to Amber Chamberlain.'

Amber turned and smiled at Ciara. 'Are you down from Dublin for the night too? Wasn't the traffic *horrendous*? That's why we're late. And they're predicting snow soon. It will be bedlam then.'

'No. I work here in the castle.'

'Oh.' For a moment Amber looked thrown, but she recovered well. 'Lucky you—working in such a lovely place.' Then she paused in thought. 'Wait a sec… I think I remember you.'

And then it dawned on Ciara. Tom had celebrated his eighteenth birthday here at Loughmore. He had invited her but the night had been a disaster, because she had known very few of the other guests and his parents had watched her unhappily all night. The following morning when she had come to work the party had still been going strong.

'The morning after Tom's eighteenth…' With a laugh, Amber held her hands to her cheeks. 'Do you remember, Ciara? You were cleaning in the games room and found me fast asleep on the billiard table. You helped me to my room.'

Ciara nodded, refusing to glance in Tom's direction. 'I remember now. Can I take your coat?'

'Please—and I would *love* a glass of champagne.' Turning to Tom, Amber linked her arm in his. 'Come on, let's go and find Jacob and Tania. They'll be dying to chat with you. They're off to St Moritz tomorrow. Will you be there as usual this New Year?'

Tom did not move, despite Amber's best efforts to lead him towards the terrace. 'Ciara, why don't you join us?'

Ciara saw the flicker of confusion on Amber's face. No doubt she was wondering why Tom was asking one of the staff to socialise with them.

All those years ago as a teenager she had been pretty much blind to the social wall that existed between herself and Tom. Youthful enthusiasm, idealism, naivety… Call it what you will, it had had her believing their different backgrounds didn't matter.

All that innocence had ended on the day she had travelled to London.

She gestured towards the dance floor. 'I need to get back to Vince… I promised him we'd have another dance together.'

Moving through the crowd, she took Amber's coat to the temporary cloakroom that had been set up in the library. The two teenage girls from the village who had been employed for the evening to man the cloakroom jumped up when she entered, frantically trying to hide their phones.

She hid her amusement and said, 'Kelly, come with me to the kitchen, I need to organise drinks for some guests, and you two look as though you could do with some of Libby's baking to get you through the next few hours.'

In the kitchen, as Kelly filled a plate with Libby's delicate savoury pastries and mini-Christmas puddings, Ciara directed one of the waiters to take a bottle of champagne and glasses out to the terrace. Then, seeing how exhausted Libby was, she forced Libby to sit down while she made her a pot of tea.

Know your place.

There was actually wisdom in that saying. When her

gran had used to say it to her she'd seen it as a putdown. But in fact her gran had only being trying to protect her. She had seen what unrealistic dreams had done to her mother—bringing a pain and humiliation that were hidden behind a wall of defiance and avoidance and a family rift that had gone on too long. Now she understood how worried they must have been when they'd seen history about to repeat itself.

They had only been trying to protect her from her own foolishness and naivety.

This time around she knew her place.

CHAPTER THREE

THE FOUR-BY-FOUR SLEWED towards the hedge on the narrow road. Tom steered into the skid, feeling the car scraping against brambles and seeing a shower of snow thumping against the side windows before he finally managed to bring the vehicle to a stop.

He switched off the engine. The fresh snow on the side of the vehicle slid to the road with a thud and then there was nothing but absolute silence. Nothing stirred. Not a single bird was to be seen in the early-morning milky blue sky. Not a cry nor a bleat from an animal. It was as if the earth was having a sleep-in, having exhausted itself in the intensity of the snowstorm that had hit the east coast of Ireland the previous night.

Below him in the valley the vibrant emerald fields of Loughmore had disappeared under a blanket of sparkling white snow. Switching the engine back on, he crunched his way through the snow-covered perimeter road of the estate, where the high limestone wall to his right marked the boundaries with the neighbouring farms. After a few minutes he finally caught a glance of his last destination for the morning: Butterfly Cottage.

It was nestled in a copse, and he could just about make out its thatched roof beneath the snow.

He drove down the long incline into the heart of the valley, the four-by-four skidding on the more sheltered parts of the road. Last night, the initial flourish of snow had frozen hard, to be followed later by a heavier and more prolonged snowfall.

At the cottage, the garden gate refused to budge, so he had no option but to leap over the low wall that surrounded the property, built to stop the estate's cows and sheep from wandering into the garden.

On the other side of the wall he muttered to himself as he landed into a particularly deep snow drift and snow flooded the inside of his wellington boots.

His knock on the rose-pink-painted cottage door echoed into the valley. He had to knock a second and then a third time before the door swung open.

Dressed in a fluffy yellow dressing gown, her hair mussed up and her cheeks pink, Ciara stared at him through sleepy eyes. 'Tom… I mean, Your Grace, what are you doing here?' Then, pausing, she peered over his shoulder. 'Oh, my God! I can't believe how much snow there is.'

Her eyes grew wide and her gaze shot back to his.

'My alarm didn't go off! I slept in! I'll be up at the gardens as soon as I can. I know snow was forecast, but I hadn't realised so much would fall. I don't usually work on a Sunday, but I would have been up inspecting the gardens earlier if I had known.'

'I'm not here because I expect you to be at work.'

'Why are you here, then?'

'The electricity in the castle went out overnight. The emergency generator took over—'

Ciara interrupted him, her expression alarmed, 'Were the outside buildings affected? The greenhouses?'

'No, they're all okay.'

She gave a grateful exhalation and then with a deep shiver added, 'It's Baltic out here—come inside before we both perish.'

The living room of the cottage was directly inside the front door. A Christmas tree, laden down with decorations, sat in one corner. Christmas cards were strung over the mantelpiece, and an array of angels and Santa Clauses and reindeers were spread on every other available surface.

Moving over to the small cottage window overlooking the front garden, Ciara leant down and propped her elbows on the deep windowsill. She shook her head as she stared at the wintry scene outside. 'I have never seen so much snow. Thank God we covered some of the more vulnerable plants with fleeces.'

There was a light switch to one side of the front door. Tom switched it to on. The brass light at the centre of the room remained unlit.

Ciara gave a groan. 'Oh, seriously… No wonder my radio alarm didn't go off.'

'You're not the only one. I've called in to all the other estate cottages this morning to make sure everyone is okay—several others are without electricity too. You're the last on my list, being the furthest out. I'd hoped you wouldn't be affected too.'

Ciara looked at him in surprise. 'You've called in to every cottage? How did everyone react?'

Now that he thought about it, his arrival *had* caused a certain level of consternation in each of the cottages. 'They were a little thrown, I suppose. What's the problem with me calling?'

Beneath her yellow dressing gown she was wearing old-fashioned white cotton pyjamas, with a lace detail running down the front of the top, the bottoms ending at mid-calf, with yet more lace detailing. The cute pyjamas and fluffy dressing gown, her mussed up hair and rosy skin, along with the remaining heat in the room from last night's fire, all combined to give him the strangest urge to take her in his arms and hold her. Inhale her sleepy scent.

He glanced away from her.

'Calling in to the cottages…it's not something your dad would have done,' Ciara said gently.

'No, I don't suppose it is.'

She regarded him as though she were trying to understand him, and then a soft smile broke on her lips. 'It's a thoughtful thing to do, though.'

Warmth seeped through him at her smile. An alarming tightness gripped his heart.

He tried to refocus. 'What will you do? Is there someone you can stay with until the electricity is restored?'

'It's okay—I'm leaving later today anyway, to spend Christmas with my mum. After I've helped out at the kiddies' party at the castle. Hopefully the electricity will be restored before I get back.'

'The road out of Loughmore is impassable.'

Her mouth dropped open. 'Oh, for crying out loud!'

'Liam Geary rang the council. They won't be able to clear the road before Christmas Day.'

'So we can't get out?'

'Nor people in to Loughmore. The weather has hit the south of England too. My mother and sisters are having to postpone their journey until after Christmas.'

Ciara leant against the windowsill, her eyes wide. 'That's terrible.'

'My mother accepts it's outside her control…and I think it might actually help her to stay at Bainsworth. It may be painful, as it's the first Christmas without my father, but at least there she has happy memories of past Christmases. And I'm sure they'll make it in time for the New Year Eve's ball. What will you do now that you can't get to Dublin?'

Ciara shrugged. 'I'm not sure… I'll chat with Libby. She's working on Christmas Day. I might go and spend it with her at the castle.'

'I've told Libby and the other staff who were scheduled

to work over Christmas to take the time off. They're staying to run the children's party later today but then taking Christmas Eve through to Boxing Day off.'

'But that means you'll be in the castle completely on your own for three whole days.'

'I was hardly going to get them all to come in to look after *one* person. I'm sure they would all much prefer to be at home with their families.'

'But what will you *do*?'

Tom could not but help laugh at the horror in Ciara's eyes. 'Work. Cook dinner for myself. Up until this year I've spent a decade looking after myself—apart from a cleaner who comes in a few days a week. I can perfectly manage without staff.'

'But that's no way to spend Christmas Day. Christmas should be about having fun and sharing it with others. Creating memories.'

He wasn't going to admit it to Ciara, but part of him was glad it had snowed. At previous Christmases he had felt duty-bound to spend it with his family. Invariably he'd leave early, feeling claustrophobic because of his father's unending silent scrutiny and his mother's recounting the tale of yet another classmate of his who had married recently. His sisters were no better, in their mission to set him up on blind dates with friends and acquaintances of theirs.

Tom had never told any of them, because he knew they would only make his life hell, but he had no interest in dating *or* relationships. His last relationship had been over two years ago, with Maki—Storm's first owner. As with every other previous relationship of his, it had ended in rows, with Maki accusing him of being too remote, too closed.

What was it she'd said? 'I've never known you, Tom. I've never understood what's in your heart.'

Cancelling Christmas at the castle was also a relief to him because he'd much prefer not to have the guilt of having the staff he was soon going to have to tell that their jobs might be redundant waiting on him on Christmas Day.

'My work means that I rarely get time to myself. I'm looking forward to having some downtime and space to think. But what about you? Have you someone to stay with?'

She gave him a hopeful look. 'Maybe the electricity won't be off for long—the suppliers won't want people spending Christmas without it.'

'Liam called the supplier. Until the road into Lough-more is clear they won't be able to repair any of the lines.'

Ciara's expression fell.

Drained after a night of virtually no sleep, he went to sit on the armrest of the yellow-and-white-striped sofa that sat in front of the fireplace. He had barely placed his hand on the armrest when he snatched it away again, jumping at the angry hiss that emanated from a dark corner.

'What was *that*?'

Clearly amused, Ciara moved in front of the sofa. Popping her hands on her hips, she stared down into the corner. 'You *must* behave, Boru.' Looking back at him, she said, 'Sorry about that. Boru is especially cranky with any man who calls.'

Tom dared to peer over the armrest. A jet-black cat with bright green eyes stared back at him and hissed again, before slowly uncurling and leaping from the sofa. He slunk by Ciara's legs and climbed the stairs of the cottage with an indignant toss of his head.

Shaking her head, Ciara stared after the retreating cat. 'God, he's the most contrary cat ever—he never does anything I ask of him.' Turning in the direction of the kitchen, to the rear of the living room, she glanced at the multi-coloured cuckoo clock sitting over the sink. 'I'd better get a move on. Sean and the rest of the gardening crew are on annual leave. I'm the only one still on the estate.'

'Back to my question—where are you going to stay until the electricity is restored?'

She grimaced. 'I don't know. Libby is allergic to cats, and all the other staff who live on the estate have families of their own. I don't want to intrude on their Christmases.'

'How about your friend Vince?'

'God, no—his Tiger tried to take a lump out of Boru the last time they met.'

'Tiger?'

'Vince's Jack Russell.' She shrugged 'I have plenty of firewood, and as the go-to or birthday present for any woman over twenty-five seems to be a smelly candle, I have enough of them to last me a lifetime. I'll be fine here.'

'But you can't stay here without electricity.'

She raised an eyebrow. 'Humankind survived without electricity for millennia. I'm sure I'll cope.'

He stared at her, the inevitable offer on the tip of his tongue. But he was loath to say it. Spending Christmas alone with Ciara was the last thing he wanted to do. There were too many memories, too much attraction, too much unfinished business still between them that he didn't want to rake up.

But he couldn't leave her here on her own—not when he had a whole castle to himself. He inhaled a long, deep breath. 'Come and stay in the castle.'

Ciara's mouth dropped open. She eventually managed to say, 'No… Thank you, but I don't… I can't…'

He pulled off his coat, rested it on the back of the sofa. 'Your car won't make it through the snow. I'll wait while you change and pack.'

Her eyes narrowed and she folded her arms defiantly. 'I *love* Christmas—I'll want to do all the traditional things… opening presents, the full works at dinner, playing games after. Are you prepared to take part in all of that?'

'I hadn't planned—'

She interrupted him. 'I'll stay here, in that case.'

He gave her a stern look, in no mood to debate this. 'Look, it makes sense—I have acres of space in the castle, and at least there you'll be closer to the gardens in order to take care of them.'

She considered that for a moment. 'That's true.' She paused, as something seemed to dawn upon her. 'And as you've told the rest of the staff not to work I can look after *you*.'

'I don't need looking after.'

She just shrugged, clearly not accepting that he did not require any help in the castle over the next few days.

Tense already, from the testing driving conditions earlier and now from this stand-off with Ciara, he stretched his arms over his head to ease the tension in his shoulders.

Ciara ran her gaze over his body, her eyes growing wider and wider as they travelled down his chest, pausing at his abs then skimming over his hips. Heat blasted in her cheeks.

'I...' She paused, backed away towards the stairs, 'I need to get changed.'

'We're not finished with our conversation.'

To that she just shrugged again, before turning and darting up the stairs.

He closed his eyes. Sucked in some air.

There was still a spark between them. A dangerous spark. Which meant that inviting her to the castle was risky. But he couldn't leave her all alone. He owed it to her.

It was up to him to control what was happening between them...not to do anything that they would later regret.

She had been right when she'd said they should have just stayed friends. In loving Ciara he had opened himself up to another person for the first time in his life. It had been both intoxicating and terrifying.

Through gentle teasing she had drawn him out. For

years he had disappointed his parents, felt the heavy weight of their disapproval and frustration at his end-of-term reports and frequent school meetings to discuss his lack of academic progress. He knew he wasn't the son they had hoped for—an all-rounder academic and sportsperson in the mould of his father.

Ciara had been the first person who'd accepted him for what he was. But he had failed her. When she had rightly cut him out of her life he'd thought *his* life would be empty and grey for ever. It had taken him years to put the pieces of his shattered heart back together again. He could never relive that pain. Even being near her now was bringing back unwelcome memories and thoughts of what might have been.

In an alcove beneath the stairs sat an old writing desk, its central green leather writing surface faded with time. On the dark wood surrounding the leather there were at least a dozen framed photos of Ciara. He picked one up, and then another.

Some were of Ciara standing with people who looked like colleagues in various garden settings. In all of them she was at the centre of the group, her arms linked tightly around the waists of those standing beside her. She looked buoyant and proud in them all. Others were holiday photos—Ciara sitting in the sun with friends, with elaborate cocktails, and a winter snap of a boat ride in Amsterdam. Another showed her wading out of an azure sea, wearing a black bikini, one hand on her forehead pushing away her wet hair.

He breathed in deeply and turned away from the image of her in the bikini.

He stared at the long row of Christmas cards over her mantelpiece. No doubt from friends and colleagues. She had led a full life since he had last seen her. He admired her for what she had achieved. Why, then, did it leave him feeling so unsettled?

He was standing at the kitchen sink, filling a glass of water when Ciara reappeared.

Wearing a silver turtleneck Christmas jumper adorned with glistening white stars, which skimmed the waistband of her tight-fitting black jeans, she looked cute and as sexy as hell.

Her gaze fell to the half-eaten cookie in his hands. He had found a tray of cookies lying on the kitchen counter and, not having eaten anything all morning, had been unable to resist taking one.

Ciara grimaced at the cookie and then darted to the fridge. 'I should have offered you something to eat before I got dressed. Would you like a sandwich? I can't offer you a hot drink…' she turned with a carton of apple juice '…but how about some juice?'

'Water is fine…and I couldn't fit in another bite after this cookie. It's rather filling.'

She gave him a disbelieving look before pouring some juice into a glass. He watched her sip it, trying to get a grip on the way her behaviour with him kept swinging from one extreme to another. Sometimes she was her old forthright self and then at other times she became almost deferential. Something was going on that he wasn't grasping.

Taking a sip of the ice-cold water, he said, 'I didn't see you again after our dance on Friday night. You didn't join Vince as you said you would.'

There was something about Tom's tone—an edge to it—that had Ciara pausing in placing the cap back on the juice carton. She glanced over at him, and then away. Did he *have* to stand there in her kitchen wearing such a tight-fitting tee shirt? She tried to shake off the image of the six-pack he had earlier exposed when he had stretched.

His long sleeved grey tee shirt had parted from jeans that hung sexily low on his hips to reveal spectacular abs…

'I ended up helping Libby in the kitchen,' she said.

'Why? It's not your job.'

'She needed help. I didn't mind.'

'Why wouldn't you join myself and Amber?'

She knew by his tone that he wasn't going to let this drop. Twisting the cap good and tight on the carton, she put it back into the fridge. Closing the fridge door, she leant against it, suddenly feeling a little dizzy.

Should she just leave well alone? Leave the past where it belonged? But something deep inside her was telling her that Tom deserved to know. Especially as he was inviting her to stay in the castle for Christmas.

Ciara liked to think that she wasn't a coward, but the thought of being stuck out here all alone in the cottage in the pitch-darkness of a winter's night was pushing her to-wards accepting his invitation. That and the fact that stay-ing with Tom over the Christmas made sense in terms of her campaign to save Loughmore. She could use the time they spent together to persuade him not to sell.

But first there were things he deserved to know.

She swallowed hard and asked, 'Your dad and you…? How were things between you in recent years?'

Tom's eyes narrowed and his mouth turned downwards. He gave a shrug that was nothing but casual. 'He had come to accept who I am.'

It didn't sound as though his father had lowered his un-realistic expectations. 'Was he proud of everything you've achieved with your restaurants?'

Tom rose an eyebrow. 'A double Olympian horseman with a first from Cambridge has very high standards.'

For a moment Ciara closed her eyes, and then in a rush she said, 'I think there's something you should know.'

He looked at her blankly.

'Your dad and my mum…' She paused and inhaled a steadying breath. 'Well, they…they had a relationship when they were teenagers. It ended when they were both twenty-one. They kept it secret…just like us. My mum only knew it was all over when she read about his engagement to your mum in the newspapers.'

Tom dropped his glass to the counter with a thud. '*Your* mum and *my* dad!'

Why did he sound so appalled? 'Don't you think she was good enough for him?'

Tom stepped away from the counter and threw his arms up, looking at her as though she had lost her mind. 'What are you *talking* about? When did I say that?'

Taking her by surprise, anger on behalf of her mum fizzed through Ciara. Fiercely she countered, 'My mum was heartbroken. She met my dad and married him soon after. And we both know how *that* ended—with him upping sticks when I was only a year old.'

Tom grimaced. Stepped back. Lowered his head from her gaze for a beat to study the quarry-tiled floor of her kitchen. Inhaling deeply, he looked back up at her, grim-faced. 'I'm sorry about what my father did to your mother.'

His apology sounded genuine…even heartfelt. It doused her anger, and in a low voice she said, 'I thought you should know… It explains so much. Especially why your dad was so opposed to us being friends.'

Tom's mouth tightened. '*And* why your grandfather in his very polite and roundabout way asked me to stay away from you.'

'Did he?'

Ciara could not keep the surprise from her voice. Her grandad was a reserved man, who kept himself to himself. Like her grandmother, he was a traditionalist and had always believed in respecting the family they served—which included never commenting on them or their behaviour.

For him to have said anything to Tom must have meant that he had been extremely worried.

Ciara felt a pang of guilt for the anxiety she must have caused her grandparents. Only now, with hindsight, could she appreciate the dilemma they must have faced back then, with their desire to spend time with their only grandchild versus seeing her following a destructive path similar to her mother's.

'I respected your grandfather. I didn't like going against his wishes.'

Ciara's heart skipped a beat at the obvious toll it had taken on Tom to go against the wishes of her grandad—a man she knew he was fond of. 'Why didn't you tell me?'

'He asked me not to say anything to you. He said he knew I would do the right thing and not hurt you.'

At that Tom stopped and held her gaze. Silence settled around them. She bit her lip, trying to ignore the ache in her chest. She had moved on from all this years ago. Hadn't she?

She grabbed a tea towel and reached for the mixing bowl that was still lying on the draining board from when she had made the cookies last night. Tom had unfortunately decided to test them. She hoped for his sake he had a strong stomach.

Drying the bowl with quick wipes, she said, 'My grandparents tried to stop my mum from seeing your dad. They knew it could never last and how infatuated she was with him.'

Opening her baking cupboard, she placed the bowl on the base of her food mixer.

Then, catching his gaze, she said quietly, 'But you know…first love—it's dangerously powerful, unfortunately.'

She turned away from him, seeing his expression grow

even tighter and picked up a tablespoon from the draining board.

'My mum hated the fact my grandparents had been right in their warnings and felt betrayed by their decision to remain employed here,' she added. 'But my grandparents felt huge loyalty towards your grandfather, who was then Duke, and it was also a time when there wasn't much employment in Ireland. In reality they didn't have much choice *but* to stay here. My mum was all against me staying with them every summer. And now I understand why. They were always warning me about getting too close to you. They must have been really worried about history repeating itself.'

Tom rinsed his glass, saying nothing.

Ciara tried not to glance at his easy movements, the way his hard muscles flexed beneath his tee shirt.

He turned and held her gaze, those silver eyes shadowed. 'My family has a poor record in how we have treated yours.'

Ciara's heart fluttered at his softly spoken words. 'I'd like to think it's all in the past now. We've all made mistakes.'

'Come and stay at the castle.'

'Are you sure that's a good idea?'

'Considering you're going to be bringing that crazy cat with you, maybe not… But it's time my family started doing the right thing by yours—starting with me offering you a place to stay this Christmas.'

The gentleness, the honesty and integrity in Tom's voice, in his steady and proud gaze, had Ciara closing her eyes for a second. Opening them again, she said, 'I don't want there to be tension between us… If I stay in the castle can we just leave the past behind us and enjoy Christmas?'

Tom considered her words for a while, his jaw working.

Then with a nod he said, 'When I leave in the New Year I'd like us to part as friends.'

Ciara tried not to blush at the implications of his words. 'Of course!'

She gave him a wobbly smile, trying to ignore the stupid hurt and disappointment inside her that that was all he would ever see her as. A friend. Nothing more.

Of course he was right.

She knew that.

It was just that her heart was having a hard time catching up with the logic of the situation, with the understanding that this was nothing more than two old friends spending Christmas together. But it was the best way to get through all of this.

'I'll go and pack.'

She was halfway up the stairs when he called out, 'I'm not sure Storm's going to be impressed with Boru, though.'

He had a point. But if she was going to spend the next few days trying to pretend that Tom Benson had no effect on her, whilst also trying to persuade him to keep Loughmore, Storm and Boru would have to do their bit and learn to get on.

'I'm sure they'll get on famously,' she said. And then she heard herself say with a laugh, 'Just like us.'

Tom raised his eyes heavenwards.

Ciara darted up the rest of the stairs, trying to convince herself that staying in the castle all alone with Tom was not a big deal.

Unfortunately it didn't work.

CHAPTER FOUR

ON A CALL to Oliver Browne, Tom's Edinburgh restaurant manager, Tom shook his head in exasperation as he heard about the flu that had wiped out half of Oliver's staff over the past few days.

Oliver had contained the crisis by recruiting temporary agency workers to replace his ill staff, but it was far from ideal. The success of Tom's Restaurants was not based only on their innovative menus, that used the best-quality regional produce, but also on the exceptional quality of service every customer who walked through the doors of Tom's received.

Tom had made it mandatory that all staff members had to attend a two-day in-house customer care course to ensure they all followed the service standards he expected.

Listening to Oliver's briefing on the fall-out of trying to run the restaurant without his usual staff at this peak time for the restaurant trade, Tom realised not for the first time that trying to run both the estate and his restaurant business in parallel was going to be a challenge—and yet another reason why selling Loughmore was the correct decision.

His phone tucked under his chin, he twisted around in his chair when he heard the library door open.

Three tiny heads peeked around the doorframe.

Spotting him at his desk, the little girls gave a high-pitched squeal and disappeared. Much giggling outside the door followed, and then the sound of a familiar voice.

He finished his call with Oliver just as Ciara entered the room, beckoning a reluctant trio in behind her.

He raised an eyebrow in Ciara's direction, his mouth twitching at the knee-length 'Mrs Claus' dress she was wearing, red velvet with white trim. Her hair was plaited to the side, and on her head she wore a matching red velvet white-trimmed hat.

Ciara threw him an unamused look. 'This was *not* my idea. Blame Libby—she's the main organiser of the kiddies' party this year and she insisted we all dress up.'

Shaking his head, he turned his attention to the three little girls whom he guessed were roughly five years old and were now staring at him wide-eyed.

Dressed in identical long-sleeved black velvet dresses, with pink and white embroidered Celtic designs on the front panel and along the base of their short flared skirts, the girls wore tiny black soft-soled dance shoes on their feet, and their loose hair was held back by black velvet bands.

'These girls are here for the party, and as they dance with the local Irish Dancing school they're taking part in a dance display for us later. They were keen to meet you, so I said we'd drop in for a few minutes to say hi,' Ciara said, by way of explanation for their unplanned visit.

Preoccupied by his call with Oliver, and the workload he needed to get through this afternoon, Tom felt a flicker of irritation—but even he was unable to resist the shy but excited trio staring at him as though he was the eighth wonder of the world.

'Hi, girls.'

The three giggled once again.

Walking to his desk, Ciara gestured for the girls to follow her.

When they came to stand directly in front of him he held his hand out to them. Reluctantly they shook it, giggling when he said to each one, 'Very nice to meet you, Miss Irish Dancer.'

'We're not called Miss Irish Dancer!' replied the raven-haired leader, who had been the first to enter the room and the first to dare to walk up to his desk at Ciara's beckoning.

'Really? So, what *are* your names?'

'I'm Grace,' said the raven-haired spokesperson.

'I'm Sophie,' said her little friend with long bright red hair and a heavy dusting of freckles.

'And…and I'm Grace too,' stammered the shyest of the three, her hands nervously twisting the heavy velvet fabric of her flared skirt.

'Hello, Grace Two.'

She shook her head, her blonde curls bobbing up and down. 'No, I'm just Grace.'

Tom leant back in his chair and slapped his forehead. 'Silly me. Hello, Just Grace.'

The three girls leant into one another, giggling even more at his foolishness.

Ciara considered the laughing trio fondly and then, meeting his eye, gave him a grateful smile. The girls' light and delicate laughter danced around the room and something unexpected shifted inside him at hearing their joy, seeing the amusement dancing in Ciara's eyes.

In that moment it hit him just how much he had missed the thrill of doing something to make her happy. How had he spent the past twelve years not realising that? Now, sitting in the library of Loughmore, seeing her brown eyes twinkle, and the way she placed a hand on her chest bone when something entertained her, the life he had led for those twelve years felt as though it belonged to another person.

He gritted his teeth, glad now that he had said he wanted

them to part as friends earlier, in her cottage. Making that statement out loud to Ciara had been an insurance policy against him doing anything stupid around her.

Like kiss her.

Especially in light of how despicably his father had treated her mum.

Plopping her arms on his desk, Grace One studied him with a hint of wonder. 'Are you really a prince?'

'Not a prince. I'm a duke.'

'What's a duke?'

'Well… I suppose I'm like a cousin to a prince.'

Grace One shook her head and looked at him, unconvinced. 'You look like a prince to me.'

'Yes, you look like the Prince in my *Sleeping Beauty* book,' Sophie added in a determined tone.

'*And* you live in a castle,' Grace Two added, and then, shyly tugging once again on the fabric of her skirt, she added in a whisper, 'It's so beautiful…' She pronounced beautiful '*beaut-fil*', and his heart melted at the blush that formed on her cheeks when he smiled at her.

But her two friends continued to study him unhappily, as though convinced he was holding back on admitting that he really was a prince.

He looked helplessly in Ciara's direction. She bit her lip, clearly fighting to hold back laughter. He eyeballed her. It had been her idea to bring the girls to visit him—the least she could do was help him out.

Clearing her throat, Ciara bent down beside his desk and looked towards the three girls. 'A duke is just as special as a prince, girls. And *our* Duke is extra-special because he is also a very famous chef, who performs magic in the kitchen. People all over the world love his work. I think that's even cooler than being a prince, don't you?'

Thrown by the pride in Ciara's voice, Tom shuffled in his seat. He frequently received positive critical reviews of Tom's Restaurants, but to hear Ciara's words felt a thousand times more gratifying.

He cleared his throat, taken aback by the sudden lump that had formed in his throat. It had been Ciara who'd encouraged him to follow his dreams to be a chef. She had seen the buzz he got from creating new dishes, the pleasure he found in the delight he evoked in people when they tasted his food. She had understood his desire to create a name for himself, independent of his title—his need to prove to his father that he could be a success in his own right, that he wasn't going to be a failure all his life.

And for the past twelve years, no matter how much he tried to deny it to himself, every career step he had taken had also been about proving to *her* just what he was capable of. But even though her praise was pleasing, it was also disturbing… He shouldn't care so much of what she thought of him.

Pushing those thoughts away, he focused on the girls. Ciara's words seemed to have taken away some of their disappointment that he wasn't a prince as they were once again regarding him with renewed enthusiasm.

Grace One propped a hand under her chin and asked, 'Have you met the Queen?'

'Yes, many times.'

In unison, all three whispered, 'Wow…'

'How about Cinderella?' Sophie asked, with hope gleaming in her eyes.

'No, not yet. But maybe some day I will.'

'Will you marry her?'

This was worse than an interrogation from any journalist. He looked in Ciara's direction. A flicker of unease passed over her expression.

'Time to go and visit Santa, girls,' she said quickly. 'Say goodbye to the Duke.'

Despite Ciara's best efforts to get the girls to leave,

Grace One refused to budge and asked, 'Prince, will you come and visit Santa with us?'

For once Tom was grateful for the endless paperwork strewn over his desk. Usually he had his administrative staff to deal with the bulk of it, preferring to conduct business either by phone or in his regular visits to his restaurants, but there was certain paperwork only he could deal with. And it frustrated the hell out of him thanks to his dyslexia.

Gesturing towards it, he said, 'Sorry, girls, but I have a lot of work to do.'

'*Please*, Prince,' pleaded Sophie.

'Santa's really nice, Prince. You can tell him what you want for Christmas,' Grace Two added passionately, her eyes alight with the magic of Christmas despite her underlying shyness.

It was going to be nigh on impossible for him to say no to their cute pleadings without coming across as a complete grouch.

'Come—it will be fun,' Ciara added. 'It will only be for ten minutes. You can get back to work after that.'

With a sigh, he stood. The three girls hopped up and down and clapped their hands. He followed Ciara and the girls out of the library, strangely moved by the girls' excitement.

In the hallway, he was taken aback when Grace One and Sophie took hold of his hands. The tiny vulnerability of their delicate fingers, the trust and innocence of their action, cracked something inside him that he struggled to name, to understand.

As a trio they followed Ciara, who was holding shy Grace's hand, along the corridor towards the main entrance hall. Along the way they met Stephen, who frowned when he saw what was happening.

As they passed one another Tom could not resist saying, 'Nice waistcoat, Stephen.'

Today, instead of his usual formal black waistcoat, Stephen was rather self-consciously—no doubt in a nod towards Libby's instruction that they all wear fancy dress—wearing a bright red waistcoat covered in tiny green trees.

Stephen's mouth pursed.

When they had moved on a short distance Ciara turned to Tom, and they shared the connection of mischievousness that had been such a part of their teenage years.

But then Ciara looked stricken and she snapped her gaze away, as though remembering that those days of closeness were long behind them.

At the entrance hall, Ciara and Grace continued to lead the way—up the garlanded main stone staircase all the way to the second floor. Tom followed with a heavy heart, wondering just how awkward this Christmas was going to be.

To his surprise Ciara led them down the long corridor of the west wing, until they met an elf standing at the closed doorway of what had once been the family nursery.

Crouching down to be at eye level with the girls, the elf, dressed in a green tunic with red trim, green tights and pixie boots, with a green and red pixie hat balancing precariously on her head, said, 'Hi, girls. Santa is with another little girl and boy at the moment, but he said you can play in his toy workshop, if you like. It's full of special toys he thinks you will love.'

The three girls nodded enthusiastically, and when the elf stood and opened the door all three gasped.

The old nursery was unrecognisable. Converted into a North Pole toy workshop, endless fairy lights hung from its ceiling and the air was heavy with the scent of ginger and cinnamon, thanks to an enormous gingerbread house sitting on a small table at the centre of the room, with the antique dolls that had belonged to generations of Bensons surrounding it.

Against one wall sat a carpenter's bench filled with wooden carvings, where every conceivable farm animal jostled for space with toy soldiers. A gift-wrapping section sat next to the bench, its table brimming with brightly co-loured presents, and a pretend production line was on the opposite side of the room, where the Benson family Steiff teddy bears sat with quiet dignity, going round and round.

Following the elf, the girls tentatively entered the room—and then made an immediate beeline for the four-storey antique dolls' house that had often been the bat-tlefield for many arguments between Kitty and Fran as children.

They had both coveted the bridal doll that was part of the house, and had continually argued over her. Fed up with their bickering, Tom had hidden the doll one summer, and she had only reappeared—much to everyone else's sur-prise—on the day they were returning to England.

Now, all these years later, Tom could finally appreciate how exquisite the dolls' house was as he stood by the girls and heard them breathlessly whispering to one another.

'Look at all the people working in the kitchen.'

'Why are they all wearing such funny dresses and hats?'

'Oh, see all the tiny furniture and the cups and sau-cers…and tiny glasses! And see…see the baby in her cot. There's a tiny teddy bear in with her!' raven-haired Grace called out.

Sophie added, with even more excitement, 'Look at the funny pictures of chickens.'

Tom chuckled at Sophie's description of what in fact were miniatures of a series of paintings of pheasants that hung in the formal drawing room of the castle.

Leaving the dolls' house to the girls' inspection, he found his attention grabbed by the electric train set running on the table opposite. His old train set! And all around the tracks were the vintage model pieces he had inherited from both his father and grandfather—the railway station with its nineteen-twenties tweed-dressed commuters, the wooden and redbrick signal box, the granite station water tower, the long locomotive shed…

And then he laughed, when further along the table he found his collection of toy cars. Someone had made the effort to line them all up into straight formal lines, but obviously throughout the day small hands had sent most askew. Almost instantly he found his childhood favourite—a silver Jaguar XJ220. It had started a love affair with Jaguar cars that continued up to this day.

Holding the car in his hand, the weight still so familiar, he saw the girls had now moved on from the dolls' house and were noisily arguing as to which of the antique dolls placed at the gingerbread house table should be called Elsa.

A tightness gathered in his chest. This nursery, and Loughmore itself, had been a refuge for him. As a young child it had given him an escape from the constant humiliation of failing he had endured. Now no future generations of Bensons would ever get to play in here.

Coming to stand beside him, Ciara studied the grey steam locomotive and green carriages as they ran round and round the track. Her red velvet dress was cut to expose the pale skin of her shoulders. He gazed at the delicate lines of her collarbone, feeling a powerful urge to place his lips there, to hold her in his arms, inhale her. It threw him with its intensity.

He looked away, annoyed with himself. And her. Irritation boiled in his stomach. Was all of this—the girls' visit, their persuasion in bringing him to his childhood nursery, the ridiculously cute outfit—all part of Ciara's scheme to stop him selling Loughmore?

Sweeping his hand around the room, he asked, 'Whose idea was all of this?'

Ciara looked at him with a puzzled expression. 'The Duchess gave permission a few years ago for the nursery suite to be used as a grotto. It was Libby's idea and it's been a huge hit with the children. You're unhappy about it?'

'Yes, because…'

Before he could say any more they both turned at the sound of the girls singing as they each cradled a doll and sang them a lullaby.

Their little voices filled the room.

My heart is with you,
Oh, baby of mine,
Let the light of my love shine,
For ever on you.

Ciara turned away from the girls. She was smiling. But tears shone brightly in her eyes.

He flinched, shut his eyes against the tightness enclosing his heart.

Resting both hands on the edge of the table, Ciara bowed her head as though she was studying the landscape of the model railway in great detail. Moving beside her, he placed his hand next to hers. They were almost touching. When she didn't pull away he gently placed his little finger over hers. She looked towards him. Tried to smile. But failed. Tears still glistened in her eyes.

He wanted to do more—wrap her in his arms, whisper that he understood—but he couldn't. Not with the others in the room. And then one of the two internal doors of the nursery swung open. They shifted away from one another just as another elf appeared from what had been the nanny's sitting room.

The elf spoke to Ciara and then, turning to the girls, said

'Grace, Sophie and Grace—Santa can't wait to meet you.' Then, turning to Tom, the elf added, 'You too, Your Grace.'

Tom restrained himself from rolling his eyes.

The three girls were suddenly hit with a bout of acute shyness, and it took both Ciara and the elf to persuade them in to see Santa.

Nanny's sitting room had been transformed into Santa's Grotto, complete with giant chimney-piece and a sparkling Christmas tree. And at the centre, red-cheeked and rotund, sat a jolly Santa Claus on a red velvet throne.

'Well, if it isn't Grace Carney, Sophie O'Brien and Grace McCarthy. The three prettiest dancers I have ever seen.'

Tom bit back a smile when he recognised Liam Geary's voice coming from beneath a wildly extravagant white beard.

The three girls stared at Santa Claus, puzzled as to how he knew them.

'Now, Grace Carney, where's your brother Jack this year?' Santa asked.

Grace pouted and then shook her head with a dramatic sigh. 'He's downstairs, Santa. He said visiting you is for babies.'

'Babies?' Santa replied. 'How can it be for babies when even the Duke is visiting me?'

Grace nodded in agreement, but then leant towards Santa and said in a stage whisper, 'He's a *prince*.'

Encouraging the girls to come closer, Santa had a long chat with each of them, enquiring about school and their families, and then what it was they wanted from him this year. After promising to go to bed early the following night—Christmas Eve—the girls gave a squeal of excitement when big fat presents for each of them dropped down the giant chimney.

Santa was in the process of saying goodbye to them when Sophie interrupted him.

'What about the Prince, Santa? What will you bring him?'

'What does the Prince want?' asked Santa.

Not pausing for a beat, Tom said, 'Peace and quiet and a twenty-year-old malt.'

Santa spluttered out a laugh.

The three girls regarded him with puzzlement before Grace said determinedly, '*I* think the Prince should meet Cinderella and marry her.'

Ciara shook her head. Somebody needed to tell the girls that fairy tales simply didn't happen in real life. As if a prince would really marry a charlady from a dysfunctional family who believed that her hallucination of a rat turning into a coachman was actual reality.

Opening the door out onto the corridor, she called to the girls, 'It's time to leave, girls. I'm sure your mums will be wondering what has taken us so long. And Miss Murphy will be looking for you too.'

At the mention of Miss Murphy the three girls squealed and bolted for the door. Miss Murphy was renowned for not only being one of the best dance teachers in the country but also for her fearsomeness. She ran her dance school like a military academy.

The girls skipped down the stairs in front of Tom. She quickly followed, still embarrassed by the way she'd nearly cried in front of him. What had *that* been about? She had been enjoying the girls' reaction to the toy workshop one minute, and the next thing, when she heard their soft lullaby, she had felt as though someone had cracked her heart right open.

Inhaling a deep breath as they neared the ground floor, she knew she needed to refocus. Today was about getting

Tom involved in the party—about developing an attachment in him towards Loughmore. Earlier, when he had driven her to the castle from her cottage, she had tried to persuade him to attend the party but he had refused, citing work as an excuse. She had been racking her brains for the past few hours as to how to get him involved, and then she had been gifted those three girls, who had ambushed her the moment they had arrived at the party with questions about the Prince and why he wasn't at the party.

At the bottom of the stairs the three girls ran across the marble floor, but suddenly Grace Carney came to a skating stop while the other two carried on in the direction of the ballroom. Rushing back towards Tom, she stretched her neck back to meet his eye and said, 'Prince, will you come and meet my brother Jack? He says you don't exist.'

Ciara was seriously tempted to high-five Grace Carney—she was the gift that kept on giving today. This was a great way to get Tom more involved in the party.

Before he could say no, she said quickly, 'Come along for five minutes. You can say a quick hello to Jack and everyone else there—the whole village has made a huge effort to get here today in the snow. They would appreciate you popping in.'

Tom eyed her warily. 'I need to get back to work.'

Ciara looked from Tom down to Grace. As though waiting for a signal, the moment Ciara gave her a mischievous grin Grace grabbed hold of Tom's hand and without a word began to drag him in the direction of the ballroom.

Once inside the ballroom, Grace pulled Tom over to where her twelve-year-old brother Jack was sitting at a table with his mother, scowling in the direction of the primary school *céilí* band, who were performing on the temporary stage at the top of the room.

Grace came to a dramatic stop in front of her brother

and, placing her hands on her hips, said, 'Jack, this is the Prince. I *told* you he existed. See—I'm not silly.'

Jack looked in Tom's direction and folded his arms, clearly not impressed. He studied Tom before asking, 'What team do you support?'

Mimicking Jack, Tom too folded his arms and answered, 'Brighton.'

Tom's answer elicited an eye-roll from Jack even more dramatic than anything his sister was capable of producing.

Clearly flustered, Jack's mother intervened. 'Jack, *behave*! Your Grace, I'm sorry.' Standing up, she added, 'Thanks a million for hosting such a special party—it's the highlight of all the children's year.' Pausing, she looked in the direction of Jack and frowned. 'Perhaps not the pre-teens, though…you know what it's like. They can be such a handful.'

Then, stopping, she clasped a hand dramatically to her cheek.

'I should have offered my condolences. We were so sorry to hear about your father. He was a good man to the village—always willing to support us in the restoration of buildings and any charitable causes that existed. He'll be missed.'

Tom gave a tense nod.

Jack's mum regarded him with a puzzled expression, but then she said in a rush, 'Of course I'm sure you'll follow in his footsteps and be a good neighbour to the entire village.'

Tom nodded, and was in the process of backing away—no doubt in a bid to return to his work—when he was surrounded by a group of villagers who all spoke to him, offering their condolences and welcoming him back to Loughmore.

When the crowd had dispersed Ciara assumed Tom would make a dash for the door—especially as the local musical and drama group had begun a clap-along acapella version of every cheesy Christmas hit ever to have existed.

Ciara loved it. But, given Tom's pained expression, which was nothing in comparison to Jack's—who actually looked as though the singing was making his ears bleed—she guessed neither of them were particularly loving the singalong.

Tom spoke to Jack's mother, and then to Jack. Immediately Jack stood up and followed Tom out of the room, both looking as though the hounds from hell were chasing them.

When they reached the hallway, Tom said something to Jack and Jack's scowl shifted into a beaming grin.

Ciara's smile faded. How different things could have been.

Later that evening Tom sighed when the library door swung open once again. Even before she appeared he guessed it was Ciara, because no one could swing a door open with such energy as she managed to.

Storm bounded in before her and, spotting him, charged across the floor with an enthusiasm even greater than usual and with one mighty leap jumped straight onto his lap.

Now dressed in faded blue jeans, brown suede ankle boots and an open navy and green plaid shirt over a white cotton tee shirt, Ciara propped herself against the floor-to-ceiling bookcase just inside the door. 'I suppose you can guess that Storm was missing you.'

Patting Storm, Tom asked him, 'Is Boru still terrorising you, boy?'

As if to say yes, Storm laid both of his paws on Tom's chest.

Ciara gave a guilty smile before her gaze shifted away. Her cheeks reddening, she said, 'Willy Wonka my all-time favourite movie is on TV in fifteen minutes. Will you watch it with me?'

Tom studied her for a moment. What was she up to? Pushing back his chair, he folded his arms and nodded to his phone. 'Thanks to this afternoon's diversions I'm snowed under here. I still have a mountain of phone calls to make.'

'Are you sure? Libby made some homemade chocolates… We can have some while watching it. Christmas isn't Christmas without watching some of the old classics.'

Right. It was time they had a frank conversation or the next few days were going to be torture.

Standing, he moved around the desk and towards her, the floorboards creaking as usual as he passed the leather club chair. 'You don't have to try to be my full-time entertainment rep, you know.'

'What do you mean?'

He settled himself beside her, one arm resting on a book shelf. 'You're not going to change my mind about selling Loughmore with your cute Christmas campaign.'

Ciara looked at him, outraged, and then huffed and puffed for a while. He raised an eyebrow, not buying her indignation for one moment.

She stepped away from the bookcase. Folded her arms. Unfolded them. Raised them in a gesture that might be one of resignation or outrage—he couldn't quite decide.

'Okay—fine. I'll admit I won't stop trying to remind you of why you should keep Loughmore, but there was nothing orchestrated about the girls wanting to meet you. And it was their idea to ask you to visit Santa with them. Thanks for being so kind to them, by the way…' She paused and placed her hands in her back pockets, biting her lip in amusement. 'When they were leaving earlier they asked me to say goodbye to the Prince for them.'

His eyes wandered to the way the deep curve of her breasts beneath her tee shirt was revealed as her shirt shifted backwards. He was *not* going to think about how she had looked…how she had felt and tasted when they had made love all those years ago.

He looked away. Willed his pulse to calm down.

Clearing his throat, he tried to focus on what they were talking about rather than the sudden urge to reach forward and pull Ciara to him. God, what he wouldn't do to be able to wrap his arms around her waist, feel the softness of her against him once again.

'What is it with little girls and princes? What's the attraction?'

'Gosh, let me think. A good-looking, sometimes decent guy who lives in a magical castle… What's there not to like?'

'*Sometimes* decent?'

'For crying out loud—you're considering selling the magical castle!' Pausing, she ran her fingertips along the spines of the leather-bound books on the shelf beside her. Then, with all traces of teasing gone, she said, 'You missed the girls dancing, by the way—they were brilliant for their age. Where did you and Jack disappear to?'

'When I saw the lead singer of the musical group dragging audience members up on the stage to join in, I decided poor Jack needed rescuing. I took him out to the stables. He told me he's asked Santa for a pony for the past few years but has never got one—I think that's why he gives Santa such a bad rap. I let him ride Goldstar in the inside arena. He's a natural.'

'Wow, I bet you've made his Christmas.'

Her smile fading, Ciara looked away from him. She stepped back on one foot, worrying at her lip all the while.

When she looked up again she held his gaze and then, in a soft voice close to a whisper, said, 'Jack is the same age as…'

His heart plummeted. He inhaled a shaky breath and said, 'Yes, he is.'

'Do you think...?' She paused, her mouth working.

He knew he shouldn't, but the pain, the sadness in her, had him stepping even closer. Into that space that changed everything between a man and a woman.

'Do I think about...?'

He paused too, raw fear coursing through him. It was only one word. A simple word. *Our.* But he felt he had no right to it. How would Ciara react if he used it? Had he forfeited his right to use it that day in London when he had let her down so awfully?

Clearing his throat, feeling as though he was about to step off a precipice, he said, 'Do I think about our baby?'

She blinked.

His heart banged against his chest. He was vaguely aware of Storm head-butting his ankle, looking for a rub.

Her chest rose heavily. Then she nodded, and nodded again. Silently saying yes, that was what she wanted to know.

The urge to hold her, to tuck her forehead against the hollow of his throat, wrap himself around her and keep her safe for ever, was unbearable and also absolutely senseless.

So instead he briefly touched the pad of his thumb against her cheek and said softly, 'Yes, sometimes I do.' He stroked her arm, felt the powerful shudder that ran through her body. 'Earlier...you were upset.'

She held his gaze for a few seconds before rolling her eyes, mocking herself. 'I'm just a sentimental fool sometimes. Don't take any notice.'

Thrown by the change in her mood, he paused and considered her. This was classic Ciara. Whenever anything got too serious, too emotional, she more often than not turned it into a joke. Should he challenge her on it? Would doing so only complicate everything?

In the end he said, 'You're a lovely fool, though.'

That had her laughing. 'Wow! That's one of the nicest things anyone has ever said to me.'

'Really?'

That elicited another eye-roll, but this time it was directed at him. 'No! Of course not.' She tilted her head, that rosebud mouth breaking into an intimate smile just for him. 'But it's still kind of cute.'

He should step away. Go back to his work.

He knew all this but found himself saying, 'You know what? I'm tired. Let's go and watch *Willy Wonka*—I never tire of watching Augustus Gloop being sucked up the chocolate pipe.'

With a doubtful expression Ciara watched him move to the library door and open it. 'Are you sure?'

'I'm sure. But if Libby has made any rum and raisin chocolates they're all mine.'

About to pass him as he held the door open, Ciara paused, her expression put-out. 'But they're my favourite.'

With a satisfied grin he replied, 'Oh, I know that.'

Ciara shook her head, amusement glittering in her eyes. Neither of them moved. They stayed grinning at each other. And there it was again—that connection, an emotional awareness, a pull, a dangerous spark between them that had him more than worried about how he was going to survive three whole days alone with Ciara Harris.

Tearing his eyes away from those soft, glittering brown eyes, he scooped up Storm from where he was resting on his foot. 'Come on, brave fellow. It's time you stood up to that crazy cat.'

CHAPTER FIVE

Christmas Eve...

Standing in the sunken garden to the east of the castle, watching the silver early-morning light catching the brilliance of the snow lying on the lawns running down to the lake, Ciara paused and breathed in the silence.

She loved Loughmore. She loved how difference lived in harmony here. The castle, so grand and regal, could easily dominate the estate cottages, but instead it only emphasised their small, cute perfection. The formal gardens with their polite structure were the same; their order only emphasised the wonder, the rawness, the rich natural evolution of Loughmore Wood and the Wicklow Mountains beyond.

She loved the centuries of history layering the castle so thickly you could almost touch it. She loved it all. And even though last night, as she had watched the film with Tom, his laughter had brought back so many bittersweet memories that she had been left wondering just how long she could handle being so close to him without losing her mind, standing in the garden right now reminded her of why she had to see this through and persuade him not to sell.

They had watched the movie in the Duke's Sitting Room. It was where Tom's father had retired after dinner every night and where he'd entertained close friends.

Of course now it was Tom's sitting room, and it had felt awkward being in the small and intimate space with him... well, small when it came to a castle. It was at least three times the size of Ciara's own living room.

Ciara had made sure to sit in a single chair a safe distance away from where Tom had sat on the sofa, his long legs propped on a foot stool. She had thought watching a movie with him wouldn't be a big deal.

Boy, had she been wrong.

Instead of watching the movie, her eyes had kept slipping over to gaze at him. Her heart had danced at his quiet smile when Charlie had found his Golden Ticket. And then her heart had sunk when she'd stared and stared at the perfection of his neat ears, the smoothness of his forehead, the refined sharpness of his cheekbones and the nobility of that perfectly straight nose. At the strength of his neck that was matched by the broadness of his shoulders, the hard, masculine shape of his mouth that gave only the tiniest hint of how passionate and overpowering his kisses were.

Storm had lain on the sofa beside him, snoring contentedly as Tom's long, lean fingers stroked him. And she had remembered how he'd used to stroke her back after they'd made love, making her sigh with bone-deep contentment and struggle not to fall asleep under his soothing touch.

Her heart had sunk because in that moment she had admitted to herself that no other man had ever come close to Tom. She had dated other guys, trying not to compare them to him, but he had always been there. The benchmark for the knee-weakening, butterflies-in-the-stomach chemistry that drew you to a partner.

Halfway through the movie Tom had caught her staring at him. By this time—much to her dismay—a slow, torturous blaze of physical longing for him had been sweeping through her. The atmosphere in the room had instantly changed.

She had forced herself to stare at the screen, but from the corner of her eye she'd been able to see Tom gazing in her direction.

Growing increasingly hot, she had longed for the movie to end. When it had, she'd shot out of her chair, attempted a laid-back yawn and said she'd head to bed.

She had nodded when he had gently asked if her bedroom was okay, if there was anything she needed, not trusting herself to speak in case she said, *Actually, Tom, I'd like to kiss you and have your hands on my skin. I want to feel the strength of your body pressed against mine. Frankly, I want to get all hot and bothered with you.*

He had walked with her as far as the stairs, the stillness of the castle emphasising their footsteps on the marble floor, their aloneness in the vastness of the building. She had glanced briefly in his direction and been taken aback by the tension in his expression. Then she'd muttered a goodnight and bolted up the stairs. Glad she had chosen a bedroom at the opposite side of the castle from his.

Her announcement that she was moving in to the castle for the Christmas period had been received in stunned silence when she had told the other staff. Their disquiet had dissipated, however, when she'd explained she needed to stay close to the gardens and that she would ensure the Duke was taken care of over the Christmas period even if he *was* insistent on everyone else not working for the three days.

Now, turning her back on the view, Ciara climbed up the steps at the rear of the sunken garden and stood beneath the row of Italian Cypresses that lined the raised banks. Heavy snow was starting to coat some of the branches. Raising the pole she held in her gloved hand, she stepped back as far as she could and, reaching up, knocked the worst of the snow from the first tree.

For the next while she moved along the row of trees,

enjoying the satisfying thump of landing snow. Until she miscalculated the weight of snow on one tree *and* the fact that there was a Brachyglottis greyi immediately behind her, therefore blocking her ability to step out of the way of the falling snow without trampling the poor shrub.

She gasped as an avalanche headed in her direction. Snow pounded her head. Encased in white coldness, she struggled for breath. And then she yelped and screamed as snow slid down her neck and ran like an ice floe down her back.

She dropped the pole. Tugged off her jacket. Next came her jumper. Untucking her shirt from her jeans, she did a little dance in a bid to toss out the snow that hadn't already melted.

And then she heard laughter.

Standing on the path at the other side of the sunken garden was Tom, with Storm at his side, shaking his head, clearly amused at her predicament.

He eventually managed to pull himself together enough to ask, 'Do you want any help?'

She gritted her teeth. And then called back, 'No, I'm good.'

Her response only seemed to amuse him even more. 'Now, how did I guess that you were going to insist that you're fine?'

Ciara eyed him. He was asking for it…

She pulled on her jumper and then her coat before she called over to him, 'Actually, Tom, I could use your help. There are some high-up branches I can't reach.'

Immediately he climbed down the steps of the garden. Halfway down he turned and called to Storm to follow him, but Storm ignored him in favour of sniffing at a modern metal sculpture of an Irish Red Deer.

As Tom passed the fountain in the centre of the garden

Ciara bent down and pretended to retie the lace of her work boot. When he was ten feet away she stood up.

Tom came to a stop. He narrowed his eyes, sensing danger.

From behind her back she produced a snowball. It wasn't as perfectly compact as she would have hoped. But it would do.

Quick as lightning, Tom ducked down, his hands scooping up his own heavy pile of snow.

Ciara threw her snowball. It hit him on the shoulder, snow exploding everywhere.

Shaking his hair free of the snow, Tom stood up. With a slow, disturbingly sexy grin he patted his snowball into a perfect circle.

When he threw it Ciara ducked, and gave a shout of delight when it missed her.

Tom came closer.

Unable to stop herself, Ciara gulped at the intensity of his expression. There was only going to be one winner of this snowball fight and it wasn't going to be her.

She knew she should at least stand her ground. Fight him. But seeing Tom bearing down on her, his eyes a terrifying combination of lethal amusement and purpose, she fled.

She darted in between the cypresses and out onto the path on the other side, heading towards the sanctuary of the arboretum. The path was slippery, but still she ran, thankful for her heavy-soled boots. Behind her she heard Tom curse as he slipped and skidded on the path.

She stopped and pointed out, 'You need to wear proper outdoor shoes, not brogues.'

His response was to duck down and gather more snow.

She gave another cry of satisfaction when he once again missed her.

Beneath his grey overcoat he was wearing a red jumper

and dark jeans. He had a grey and white woollen hat on his head. His breath came out in puffs of steam. He looked hacked off.

He had never looked so gorgeous.

God, she was weak for him.

Tom studied the icy path and then the snow-covered lawn. Before he had even edged towards the lawn she knew what he was about to do.

She waved her hands. 'No! You can't run on the lawn. Sean will kill me…you'll damage the grass beneath. We'll be seeing your footprints for months.'

He lifted one foot over the lawn. Daring her to stop him.

'I mean it, Tom, don't walk on the grass.'

'Fine. But then you must come back here to me.'

She looked at the lawn and then at him. She'd take her chances with Sean. Twisting around, she began to run.

She could hear the soft crunch of snow behind her to her left. And it was coming closer and closer. She yelped. And then an arm was on her waist, lifting her away from the path.

They fell onto the lawn.

At first she landed on Tom, but then they were rolling as she fought him.

When they came to a stop—she on her back, Tom above her—she grabbed a fist-load of snow. But just as she was about to throw it Tom grabbed her wrist and forced her to drop it.

And then they lay there, both panting hard, their laughter fading. Unconsciously she shifted beneath him, a powerful surge of physical need engulfing her.

His eyes raked over her face. Settled on her lips.

Her heart came to a stop.

He dipped down.

Her heart spluttered as for the first time in twelve years

she saw the navy flecks in his eyes. His breath mingled with hers.

She felt light-headed, dizzy with the need for him. Unconsciously she lifted her head, her lips parting.

His gaze grew darker.

A deep thrill twisted inside her.

And then his lips were on hers. Soft. Warm. Testing, as if to ask if this was what she wanted.

With shaking hands she rested her fingers on his hat, pulling him towards her.

He made a guttural sound in the base of his throat.

Every cell in her body responded with an upward surge of elation. This was so familiar—but even better than she remembered. This was everything she had missed for so many years. The finger-tingling passion of being on the receiving end of a kiss from the man you wanted to be at one with, who made your heart ache in a thousand ways.

She shifted her body again, wanting even more of his weight upon her.

His kiss became more demanding. She met him with the same hunger.

He yanked off her hat. Clasped his hands beneath her hair, his fingertips on her scalp. Deepened his kiss even more.

She cried out. Wrapped a leg around his. Lost to the brain-zinging taste of his mouth on hers.

Warmth, need and disbelief spun and spun inside her. She tightened her fingers against his skull, dizzy with the passion of his faint-inducing kiss.

But then, with a groan, Tom was pulling away, twisting his head to the side.

Storm was standing there, looking baffled by the sight of his master rolling about in the snow.

Tom dipped his head down against her throat for a second. Groaned. And then lifted himself off her. With a rueful smile he helped her stand up.

Ciara busied herself by dusting herself down. Desperate to hide the lust that must still be in her eyes given the heavy, sensual beat still pulsating in her body. Desperate to hide how disappointed she was that their kiss was over.

Tom brushed the snow off his coat too and then, studying the imprints of their bodies on the grass, he pointed and asked with a grin, 'So how are you going to explain *that* to Sean?'

Ciara groaned. She was happy to keep this light-hearted because she didn't even want to *start* to think about the implications of what had just happened between them. 'God, I don't know. Maybe I'll say a cow broke into the garden.'

Bending she swept some snow into the vacant space, praying the grass wasn't overly damaged.

Straightening, she added, 'I'd better get back to work.'

She heard the slight tremble in her voice. She was cold…but in truth it was the emptiness, the sense of loss, the confusion over their kiss that was causing her to shiver.

Tom reached for her elbow. 'What happened just now…' His voice trailed off, his expression giving nothing away.

She shrugged, desperate to get away. 'A kiss for old times' sake?'

His eyes narrowed. 'I guess…' And then with a sigh he said in a soft voice, 'There's still something between us, isn't there?'

A spectacular lump formed in her throat. His voice was so tender, so honest, so sad. She blinked back tears. 'Yes. But that doesn't mean it's right.'

He nodded at that. 'Last time we didn't say goodbye to one another the way we should have. Let's not let that happen again.'

She forced a smile. 'But we aren't going to say goodbye. I'll see you here in Loughmore whenever you come. I'll even give you a tour of my projects every time you visit, so you can see why you made the right decision in keeping Loughmore.'

Shaking his head, Tom called to Storm and, trying to hide his amusement said, 'You're incorrigible.'

Ciara watched him walk away. Alarm bells in her brain were telling her that she needed to be careful, protect herself. She needed to ensure that there were more people around. It was too dangerous when it was only the two of them.

She called after him. 'Is it okay if I invite some people over tonight for drinks?'

When he turned with a quizzical look she blushed, but forced herself to say, 'I think it would be good for us to have some company.'

He blinked as he realised what it was she was saying. With a nod, he turned away—but then turned back again. 'It was you who encouraged me to become a chef all those years ago. I think it's time I said thank you, so I'll cook Christmas dinner for us tomorrow.'

'But you're the Duke... I should be cooking for you. That's what I've planned. Libby has left me all the ingredients I need and detailed instructions.'

Tom flinched. 'When you were packing at the cottage yesterday I tested the cookies you had left out... I assume it was you who made them?'

Ciara nodded. 'And?'

'They were...*interesting*.'

Ciara could not help but laugh. 'I think you mean inedible. Okay, you make dinner. To be honest, I was dreading it.'

Once again Tom and Storm walked away.

She wanted to shout after him to get off the grass.

But God knew this was *his* castle, after all... And in a

few months' time it might not matter anyway if Tom was serious about selling.

Which would mean she would never see him again.

He turned when he reached the steps, gave a slight nod before he disappeared from view.

She swallowed against the tight lump in her throat. Then took her phone out of her jacket pocket and began to phone her friends who lived nearby to invite them over for drinks.

Popping open a bottle of champagne that evening, Tom filled the glasses of all those present—Liam Geary and his wife Maeve, Libby, Vince McNamara and Ciara—before proposing a toast, 'Wishing you all a happy and peaceful Christmas.'

Everyone dutifully tapped their glasses, but there was an awkwardness in the room. Liam kept fingering his collar while Maeve looked decidedly pale…especially in comparison to Libby, who looked as though she was seriously overheating.

Only Vince seemed immune to the unease. He had swept into the room a little earlier in the company of Libby, gasping loudly at his surroundings before enthusiastically complimenting the décor.

The drawing room had always been Tom's favourite room in Loughmore, but it still surprised him just how proud he had felt at Vince's admiration for the thirty-foot-long room, with its ornate gilded ceiling, rich red tapestry rugs, the two Christmas trees flanking the marble fireplace, the red and gold thread curtains and the antique side tables and sofas commissioned by the Sixth Duke of Bainsworth in Paris.

Toast over, they all stood at the centre of the room, Libby, Liam and Maeve avoiding eye contact with him.

An uneasy silence fell, until Ciara intervened by saying, 'I mentioned to you that Vince's husband Danny is away skiing? Unfortunately he didn't make it back to Lough-more before the snowstorm... It was to be their first Christ-mas together.'

Tom turned to Vince. 'I'm sorry to hear that.'

Vince gave an unconvincing shrug of bravado before putting his arm around Libby's shoulders, 'I may not have Danny tomorrow, but I do have Libby—we're spending the day together. And as for Danny—he's in Dublin being spoilt rotten by his mother as we speak.'

Tom smiled at the affection in Vince's eyes when he said Danny's name.

Maeve obviously saw it too, because she said in a voice full of warmth, 'Marriage suits you, Vince. I don't think I've ever seen you so happy.'

Vince batted his hand and grew a little red while tears formed in his eyes. He nodded, and then with a laugh admitted, 'It *is* wonderful...to find someone you love so much and who loves you back with equal passion... I never knew I could feel so loved, so secure. What more would you want in life?'

Liam and Maeve nodded in agreement before sharing a private look.

Tom twisted the stem of his champagne glass and willed himself not to glance in Ciara's direction. But that lasted all of five seconds. He looked over at her. She met his gaze be-fore dipping her head, a small blush forming on her cheeks.

His heart punched hard against his ribs. Why had he kissed her this morning? Why was he complicating things when he had sworn to himself he wouldn't? He had said they'd be friends. Friends didn't kiss. And certainly not the kind of hot, lustful, memory-provoking kiss they had shared this morning. Why was he leaving himself open to the pain and bewilderment of twelve years ago all over again?

But the worst part of it all was that he should bitterly

regret the kiss, but he didn't. How could he when it had been so glorious, so intimate, so beautiful. Kissing Ciara was like nothing else. It sent his senses crazy but it also gave him an emotional warmth, a sense of belonging, a sense of being true to himself that was as wonderful as it was bewildering.

Libby broke the silence in the room. 'Right. That's my New Year resolution sorted out. I'm going back to online dating. There has to be someone out there for me. You too, Ciara... Let's be dating partners.'

Ciara. Dating. Hundreds of men staring at her profile picture. No way.

He turned to Libby. 'Online dating can be dodgy.'

Libby gave him a doubtful look. 'I suppose...'

Libby looked so crestfallen, and so nervous of him once again, that he gave her a smile and said, 'I have a number of guys working in my restaurants who are single. I can introduce them to you...you'd share the same passion for cooking.'

Libby looked startled at first by his suggestion, but then her face lit up. 'Wow...if you wouldn't mind.' Pausing, she gave a little laugh. 'I didn't think you would be a match-maker, Your Grace. Sounds like our love lives might be improving next year, Ciara!'

Ciara gave Libby a dubious look. 'Perhaps...' Then, looking around the group, she said with a little too much enthusiasm, 'Why don't we play a party game?'

Tom could not help but moan.

Liam laughed and said, 'I'm with you, Your Grace.'

Tom threw his eyes to heaven. 'For crying out loud, people—stop calling me that. I'm *Tom*.'

They all nodded, and the tension in the room eased even further as their nods were joined with broad smiles of relief.

He spoke to the group, but to Liam and Libby in particular. 'I may be the Duke, but I see all our roles as being of equal value and importance. I know in the past my father kept everything very formal, but that's not my style. I run my restaurants on the basis of trust and respect, with everyone from the waiting staff up to my executive chefs treated with the same value. I want the same with my estates.'

Vince raised his glass and said, 'Hear, Hear.'

They all good-naturedly tapped their glasses again.

Then Vince added, 'Now, can we get on with a party game? I propose charades.' Wrapping his arms around Libby's and Ciara's waists, he drew them to the stuffed velvet sofa at one side of the fireplace, 'Libby and Ciara—you'll be on my team.' When all three had settled on the sofa, Vince said with a cheeky grin, 'Tom, Liam and Maeve—you can be on the losing team.'

Liam exchanged a look with him. It was game on.

Ciara was the first up. The two groups had spent some time coming up with suitable titles for the opposing teams, which they had typed into the memo section of their phones.

Ciara read the title on Liam's phone screen. Her eyes twinkled and she hit him with a much too self-satisfied grin. 'That's easy.'

Maeve threw a dirty stare towards Liam, who was sitting beside her on the sofa. 'I told you it was too easy.'

Ciara turned to her group.

Vince enthusiastically responded to her gestures. 'It's a book. Four words. The third word is *the*.'

Libby joined in, 'The second word is small... An... is...it...to...'

Ciara shook her head.

'Of!' Vince shouted.

Ciara gave a thumbs-up.

'Fourth word...'

Libby and Vince stared at Ciara as she moved up and down the floor, flapping her arms at her sides.

'Bird. A penguin. A crow.'

'A robin. A thrush. A chicken.'

'An ostrich!' Libby shouted.

For some reason this cracked Ciara up. She shook her head, tears of laughter bubbling in her eyes. She tried to do her acting out again but kept stopping, overcome with laughter.

The gold sequinned dress she was wearing stopped at mid-thigh. Her legs seemed to go on for ever until they reached the pale gold stiletto shoes on her feet. Her hair was tied up in a loose chignon. She looked absolutely beautiful, standing before the fireplace, the sequins in her dress flashing as they caught the lights from the Christmas trees and the flames from the fire... And Tom realised in that moment that it would be so easy to fall in love with her all over again.

He flinched at the idea. Ciara would never love him back. How could she after all the pain he had caused her?

In their time together they had never uttered the words *I love you*—perhaps both of them had known they were too young for such a momentous statement, too scared of the implications.

Her teasing, her batting away of his compliments, had eased, though, in the weeks before they had made love—and in the weeks that had followed. She had softened, had listened to him with an intensity that had cracked open his heart. And she had walked straight in. Their love for one another had been there in their lovemaking. In the way she had gazed into his eyes with an unwavering honesty, vulnerability, trust.

A trust he had destroyed.

Now, across the room, Libby and Vince were shouting out every bird name they could think of, totally ignoring

Ciara's hand-waving as she tried to silently tell them they had gone down the wrong track with their obsession with bird names.

Throwing her hands up in the air, she eventually caught their attention by pushing her right index finger forward.

'First word,' Vince said.

Ciara pointed back to Tom.

He could not help but smile at the seriousness of her expression. She was determined to win.

'Tom… Your Grace…' Vince called out.

Ciara nodded, but then shook one hand from side to side, to indicate that it was something similar.

With pleasure, Tom called out, 'You only have fifteen seconds left.'

That started an avalanche of answers from Vince. 'Duchess… Queen… Boss… King.'

'King of the Jungle!' Libby called.

'King of the Castle!' Vince shouted.

By now Ciara was once again shaking with laughter.

'Time is up,' Tom announced.

Libby and Vince groaned.

Ciara threw her hands up in the air, and with laughter bubbling in her voice said to her teammates, 'It was *Lord of the Flies*, you twits.'

Later, after seeing the others to the door, Tom found Ciara in the kitchen. She gave him a quick smile before placing the now empty bottles of champagne into the glass recycling bin. Then she began to fill the dishwasher with the cups and saucers they had used.

She gave a chuckle. 'Libby looked as though she was going to pass out when you insisted on making tea and coffee for everyone.' Then, after a pause, she added, 'It was a fun night. Did you enjoy it?'

There was tentativeness in her question.

He eyed her, pretending to think deeply.

She straightened, a cup still in her hand. Waiting for him to answer.

Eventually he answered with a grin, 'It was fun. Especially beating you at charades.'

She scowled at him, but then laughed.

A happiness, a contentment, spread through him like warming brandy. God, he loved being able to make her smile.

Her eyes moved beyond him, and he turned and saw she was looking towards the kitchen clock.

In a low, eager voice she said, 'It's only half an hour until midnight. Right now is my all-time favourite time of year. Don't you think there's something magical in the air?' She paused and tilted her head. 'I always think that if I listen hard enough I might hear Santa's sleigh.'

'Just how much champagne did you have?'

She glared at him light-heartedly. 'My own Christmas grouch!'

She had called him a grouch. He should be put out. But instead a deep pleasure fizzed through him. *My own...* She had said those words with such warmth.

Taking the cup from her, he placed it in the dishwasher. Then, shutting the door, he said, 'Let's go greet Santa.'

He told her to change into something warmer, and to wear outdoor shoes, and then turned away when she bounded up the stairs, her short skirt bringing back the memory of her leg curling around his earlier that morning. He had burned with the desire to yank off her coat... to lift her jumper and feel the soft skin of her stomach. To place his lips there and then move upwards to the sweet swell of her breasts.

Within five minutes she was racing back down the stairs, zipping up a padded jacket.

He took her outside and they followed the path down to

the lake. At the lake house he pulled out two of the wicker garden chairs stored there for summer picnics on the lake and a couple of blankets. Positioning them on the wooden jetty, he told Ciara to sit on one, passed her a blanket and, after switching off the lake house light, joined her.

It was a brilliantly clear night. Millions of stars hung over them and the moon was a gentle crescent.

Sitting, he said into the still night, 'I reckon this is the best place to see Santa.'

Her laughter rippled out along the lake. 'I take it all back—maybe you're not a grouch after all.'

For the past couple of days he had thought her enthusiasm for Christmas was based on her campaign to stop him selling Loughmore. But now he realised it was genuine.

'Why do you love Christmas so much?'

She shifted in her seat, pulling the blanket more tightly around herself. She tilted her head back and stared at the stars for a while before answering. 'When I was growing up, as you know, it was just myself and my mum. We had no other family to spend Christmas with and it was all a little sad, to be honest. We used to eat Christmas dinner in front of the TV. My mum wasn't into decorating the house too much. It was nothing like the fun family celebrations I saw in the movies. My memories of Christmas are all a little grey… I guess I'm trying to make up for that now.'

Adjusting her hat with gloved fingers, she pulled it down too far, the brim covering her eyes. She giggled to herself. Lifting the brim, she caught his gaze. His heart stumbled at the warmth, the hope, the excitement in her eyes.

'Christmas should be joyful. It should be a time you spend with people you love.' She stopped abruptly, looking at him wide-eyed. 'Like tonight—I love Vince and Libby to bits. They're good friends. And Liam and Maeve have been really supportive since I came to Loughmore.

Their sons live abroad, in Vancouver and Perth. They miss them greatly—I think Maeve likes to mother me in their absence.'

She gave him a quick smile. Flustered.

'So—what was Christmas like in the Benson family?'

'Noisy. Chaotic. My parents always had friends and family to come and stay for the Christmas period. As you would have seen by the large number of guests who came here to Loughmore during your summer stays, my parents liked to entertain.'

'You didn't like them entertaining?'

'It always felt like we children were lost amongst all those guests. Now, with hindsight, I can see it was my father's way of ignoring all the things that were wrong in his life.'

'Like what?'

'His marriage. The financial strain running such a vast estate brings. My father was deeply ambitious and driven. He felt he had to live up to the title of Duke—be superhuman somehow, larger than life. All his achievements— socialising, entertaining, his obsession for polo—were how he thought a duke should behave. He was an overly proud man, who would never ask for help from anyone. And he didn't accept weakness in others.'

'And you were caught up in all that?'

'Fran, Kitty and I spent very little time with our parents. As you know, we were sent to boarding school from the age of seven, and when we were at home the houses were always full of visitors that had to be entertained.'

'I often wondered about your mum—didn't she miss you when you left home at such a young age?'

His mother had been a remote figure when he was growing up. He had felt as though all her energy had been consumed in keeping his father happy. No wonder he had fallen so hard for Ciara—elated to finally have someone so gregarious and giving in his life.

'My father had such a big and powerful personality, it dominated their marriage. I know she loved him, but it was as though she was constantly trying to please him, placate him. She's changed since my father died. Since he's gone she's more relaxed. When he was alive we had a difficult relationship. She always took his side.'

'Against you?'

'He threatened me with disinheritance when I became an apprentice chef. My mother stood by his stance.'

Ciara sat forward in her chair. Touched her hand against his knee. Settled her troubled eyes on him. 'Tom, why didn't you tell me?'

Because I knew you would worry, feel responsible for encouraging me to follow my dreams. I wanted to protect you, Ciara. I wanted to make you proud. I was sick of feeling like a failure.

He didn't say any of those things to her. Instead he held her gaze and thought of his mother, and how she had spent her lifetime trying to win his father's love. 'My mother was never certain of my father's love. It's almost destroyed her.'

Ciara's hand remained on his knee. Over the treetops and along the flat calm surface of the lake skimmed the sound of church bells.

Ciara blinked. Said in a whisper, 'It's Christmas Day.' She swallowed. Tears shone in her eyes. 'Happy Christmas, Tom.'

The weight of her hand on his knee, her nearness, her soft compassion, the care in her eyes, almost undid him.

For a brief second she closed her eyes, and then added in another whisper, 'I thought of you every Christmas—wondered how you were.'

That hit him like a boot in the stomach. He wanted to shout at her not to say things like that. He wanted to drag

her on to his lap, wrap his arms about her and lose every
part of himself in her.

Instead he nodded and quietly spoke the truth. 'I thought
about you too.'

Ciara sighed heavily. A sigh full of sadness and regret,
but a sigh that also said that it was all in the past. And she
was right. They needed to move on.

So, despite the urge to pull her into him, to feel her lips
beneath his again, he stood and said as light-heartedly as
he could, 'Right, you need to go to bed, Ciara Harris, or
Santa won't come and leave you any presents.'

CHAPTER SIX

THE FOLLOWING MORNING, about to enter the breakfast room, Ciara stumbled to a stop—thanks to the sight of Tom strolling towards her with that easy, sexy saunter that had always been her undoing as a teenager.

Her knees wobbled, threatening to give way, and it had nothing to do with the weight of the tray she was carrying. Yep, that saunter still managed to nail her.

His hair damp, today he was wearing slim-fitting navy trousers and a pale blue shirt, the top button undone.

Early Christmas morning and Tom Benson.

A lethal combination of pleasure and potential disaster.

Images raced through her mind—Tom in the shower just now, earlier asleep in his bed... They had only ever managed to spend one whole night together, but the image of him curled into her, the long length of his eyelashes fluttering when he muttered in his sleep, his arm lying heavily on her waist, was deeply ingrained in her memory. She had lain there as the sun had peeled away the night, astonished and scared that she could feel so much for another person.

Now she held her breath as his eyes moved over her, taking in her cream blouse with its wide bow at the neck, her black cigarette pants. She was pointlessly pleased by the attraction in his eyes.

His eyebrows flickered upwards when his gaze settled

on her bare feet, her toenails painted bright scarlet in honour of the season.

She gave him an apologetic smile. Despite the fact she had only been wearing her black patent stilettos for little more than an hour, her feet had ached in them so badly she had jettisoned them earlier, while working in the kitchen.

It was a good job Stephen wasn't around—he would have a conniption if he found her wandering around the castle shoeless. Especially as the bluebell tattoo on her right foot was visible.

A surge of embarrassment ripped through her as she remembered the various other social faux pas she had unwittingly committed as a teenager when around the Benson family. Kitty and Fran had always responded with giggles, while Tom's mother would look away with an expression that suggested she was yet again disappointed in the whole of mankind. His father would simply glare in her direction, as though wondering who'd allowed this simpleton into his household.

As Tom neared her, she tried to shake off all those thoughts. 'Good morning. Breakfast is ready. If you would like to take a seat, I'll go and fetch some tea for you.'

Tom regarded her curiously. Then, glancing into the breakfast room, he asked, 'Why is the table only set for one?'

Last night, as she had tossed and turned in bed, remembering their kiss on the lawn that morning, and the searing heat that had consumed her despite the ice-cold snow beneath her, remembering the affection in Tom's eyes later as she had failed hopelessly at her turn in charades, the pull she'd felt towards him as they had sat by the lake awaiting Christmas Day, she had known she needed to back off, to be more careful around him. She was once again losing herself to him. Forgetting all the reasons why they could never be together.

'I…well…staff don't normally eat with the family.'

With clear impatience he took the tray from her and entered the room. 'Come on, Ciara, you're more than staff.' Depositing the tray on the table, he turned to her and said, 'I thought we were friends.'

She followed him into the room. Placed her hands on the back of one of the twelve carved walnut chairs surrounding the breakfast table. 'It's all getting a little messy.'

Tom folded his arms. 'I'm sorry about our kiss yesterday.'

Despite herself, she flinched. Unable to look at him, she moved her gaze to the bay window of the room. It was snowing again beyond the sash window.

Behind her the fire snapped and hissed gently.

'What time were you up this morning?'

She turned at his impatient question. 'Just after seven.' When his expression hardened she added, 'I couldn't sleep. Rather than lie there I thought I would get your breakfast ready.'

'I don't expect you to look after me, Ciara.'

How was she going to explain that she felt safer when their roles were clearly defined? When there were boundaries set down by centuries of tradition that dictated staff were never even to *attempt* to mix with the family, to believe they were equals.

Going to the tray, she lifted off a silver pot of marmalade and a silver jug filled with milk. Trying not to blurt out the crazy thoughts rampaging through her mind.

Maybe I want to look after you, Tom. Not in the way a staff member takes care of her boss. But in the way a couple look out for one another. Do something nice to make your day pleasurable.

'I'll go and get you some tea…or would you prefer coffee?'

'For crying out loud…'

With that Tom left the room. Ciara chased after him. He was heading in the direction of the kitchen.

Once in the kitchen, he slammed the kettle onto the heating plate of the range. And then he turned to her. 'You're joining me for breakfast. Tea or coffee?'

Ciara hesitated, but then she saw the tiniest hint of amusement tugging at Tom's mouth. Her own mouth twitched. She folded her arms and gave him her best evil look. 'You were always bossy, Tom Benson.'

'And *you* were always useless at keeping a straight face.'

With a feeling of ridiculous pride, Ciara watched Tom finish his breakfast of smoked salmon and scrambled eggs on soda bread. Outside, snow still gently floated past the bay window. The fire continued to crackle, heating the room with a soothing warmth that induced the need for a quick nap—as evidenced by Storm, who was laid out before the hearth, snoring contentedly.

Tom chuckled as Storm gave a particularly loud snuffle.

Ciara felt a dizzying, out-of-body disorientation. What was she, a working-class girl from Dublin, doing sitting in the breakfast room of Loughmore Castle on Christmas Morning, having breakfast with the Eleventh Duke of Bainsworth?

She sipped her tea. Meeting Tom's eye over the rim of her cup. His smile faded. To be replaced by an intensity that matched the violent sweep of attraction hijacking her own body.

Her heart rolled in her chest.

Springing out of her chair, she began to clear the table. Needing to be busy. Needing to ignore the ever-increasing simmering tension between them.

She gave her best cheerful grin, and hoped her voice sounded breezy. Back in entertainment rep mode, to use

Tom's words. 'After I clear up, let's open our presents under the tree.'

Standing too, Tom began to clear away the dishes, saying nothing.

His silence unsettled her. Only adding to her feeling of jitteriness.

She had known being alone with him, spending so much time together, would be difficult. But she hadn't expected to be so physically drawn to him, so crazily craving to be in his company. She actually missed him when they were apart. What madness was taking her over?

She lifted the tray she had loaded. Almost buckled under its weight. She had absentmindedly overloaded it.

Taking it from her, Tom placed it back onto the table. Lightly he placed his hands on her shoulders and held her gaze. 'Breathe, Ciara…relax.'

What did he mean? She gave him a puzzled look. And then, seeing the amusement in his eyes, she laughed out loud at her ability to freak herself out so easily.

Her laughter shifted the tension in the room and together they cleared the table and cleaned up in the kitchen, with Tom telling her about his restaurants, making her giggle by recounting humorous incidents with customers.

When they'd finished they moved to the drawing room. Tom shook his head as his gaze took in the already lit fire, the twinkling lights of the two trees flanking the fireplace and the pile of Christmas presents she had earlier placed beneath one of the trees. 'There was no need…'

She shushed him by kneeling down on the rug beneath one of the trees and pushing a pile of brightly wrapped presents towards him. 'These are all yours.'

Taken aback, he stared at them. 'From whom?'

'The small rectangular present in the silver paper is from the staff here in Loughmore and the others are from me and Boru.'

He sat down on a nearby chair and studied the pile. His gaze travelled back to her. The smile he gave her warmed every cell in her body.

'Thank you.' Then, running a hand over the smooth skin of his jawline, he said ruefully, 'Let me guess—Boru has given me anti-scratch ointment.'

'No. But, you know, that's not a bad idea for next year.'

Too late she realised what she had said. There would be no 'next year'. This Christmas was going to be a one-off.

She forced down the dismay that came with that thought and nodded to his pile. 'Come on—aren't you going to open them?'

He selected the rectangular present wrapped in shiny red paper first. He opened it up, studied it and then turned the photo frame towards her. It was a photo of the castle she had taken early yesterday morning. With the grounds blanketed in snow, the castle had never looked so magical. She had driven into the village yesterday afternoon to print the photo at Murphy's Chemists, and also to pick up some other presents for Tom.

Tom gave her a dubious look. 'It's a stunning photo…but certainly not the most subtle present I have ever received.'

She feigned innocence. 'It's not often we have snow in Ireland. I thought you'd appreciate a memento to have with you when you're not here in Loughmore.'

He raised his eyes heavenwards, not buying it for a moment. Then nodding towards her pile he said, 'Your turn.'

She selected a square present wrapped in paper bearing images of hundreds of tiny jolly Santas riding their sleighs through the night sky. Libby had given it to her. Ripping the paper open, she laughed at the present inside. 'A board game based on Truth or Dare. Libby knows of my addiction to board games.'

When Tom opened his next present he sighed deeply and once again turned it around towards her. 'Really?'

A few years ago, when Tom had announced he was opening a restaurant in Paris, a renowned Parisian restaurateur had been scathing about Tom's, calling the food 'pedestrian.' Tom had stayed silent on the criticism, but a year later, after Tom's, Paris, had received a host of food awards, he had invited the other restaurateur for dinner at Tom's during a radio interview. The restaurateur was yet to take up the invitation.

Trying to keep a straight face, Ciara held out her hand for the cookbook by that restaurateur, intending to pretend to flick through the recipes. 'I thought you should keep up to date with what your competition are doing.'

Tom passed the book to her, but when she took hold of it refused to let go. 'So you've been keeping an eye on my career?'

Ciara willed herself not to blush. She pulled at the book, but still Tom would not let go. He was clearly not going to give in until she gave a response.

'Call it a passing interest.'

He laughed. Clearly not buying that either.

She ignored how pleased he looked at the fact that her teasing present to him had backfired, with her now being the one embarrassed, and grabbed another of her presents.

This one was from Maeve and Liam. It was a bottle of perfume. One she had not used before. Opening the package, she admired the ornate flower-shaped bottle top and sprayed some of the perfume on her wrists and throat. She was enveloped by a light but sensual floral scent that reminded her of sweet peas in August, with a backdrop of delicate lemon.

Then, unconsciously, she leaned towards Tom and held her wrist out. 'Isn't this incredible?'

Tom leant over her wrist. The tip of his nose touched her skin. A deep craving so hot and lusty that it threatened to split her in two shot down through the centre of her body.

For a brief moment he took hold of her wrist. She swayed at his light grasp. Then, lowering her hand, he said in a low voice that held a dangerous note, 'You should wear it all the time.'

All the time... Including in bed? She shook off that thought and lifted another of his presents. Trying to be light-hearted, she waved it about. 'Bet you can't guess what this is!'

'Let me see... A cylindrical box with something moving inside it. Tennis balls for Storm to chase? A map for buried treasure?'

Lifting another small present, Ciara showed it to him. 'Storm has his own present to open. And you certainly don't need a map for buried treasure.'

'I wouldn't be so sure of that.'

Ciara looked at him curiously but he shrugged away his words.

Calling to Storm, who was half hidden under the sofa behind Ciara, dozing once again, Tom laughed when he opened Storm's present to reveal a red and green chequered neckerchief. Placing it around Storm's collar, Tom rubbed him vigorously before opening the cylindrical box.

'Twenty-year-old malt whiskey...there was no need.'

Ciara sliced her hand through the air, silencing him. 'You asked Santa for it—of course there was a need.'

He laughed. 'I also remember asking for peace and quiet.'

'That will come...once you decide to keep Loughmore.'

Tom looked down at Storm, shaking his head. 'She gives with one hand...takes with the other.'

Ciara had one final box to open. It was a huge present wrapped in gold paper from Vince and Danny. Last night when Vince had given it to her she had tried refusing to accept it, instinctively knowing, even without opening it, that it would be a much too generous gift. But Vince had insisted she accept it, explaining that it was his and Danny's way of thanking her for looking after their menagerie of pets when they were away on honeymoon earlier in the year.

Ciara opened the box with her breath held tight. Beneath a thick layer of gold tissue paper was a white and gold strapless gown. She gasped when she pulled it out. Standing, she held it against herself, her hands flaring over the full skirt that reached to her mid-calf. It was the most stunning piece of clothing she had ever seen.

'Danny is a buyer for one of the major department stores in Dublin. He was showing me some of the winter collection online one night and I fell in love with this. It was out of stock at the time. I can't believe he found it for me.'

Her heart came to a stop when she looked back at Tom. He was studying the dress hard and then he stared at her. His voice was deep, possessive, when he spoke. 'You will look amazing wearing it.'

She laughed off his compliment. 'I need to find somewhere to wear it first.'

His gaze shifted away from her. He rolled his shoulders. Eventually he said, 'Come to the New Year's Eve ball.'

Ciara clutched the dress tighter to herself. Why had he hesitated before asking her? And, anyway, was he even being serious? Staff *never* went to the ball. Nor did any of the locals. The Loughmore New Year's Eve ball was attended by the rich and famous and titled. 'I can't.'

'Why not?'

'I'd only embarrass you—like that time at your eighteenth birthday party, when I said I hated a particular movie only to find out the producer was actually sitting at the table, listening to my every word. I thought your father was going to kill me.'

Tom tried his best not to laugh. 'It *was* an awful movie.' Then, his expression sobering, he asked, 'Will you come?'

For a moment she considered pointing out all the reasons why she couldn't but, not wanting to destroy the Christmas atmosphere, she said instead, 'I'll think about it.'

Kneeling down again, she passed his last present to him and began to fold away her dress.

Unwrapping the metallic silver paper, Tom opened the ruby-red presentation box inside. Lifting out a heavy metal key, he weighed it in his hands before saying in a low voice, 'The key to Loughmore.'

'Apparently it's tradition for the staff to give every new Duke a key,' Ciara explained.

Tom inhaled deeply and studied her with a perplexed expression. 'Didn't you try to stop this? You *know* what my intentions are.'

'And you know I don't agree with them.'

With that Tom stood and, grabbing all the paper strewn on the floor, crumpled it all into a tight ball. 'I'll go and make dinner.'

Standing too, Ciara faced him, fear at the thought of Loughmore falling into developers' hands having her say sharply, 'Tell me why you have to sell Loughmore, Tom? I still don't understand.'

He let out an angry breath, his nostrils flaring. He turned to walk away but then swung round. 'My father has left the estate in debt. I have no option.'

Dumbfounded, she stared at him. 'Tom… I'm sorry. I had no idea.'

He shook his head impatiently and turned away again.

She followed him instantly and reached for his arm. 'This must be a huge worry for you.'

He slowly turned to her, the frustration in his expression giving way to a guarded tiredness.

Blushing, she shook her head, frustrated and annoyed

with herself, 'And there I was, giving you a hard time. I wasn't exactly being any help, was I?'

Tom threw the ball of wrapping paper onto the chair behind him. 'You weren't to know.'

'Would you keep Loughmore if the finances allowed it?'

'Maybe.'

'I thought your restaurants…?'

He raked a hand through his hair. 'I don't want to burden my restaurant business with the debts of the estate. They're two separate entities.'

'Is there anything I can do?'

His jaw tightened. 'There's nothing *anyone* can do.' But then his irritation seemed to melt away and with a faint smile he admitted, 'But you asking that means a lot to me.'

Her heart skipped at the sincerity in his voice.

'As do all the presents…' He paused. 'I almost forgot *your* present. Wait here—I'll go fetch it from my office.'

Though Ciara hadn't expected a present from him, she could not help but be secretly chuffed that he had thought to give her one, and when he came back into the room carrying a small package she tried to keep a lid on her excitement.

Opening the glittering snowflake-printed paper, she felt a solid lump form in her throat. Inside the wrapping was the antique Irish wildflower identification book she had spent so many summers poring over in the Loughmore library when no one else had been about.

She held the book out to Tom. 'I can't… I can't accept this. It's too rare—too valuable.'

Tom backed away. 'It's yours. To the rest of us it's just another book amongst the thousands lining the shelves of the library. I know how much you used to love it and I want you to have it.'

Ciara's throat closed over. She did love this book. Opening it, she turned the pages. The full-page illustrations of wildflowers such as bog myrtle and Marsh-marigold on heavyweight paper, with interlining tissue guards to protect them, were as intricate and vibrant as she remembered. But what was getting to her even more was the fact that Tom had remembered her love for it.

'Now, I guess I'd better go and make that dinner I promised you.'

She looked up at Tom's words. 'I'll help.'

He looked as though he was about to argue with her, so before he could she intercepted him. 'I'd enjoy watching you cook.'

A wicked grin formed on his mouth and Ciara tried not to blush. That had sounded all wrong.

Eventually, after grinning at her for much too long, he put her out of her misery by saying, 'Okay, but you're on veg prep.'

Together they walked to the kitchen, with Storm loudly giving chase to Boru when he spotted him slinking into the Billiard Room. Ciara's heart sang to hear Tom's laughter when both animals bounded out of the room, Storm slipping and sliding on the marble floors as he tried to capture his arch nemesis.

Later that evening, Ciara wobbled on her high heels, fully understanding now why Storm struggled so much on the smooth marble floors of Loughmore. Stopping at the entrance to the dining room, she tugged on the bottom of her dress, questioning once again if she had made the wrong choice in what to wear for dinner.

It was embarrassing enough that she had looked blankly at Tom when he'd earlier suggested they change for dinner. It had taken her a few minutes to realise he meant they should dress up for the occasion…well, dress up more than they already were.

Given that she spent the majority of her days outdoors,

she didn't have many dressy outfits in her wardrobe, and as she had already worn two of her limited supply in recent days she had spent the last half an hour agonising over whether the high street dress she had purchased for the nightclubs of Ibiza when she had gone there on holidays two summers ago was suitable for Christmas dinner with a duke in his fairy tale castle.

No, was probably the correct answer to that question.

Entering the candlelit room, she willed herself to remain calm when Tom stood up from his seat at the top of the table. Dressed in a dark navy suit, white shirt and a navy tie with small red polka dots, gold cufflinks glittering in the candlelight, he looked completely at home in his opulent surroundings. His gaze slid down her body, his expression darkening, and Ciara's heart kicked wildly in her chest.

When she neared him he held out the chair to his right for her to sit on. Maggie and Stephen had set the table before they'd left for their break with their usual meticulousness. A huge centrepiece of fresh red roses scaled to accommodate the vastness of the twenty-two-seater table sat in the middle, with four tall candelabra on either side. A smaller version of the centrepiece sat between her and Tom.

They had spent hours in the kitchen together, with Tom patiently explaining what he was doing and how she could help and the radio playing Christmas songs in the background. Even though she had been hyper-aware of him, the mood had been relaxed as they'd worked together. But now all that had changed. Was it the dimness of the room? The act of eating dinner alone? The fact that her dress was probably a tad too short?

Then, as she was about to take the proffered seat, her attempt at calmness became a distant memory when he bent and kissed her cheek. His lips were warm…tingleinducingly firm. She breathed in citrus and leatherwood. Her hand reached for his arm to steady herself. But the strength, the hard muscle she found there, only made her feel even more breathless.

His lips lingered for long seconds. And then he murmured, 'Happy Christmas, Ciara.'

Her head swam.

Tom stepped back, his gaze moving over her once again. 'Please tell me you've never worn that dress out in public.'

His voice was unsettlingly husky. She tried to ignore the melting sensation in her bones.

Placing a hand on the Balmain-inspired brown and black sequin-embellished dress she shrugged innocently. 'I've only worn it to the County Wicklow Gardening Awards ceremony.'

Tom's jaw stiffened. 'You aren't being serious?'

She let him dangle for a few seconds before giving a laugh. 'Of *course* I'm not being serious! I might not be the best with social etiquette, but even *I* know this is a bit much for an event where the average age is sixty-five.'

Taking her seat, she accepted the white wine Tom offered her before he went over and took their starters from the warming oven in the adjacent Dinner Service Room.

She gripped the stem of her wine glass, fighting the compulsion to tell him to sit down—that it was she who should be serving him. And when he sat beside her, so at ease, born to be surrounded by such beauty and luxury, she felt like a complete fraud.

She did not belong here.

She bit her lip.

Tom's gaze narrowed. 'Is something the matter?'

She shook her head, too embarrassed to try to explain how out of place she felt. And also determined not to ruin their first…and only… Christmas meal together.

She tried to keep her sighs to a minimum as she hungrily ate the velvety and luscious cauliflower velouté with black truffle, but one eye-roll of pure pleasure too many had Tom grinning from ear to ear.

For their main course Tom had cooked a fillet of cod with a poached egg on a bed of crushed potatoes, with beurre blanc and roasted root vegetables.

Taking a mouthful of the delicate fish, she felt her eyes twitch with the need to close them in delight.

Biting back a smile at Tom's expectant look in her direction, she shook her head sadly. 'It's not turkey—I always have turkey on Christmas Day.'

He stabbed at his potatoes with a fork. 'So you've been reminding me—all afternoon.'

She bit back a smile. 'It's… It's…' She paused, his eyes narrowed, and tilted her head. 'It's the most fantastic dish I have ever tasted.'

Later that evening Tom reluctantly allowed Ciara drag him into the drawing room. Before the fire she had placed a large upholstered ottoman that was groaning under the weight of various board games.

Slipping off her shoes, she knelt before the ottoman. 'Indulge me for an hour.'

In her kneeling position, even more tantalising inches of her toned legs were exposed. He knew he was staring, so he forced his gaze away, and then he was captured by the beauty of the fiery depths of her hair glistening in the firelight, the seductive shimmering of the sequins of her dress. But it was her eyes, bright and gleaming, that captured his heart.

A ton of worry lodged in his chest. He was growing too close to her. Letting her into his heart. Earlier, when he had told her about the estate's debts, her empathy had broken through the burden he had been carrying around for the past few months. And later, as they had prepared dinner together, they had worked in easy companionship. Ciara, despite her teasing, had been eager to learn.

And then later, when she had tasted his food, he had felt a warm glow of pride fill his chest. It had felt good to hear her praise, to provide her with pleasure. Unfortunately it had felt a little *too* good. He knew he had to be careful. But that was easier said than done when it came to Ciara Harris.

'How about we give Libby's present a go?'

He watched Ciara pull off the cellophane surrounding Libby's present, and then open the box to reveal a board and cards inside, and considered saying that he had work he needed to attend to.

But the excitement in her eyes when she looked up had him kneeling opposite her.

Reading the instructions, she said, 'Okay, first around the board wins. There are "Truth" and "Dare" cards, all ranked in difficulty from one to five. The player gets to choose the ranking. You can forfeit the "Truth" or "Dare", but that means you do not advance on the board and you also miss your next go. Do you want to go first?'

He studied the cards. What would be the best tactic? Go first and have a head start? Or have Ciara go first so he could learn about the difficulty of the cards from what she selected. He nodded to indicate that he'd go first.

Ciara pointed to the cards set in the centre of the board. 'Truth or Dare?'

'Truth. And I'll go with a level three card.'

Ciara picked up a yellow "Truth" card and read it out loud. 'Did you have an imaginary friend when you were growing up?'

Oh, hell… This was going to be embarrassing.

He rolled his neck, trying to ignore the way Ciara was studying him expectantly.

He cleared his throat. 'Yes.'

When he didn't add any more, Ciara laughed and said, 'For crying out loud, Tom, you have to tell me more than just *yes*. Was it a girl or a boy? Did he or she have a name?'

He rolled his eyes, cursing the heat of embarrassment that was building on his skin. 'A boy…he was called Arthur.'

Ciara clapped her hands. 'How cute is *that*? How old were you?'

He swallowed hard again and paused, desperately trying to figure out how to answer her question without sounding completely lame.

Ciara's gaze narrowed. 'This is a "Truth" card—you have to spit all the details out.'

'Okay, so he first appeared when I went to boarding school at seven…and he stuck around until I was about twelve.'

Ciara's bright beam morphed into one of disquiet.

Seeing she was about to speak, he interrupted her, 'And, yes, I *know* twelve is much too old for an imaginary friend. Now it's your turn. Truth or Dare?'

Soft brown eyes held his. 'Was he a good friend?'

He blinked at the gentleness of her tone. The understanding behind her question. She knew how much he had hated school.

Arthur had seen him through the dark nights when he had longed to be at home, hearing Kitty and Fran argue, watching his mother get ready for a night out. Anything but the loneliness, the constant bewilderment he had felt at the jumble of words that had met him every day in the classroom. Arthur had also stood bravely at his side on the rugby pitches, telling him to ignore his father's yells to 'buck up' when he visited on match days.

Now, he answered Ciara's question, 'Yes, he was a good friend—but he did get me into trouble once or twice by persuading me to raid the tuck shop in the middle of the night when he was hungry!'

Ciara shook her head, laughing. 'Everyone needs a friend like that in life. Loyal, but naughty too.'

Their eyes met. Their smiles faded. They had once been such good friends. Only now did he fully realise how much of a void had developed in his life when he'd lost her friendship.

Pushing those thoughts away, he asked again, 'Truth or Dare?'

'Dare.' She paused and gave him a challenging look. 'And I'm going for a level five.'

'Are you sure?'

She squared her shoulders. Gave him a grin that was much too sexy. 'One hundred per cent.'

'You're determined to win, aren't you?'

'Of course.'

He lifted the 'Dare' card, slowly read the details, wanting to get the words right, and with a satisfied smirk said, 'We'll see about that.' And then he called out, 'You have to perform the snake dance move for ten feet.'

Ciara stared at him. 'No way! You're making that up, aren't you?'

Moving forward, she pulled the card out of his hand. Reading it herself, she studied the pictures beneath the words with a deep frown. They showed a step-by-step guide to performing the dance.

Rocking back on her heels, she shook her head in disbelief. 'God, I thought you were winding me up. The snake dance for ten feet…that's going to be really hard.'

'So, I guess you'll forfeit?'

Her eyes narrowed at his grin. 'Not a chance.'

Standing, she moved to the side of the room next to the drawn curtains. There were no obstacles here, in the walkway that had been created to allow easy movement from one end of the thirty-foot room to the other. He stood when she disappeared behind a sofa and went and stood by the room's grand piano, which would be roughly the finish line for her ten feet challenge.

Ciara was kneeling on the floor. Gathering her hair, she twisted it into a makeshift bun. Then she rolled her shoulders, limbering up.

'Have you ever tried this before?'

Lifting her hands, she positioned them either side of her chest. 'Nope.'

Then, falling forward, she planted both hands on the floor and jerked her body forward. She moved about five inches in total. Five awkward inches that were more sack-of-potatoes-being-shifted than fluid dance move.

She tossed her head. 'Don't you *dare* say a thing!'

He swallowed a laugh.

She gave him a glare before dramatically dropping her forehead to the rug with a groan.

And then he heard her laughter. Her whole body shook.

He sat down on the rug beneath the piano and called to her, laughing too, 'Come on, Ciara, you can do it.'

She lifted her head. Laughed even more. A deep, belly-aching laugh.

A burning urge to go to her, to hold her, to lie next to her, grabbed him by the throat. He winced at its intensity, at how deeply connected he felt to this woman he had so badly let down.

Further down the room, Ciara muttered to herself, 'There must be a knack to this…'

Tom studied her. 'Perhaps brace your toes on the floor behind you and push yourself forward when you lift your chest.'

She looked at him dubiously but followed his advice. This time she shifted forward for close to ten inches. It earned him an elated beam. Her next attempt was less successful. But inch by inch she moved towards him, her cheeks rosy with exertion and laughter.

When she finally reached him, she breathlessly high-fived him.

He pulled her to him for a congratulatory hug.

They parted slowly. *Too* slowly.

Ciara held his gaze and through a soft smile said quietly, 'Thanks for the encouragement... You didn't have to help me. We are competitors after all.'

'I couldn't resist helping you—you looked pretty incredible down there.'

The heat in her cheeks flamed at his words.

She went to say something in response, but then stood and fled back to her side of the ottoman. 'It's your turn. Which do you want?'

'Certainly not Dare, after your experience—I don't fancy paragliding off the tower or anything like that. I'll stick with Truth...level five.'

She gave him a wicked grin. 'So I'm not the only one out to win.' Lifting a 'Truth' card, she read, 'What's the silliest thing you have an emotional attachment to?

He threw himself down opposite her. 'Oh, give me a break.' He gave her a deadpan look. 'I don't *do* emotional attachments.'

She wasn't having any of it. She folded her arms. 'First off, Tom Benson, don't blame me... I didn't set the questions. Secondly, it was *you* who asked for a level five, so deal with it. And thirdly, don't even think about not answering truthfully.'

With an exasperated breath he whipped his wallet out of his back pocket. Opening it up, he passed to her the small piece of paper he kept folded in there.

He watched as she unfolded the tattered edges. On the page was a delicate tiny life-size drawing of a pink five-petalled flower.

'I had forgotten about this—my drawing of the Lesser Centaury we found in the woods that day...'

She paused and looked at him. Her gaze shot back to the page. She had drawn the flower on an exceptionally warm July Sunday, when they had sneaked out to swim in the lake and later walk to their favourite spot in the woods. Insects had hummed around them as they'd lain in the warm grass, the air heavy with the scent of woodland and grass and summertime growth. They had kissed. And then slowly made love for the first time.

Her gaze swept back to his. She tried to speak but in the end all she could do was give him a sad smile.

Slowly she folded the paper again. Passing it back to him, for the briefest moment she leant into him, pressing her lips against his cheek. 'Thank you.'

And then she was pulling away.

'My turn. I want a Truth. Level five.'

For a moment he was disorientated. He wanted to talk about the past. He wanted to have her lips against his skin again. But neither made any sense, so he tucked the paper back into his wallet and picked up the next 'Truth' card on the deck.

He read it twice to himself and then read it out loud. 'What is your deepest fear?'

Ciara's eyes narrowed scornfully. 'What a daft question. I don't know—the world's chocolate supply running out, heights, walking down the street with my skirt tucked into my underpants.'

He laughed, but there was a defensiveness to her expression that had him saying, 'I'm calling cop-out.'

She eyed him unhappily. 'I see nothing wrong with my answer.'

'I hate rats, but they aren't my deepest fear.'

She looked at him curiously. 'So what *is* your deepest fear?'

How would she react if he said *Daring to fall in love with you again*? Would she laugh? Tell him he had no right to do so?

He fixed her with a steady gaze. 'You're not switching this around on me—it's your question. Answer it honestly.'

Her face set into a stubborn expression. 'I don't have any fears.'

Despite her sceptical bravado he could tell that the question had clearly unsettled her. 'Why are you being so defensive?'

Her mouth dropped open, as though she was deeply affronted. 'I'm not—who goes around talking about their deepest fears, in the name of God? I've never done it and I certainly won't start now.'

'With me, you mean?'

She blinked at that, the stubbornness in her eyes giving way to uncertainty. 'It's been twelve years, so…' She trailed off.

'So why would you trust me?'

She grabbed the deck of cards and focused her gaze on them. 'Don't take it personally—it's an Irish thing… We like to pretend everything is grand even when it's clearly not.' She looked back at him, gave a wry smile. 'We don't open our hearts easily, and talking about our emotions brings us out in a rash. For crying out loud, in my family we can't even compliment each other without throwing in an insult… My mother's favourite way of addressing me is, "Ya big eejit, ya."'

'That sounds familiar.'

She looked at him with wide-eyed surprise, but there was a knowing smirk on her lips. 'Your mother the Duchess calls you an eejit?'

He sighed. 'No—and you know that's not what I meant… I mean that *we're* not great on expressing our deepest emotions either.'

Ciara grimaced. 'It gets a little frustrating sometimes, doesn't it? Having to pretend everything is fine.'

There was a vulnerability in her voice that had him wanting to reach out to her, express some of his feelings for her.

In a low voice he admitted, 'You were the first person I ever really spoke to. You were good at listening... When we split up I missed talking with you.'

Ciara bit her lip, said quietly, 'I missed chatting with you too.'

He swallowed at the honesty in her voice. 'If you ever want to talk...'

She shook her head and gave a rueful smile. 'I think you're going to be too busy with the restaurants and the estate to be listening to *me*.'

'I'll always be there for you...call me any time you want to talk.'

She gave him a dubious smile. 'That's good to know.'

A mischievous glint grew in her eye. 'You know, I much prefer chatting face-to-face with people rather than over the phone. If you keep Loughmore we'll be able to do that—wouldn't that be great?' With a happy chortle she added, 'Now, can we please get on with the game? I'm looking forward to beating you.'

Tom shook his head. 'You're impossible.' Then, with a self-satisfied smirk, he gestured to the board. 'I believe you've just forfeited this go, and the next one, so I'm cruising to the finish line. Hit me with a Dare—level five.'

Ciara threw him an evil look, lifted a card and read it, a wicked grin breaking out on her mouth. 'You must compose a poem. You have two minutes to do so before you have to recite it out loud.'

Tom dropped his head and playfully banged it on the ottoman. 'May I have another card?'

Ciara wasn't going to give him an inch. 'Nope—and you have ninety seconds left.'

He stood and walked away. His back to her, he closed his eyes, desperately searching for inspiration.

Much too soon, from behind him, Ciara called out, 'Your time is up!'

He turned to find her standing close, her arms folded.

'It doesn't rhyme,' he said.

Her grin was wicked. 'No excuses. Come on—I'm waiting.'

He cleared his throat, squared his shoulders. 'There once was a bewitching gardener, Who liked to tantalise her employer, She set out one day, To change his ways, And he could only look on in ardour.'

Ciara opened her mouth. Closed it again. And then she was laughing and high-fiving him. 'That was so terrible it was brilliant!'

They stood grinning at one another. And in that moment Tom knew he was tired of fighting his attraction to her.

He stepped closer.

Her eyes grew wide, initially with surprise and then with something much more carnal.

He placed his hand just above the sharp tilt of her hip-bone. 'I've decided I'll be a good sport and let you have a turn, even though you forfeited it.'

She looked at him quizzically. 'What's the catch?'

He stepped even nearer, the pull towards her almost buckling his knees. He lowered his mouth to her ear. 'You can have a Truth question, and the question is...would you like me to kiss you?'

Wide-eyed, high heat in her cheeks, she searched for words. 'But that's cheating...you can't set your own questions.'

His heart thundered to hear the breathless sensuality of

her voice. 'It's a special level ten question. If you answer it you get to win the game.'

She pulled in a long, deep breath that sounded like a caress. 'Well, in that case...'

His fingertips touched lightly against the heavy silkiness of her hair. 'Remember...you have to tell the truth.'

Her eyes darkened. Her mouth parted ever so slightly. She tilted her head, edged forward, her eyes focused on his mouth. 'You know the answer to that question already... you're just being cruel in making me answer,' she said.

'I want to hear you say it.'

'Yes, I want you to kiss me.'

The delicate narrowness beneath her ribs, above the flare of her hips, was gloriously feminine. He pulled her to him, his mouth finding her ear. He nibbled her lobe. She buckled against him. His lips moved down her throat, his arm holding her tight against him.

Her fingertips trailed over his biceps, then his chest, until finally they clung to his shoulders.

His lips trailed up over the delicate softness of her throat. She trembled. Called out his name into the silence of the room.

His head spun with the need for her.

But he was not going to rush this.

While his mouth continued its slow trail over the silky skin of her throat his hands skimmed the soft shape of her hips, over the high flare of her bottom.

She tilted into him. Sighed again.

His fingers edged down. Grazed over the point where her dress gave way to the soft skin of her thighs.

'You asked if I wanted you to kiss me... I don't remember you mentioning anything about torturing me.'

He chuckled at her husky outrage, letting his mouth follow a path to her other ear, feeling his pulse pounding at her murmurs and cries, inhaling her floral scent. His body kicked in remembrance of how sweet, how passionate her body had felt beneath his all those years ago.

He grinned against her skin, and continued to trail his lips against her throat while warning her, 'You're not going to rush me.'

She shuddered again…gave a small cry.

He pulled back, revelling in her desire-fuelled unfocused gaze, the blaze of heat on her cheeks. His mouth hovered over hers. Silently tempting her. Every inch of him was screaming.

And then his lips were on hers.

He groaned at their sweet fullness.

He deepened the kiss. Her lips parted.

He swept into her mouth, pulling her tight against him. Her body—firm, softly flaring—pressed into him. Her hips pressed into his thighs, her breasts against his chest.

He clasped his hands even tighter around her waist. Her hips rocked against him.

Breaking away from the kiss, she ran a torturous warm and sensual path of kisses down his throat, her hands clumsily undoing the top three buttons of his shirt. Her lips trailed down his chest, scorching him. He groaned deeply, the noise reverberating around the room.

He stepped backwards, about to lose any sense of control, pulling her with him. He came to a stop when the wood panelling of the room pressed into his back. He twisted her around, pressed her against the wall.

His mouth found hers again. They kissed—an all-consuming, head-spinning, perfect kiss.

She shifted her body beneath his weight and for a few moments he lost himself in her gentle rocking against him. Too weak with longing to pull away. But from somewhere deep inside he finally dredged up enough energy to shift away. Not far. Just an inch or two. But enough to start making sense.

He buried his head in her hair and whispered, 'This is about to get out of control.'

'I think it already has.' Her voice trembled with the effort to speak.

He pulled even further back. Knowing he had to kill this.

Placing a hand on the wall behind her, he gave her a steadying look. 'This isn't going to change my mind about selling Loughmore, you know.'

She blinked, and blinked again, the desire in her eyes fading to comical outrage. She smacked him on the arm. 'Tom Benson...what *do* you take me for?' She waved her hand vaguely between them. 'That...that kiss...had strictly *nothing* to do with you keeping Loughmore.'

'So what *was* it about?'

She tossed her head and darted under his arm. At the drawing room door, she stared at him defiantly. 'It was about me winning the game...nothing more.' Then, with a toss of her head, she added, 'And can I point out that it was *you* who asked the question, so don't be blaming me if you can't handle the consequences. Now, I think it's time we had dessert. Libby won't be happy if she finds out we haven't tried her plum pudding.'

With that she left the room with a confident stride, her head held high.

Tom fell back against the wood panelling. Inhaled deeply.

One more day. Then the rest of the staff would be returning to work.

One more day of resisting Ciara.

He was capable of that, wasn't he?

He was capable of not doing something stupid...of not opening up old wounds and creating new ones...wasn't he?

CHAPTER SEVEN

THE DOOR OF Daly's Pub was blasted open. A procession of eccentrically dressed people carrying musical instruments walked into the centre of the room. A loud cheer went up from the already assembled customers in the ancient pub that operated not only as a bar but also as a grocer's and hardware store.

Perched at a table beside the open fire, Tom leant towards Ciara, 'What's going on? Why are they wearing those oddly-shaped straw hats?'

Ciara laughed. 'You know what? I actually have no idea! They're called the Wren Boys; its traditional for them to go from pub to pub on the twenty-sixth of December, St Stephen's Day, and play music and collect money for charity.'

The Wren Boys picked up their instruments, and at the command of a teenager, who tapped his bodhrán three times with his wooden tipper, began to play a toe-tapping céilí tune.

Their straw hats were cone-shaped, and hid many of the faces beneath, but he spotted small Sophie from the kiddies' party, who lowered her tin whistle to wave at him shyly, her red hair giving her away.

He had reluctantly agreed to come here this afternoon, eventually giving in to Ciara's protests that he had worked enough for the day and needed some exercise—the mile walk to the village being a perfect excuse to partake in a hot port in Daly's before they made the journey home again.

He took a slug of his port and looked towards Ciara, who was clapping her hands in time with the music, her eyes blazing with delight. Dressed in jeans and a thick cable-knit cream polo neck jumper, her hair tied back into a high ponytail, she looked radiant.

And he longed to kiss her again.

Which would be beyond stupid.

Selling Loughmore was a difficult enough decision. Adding the complication of Ciara into the mix was simply asking for a whole heap of trouble.

Looking about him, taking in all the faces of the other customers who had all earlier come and shaken his hand, offered to buy him a drink, taking in the old charm of the pub's interior, bursting at the seams with memorabilia and framed newspaper clippings of village events, many based around the castle, he wondered once again at Ciara's motivation for persuading him to come here.

Had yesterday, today, all been just part of her campaign to save Loughmore?

A kiss between old flames.

Those words came back to taunt him again.

Or was all this nothing more than a trip down memory lane for her?

He gritted his teeth. He was falling for Ciara. Damn it. What type of fool *was* he? To allow himself to fall for her when she would never love him back after all the hurt and pain he'd caused her.

The jaunty music and clapping flowed around him while a claustrophobic hollowness, panic, grew within him.

When the music had come to a stop, and the collection buckets had been passed around for donations, the Wren Boys left the pub to rousing applause.

Standing, he pulled on his overcoat. 'I need to get back to the castle.'

'But we haven't finished our drinks yet.'

He stepped away from the table. 'It'll be dark soon. I'd prefer to leave now.'

'It's only three—it doesn't get dark for at least another hour.'

With a shrug, he turned and walked out of the pub.

Halfway down the main street Ciara caught up with him, dragging on her green parka jacket. They passed the limestone church built by his forefathers, its grounds covered in a thick blanket of snow, and passed the People's Park, with its bandstand, seeing a few brave families making use of the playground despite the low temperatures—one little boy screaming in delight as his father pushed him ever higher on the swing. They passed a few people who wanted to stop to chat with them, but Tom ploughed on, only giving a quick hello.

It was only when they were behind the high castle walls, in the privacy of the pedestrian walkway to the castle, that he turned to Ciara, the burning need to try to understand what was going on between them propelling his angry words.

'Right—enough games, Ciara. All this…everything you have orchestrated to try to persuade me to keep Loughmore…has to stop right now.'

Ciara left out an angry breath and studied Tom, totally unamused. What on earth was *wrong* with him? They had left half-drunk drinks behind them in the pub.

Anger, tension, and a frustration she didn't quite understand bubbled away inside her. When she spoke she struggled to keep her voice calm.

'I'm not playing games. Yes, I want you to keep Loughmore. For your sake as much as anyone else's. But I've been totally upfront about that, so how exactly am I playing games?'

Tom worked his jaw and then stormed away, down the path.

With a deep sigh she followed him as he entered Loughmore Woods. Most of the trees were bare, allowing weak shafts of sunlight to land softly on the snow-covered earth, where fronds of bracken poked out as if to say hello.

To Tom's back she called, 'Do you want to know why I like working as a horticulturist? Because plants are so uncomplicated in comparison to you men.'

Tom came to a stop at the top of a small incline in the path. He waited there until she joined him. She tried to keep her expression carefree and unfazed, but there was a darkness to Tom's expression that was making her decidedly jittery.

'At least men aren't Machiavellian in everything they do.'

Ciara gave a huff of disbelief. 'How can I be "Machiavellian" when I've been straight up with you about everything?'

Tom yanked a grey woollen hat from his coat pocket and pulled it on. 'Tell me—have our kisses been just about me keeping Loughmore?'

The hat sat perfectly on his head, moulded to his skull, deepening the silver of his eyes. Her heart lurched in attraction.

How was she going to answer his question? Should she pretend that the kisses were part of her efforts to save Loughmore? That they were meaningless, *hadn't* been glorious and beautiful, *hadn't* kept her awake for the last two nights with wicked thoughts of what they might lead to, *hadn't* wrenched open her heart to this man she had once loved with every fibre of her body?

His eyes held hers… How on earth was she supposed

to pretend that his kisses weren't tearing her apart when he looked at her with such hypnotic intensity?

She willed herself to look away, but the need to be connected with him, to be at one with him, was too great. Her heart was beating solidly against her chest, her throat hot with emotion.

'No, the kisses were different—and so was most of everything we've done over the past few days, Tom. We were friends...' She trailed off as a dawning realisation hit her.

Could it be that she had been fooling herself all along? Pretending that her need, her motivation for spending time with him, was all based on saving Loughmore when the truth was she selfishly wanted to spend time with him?

Tom's mouth settled into a hard line. 'We were more than friends, Ciara.'

She felt herself blush at his softly spoken words.

He inhaled deeply, worked his jaw again, and said, 'You said before you regretted it. Is that true?'

The heat in her throat spread to every limb. She bit her lip, looked down the path, burning with the desire to run but knowing there was no way she was capable of walking away from him. For so many years she had survived by hanging on to the untruths she had convinced herself of—that she had moved on from Tom, that she regretted they had ever become lovers.

But now all those untruths were unravelling.

Yes, she regretted what had happened in the weeks and months following their summer together, but she didn't regret their lovemaking. How could she when it had been so perfect, so exquisite, so soul-connecting and intimate with the man she had loved?

She knew they both deserved to hear the truth spoken out loud. Pulling in some air, she said, 'No, I don't regret it...what we had was special.'

Tom blinked hard. His eyes flitted away in a moment's

hesitancy before they returned to her with renewed intensity. 'The rest of the staff are back working tomorrow.'

Her stomach flipped in response to the huskiness of his tone. 'I know.'

Tom looked up at the canopy of bare branches hanging over them, his chest rising and falling heavily. He hit her again with those silver eyes. 'I want to be with you tonight.'

The air whooshed out of her lungs. Tears prickled at the sides of her eyes. This was ridiculous. She should laugh and tell him he was being crazy.

It *was* crazy.

But, looking into those silver eyes, she *knew* this man— knew how honourable and good he was, how alive she felt in his arms, knew the bone-deep connection she felt with him. And she said on a whisper, 'I want that too. But only if you swear to believe that it has nothing to do with you keeping Loughmore.'

'What *is* it about?'

She had no idea. She searched for the right words, but none came. And in that moment she realised that she was tired of thinking. Tired of pretending her body and soul didn't need him, even if it was only going to be for a few precious hours.

In a low voice she answered, 'Maybe it's just about living for the moment…taking happiness when you can.'

For a heartbeat they studied each other. And then they were both moving forward.

Days of tension and attraction and denial, years of memories and longing tumbled together. They kissed furiously, their hands gripping each other.

Tom held her tight against him, his arms imprisoning her. Her head swam at his closeness, the passion in his kiss, the hardness of his body.

Fresh snow had started to fall around them, falling on the burning skin of her cheeks. In silence they walked through the woods and skirted the orchards. Tucked into his side, she felt her body hum, while her heart crashed around in her chest in anticipation…and disbelief.

She greedily pushed away all thoughts as to why this was a terrible idea and instead felt liberty for the first time in twelve years. She was going to give her body what it needed. One long sultry night with the man who answered her every physical need.

They entered the castle via the main entrance.

Storm bounded noisily towards them in greeting, pawing the leg of Tom's trousers and clearly unimpressed that his full attention was on Ciara, who was pressed against the giant wooden door, about to collapse beneath the force of his kisses.

With a groan Tom broke away to greet Storm, and when the dog finally pottered away he held her hand and together they rushed up the stairs.

He took her to his bedroom suite. Inside, he kissed her, undressed her. Laid her down in her bra and panties beneath the canopy of his four-poster bed and ate her up with hungry eyes.

'You're even more beautiful than I remember.'

She squirmed at the wonder in his voice, at the need darkening his expression. She held her hand out to him, wanting him at her side, lying on top of her. She wanted to scream with her need for his uplifting, soothing, reassuring weight.

Yanking off his clothes until only his denims remained, he knelt at the base of the bed. Ciara gasped when his lips gently landed on her bluebell tattoo, and then her ankle. Slowly he trailed kisses up her calf, murmuring words about the pleasure he found in her body.

It was torture.

Sensual torture.

She wanted him beside her. She wanted his mouth

on hers. His hips rocking against hers. She begged him to stop. But he refused. She writhed as his lips moved onwards, over the delicate skin of her inner thighs. She gasped once again when he went even higher, gasped in disappointment when his lips merely skimmed over her panty line before his lips and tongue began to wreak havoc on her stomach. She arched upwards when his lips landed on the exposed valley of her breasts, his cheek rough with evening shadow brushing intentionally against her stinging nipple.

Unable to take any more, she wrapped her hands around his head and hauled him up to her. She tugged his head down, found his mouth with her lips, groaned deep and heavy at the sensation of tasting him, feeling the elation of his weight spreading across her limbs.

When he entered her, her body arched and her heart broke open with more than a decade full of emotion. Afterwards, lying in his arms, her heart was confused. But he kissed away her vulnerability and made love to her again, with a tenderness that rubbed her soul raw.

Four lousy hours. That was how long Tom had lasted before he had given in to the compulsion to go and seek Ciara out.

He had woken this morning disorientated by the absolute exhaustion in his body but feeling contentment in his soul—only to see the cause of that disorientation about to creep out through his bedroom door.

She had turned when he'd called out to her, her stern pleas for him to be quiet, saying that some staff might already be back at work, at odds with the heat in her cheeks and her darting glances as he moved across the floor to her.

She had begged him to put on some clothes, but hadn't resisted too much when he'd dragged her into his bathroom and undressed her. In the shower they had washed one another. He had gently stroked every inch of her body with a burning need to worship her.

Now, just before lunchtime, despite his pledges to himself that he would play it cool and keep everything that was happening between them casual and relaxed, here he was, searching for her in the gardens with a crazy desperation to see her again.

He eventually found her in one of the glasshouses, bent over a table full of plant trays. She did not respond when he called out her name.

He stood watching her, a jolt of pleasure streaming through him at the memory of looking up into her dazed, passion-filled eyes as she'd straddled him last night, her glorious hair fanned across her naked breasts.

And then, as though sensing him, she turned, tugging out the earbuds from her ears, her smile uncertain.

Keep it cool and relaxed, Tom. No pressure. Don't expose yourself.

'Hi, I thought I'd come and see how you're doing...'

That was the right balance between being a gentleman, caring for a woman you'd slept with, and being casual, wasn't it?

For a moment she looked nonplussed, unsure of what her response should be, but then, gesturing to the trays on the table behind her, she answered, 'I'm just checking on the winter salads—Libby wants to use them for the starter at the New Year's Eve ball.'

He plucked some rocket from one of the trays. Sweet but peppery, it tasted amazing. 'This is really good.'

Ciara ran her hands over the tall glossy leaves of a tray of Swiss chard. 'We're really proud of the quality of the vegetables and fruit we grow here. In fact, we're now supplying some of the top restaurants in Wicklow and Dublin.'

She paused, turned towards him and fixed her hair behind one ear. He was immediately on the alert. Ciara always touched her hair when she was about to say something she was uncomfortable about.

'I've been thinking—'

He interrupted her with a groan.

She gave him a stern look. 'Let me make it clear...' She reddened and waved her hand vaguely between them. 'What I'm about to say is in no way connected with last night, before you start accusing me of some great Machiavellian plot. It's merely a suggestion.'

She shifted further away to the end of the table, which was lined with trays of Mizuna.

'I understand now why you have to sell Loughmore, but maybe there's a way around it. You've seen the quality of the organic produce we grow here in Loughmore—why don't we grow even more? And, I don't know if you remember, close to the village there's an old barn that could easily be converted into a restaurant—why don't you open a Tom's here? The castle could be opened up during the months you aren't here too. Tours could be given and I can run workshops on wildflowers and heritage plants. And those old stables that aren't used any more would look fantastic converted into shops. Libby's sister Heather is looking for a suitable location to open an art gallery, and there are lots of other artists based in County Wicklow who would love the opportunity to work in a community. Tourism is growing in the county all the time. We can tap into it.'

She paused for a breath, her eyes willing him to be as enthusiastic as she was.

'We can make Loughmore financially viable for you.'

If only it was that easy. 'The estate is in too much debt.'

Ciara gave him a contrite grimace. 'Earlier this morning I looked up Tom's restaurants' financial results from last year. I don't understand why you can't service the estate's debts with the profits you have made.'

Taken aback by how much thought she had put into this, but disliking her interference, he let out an angry breath. 'Those profits are being ploughed back into expanding Tom's.' He gritted his teeth. 'I appreciate your input, but the estate has to fund itself.'

'But *why*?'

'They're two separate entities. I don't want to saddle the restaurant business with debt issues my father created.'

She folded her arms and considered him with a puzzled frown. 'But they both belong to you now. They're both *part* of you. You should protect them. You grew one from nothing, which is amazing, but you should equally cherish your inheritance.'

'And what if I said I never wanted to inherit it in the first place?'

'Why would you say that?'

Because Loughmore reminds me of you, Ciara...of what I did to you. The shame of how I treated you. It reminds me of the baby we lost. It reminds me of how you refused to answer my calls. It reminds me of how you turned your back on me that night in your mother's house and told me you never wanted to see me again.

'The restaurant trade excites me. The estate doesn't.'

Ciara came and stood beside him. She was wearing a brown padded jacket, the same shade as her eyes, zipped up so that it almost reached her chin. She looked at him with an honesty that took him straight back to his bedroom last night and the way her eyes had clung to his when they'd made love.

'You'll grow to love Loughmore. I know you will. Please don't rush into this decision. Loughmore deserves better. So do you.'

He shook his head, not understanding. 'What do you mean?

'Your dad has just died. You've taken on a huge amount

of responsibility on top of the restaurant empire you're already running. It's a lot for one person to manage.'

Her words were hitting raw nerves he hadn't even known he possessed. 'I've wide shoulders. I'll cope.'

Ciara didn't look convinced. 'Are you *really* ready to let Loughmore go?'

Frankly, he didn't know what he wanted any more. He had left London less than a week ago, intent on selling Loughmore, restoring the estate's finances and for once and for all putting the ghost of his love for Ciara firmly behind him.

He rolled his shoulders, plucked more rocket, ate it and shrugged. 'I believe so.'

Ciara's hand tentatively touched against the sleeve of his wax jacket. 'I'm not trying to give you a hard time. I want to *support* you.'

He swallowed hard, taken aback at just how acutely moved he was by the truth of her words. He pulled her into his arms and hugged her, muttering 'I know.' He took a few seconds' pleasure in her warmth, touching his lips against her hair, before he reminded himself that he was supposed to be acting laid-back and stepped away.

She wrapped her arms tightly about her waist, rocked back on her heels. She wasn't quite able to hold his gaze. 'Last night... Please know that was just about you and me. Nothing about you keeping Loughmore.'

He could not help the grin that grew on his mouth as images of last night flashed before him—her shyness at first when he had undressed her, her gasps as she had lain beneath him calling his name, her body arched into him... 'Did you enjoy it?'

Her eyebrows shot upwards. She looked at him, speechless for a few seconds, and then her lips quirked, 'It was pleasant.'

He moved in next to her. Stared down into her laughing eyes. 'Just *pleasant*?'

She pursed her lips. 'Yes… I think "pleasant" is the right word to describe it.'

He reached for the waist of her jeans, pulling her hips against his thighs. 'Well, we'll have to make it spectacular tonight.'

She blinked in surprise, blushed, but then let out a theatrical sigh. 'I'm afraid there's no tonight. I'm going home now that the roads have been cleared. And Vince has invited me over to have dinner with himself and Danny.'

He lowered his mouth. She tried to resist him but within seconds was melting against him, sighing with pleasure.

He pulled away long enough to mutter, 'Tell Vince he has another guest coming for dinner.'

CHAPTER EIGHT

TOOTHBRUSH IN HAND, Ciara crept from her bathroom into her bedroom. Was that a car she had heard, approaching the cottage? At her bedroom window she gingerly parted the curtains in time to see the inner light of Tom's four-by-four flick on as he opened the driver's door.

A thousand tiny bubbles of excitement popped inside her. She gave a squeal—and then grinned at her own inanity.

She hadn't expected him tonight. In spite of the fact that he had appeared at her door for the past three consecutive nights.

She had tried objecting, telling him people would find out, but he had refused to listen. And in truth she hadn't put up much of a fight. Not when he was leaving for London in two days.

Their time was running out.

She grabbed that thought and discarded it somewhere deep inside her. She was dreading the emptiness she was going to face, but hungry to grab hold of what little time they did have left.

Wearing a heavy navy overcoat and a peaked tweed hat, Tom made his way up the cobbled garden path and she danced from foot to foot, her body jittery with attraction, her heart dancing to its own peculiar tune. As he neared the front door she raced downstairs in her bare feet.

She grinned at his gentle rapping and inched the door open. 'Shouldn't you be at the castle, entertaining your mum and sisters?'

He leant much too sexily against the doorframe, those silver eyes beneath his peaked hat trailing over her ivory silk dressing gown. 'Looks to me like you were expecting company tonight.'

Okay, so maybe she *had* dressed for him—just in case he decided to make it four nights in a row. But she wasn't going to admit that to him.

She folded her arms, not budging from the door. 'You haven't answered my question.'

'My family were tired after their journey here today. They went to bed early. Now, are you going to let me in?'

Ciara's heart thudded at the dark desire in his eyes. 'What if they find out you've come here?'

He shrugged. And then gave her the sexiest grin ever. 'Do you know what I want to do with you tonight?'

She gulped. 'No—what?'

He nodded towards the dying fire, glowing softly in the hearth. 'First I'm going to get that fire blazing again.' Raising his right hand, he went on, 'Then I'm going to open this champagne.' Searching his coat pocket, he extracted a smaller bottle, filled with pink body lotion. 'And then I'm going to lay you down before the fire, undress you ever so slowly, and massage every inch of your gorgeous body.'

Ciara dragged in a shaky breath, trying to calm the pressure of excitement and longing weighing heavily in her bones.

'I must admit I'm in need of a massage. There was a lot of snow that had to be cleared away on the grounds today, in preparation for the ball tomorrow night. I was thinking of booking in for one tomorrow at the local spa.' Swinging the door open, she gave him a cheeky grin. 'But I guess you'll save me the trip.'

* * *

Later, they lay on her sofa, covered in a thick throw, Tom's warm body wrapped tightly against hers.

A sigh of pleasure escaped from deep inside her.

Behind her Tom chuckled, his lips gently kissing and teasing her neck.

She snuggled into him, loving this moment of feeling desired, protected, safe.

His lips moved to her ear. She blushed even more fiercely when he began to list all the parts of her body he adored.

She laughed as his list went on and on. Then, turning to him, she shook her head teasingly. 'Tom Benson, you're such a charmer.'

That earned her another wicked grin.

And then his mouth was on hers. His kiss was gentle. Tender. His hand moved slowly over her bare skin…a delicate caress. She pulled away, unable to handle just how vulnerable and confused it made her feel.

She gave a smile, trying to pretend all was fine when in truth she was beginning to feel really scared. His silver eyes held hers and she flipped onto her back, afraid of what he might see.

'So, are you coming to the ball tomorrow night?'

Ciara twisted her head back at his softly spoken question, her heart plummeting. The real world was out there, ready and waiting to point out why all this was a really bad idea.

Grabbing her dressing gown from the floor, she pulled it on. Standing, she backed away from the sofa and, despite the growing panic swirling in her stomach, laughed and rolled her eyes.

'Of course I'm not going. As I've told you plenty of times over the past few days, I'm a member of staff—I don't belong at the New Year's Eve Ball!'

Seeing his expression harden, she felt compelled to fill the tense silence that followed.

'I'm not sure how the other staff would react—or anyone else for that matter. How would we explain it to your family? It's better that I don't go, but I'm sure you'll have a wonderful night.'

Reaching for his trousers, Tom tugged them on. 'We don't need to explain our actions to others. We're grown adults. But if it makes you happy we can say your invitation is my way of thanking you for keeping me company over Christmas.' She was about to speak but Tom got there before her. 'I've also invited Vince and Danny. I thought you'd like to have them there.'

Grabbing hold of her nightdress, that was still on the floor, she wrapped it in a tight ball and placed it on the stairs. 'I really don't want to go. It's not a good idea...' She trailed off, seeing Tom's mouth flatline into a grimace.

The New Year's Eve ball was, by all accounts, a spectacular affair. She should be jumping at the chance of going. And she'd have Vince and Danny for company. But it would deliver her smack-bang into the reality that she didn't belong in his world of wealth and power and social etiquette.

'I don't understand why you're inviting me.'

Tom paused in buttoning his shirt. His hands dropped to his hips.

Standing there, bare-foot, his trousers slung low on his hips, his open shirt exposing the knotted muscles of his abs, the smooth firmness of his chest, Tom eyed her with incredulity. 'Are you *serious*? After the past few days— what we've shared—how could I *not* invite you?'

Oh, God, why had she opened this can of worms? Why hadn't she just made up some excuse as to why she couldn't go, rather than argue the point with him? Now they were heading in the direction of needing to have 'a talk' about how this would all end rather than just saying goodbye to one another…however *that* was supposed to have worked.

She hadn't put much thought into it, unfortunately. Oh, Lord, it was going to be awkward and horrible. She inhaled against the panic growing inside her, the sickening loneliness coating her heart.

'It's very honourable of you to invite me, but I honestly wouldn't have been offended if you hadn't. I had no expectations that you would do so. We both went into the past few days with our eyes wide open—we knew it was just two old flames rekindling what they'd once had. Let's not complicate it.'

A dash of red grew on Tom's cheeks, highlighting the sharp curve of his cheekbones. 'I'm inviting you as a friend. I'm hoping you'll enjoy the ball and have fun. And, as I said already, it's my way of thanking you for your company over Christmas.'

Ciara was about to say something, but Tom got there before her, a sharpness to his voice, 'And before you even think it, never mind *say* it, I don't mean that I'm thanking you for your company in bed.'

Plucking the now empty champagne glasses off the floor, she felt her resolve not to go to the ball wane. It was obviously important to him, and she knew she should accept his invitation graciously, without making a huge song and dance over it.

Straightening, she gave him a warning look. 'Well, if I manage to insult one of the guests or commit some other social faux pas you have only yourself to blame.'

His expression remained grave but his eyes crinkled ever so slightly. 'You won't—and even if you do you're so adorably sincere people will forgive you.' Moving next to her, he placed his hand on her waist and said quietly, 'I'm glad you're coming.'

She gave a wobbly smile. The feeling that events were overtaking her, that she no longer had any control of her life and how she felt for this man, was weighing heavily on her chest.

Tom disappeared into the kitchen, but soon returned with the champagne bottle. 'We have at least half a bottle to finish.'

Part of her wanted nothing more than to spend the night with him, to go upstairs and lose herself physically with this man who managed to turn her inside out. But another, more vehement part of her demanded she start protecting herself. Sleeping with him was stripping away every protective layer she had wrapped around herself in the years following their split.

She forced herself to give him a playful grin. 'I reckon I need my beauty sleep tonight. Time for you to head home.'

Tom looked at her, bemused.

She moved to the front door.

Tom did not follow.

She tried not to wince at the confusion, the hurt in his eyes... It was just his male pride, wasn't it?

He turned and yanked on his sweater and overcoat before joining her at the door. He eyed her unhappily for a brief moment, before turning his attention to unlatching the door.

'I'll be tied up with the arrival of our guests, so I probably won't see you tomorrow, but I'll come and collect you for the ball at seven.'

'You'll be busy. I'll make my own way there.'

He shook his head. 'I'll collect you at seven.'

Then, with the briefest of kisses on her cheek, he walked away. She bolted the door to the sound of his car's engine roaring to life, and as she made her way upstairs she heard the powerful car eat up the silence of the night as it furiously climbed the valley's track.

* * *

The Loughmore New Year's Eve ball was every bit as fabulous and glamorous as Ciara had heard.

Pre-dinner drinks had been served in the Great Hall, to the accompaniment of a string quartet. And the five-course dinner, which had featured crab cappuccino to start, followed by a winter consommé, then a main course of tender slow-cooked ox cheek, and salted caramel tartlets and a selection of Irish cheeses to finish, had taken place in the candlelit Orangery.

Guests had then been invited to the Ballroom for dancing, but she had yet to make her way there—thanks to Vince and Danny's insistence that she join them in the Garden Room, which had been converted into a cocktail bar for the evening. There they had soon joined a raucous table of Tom's friends from London, who were partaking in drinking games much to the enjoyment of Danny.

Vince was on call, so unable to drink, and Ciara had taken part in one game but called it quits after that, finding the bitter alcohol not to her liking.

Now, as she watched Danny and Vince lean in towards the table, sharing jokes and anecdotes with the rest of the group, she sent up silent thanks that they were at the ball. Without them she would have felt at a loss, surrounded by the confidence and social ease of all the other guests, the majority of whom seemed to know one another.

Unfortunately some seemed to remember her too, from their visits to the castle over the years, and she had had to explain that, yes, she *was* still a staff member, which had received various levels of response, but mostly taken aback surprise—whether because she still worked on the estate or was a guest at the ball, she wasn't sure.

Earlier that day she had called Tom to say she had organised for Vince and Danny to collect her from her cottage for the ball, thereby freeing him to spend more time with his guests.

After a long pause he had said, 'If that's what you'd prefer.'

She had grimaced at the coolness of his response but known it was the right call. Last night, after he had left, she had realised just how bad an idea it was for him to collect her. It would send all the wrong signals—make their relationship look like something more than friendship.

She had to think of the future—of living in Loughmore with the speculation of others about her relationship with her employer. It would be horribly awkward. Not only with the rest of the staff but also in her interactions with his family. And what if he went ahead with his decision to sell Loughmore? How would her colleagues react if they knew they had once been lovers? Would they blame her somehow for his decision to sell?

When Vince and Danny had turned up at her door she had never felt more grateful for their playful *joie de vivre*. Danny had fussed over her hair, insisting it hang loose rather than remain in the bun she had twisted it into, and the two of them had bustled her out through the door, refusing to listen to her doubts as to whether she should attend the ball at all.

On their arrival at the castle she had felt a dizzying confusion of emotions as she had stood in line, waiting to be greeted by Tom and his family in the entrance hall. Giddiness at just how handsome he looked in a midnight-blue tuxedo, his hair sleeked back, had had her skin blushing in memory of their recent lovemaking.

But there had also been that persistent feeling of being an imposter—of not belonging at the ball. And worse still the overwhelming loneliness, the sense of distance and detachment that had come as she'd observed him, so calm and distinguished in his role as Duke. She would always be an outsider in that part of his life.

Tom had headed the welcoming line and had greeted both Vince and Danny warmly. When it had been her turn his eyes had held her gaze for a brief, blazing second before his mouth had murmured against her ear, 'You look stunning.'

Thrown by how she had longed to step towards him, to have him wrap his arms around her, she had darted backwards and caught his mother, who was next in line, gazing at her curiously.

Reddening, Ciara had stepped forward, forgetting that she should wait for Tom to introduce her in her panic and said, 'Your Grace, my name is Ciara Harris. I'm a horticulturist employed here at Loughmore.' At this the Duchess's eyebrows had risen and Ciara had heard herself say, 'Years ago I worked here as a cleaner. My grandparents were Jack and Mary Casey...'

The Duchess had continued to gaze at her curiously. Darting a glance at Tom, who had been staring at her with a perplexed expression, Ciara had felt compelled to explain her presence at the ball.

'Tom invited me tonight as a friend...we used to hang out together during the summer.' Then, at a loss as to what else to say, she'd smiled wanly at the other woman.

The Duchess, her dark brown hair tied back in a chignon, her make-up subtly but beautifully applied to her perfect ivory skin, had given the tiniest hint of a smile, 'Of course I remember you, Ciara.'

Thrown by the gentleness of the Duchess's tone, Ciara had nodded and then scurried away, cringing inside at her runaway mouth and lack of social graces.

She had only seen Tom from a distance for the rest of the night. Which was understandable. He had a hundred and fifty other guests to attend to. And in truth she had been avoiding him.

He was leaving for London tomorrow.

She inhaled a deep breath. She had walked into this situation knowing all along that getting involved with Tom again was asking for trouble. Well, trouble was here, with a capital T, and she had no one but herself to blame for the loneliness blossoming in her chest. She had to deal with it whether she liked it or not.

She stood and held her hand out to Vince. 'Come and dance with me.'

Tom followed his mother as she walked towards the door of the ballroom, concerned at the tiredness etched on her face. He caught up with her by the Christmas tree positioned to one side of the wide double doorway, saw the white flashing lights from the tree emphasising the dark circles under her eyes. He hesitated, thrown by the vulnerability in her expression.

He cleared his throat. 'Would you like to dance?'

His mother blinked. Swallowed. 'Thank you, but I'm feeling rather tired. I know it's probably rude of me, but I'm going to retire for the night.'

Tom placed a hand on her forearm, this new softness and openness in his mother since his father's death still disarming him. 'Tonight…all of Christmas…must have been difficult for you.'

His mother nodded, and then in a low voice said, 'I miss him… As you and I both know, your father had his faults—but I did love him.'

Her hand came to rest on his arm, an action so surprising, given her history of little physical contact with her children, that his heart leapt wildly in his chest.

'Darling, why don't you ask her to dance?' she said.

'Ask who?'

His mother nodded towards the dance floor, where Ciara was dancing with Parker Kidston, an old schoolfriend of his.

'Ciara Harris, of course.'

Ciara's dress swirled around her calves as Parker twisted her around and around, the gold threads in the white silk catching the light from the overhead chandeliers. Her hair, loose around her bare shoulders, shone in the light too, its rich autumnal tones reminding him of their walk back to the castle through the woods after Daly's Pub, her body tight against his, their steps in perfect harmony.

Now, as he watched her laugh when Parker twisted her beneath his arm, jealousy punched him square in the stomach. 'Why would I do that?'

His mother's cornflower-blue eyes settled on his. 'Because I saw how you looked at her earlier in the Great Hall.'

He looked away from his mother's gaze and back towards the dance floor. Last night when Ciara had asked him to leave there had been a distance in her eyes, in her voice, that had chilled him. The same earlier, when she had called to say Vince and Danny would collect her for the ball and there was no need for him to do so. She had sounded remote…keen to end the call.

'It's complicated.'

'I'm sure it is.'

He twisted back to regard his mother, confused by the regret in her voice. 'Don't you disapprove of her, like you did before?'

'When you were teenagers, you mean? Of course I disapproved then—you were nothing more than children. Now who you date is your choice, but I admit I still worry. Your role is a difficult one. You need someone who will support you in good times and bad. Someone who understands the demands of being a duchess. If you marry—and I sincerely hope you do—your wife will not just be marrying *you*, Tom, she'll be marrying this estate and all the responsibilities that come with it. It's a lot to ask of any woman—make sure she's prepared for it.'

Thrown, Tom shrugged and gave a rueful laugh. 'You're jumping the gun...it's early days with Ciara and I.'

For the longest time Tom could ever remember his mother held his gaze. Something shifted in him at the openness, the concern, the love he saw there.

'I don't want you hurt again like you were all those years ago after your last summer here in Loughmore. Am I right in guessing it was because of Ciara?'

Tom nodded in response, and his mother considered him with a remorseful expression. 'I wanted to speak to you. But your father was so cross at the time over your decision to become a chef he asked me not to see you. It's something I deeply regret.'

Sharp pain kicked hard in his chest when he remembered the eighteen-month period after he'd split with Ciara, when he had had no contact with his parents. Unable to hide the bitterness inside him he said sharply, 'I needed your support but you both shut me out.'

His mother winced, but still held his gaze. 'I know. I'm sorry.'

Tom insisted on walking with his mother to her suite. They did so in silence.

Outside her door, she turned to him and said, 'All I wish for you in life is a wife who loves you with all her heart. I didn't have that with your father...it was hard to live with.' Then, with a faint smile, she added, 'But don't rush into any decisions—make sure that the person is right for you. Sometimes we think we can change the person we love, make them something they're not. I thought I could get your father to love me, and in his own way he did, but I never truly had his heart.'

Tom walked away from his mother's suite, heard her

door softly closing behind him. He winced in memory of the sadness etched in her eyes.

Back in the ballroom, he grabbed a whiskey from a passing waiter and was soon joined by a group of Fran's old university friends, whom he knew through their frequent visits to Bainsworth over the years. He nodded distractedly at their chatter, his gaze wandering over the dance floor, searching for Ciara. Where *was* she?

He took a gulp of the whiskey, barely noting its burning flow down his throat. He gripped the tumbler tighter, confusion raging through him.

He wanted to be with Ciara, to hold her in his arms again, inhale her vanilla and rose scent. Feel his heart explode with happiness when she smiled. He wanted their sizzling attraction...their friendship. He wanted their chatter and ease.

Why was he doing this? Allowing himself to fall in love with her? He had seen the toll it had taken on his mother— to be in love with a man who didn't love her back with the same intensity and need and intimacy.

It was happening already—Ciara was pushing him away, distancing herself from him. Tonight whenever he'd caught her eye she'd looked away. What had happened twelve years ago was about to happen all over again.

His stomach lurched at that thought.

But he had no one to blame but himself.

From the stage, the lead singer of the band announced that there were only fifteen minutes until midnight. She invited the guests to collect their coats from the cloakroom in order to welcome the New Year out on the terrace.

Tom shook himself. He was the host of this party.

He beckoned the guests towards the cloakroom, and out in the Great Hall accepted Stephen's offer of his overcoat and allowed Kitty to drag him out onto the terrace.

* * *

Laughing, Ciara ran with Vince down the corridor to the temporary cloakroom, stopping when she almost lost one of her shoes.

'Hurry up—we're going to miss the midnight celebrations.' Vince urged her on.

He had found her in the kitchen, sharing a pot of tea with Libby. She had popped in to say hello and had found herself staying there for well over half an hour, glad to take refuge in the familiar surroundings of Libby's kitchen after seeing Tom and his mother deep in conversation in the ballroom, their glances constantly shifting in her direction.

What had they been saying? Had his mother learnt about their relationship? Was she warning him about the inappropriateness of getting involved with a member of staff?

At the cloakroom, Vince eyed the attendants, Kelly and Sinead, who were closing the cloakroom door. 'Sneaking out to watch the fireworks, girls?'

When both the girls reddened and mumbled 'yes,' Vince laughed. 'Good for you.' Nodding towards the near empty coat racks beyond the partially open door he added, 'I see we're the last to head out. Can Ciara and I have our coats as quickly as you can?'

Then, running back to the ballroom, they joined the rest of the guests out on the terrace. The crowd were already assembled into one large circle that extended around the entire periphery of the forty-foot-plus flagstone terrace.

The band had also moved out onto the terrace with their instruments, and the lead singer called out on the portable microphone. 'It's twenty seconds to midnight, folks!' and then began the countdown.

Vince led Ciara through the crowd until he found Danny. They joined the circle of partygoers, Ciara holding Vince's hand on one side before sharing a smile and holding hands with the elderly gentleman on her other side.

'Five, four, three…' the crowd called out.

Ciara's gaze darted around the crowd. Where *was* he?

'Happy New Year, everyone!' the lead singer called out.

Desperation took hold of Ciara. She wanted at least to be able to *see* him.

And then she spotted him, further down the circle, embracing Kitty, shaking the hands of others around him. He was smiling. Relaxed. Everything she wasn't.

The band began the opening bars of 'Auld Lang Syne.' Ciara's heart fell heavily.

The crowd around her began to sing. She joined in for the first few lines. '"Should old acquaintance be forgot, and never brought to mind…?"' But the words, not for the first time, choked her.

She shut her eyes for a moment and then glanced towards Tom. Everyone around him was singing but, grim-faced, he was staring in her direction.

She winced.

For a crazy moment she wanted to go over and stand before him and yell, *Do you know that every year I thought of you when I sang those words? That I had to leave every party early, afraid that if I started crying I would never stop? Do you know I missed you that much, Tom? Did you even think of me? Why did we ruin what we had by sleeping together? Why was I stupid enough to fall in love with a man I could never be with…who when faced with the prospect of being tied to me for ever through our baby looked dismayed.*

She broke her gaze away. Sighed with relief when the singing stopped and the fireworks spectacular began. The crowd gasped as the sky lit up in a symphony of red and blue explosions, the colours catching the sparkling snow still blanketing Loughmore…

* * *

Fireworks over, Tom was talking to an old friend of his father's in the Great Hall while handing his coat to an awaiting Stephen when Ciara approached him in a rush.

Giving Lord McCartney an apologetic smile, she said, 'My apologies for interrupting, but I just wanted to say thank you for a wonderful evening. I have to leave now—'

Tom took her arm. 'David, will you excuse me for a moment? Ciara and I need to talk.'

He led her in the direction of the Morning Room, biting back the temptation to demand to know why she was leaving early until they were behind closed doors.

But when he threw open the doorway of the room he came to a stop. Fran was perched on one of the sofas, the voluminous skirt of her red taffeta gown spread around her, surrounded by a bevy of friends. Empty champagne bottles were strewn across every surface.

Fran gave a squeal of excitement, followed by a little hiccup. 'Tom! Come and join us! We were just discussing the Somerset Ball.' Smiling at a group of friends seated on the opposite sofa, she added, 'The girls were all wondering if you plan on attending. Isn't that right, Alicia?'

Alicia Percy-Villiers gave Fran a vile look, which only caused Fran to laugh in delight. Then Alicia stood and regarded him, while smoothing out the gold silk of her ball gown. 'We missed you in St Moritz this year.'

Alicia's gaze wandered towards Ciara. As did Fran's. Fran stood and walked towards them. 'I'm Fran—Tom's sister. I don't think we've met before…' Pausing, Fran considered Ciara. 'Although I must say you *do* look familiar.'

Beside him he felt Ciara stiffen. Sharply he said, 'Ciara is a friend of mine.'

Ciara, reddening, cleared her throat. 'I worked here during the summer as a teenager—that's why you recognise me.'

Fran slapped her own cheek lightly and rolled her eyes dramatically. 'Of *course*—Ciara. I should have remembered you. Gosh, I reckon I might need to lay off the champagne for a while. What are you doing now?'

There was an awkward pause before Ciara answered. Everyone in the room was waiting for her response. 'I'm still working here—now in the gardens.'

Fran's gaze ran from Ciara to Tom and then back to him again. She was clearly trying to understand exactly what was going on between him and the gardener. 'Cool.'

The faces of the rest of the guests in the room held the same expressions of curiosity.

Hating their interest, hating the pointless class divide that had Ciara constantly feeling the need to explain her presence in his company, he said sharply, 'Ciara is a respected and much sought after horticulturist—we're lucky to have her here in Loughmore. Her research into rare and heritage plants has been published in many scientific journals.'

Ciara looked at him, aghast, while the rest of the people in the room stared at them with a hint of scandalised interest.

Ciara moved towards the door. 'I need to go. Vince is waiting for me.'

Placing a hand on Ciara's arm, to prevent her leaving, he turned to his sister. 'Fran, Ciara and I need to speak in private.'

Fran made a playful noise of intrigue, determined to tease him. 'Oh, now that sounds *very* mysterious.'

Fran's laughter died, though, when he hit her with a glare.

Beckoning her friends to the door, she said, 'I reckon it's time for us to hit the dance floor.'

The group slowly made their way out of the room.

When she passed them by Alicia gave him a coy smile

and said, 'You still owe me a dance from the Rhodes ball, Tom.'

When he shut the door on their laughter and calls for more champagne Ciara folded her arms and regarded him crossly. 'For her sake, I hope Alicia is wearing steel-toe-cap shoes.'

He ignored her jibe and asked instead, 'Why are you leaving?'

Her mouth tightened. She looked as though she was in the mood for a fight. *Good.* Because so was he.

'I don't need you defending me by exaggerating the importance of my job,' she said.

'Some people need to be educated and taken off their high horses. And I wasn't exaggerating. Don't forget I have access to your personnel file—your CV is very impressive. Now, are you going to answer my question?'

She yanked the belt of her long camel-coloured wool coat tighter. 'Vince wants to call in to see Paddy Hayes—he's eighty-five and lives on his own. He hasn't been well recently and Vince wants to check up on him, give him some company. It's sad to think of him all alone on New Year's Eve. I said I'd take a lift home with himself and Danny on the way.'

She stared at him defiantly, the pink in her cheeks the same shade as the gloss on her lips.

He worked his jaw.

She folded her arms.

The stand-off between them ensued.

But then something dangerous shifted in the air between them. The irritation in her eyes was replaced with a hunger that sideswiped him.

With a curse, he was crossing the short distance between them, his mouth finding hers, his hands frantically undoing her belt. Her coat dropped to the ground. His mouth trailed over the smooth skin of her bare shoulders, his hands on the silk of her gown, pulling her tight against him.

He heard himself whisper, 'I've been wanting to do this all evening.'

Against his ear she moaned deep in her throat, her body shuddering against his. Breathlessly she whispered, 'I need to go. Vince is waiting for me.'

His mouth captured hers again. She kissed him back wildly, her hands running through his hair.

They kissed, hard and furious, hot desire moulding their bodies together.

He pulled away long enough to mutter, 'I'll drop you home later.'

His mouth captured the soft pillows of her lips again, but after a few seconds she pushed against him and moved away, shaking her head. 'You're busy. I should go.'

He watched her bend to pick up her coat and that feeling of her closing him out of her life returned with a vengeance. He swallowed the pride that was telling him to let her go and bit out, 'I want to drop you home.'

Her phone began to ring. She grimaced when she pulled it out of her coat pocket. 'It's Vince. I have to go.'

He ground his teeth. 'Why?'

She paused, bit her lip before answering. 'I'm leaving early tomorrow morning for Dublin. I'm spending the day with my mother.'

He folded his arms, trying not to let his surprise at her plans show. He had thought they would spend tonight together—tomorrow too. 'You know I'm leaving for London in the afternoon?'

She winced ever so slightly at his words, but then a hardness came over her expression. Squaring her shoulders, she answered calmly, 'Yes, I know.'

Anger flared inside him. 'Why have you been avoiding me all night?'

'I haven't…' Pausing, she exhaled loudly and tilted her chin defiantly. 'You said you wanted us to part as friends—let's do that.'

'I'm not sure friends sleep together.'

She placed a hand on the console table beside her, leaning her weight against it. Her head dropped, and when she looked up there was no fight left in her eyes.

'Please, Tom. I don't want it to be like twelve years ago. I don't want us to part arguing like this.'

The air in his lungs whooshed out. She was right.

Her phone rang again.

Reaching forward, he took it from her and answered. Told Vince he would take Ciara home himself.

Ciara threw him an angry glance, and when he'd hung up he spoke before she could. 'You're right. I don't want us arguing.' Something rather large seemed to be stuck in his throat at this point, and he had to swallow hard to shift it. 'Come and dance with me.'

She eyed him dubiously. 'But you hate dancing.'

He managed to force a smile to his mouth. 'Yes, but I know how much you enjoy it.'

In the ballroom, he breathed out a sigh of relief that the band were playing an up-tempo song. He guided Ciara out on to the dance floor, where they joined a group of old family friends from Dublin.

God, he hated dancing. But he forced himself to smile, to pretend that he was having a great time. And when the tempo changed to a slow dance he held her in his arms at a respectful distance.

His mind felt numb, but he managed to chat to her about her plans for tomorrow. Told her of the opening of a Tom's in Bordeaux next week. And when she said she'd like to go home he drove her there, through the white silence of the snow-covered countryside.

He walked her to the door with a sense of unreality.

She opened her front door and turned to him. In the darkness she gave him a fleeting smile. 'Thanks for the lift.'

He nodded. Working all the time to keep the conversation light, casual, with none of the pain and hurt of twelve years ago. 'I haven't made my decision on selling Loughmore yet, but you will be the first to know when I do.'

She stepped out of the shadows of the doorway, her expression sad and resigned. 'If there's anything I can do to help, let me know.'

He stepped back, wanting to hold her again, kiss her, but knowing that to do so would be to cross that friendship barrier she so obviously wanted restored. 'I'd better get back to the party. Sleep well.'

She stepped closer again, following him, her eyes holding his with a tender sadness. 'It was a wonderful Christmas.'

He needed to get away. He nodded quickly. 'Yes it was.' And turned away.

'Tom, I…'

Halfway down the path he turned at her call, hope spinning in his chest. 'Yes?'

'I…' She hesitated for a moment and then said quietly, 'Take care of yourself.'

In the car, he sat and watched her close her door and then saw the downstairs lights come on. Already missing her. But knowing he had no option but to move on with his life.

CHAPTER NINE

'GOD ALMIGHTY, CIARA, you're looking awful—are you sick?' Standing on the doorstep of her redbrick terrace house, in pink slippers and a dressing gown, Ciara's mum eyed her with undisguised horror.

Just great. Not only did she feel lousy, but apparently she looked even worse.

Keen to divert her mum's attention, she held out the bag of gifts she was carrying. 'Happy New Year, Mum.'

Her mum whisked the bag out of Ciara's hand. 'Ah, love, you shouldn't have. You know I didn't want anything.'

With her mum busy rifling through the bag Ciara took the opportunity to slip into the house, muttering, 'I could kill for a cup of tea.'

While Ciara boiled the kettle her mum fussed around her.

'Will you have a mince pie, pet? Or how about some of your gran's Christmas cake? She posted it to me all the way from Renvyle. I told her not to, but as usual she didn't pay a blind bit of notice to what I said. For the cost of posting it I could have bought ten of them in Dunne's Stores, but would she listen? And I ended up having to go down to the sorting office to collect it because I wasn't at home when my post lady arrived.'

Normally Ciara would have just shrugged at her mum, changed the subject for an easier life, but there was something inside her this morning—was it tiredness from her sleepless night, or a need for some love and understanding in her world, a need for forgiveness and harmony?—that had her turning to her mum and saying quietly, 'Maybe sending the cake is Gran's way of showing you she loves you.'

Her mum leant against the counter-top. 'You really *are* sick, aren't you?'

Ciara rolled her eyes. Mentions of love, affection, or any emotions for that matter were without doubt borderline taboo in her family.

'I only had breakfast an hour ago. That's why I'm not hungry.'

Taking two mugs with bright red poppy designs from a mug tree on the counter, her mum asked, 'Why are you here so early, anyway?'

For a moment Ciara thought about making up an excuse, but instead she spoke the truth. 'I wanted to see you.'

In the process of pouring boiling water into the cups, her mum lowered the chrome kettle to the laminate surface of the counter-top and said, 'Now you've *really* got me worried.'

God, trying to talk to her mother about anything substantial was impossible. Taking some milk from the fridge, Ciara wondered what exactly she was hoping to achieve today.

She had slept terribly. And woken early to an emptiness inside her that was even worse than the night before. So much for her hope of sleeping it off.

She had gone to bed last night determined to start the New Year with strength and resolve—with a determination to put everything about Tom behind her. But she hadn't reckoned on the loneliness that had had her showering and dressing and shooting out through the door in record time.

She had needed to get away from her cottage, from the

estate. Away from the hope that Tom might call in to see her one final time. It was all over. Tom was going back to his life in England and the sooner she accepted that fact the better.

Passing the milk to her mum, she said, 'I thought we could go for a walk in Phoenix Park this morning—maybe head to the sales this afternoon.'

'Ah, love, I have the New Year's Day bingo in the parish hall this afternoon.'

'Mum, for crying out loud.'

'What?'

'Can't you for once…? Can't you spend some time with me?'

Was she really saying these things to her mother? Asking her for her company, her support? What was the point? What did she expect? That after all these years she and her mum might actually have a proper conversation that wasn't full of wisecracks and avoidance.

Her mum studied her, her mouth pursed tightly. 'I read in the newspapers that the new Duke was in Loughmore for the Christmas. He's upset you again, hasn't he?'

For a nanosecond Ciara considered answering her mother, but then she moved towards the hallway, muttering, 'I need to go to the bathroom.'

Bounding up the stairs, instead of going to the bathroom she headed into her old bedroom. There she stared at the 'Plants of Ireland' posters she had bought in the National Botanical Gardens for her seventeenth birthday and had later hung on her headache-inducing purple bedroom walls.

Her birthday was in June, and she remembered her seventeenth birthday so well—in particular her ever-growing excitement at the prospect of seeing Tom again. After visiting the gardens—which she had had to drag her friends around—they had gone into Temple Bar where she had got her bluebell tattoo.

Her mum had hit the roof, and Tom hadn't been keen at first, telling her she shouldn't have marked her skin, but eventually he had grown to like it. At least she hadn't got a tattoo of his name, which was what she had *really* wanted to do. Thank God even her seventeen-year-old infatuated self had seen how cringeworthy *that* was. But whenever she looked at her bluebell she thought of the swathes of bluebells that carpeted Loughmore Woods in the springtime—and then, of course, her thoughts turned to Tom.

Out in the corridor she heard her mum going into her bedroom. Part of her didn't want to talk to her mum about Tom. She didn't want to lift the lid on her mum's anger with his dad and with Tom himself. She didn't want to have to put into words the turmoil inside her right now, because to do so would make it all too real, would stop her moving on.

But another part of her *did* want to talk to her mum—the one other person who understood what it was like to fall for someone out of your reach; the one other person who understood what had happened between herself and Tom all those years ago. Part of her wanted to make sense of everything in talking.

But did she seriously think talking to her mum was an option? They just didn't have that type of relationship. Theirs was a 'batten down the hatches' type of relationship, where anything difficult in life was ignored or laughed off with gallows-type humour. And that was not going to change now.

Out in the corridor, she knocked on her mum's bedroom door and went inside when her mum called for her to do so.

Her mum, now dressed in a knee-length plum wool dress, was at the dressing table, brushing her shoulder-length brown hair. Slim, with almond-shaped eyes and cheekbones to die for, she was truly beautiful. Sadness seized Ciara's throat. Her mum had never met anyone after her dad had left them. Did she ever turn the key after a day's work and wish she had a hug waiting on the other side of the door?

She smiled at her mum's reflection. 'Let's head into town. I'll buy you lunch. You can be back in time for your bingo.'

Her mum shifted along the stool she was sitting on, 'Come and put some make-up on.'

Ciara went and sat beside her. 'Do I look that bad?'

Her mum laughed. 'Nothing some war paint can't mend.'

Ciara rolled her eyes, taking the moisturiser and foundation bottles her mum held out to her. 'There's no fear of anyone getting a big head in this house, is there?'

For a few minutes both women worked in quietness, applying foundation and concealer and then working on their eyes.

Her mum pumped at her mascara. But instead of applying it she looked at Ciara's reflection for the longest while.

Thrown by her mum's scrutiny, Ciara lowered her eye shadow brush. 'I don't wear a lot of make-up at work. I'm out of practice.'

Her mum shook her head. Gave her a hesitant look. 'The night the Duke came here…when we found him on the doorstep… I didn't want to admit it at the time… I was worried about you…but he was genuinely upset. He was very respectful to me, and he apologised for upsetting you. He seemed like a nice person.'

Thrown, Ciara focused on dabbing her brush against the eye shadow palette. 'He *is* a nice person—but that's all in the past.'

Her mum made a disbelieving sound before adding, 'It sure doesn't sound like it is…or look that way, given how pale you are today.'

Emotion fisted in Ciara's chest and she reddened at the gentleness of her mum's voice. For a brief moment they held each other's gazes, feeling a connection forming between them that was as disconcerting as it was wonderful.

Her mum gave a small grimace. 'When he was leaving he said, "I'm sorry for the pain I've caused her...she's everything to me. Please tell her how much I love her." I should have told you.'

Ciara's mouth dropped open. 'He said *that* to you?'

'I didn't tell you because I didn't want you involved with him.'

Ciara edged back on the stool, disbelief confounding her. He had said he *loved* her! To her *mother*! Why had he never told *her*?

But then sense kicked in. He had said those words in the heat of the moment, in the sadness of that night. Even if he had told her himself it wouldn't have changed anything. They were still from different worlds, with their own lives to forge.

Her mum was staring at her, nervously waiting for a response. 'It's okay, Mum, it wouldn't have mattered if you *had* told me. It was all over between us anyway.'

Her mum pumped her mascara again and lifted the heavily loaded wand. She was about to apply it to her eyelashes, but then lowered it again and asked quietly, 'Did you love him?'

Ciara waited a moment for a wisecrack of some sort, but none came. Instead her mum looked at her with empathy, with an understanding that grabbed her heart and tugged hard. She swallowed. 'Yes...yes, I loved him.'

Her mum breathed in deeply. 'What happened over Christmas?'

Her heart was thudding in her chest, and part of her wanted to run away, but somehow she managed to answer. 'We spent it together, but we've agreed to be friends only.'

Seeing her mum's deep frown, she added, 'It's not a big deal…it's better this way.'

'Do you love him now?'

'There's no point, is there?'

Her mum didn't look convinced. 'If he wasn't a duke would things be different?'

Ciara grabbed hold of one of her mum's lipsticks. Opening it blindly, she stared at it but failed to register what colour it was before she closed it again.

She gave her mum a rueful smile. 'No. Now, we'd better get a move on or you'll miss bingo later.'

She bolted out of the bedroom and headed downstairs, with the rest of the answer she would have given her mum if they'd been closer—if the words hadn't been too private and painful—spinning around her brain.

No, things wouldn't be different, because I still wouldn't understand what he feels for me, never mind actually believe that he could ever truly love me… I'm not what he needs.

A week later Tom threw his overnight bag next to the coatstand in the hallway of his Kensington apartment and sat down onto the parquet floor to cuddle Storm. Storm nuzzled into him, his tail wagging frantically as though Tom had returned from an epic Arctic adventure instead of an overnight stay in Bordeaux.

Tom would have happily sat on the floor all night, taking comfort from Storm's affection, but after a few minutes of indulgence Storm grew bored and padded off—no doubt in the hope of finding one of Tom's ties, which he was partial to chewing.

Standing, Tom read the note left by his cleaner and dogsitter Helena, assuring him that Storm had been fine in his absence, then rifled through his post. He opened his fridge, decided he couldn't be bothered eating, turned on his laptop and poured himself a drink.

Ten minutes later he switched off the laptop, resigned to the fact he was in no mood to work. He stared instead at the whiskey in his tumbler. It was the twenty-year-old malt Ciara had given him for Christmas.

Today, in Bordeaux, at the opening of Tom's Restaurant in the Bassins à Flot district of the city, he could have sworn he had heard her laughter. He had turned away from the British Ambassador, who had travelled to Bordeaux for the opening, and searched the restaurant, but of course it had all been in his imagination.

The same as it had been when he'd thought he had seen her walking down the Royal Mile in Edinburgh earlier in the week, when the delight in his heart had knocked him sideways, and the bitter disappointment when he'd chased after her to find it was a different person had almost knocked him out.

He missed her.

There were no other words.

He eyed his phone.

She had said they would be friends.

What was the harm in ringing her? As he would with any other friend.

He dialled her number.

A storm of butterflies hit his stomach.

It rang and rang and rang.

He was about to hang up when she answered.

'Tom.' Her voice held surprise, delight, doubt.

He cleared his throat. 'Hi. I thought I'd call…see how you're doing.'

He heard her footsteps on the other end of the phone. Where was she? What was she doing? It felt so wrong to know so little about her day-to-day life. Not to be there with her.

And then it hit him. Square in the eyes. He was in love with her.

He wanted Ciara Harris in his life.

'I'm fine. I was just watching TV with Boru...having a cup of tea.' She paused and gave a little laugh. 'My life must sound so dull to you.'

He was in love with her!

His hands shook, and the sound of her light, musical voice had him saying gently, 'It sounds perfect.'

'It does?'

Yes, it does. I wish I was sitting there with you. The fire burning. You cuddled against me. Knowing we would soon be going to bed together. Knowing I would have you lying by my side every night for ever and ever. That's what I want most. To know that every night we would lie together, as husband and wife, in our bed, in that cocoon of privacy and love and tender moments.

Tom shook himself. At a loss as to where all these thoughts and emotions were coming from. At a loss as to just how intense, how powerful, how *real* they were.

'Tell me about your day?' he asked.

They chatted for a while. Ciara told him about the garden tour she had given that morning, to the children from Loughmore School. He told her about his trip to Bordeaux, and the beauty of the city. When he had finished, he wavered, knowing he should get his head straight before he said anything else.

But it was so good to speak with her, to hear her laughter, so he said into the silence of the line, 'I wished you were there with me.'

He heard the tiniest exhalation and then, 'I'd better go... it's getting late.'

He winced, her words as effective as a hand physically pushing him away. Old fears surfaced, and he could not help the bitter note in his tone when he said, 'You haven't asked me about Loughmore—if I've come to a decision over selling it.'

On the other end of the line he heard her pull in a breath. 'I know how difficult it must be for you at the moment, deciding what to do, and I don't want to add to it. You know how I feel about it all, but I'm sure you'll make the right decision—for both you and Loughmore.'

Thrown by her answer, by her acceptance, her support, her belief in him, he said, 'I'll call you again soon.'

A familiar television programme's theme tune played in the background. Quietly, she said, 'I'm not sure that's a good idea.'

Bewildered he asked, 'Don't you want me to call?'

The theme tune continued to play, and then in a tired voice she said, 'It's too hard saying goodbye.'

Tom stared at his phone, heard the disconnected buzz playing out from the speaker.

She had hung up on him.

His bewilderment switched to anger, then fear, then back to confusion.

What did she mean?

But one thing was for sure: Ciara sounded as lonely as he did.

Why, then, did she keep pushing him away?

Was she as scared as he was of being hurt again?

CHAPTER TEN

CIARA SHUT DOWN her laptop and tidied away her paperwork, hearing the applause from the gardening and forestry teams at Bainsworth Hall continuing as she did so.

Taking a seat beside Henry Page, Head of Parks and Gardens at Bainsworth, she acknowledged his thanks for her presentation and nodded in agreement when Henry said he was looking forward to increased co-operation between Loughmore and Bainsworth in their joint conservation efforts.

She hoped and prayed she was appearing professional and unruffled to all those assembled in the room, because inside she felt as if she was going to crumble at any moment.

She had been given only two days' notice of this meeting. On Monday morning Sean had casually strolled into the walled garden and told her that Henry Page had called and asked if Ciara would speak at the annual Bainsworth Hall Parks and Gardens team meeting on the topic of heritage planting.

Normally Ciara would have been excited at the prospect of sharing her knowledge and having the opportunity to see the famed gardens of Bainsworth for the first time. But for the past two days a growing knot of despair had taken hold—a knot that had only tightened when the estate car that had met her at the airport had driven through the entrance gates of Bainsworth and along its tree-lined avenue to reveal the astonishing beauty and grandeur of the Palladian-style hall.

To be here, at Tom's primary residence, felt unnatural. Alien, even. It intensified how much she missed him. It emphasised just what a gap existed in the lives they both led.

She still did not know what decision he had taken over Loughmore. Could she take Henry's words as a good omen for what the future held?

She stood as the team began to file out of the converted barn where the day's team meeting had taken place.

'It's a shame you can't join us for dinner, Ciara.'

Ciara gave Henry a smile of apology, checking the time display on her phone. 'My flight back to Dublin leaves in three hours. I'd better leave for the airport soon.'

'A car is booked for you in an hour's time, but first the Duke has requested to meet with you.'

Ciara, in the process of putting her paperwork into her shoulder bag, paused and looked at Henry with consternation. 'He's here at Bainsworth?'

'Yes, he arrived this lunchtime.'

She hadn't known he would be here. She had assumed he'd be in London. She picked up her phone, checked the screen again. 'I don't think I've time—will you give the Duke my apologies?'

Henry walked around the large conference table towards the exit door. 'Don't worry, we'll make sure you get to your plane on time.'

The knot in Ciara's stomach tightened. On wobbly legs she followed Henry out onto the pebbled pathway that ran past the six-acre walled garden of Bainsworth Hall, which she had toured with Henry earlier in the day, and out onto the Italian terraces that ran behind the hall.

A thousand thoughts raced through her mind.

Why hadn't Tom told her he would be here?

She grimaced as she remembered how she had ended their call last week. What on earth had she been thinking? Why had she admitted just how hard she found it talking to him? Why did he want to meet with her now? Was it to tell her about his decision on the future of Loughmore?

Walking up the central path through the terraces, they passed the vast fountain that sat before the rear entrance portico, its twenty-five water jets filling the air with a faint mist.

After taking the limestone steps up to the portico they entered the hall and passed through a state room full of statuary and tapestries. Ciara tried to listen to Henry's guided tour as they moved through a gilded drawing room with a dazzling royal blue and gold carpet, but she was too nervous to take much in.

Beyond the drawing room, they walked along a wood-panelled corridor filled with marble busts. Henry came to a stop outside an open door and tapped lightly on the wood.

Ciara's heart went into orbit when she heard Tom call out, 'Come in.'

Sitting behind a desk that was positioned before the enormous sash windows of the office, Tom stood when they entered.

Dressed in a charcoal suit and a pale pink shirt, the top button undone, he looked sexy and powerful, and her mouth grew dry while her heart pounded in her ears. For a brief moment she felt hot tears at the back of her eyes, but she pulled herself together in time to say, 'Your Grace...' following Henry's introduction.

Tom rolled his eyes.

Henry looked from Tom to her, clearly confused at Tom's reaction, and then disappeared out of the room.

Tom walked towards her, his gaze travelling down over her navy pin-striped trouser suit, pausing at her red stiletto shoes. Then his eyes captured hers. Attraction zipped between them.

'It's good to see you.'

Goosebumps pebbled on her skin at the huskiness of his tone. How tempted she was to walk towards him, to place her head on his shoulder, wrap her arms around his waist.

Despite the dryness in her mouth, she forced herself to say, 'You too—but I'm afraid my flight to Dublin leaves soon, so I'd better get going.'

'It sounds as though you can't wait to get away from me.'

Despite his teasing tone, there was a strain in Tom's expression that grabbed her heart. 'What? No! I'm just worried about my flight, that's all. I didn't know you would be here, that you would want to meet with me. You should have told me.'

He shrugged and went and shut the office door. 'Would you have come if you'd known I'd be here?'

Thrown by his closing the door, and by his tone—which implied he already knew the answer to his question—Ciara studied him, realisation slowly dawning. 'Was it your idea for me to come here? To speak to the gardening team?'

He came closer…too close, in fact. She could smell his aftershave, and every cell in her body melted as the image of his naked limbs wrapped around hers flashed before her eyes. She barely heard his quietly spoken response.

'I wanted you to see Bainsworth. I thought after seeing it you'd agree more easily to coming here to work on the walled garden renovation project.'

Her already overloaded brain creaked and tried to make sense of what he was saying. 'But why would I come to Bainsworth? My job…my life…is at Loughmore.'

Tom looked at her for long moments, those silver eyes capturing her soul. 'You can divide your time between the two estates.'

'Why would I do that?'

He blinked, worked his jaw. 'To spend time with me.'

She wasn't following, and she certainly wasn't ready to deal with the possible implications of what he was saying, so she asked instead, 'Does that mean you're keeping Loughmore?'

'You were right when you said I had a responsibility to look after the entire estate. I was planning to sell it for the wrong reasons. I was planning to sell it because Loughmore held too many painful memories.'

She winced at his words. 'I think I should resign.'

She craned her neck as he came to stand in front of her again. She hadn't seen him wear this suit and shirt before. For some reason that thought made her feel ridiculously sad. There was so much about his life she had no knowledge of.

His hand reached forward, his fingers lightly, tenderly touching the lapel of her suit. His eyes swallowed her up with gentle certainty. 'I missed you.'

Why was he saying these things to her? It was going to mess up their already uneasy understanding that they would only be friends.

'Did you hear what I said?' she asked.

'You're not resigning. And you're not pushing me away again. I'm here to stay in your life.'

'Please, what's the point? I'm a gardener...you're a duke. We have no future.'

Perching himself on the back of a nearby sofa, Tom reached and pulled her between his parted legs. 'Who we *are* doesn't matter. What matters is that I want to be with you.' He gave her a tentative smile. 'I'm hoping that you want to be with me too.'

She tried to pull away, but his arms on her waist held firm. She placed a hand on his chest, tried to lever herself away. 'But what's the point? You should be thinking about marrying. You need someone with the right background—someone who knows how to be a duchess.'

'I want to be with *you*.'

'For how long, though? I'm a working-class girl from Dublin. We both know I'd be a liability.'

He shook his head, a small smile drifting onto his lips. 'You're wrong, you know. The estate needs a duchess who is smart and intelligent, who can lead the people who work for us. I've seen how you interact with the staff at Loughmore—they love you. You're warm and open…fun to be around. I need a duchess who *gets* me, who supports and believes in me. Someone I can rely on—someone I know will stick by me through life's up and downs.'

He paused, and the certainty in his eyes, that faint smile, disappeared.

He swallowed hard before he asked in a bare whisper, 'Are *you* that person, Ciara?'

It sounded like an ultimatum from Tom, but in truth it wasn't. He was reaching out. Trying to engage her. And it terrified her.

'I don't know.'

Tom blinked. The weight of his hands on her waist lightened momentarily, but then he pulled her even closer, the powerful muscles of his inner thighs pressing against her legs. 'I love you, Ciara. But do you love *me*?'

Stunned, she looked away from his gaze, unable to handle the blazing intensity in his eyes. He'd said he loved her. But he didn't mean it—not really. They were from different worlds, with no future together, and one day soon he'd realise that and walk away. Just as he had done twelve years ago, when he had walked away on that London street. Just as her father had done, leaving behind only a handful of photos that showed him holding her in his arms, beaming proudly into the camera. The picture of a contented dad.

Time and the reality of life destroyed even the strongest love.

She swallowed hard, attempted a laugh. 'You don't mean that. We've been caught up in memories and...and lust.'

'Ciara...'

She winced at the sadness in his voice. And then his hand was on her chin, forcing her to look at him.

He breathed in deeply, as though fortifying himself. 'You have my heart, my soul, my every waking thought. I love you—of that be in no doubt. The question is, again, do you love *me*?'

She looked into the eyes of the one person who made her feel complete, at ease. Who thrilled her. Who filled her life with happiness and hope and dreams. And she answered truthfully, 'I'm scared.'

His forehead dropped gently against hers. Her heart went into freefall. His warmth, his scent, the chemistry playing between them was almost undoing her.

'I'm scared too, but losing you scares me even more,' he said gently. He shifted his head, whispered against her ear, 'Tell me why you're scared. Let me help you.'

Held in his embrace, hearing his softly spoken words, she desperately wanted to pull away. But, as if sensing what she was thinking, Tom curled his hand lightly around the base of her neck, where her hair was pulled up into a high ponytail, his fingers stroking her soothingly, as though trying to ease her panic.

And it worked. In the cocoon of his embrace, his touch, in knowing that he loved her, she felt her panic lessen and found the solace and strength and courage to admit for the first time what was truly in her heart.

'I'm scared that some day you'll realise I'm not what you want, what you need in life. You've apologised a hundred times for how you reacted in London, when I told you I was pregnant, but deep down I still worry that is how you truly feel. That you will reject me like your father rejected my mum.' She pulled back, stared him in the eyes, forcing her words out from a throat that felt narrow and raw. 'I'm scared of losing another baby. I'm scared of losing you again, Tom. I couldn't bear it.'

His thumb rubbed against her cheek, which was burning hot with the emotion of her admissions. 'So it's easier not to fall in love with me?'

'Yes.'

Tom understood only too well how scared Ciara was feeling. For the past week he had battled his own fears, questioning the wisdom of the path he was taking, waking in the middle of the night racked with doubt. He knew he was running a huge risk, opening up to Ciara about his feelings for her. It would without doubt bring an end to their attempt to be friends and, worse still, it meant he was putting his heart on the line and opening himself up to the potential humiliation and pain of hearing her say she did not love him back.

But in the emptiness of his life without Ciara he had come to realise he needed to find the courage inside himself to reach out to her and fight for their relationship. By their own admission they did not wear their hearts on their sleeves, but that had to change.

'I love you, Ciara. Even though I tried to pretend I had moved on from you when we split, I never stopped loving you. The first time I realised I loved you was that day when we went swimming in the lake—do you remember I hid under the jetty and you called and called for me? When I came out you were crying. No one had ever cared so much for me.'

Her eyes grew wild and angry in remembrance. 'I wanted to kill you.'

He grimaced, held his right bicep. 'I reckon I'm still bruised from where you hit me.'

'You *so* deserved it.'

He could not help but grin at the passionate anger glittering in her eyes. 'Do you believe me when I say that I love you?'

'I'm trying to.'

'It tore me apart when we split. I was ashamed of how badly I reacted when you told me you were pregnant.' A tightness gripped his throat. 'On my flight to Ireland I had worked out a plan for how we would manage. I would move to Dublin to be with you, work double shifts to support you through university while you were pregnant. Once our baby was born I reckoned I could work evening shifts, so that I could mind him during the day...' He swallowed against the ache gripping his throat. 'On the flight back everything was a void. I felt so empty. I had no future.'

Tears shone in Ciara's eyes. He felt tears well at the back of his eyes too. Pretending everything was okay was so ingrained in him that he struggled to continue, but knew their relationship needed this blunt honesty—no matter how difficult it was to open up, to effectively hand his heart on a platter to Ciara.

'What I feel for you now is even more intense than my love for you before. Being with you over Christmas reminded me of what we had, but I've also fallen in love with the woman you've become—a smart, savvy professional, who's loyal to those she loves. And people love you back. And are loyal to *you*. That's what I need in a duchess most of all—a leader who's respected and loved, who creates loyalty. You'd make a perfect duchess.'

Ciara rolled her eyes. 'A gardener with a tattoo? Hardly. As for being smart—if I was smart I wouldn't be in love with *you*, would I?'

Really? Was *this* the way she was going to tell him?

His heart gave a funny little kick. A broad beam popped onto his face. 'You love me?'

Ciara stepped away, folded her arms and considered him unhappily. 'I'm warning you, Tom, you'd have a much easier future with someone else.'

She loved him! He wanted to take her into his arms, hold her. But this conversation wasn't over yet. Not by a long shot. They had things that needed to be cleared up.

'You said last week that it was my decision as to whether I sell Loughmore or not. You trusted me on that. It means everything to me that you gave me that trust. I thought after my reaction to your pregnancy you'd never trust me again, but you *did*. It gave me hope that you loved me as much as I love you. But why won't you trust me now, in deciding who I want to marry, who I want to spend my life with? I want to have children with you, Ciara. I want to share my life with you.'

'People will talk…disapprove…think you're cracked.'

'And together we'll prove them all wrong.'

She gripped her folded arms even tighter, her eyes clouding with worry. In a quiet voice she asked, 'What if I miscarry again?'

His heart crumbled as he saw her distress. He took her into his arms. Held her. Planted a kiss against her forehead. 'We'll deal with that too.'

'Your family won't approve.'

'Well, we're even on that—nor will yours. Life will have its up and downs, Ciara. I'm not promising you a fairy tale, but we'll be a team. We'll face whatever life throws at us. But the one thing that will kill us as a couple is if we aren't honest with one another—open about what's upsetting us.'

Tom was right. Not being honest, not trusting each other, being too scared to look for support, was what had driven them apart before.

She squeezed her eyes shut, dragged in a breath and, stepping back, admitted, 'I'm terrified you'll walk away from me like my dad did—like your dad walked away from my mum. I'm terrified I'm not what you need…that all we have is this stupid chemistry between us and memories.'

Tom shook his head, his silver gaze never leaving her. 'I promise I will never leave you. How could I when you are the centre of my life? You give me meaning, hope. And as for what I need in my life—well, I reckon what I need more than anything is a feisty redhead who is insightful and empathetic. Who supports me like no one else. Who makes me laugh. Who *gets* me. No one gets me like you do, Ciara. With you I feel complete. I feel alive. Yes, I'm attracted to you to the point of madness—but it's more than that. With you I'm at ease… I'm my true self. Not the Duke of Bainsworth, with all the responsibilities and traditions that go with that. I'm Tom—pure and simple. A man in love with the most incredible woman in this world.'

Ciara could not help but blush—at Tom's words, and even more at the tender love and affection shining in his eyes.

'I got on with my life when we were apart, and I'm proud of how I survived, but there was this emptiness inside me,' she said. 'I tried to ignore how much I missed you, but on your birthday, at Christmas, on Valentine's Day…frankly every day of the year… I thought about you. I felt so *proud* of everything you were achieving.'

Her chest felt as if it was going to explode with the hurt and sadness of all those years.

'But I had lost my soul mate—the person who teased me, who held me when I was down, who told me things would work out. The person who listened to my dreams and didn't dismiss them. And I could do nothing to make that right.'

Tom held out his hand to her, and when she took hold of it he pulled her towards him. Undoing the single button of her suit jacket, he wrapped his arms around her waist, the heavy warmth of his forearms melting through the light cotton of her blouse.

'We've found each other again—let's not waste any more time.'

His hands on her back stroked against her spine. She edged into him.

In a husky voice that matched the dark passion in his eyes, he whispered, 'I want to be with you—today and every day for the rest of our lives.'

A shudder of hope, tenderness and desire ran down the length of her body. 'Sean is expecting me back to work tomorrow.'

'You and I are flying to Dublin tonight on my plane. I need to start work on all those plans you have suggested for making Loughmore financially viable.'

She nodded, but in truth she was still confused. Tentatively she asked, 'So…how do you want to play this? Will we date? See how things work out?'

Tom reared back, stared at her as though she'd just suggested they commit the crime of the century. 'Are you kidding me? After so many years apart, we're not wasting any more time, Ciara Harris!'

Bemused, Ciara watched him walk to his desk, take something from a drawer. Her heart went into orbit when he knelt before her, opening the green velvet box in his hands to reveal an exquisite emerald ring.

'Ciara Harris, will you do me the honour of marrying me?'

Ciara could not help but giggle at the formality of his words, but she soon sobered when she saw the tension in his expression. 'Isn't this all happening a bit too fast?'

'Will you feel any different about me in six months? A year's time?'

He had a point. 'No, I'll still love you to bits.'

'Then why wait?'

She couldn't make this too easy for him. She needed to see him sweat—if only a little bit. 'Only if you promise to come to dance lessons with me before the wedding.'

Still kneeling on the floor, Tom shook his head. 'Now. *that's* a deal-breaker if ever I heard one.'

Ciara laughed, loving the playful mischievous swirling around them, the loving teasing between them, the life-affirming freedom of knowing the person she loved loved her back with the same passion and intensity.

'I love you, Tom Benson. Yes, of course I will marry you.'

His eyes alive with love, Tom placed the ring on her finger, stood, lowered his mouth to hers and whispered, 'And I love *you*, Ciara Harris,' before his mouth caressed her lips with a kiss full of tenderness and dreams and hopes and promises.

EPILOGUE

THE FOLLOWING CHRISTMAS snow did not arrive at Lough-more. Instead a bright sun gently warmed the land in the days leading up to Christmas Day.

It was on such a gentle day of pale blue skies that Ciara travelled towards the church in Loughmore Village in a horse-drawn carriage, with her grandad on one side, Libby on the other. From the moment they had boarded the carriage, outside the castle, her grandad had held her hand, pride gleaming in his eyes.

At first when they had announced their engagement both families had been alarmed, but for the past year she and Tom had worked hard to include them all in the wedding plans. And as the months had passed by, and both families had seen close at hand not only their love and support for one another, but the way they wanted to become part of their new extended families, they had come round to accepting their marriage.

Sitting on the opposite bench, her flower girls giggled as the carriage hit the brow of a steep hill and the four horses began to canter down the opposite side. Grace Carney, Sophie O'Brien and Grace McCarthy all looked angelic in their floor-length white tulle skirts and white fake fur jackets with matching mufflers.

Fiddling with the ivy wreath in her hair, Grace Carney stopped giggling and fixed a look of deep concentration on Ciara. 'If you and the Prince have a baby will she be a princess?'

Ciara bit back a smile, remembering Tom's whispered words last week, before she had left Bainsworth to return to Loughmore to prepare for the wedding, about how they were going to spend their entire honeymoon on the Bensons' private St Lucia resort making babies.

A week away from him had been torture. For the past year they had rarely spent any time apart. Tom had worked mostly from his offices at Bainsworth and Loughmore, between which they were now dividing their time.

She edged towards the girls—not an easy feat with the weight of her full-skirted lace dress and its long train. She had fallen in love with it in a Paris showroom, and Danny and Libby, her wedding-dress-buying companions, had both cried when she'd stepped out of the dressing room and insisted she buy it immediately.

Now she answered Grace's question. 'Not a princess but a *lady*.'

All three girls were rosy-cheeked from the cold, but shy Grace blushed even more as she asked hesitantly, 'Ciara, will...will you dance with me at the party?'

Ciara's heart swelled at Grace's shyness and she blinked back fresh tears. Was she *really* about to marry Tom Benson, the love of her life, surrounded by all the people she loved in this world? Not for the first time she wanted to pinch herself to see if this was really happening to her.

'Of course I'll dance with you, Grace.'

Beside her, Libby grumbled. 'God, I'm not sure I'll be able to dance in this dress—it's digging into my ribs.'

Ciara eyed Libby and laughed. They both knew Libby's full-length champagne tulle dress with matching fake fur jacket fitted her perfectly. She was only complaining because of her nervousness—something Ciara had been teasing her about all morning, pointing out it was *she* who should be nervous, not Libby.

And that was the curious thing. She wasn't nervous. Instead she felt a calmness. A peace of mind and a joy that she was about to marry the man who loved her so deeply.

Every day for the past year he had shown his love to her. Often in small ways. A phone call when she needed it. Whisking her away for walks in the woods when she was stressed with the work of helping transform some areas of Loughmore into visitor centres alongside the newly appointed Loughmore Events Manager and her team.

He had also insisted that they spend a week with her grandparents in their home in Renvyle. It had been a week full of love and laughter, of early-morning swims in the Atlantic and sunset horse-rides on the deserted beaches of Connemara.

And he had invited her mum to cut the ribbon on the opening night of Tom's, Loughmore. She had performed with her usual 'not-fussed' demeanour, but deep down Ciara had seen her mum's delight at appearing in all the national newspapers standing alongside her famous soon-to-be son-in-law.

And then there had been his insistence that their wedding guest list wouldn't just involve the usual dignitaries, but also all their friends and the staff.

Libby's glossy chestnut hair was hanging loose, just as Ciara's was, and Libby was wearing a tiara made of a single strand of diamonds. Ciara was wearing the Benson family diamond and platinum halo tiara and a long veil.

Ciara took Libby's hand. 'You look gorgeous—and I bet Evan will agree.'

Libby shrugged, trying very hard not to look delighted. Ciara held her hand even tighter, feeling how it was trembling. Libby and Evan had been dating for over two months now. Evan had transferred from Tom's, Cambridge, to head up the new Loughmore restaurant, and both chefs had instantly hit it off.

A few weeks into their relationship Tom had finally admitted to Ciara that he had asked Evan to transfer to Loughmore because he'd had an instinct Evan and Libby would make an ideal couple.

There were crowds lining the streets of Loughmore, and when the carriage came into view applause rang out. Some called to her grandad, who was now beaming from ear to ear, others called to the flower girls, who were waving wildly to all they knew.

Ciara's calmness deserted her, to be replaced by rampant butterflies in her stomach.

Outside the church her mum fussed around her, fixing her dress as newspaper photographers snapped away.

Then her mum gave her a quick hug and whispered into her ear, 'You look deadly, pet—the absolute bee's knees. Now, be a good girl and try not to make a holy show of yourself by tripping in the aisle.'

She disappeared into the church.

His eyes fixed on the stained-glass window towering over the altar, focused on breathing in deeply and exhaling slowly, trying not to allow his leg to jig up and down, Tom heard laughter moving down the aisle.

Ciara! She was here!

From the corner of his eye he spotted her mum taking her seat on the opposite side of the aisle. At first wary of him, Ciara's mum Bernie had slowly softened towards him over the past year. A large lump had formed in his throat earlier, when she had fussed over his lopsided buttonhole. Re-pinning it, she had called him a 'big eejit' before giving him a quick hug and scuttling off to talk to his mother. Much to his surprise, his mother had instantly taken to

Bernie, explaining that she enjoyed Bernie's frankness and wicked sense of humour.

'Maybe she's having second thoughts?'

He eyed Fran, who was seated behind him and had sat forward to tease him with an evil look in her eye.

Kitty decided to join in too. 'We told her to run at the hen party, but she wouldn't listen.'

His sisters had initially been cautious around Ciara, intent on protecting their big brother and more than a little put out that their matchmaking hopes for linking him up with one of their friends were over. But over the Easter weekend, which they all spent at Bainsworth Hall, they had got to know Ciara's irreverent humour and loveliness and quickly decided to be on 'Team Ciara'.

The minister stepped out in front of the altar. Beamed down towards the end of the church.

Charlie Perry, an old schoolfriend of his who was now a guitarist in a world-famous band, began to play Pachelbel's 'Canon in D,' the soulful notes rising up to the vaulted roof of the church.

Tom stood, blinking back tears. He had lost her for too long. He had lost the person he was. But now life was once again full of colour and possibilities and love.

He turned. His heart somersaulted. Beyond the giggling flower girls and a blushing Libby the love of his life was walking towards him, with Charlie's tender rendition of the music guiding her every step.

Fresh tears flooded his eyes. He wiped them away, not caring that all the guests would see. He loved this beautiful, strong and intelligent woman whose heart was spun from gold.

When she finally came to stand beside him he hugged her grandfather and then turned to her. They were both crying. They both knew what it was to lose one another.

And how precious, how miraculous it was to find one another again.

He pulled her into him, felt their tears mingling. He whispered, 'I'll love you for a thousand years and more.'

She pulled away, sniffed, laughed. She held his hand and smiled, her eyes blazing with love. 'I've dreamt about this moment for years and years… I never thought it would actually happen.'

He touched his thumb against her cheek, wiping the tears away. 'Ready?'

She nodded. And together they turned to the minister knowing friendship and hope and above all love would bond them together for ever.

* * * * *

THE RANCHER'S CHRISTMAS PROMISE

ALLISON LEIGH

For my family.

Prologue

"You've got to be kidding me."

Ryder Wilson stared at the people on his porch. Even before they introduced themselves, he'd known the short, skinny woman was a cop thanks to the Braden Police Department badge she was wearing. But the two men with her? He'd never seen them before.

And after the load of crap they'd just spewed, he'd like to never see them again.

"We're not kidding, Mr. Wilson." That came from the serious-looking bald guy. The one who looked like he was a walking heart attack, considering the way he kept mopping the sweat off his face even though it was freezing outside. March had roared in like a lion this year, bringing with it a major snowstorm. Ryder hadn't lived there that long—it was only his second winter there—but people around town said they hadn't seen anything like it in Braden for more than a decade.

All he knew was that the snow was piled three feet high, making his life these days even more challenging. Making him wonder why he'd ever chosen Wyoming over New Mexico in the first place. Yeah, they got snow in Taos. But not like this.

"We believe that the infant girl who's been under our protection since she was abandoned three months ago is your daughter." The man tried to look past Ryder's shoulder. "Perhaps we could discuss this inside?"

Ryder had no desire to invite them in. But one of them *was* a cop. He hadn't crossed purposes with the law before and he wasn't real anxious to do so now. Didn't mean he had to like it, though.

His aunt hadn't raised him to be slob. She'd be horrified if she ever knew strangers were seeing the house in its current state.

He slapped his leather gloves together. He had chores waiting for him. But he supposed a few minutes wouldn't make much difference. "Don't think there's much to discuss," he warned as he stepped out of the doorway. He folded his arms across his chest, standing pretty much in their way so they had to crowd together in the small space where he dumped his boots. Back home, his aunt Adelaide would call the space a *vestibule*. Here, it wasn't so formal; he'd carved out his home from a converted barn. "I appreciate your concern for an abandoned baby, but whoever's making claims I fathered a child is out of their mind." Once burned, twice shy. Another thing his aunt was fond of saying.

The cop's brown eyes looked pained. "Ryder—may I call you Ryder?" She didn't wait for his permission, but plowed right on, anyway. "I'm sorry we have to be the bearer of bad news, but we believe your wife was the baby's mother, and—"

At the word *wife*, what had been Ryder's already-thin patience went by the wayside. "My *wife* ran out on me a year ago. Whatever she's done since is her prob—"

"Not anymore," the dark-haired guy said.

"What'd you say your name was?" Ryder met the other man's gaze head-on, knowing perfectly well he hadn't said his name. The pretty cop's role there was obviously official. Same with the sweaty bald guy—he had to be from social services. But the third intruder? The guy who was watching him as though he'd already formed an opinion—a bad one?

"Grant Cooper." The man's voice was flat. "Karen's my sister."

"There's your problem," Ryder responded just as flatly. "My so-called *wife's* name was Daisy. Daisy Miranda. You've got the wrong guy." He pointedly reached around them for the door to show them out. "So if you'll excuse me, I've got ice to break so my animals can get at their water."

"This is Karen." Only because she was a little slip of a thing, the cop succeeded in maneuvering between him and the door. She held a wallet-sized photo up in front of his face.

Ryder's nerves tightened even more than when he'd first opened the door to find these people on his front porch.

He didn't want to touch the photograph or examine it. He didn't need to. He recognized his own face just fine. In the picture, he'd been kissing the wedding ring he'd just put on Daisy's finger. The wedding had been a whirlwind sort of thing, like everything else about their relationship. Three months start to finish, from the moment they met outside the bar where she'd just quit her job until the day she'd walked out on him two weeks after their wedding. That's how long it had taken to meet, get hitched and get unhitched.

Though the unhitching part was still a work in progress. Not that he'd been holding on to hope that she'd return. But he'd had other things more important keeping him occupied than getting a formal divorce. Namely the Diamond-L ranch, which he'd purchased only a few months before meeting her. His only regret was that he hadn't kept his attention entirely on the ranch all along. It would have saved him some grief. "Where'd you get that?"

The cop asked her own question. "Can you confirm this is you and your wife in this picture?"

His jaw felt tight. "Yeah." Unfortunately. The Las Vegas wedding chapel had given them a cheap set of pictures. Ryder had tossed all of them in the fireplace, save the one the cop was holding now. He'd mailed that one to Daisy in response to a stupid postcard he'd gotten from her six months after she'd left him. A postcard on which she'd written only the words *I'm sorry*.

He still wasn't sure what she'd meant. Sorry for leaving him without a word or warning? Or sorry she'd ever married him in the first place?

"You wrote this?" The cop had turned the photo over, revealing his handwriting on the back. *So much for vows.*

Ryder was actually a little surprised that it was so legible, considering how drunk he'd been at the time he'd sent the photo. He nodded once.

The cop looked sympathetic. "I'm sorry to say that she died in a car accident over New Year's."

He waited as the words sank in. Expecting to feel something. Was he supposed to feel bad? Maybe he did. He wasn't sure. He'd known Daisy was a handful from the get-go. So when she took a powder the way she had, it shouldn't have been as much of a shock as it had been.

But one thing was certain. Everything that Daisy had told him had been a lie. From start to finish.

He might be an uncomplicated guy, but he understood the bottom line facing him now. "And you want to pawn off her baby on me." He looked the dark-haired guy in the face again. "Or do you just want money?" He lifted his arm, gesturing with the worn leather gloves. "Look around. All I've got is what you see. And it'll be a cold day in hell before I let a couple strangers making claims like yours get one finger on it."

Grant's eyes looked like flint. "As usual, my sister's taste in men was worse than—"

"Gentlemen." The other man mopped his forehead again, giving both Ryder and Grant wary looks even as he took a step between them. "Let's keep our cool. The baby is our focus."

Ryder ignored him. He pointed at Grant. "My wife never even told me she had a brother."

"My sister never told me she had a husband."

"The situation is complicated enough," the cop interrupted, "without the two of you taking potshots at each other." Her expression was troubled, but her voice was calm. And Ryder couldn't miss the way she'd wrapped her hand familiarly around Grant's arm. "Ray is right. What's important here is the baby."

"Yes. The baby under our protection." Ray was obviously hoping to maintain control over the discussion. "There is no local record of the baby's birth. Our only way left to establish who the child's parents are is through you, Mr. Wilson. We've expended every other option."

"You don't even *know* the baby was hers?"

Ray looked pained. Grant looked like he wanted to punch something. Hell, maybe even Ryder. The cop just looked worried.

"The assumption is that your wife was the person to have left the baby at the home her former employer, Jaxon Swift, shared with his brother, Lincoln," she said.

"Now, that *does* sound like Daisy." Ryder knew he sounded bitter. "I only knew her a few months, but it was still long enough to learn she's good at running out on people."

Maybe he did feel a little bad about Daisy. He hadn't gotten around to divorcing his absent wife. Now, if what these people said were true, he wouldn't need to. Instead of being a man with a runaway wife, he was a man with a deceased one. There was probably something wrong with him for not feeling like his world had just been rocked. "But maybe you're wrong. She wasn't pregnant when she left me," he said bluntly. He couldn't let himself believe otherwise.

"Would you agree to a paternity test?"

"The court can compel you, Mr. Wilson," Ray added when Ryder didn't answer right away.

It was the wrong tack for Ray to take. Ryder had been down the whole paternity-accusation path before. He hadn't taken kindly to it then, and he wasn't inclined to now. "Daisy was my wife, loose as that term is in this case. A baby born to her during our marriage makes me the presumed father, whether there's a test or not. But you don't know that the baby was actually hers. You just admitted it. Which tells me the court probably isn't on your side as much as you're implying. Unless I say otherwise, and without you knowing who this baby's mother is, I'm just a guy in a picture."

"We should have brought Greer," Grant said impatiently to the cop. "She's used to guys like him."

But the cop wasn't listening to Grant. She was looking at Ryder with an earnest expression. "You aren't just a guy in a picture. You're our best hope for preventing the child we believe is Grant's niece from being adopted by strangers."

That's when Ryder saw that she'd reached out to clasp Grant's hand, their fingers entwined. So, she had a dog in this race.

He thought about pointing out that he was a stranger to them, too, no matter what sort of guy Grant had deemed Ryder to be. "And if I cooperated and the test confirms I'm *not* this baby's father, you still wouldn't have proof that Daisy is—" *dammit* "—was the baby's mother."

"If the test is positive, then we know she was," Ray said. "Without your cooperation, the proof of Karen's maternity is circumstantial. We admit that. But you were her husband. There's no putative father. If you even suspected she'd become pregnant during your marriage, your very existence is enough to establish legal paternity, DNA proof or not."

The cop looked even more earnest. "And the court can't proceed with an adoption set in motion by Layla's abandonment."

The name startled him. *"Layla!"*

The three stared at him with varying degrees of surprise and expectation.

"Layla was my mother's name." His voice sounded gruff, even to his own ears. Whatever it was that Daisy had done with her child, using that name was a sure way of making sure he'd get involved. After only a few months together, she'd learned enough about him to know that.

He exhaled roughly. Slapped his leather gloves together. Then he stepped out of the way so he wasn't blocking them from the rest of his home. "You'd better come inside and sit." He felt weary all of a sudden. As if everything he'd accomplished in his thirty-four years was for nothing. What was that song? "There Goes My Life."

"I expect this is gonna take a while to work out." He glanced at the disheveled room, with its leather couch and oversize, wall-mounted television. That's what happened when a man spent more time tending cows than he did anything else. He'd even tended some of them in this very room.

Fortunately, his aunt Adelaide would never need to know.

"You'll have to excuse the mess, though."

Chapter One

Five months later.

The August heat was unbearable.

The forecasters kept saying the end of the heat wave was near, but Greer Templeton had lost faith in them. She twisted in her seat, trying to find the right position that allowed her to feel the cold air from the car vents on more than two square inches of her body. It wasn't as if she could pull up her skirt so the air could blow straight up her thighs or pull down her blouse so the air could get at the rest of her.

She'd tried that once, only to find herself the object of interest of a leering truck driver with a clear view down into her car. If she'd never seen or heard from the truck driver again, it wouldn't have been so bad. Instead, she'd had the displeasure of serving as the driver's public defender not two days later when he was charged with littering.

"I hate August!" she yelled, utterly frustrated.

Nobody heard.

The other vehicles crawling along the narrow, curving stretch of highway between Weaver—where she'd just come from a frustrating visit with a new client in jail—and Braden all had their windows closed against the oppressive heat, the same way she did.

It was thirty miles, give or take, between Braden and Weaver, and she drove it several times every week. Sometimes more than once in a single day. She knew the highway like the back of her hand. Where the infrequent passing zones were, where the dips filled with ice in the winter and where the shoulder was treacherous. She knew that mile marker 12 had the best view into Braden and mile marker 3 was the spot you were most likely to get a speeding ticket.

The worst, though, was grinding up and down the hills, going around the curves at a crawl because she was stuck behind a too-wide truck hogging the roadway with a too-tall load of hay.

Impatience raged inside her and she pushed her fingers against one of the car vents, feeling the air blast against her palm. It didn't provide much relief, because it was barely cool.

Probably because her car was close to overheating, she realized.

Even as she turned off the AC and rolled down the windows, a cloud billowed from beneath the front hood of her car.

She wanted to scream.

Instead, she coasted onto the weedy shoulder. It was barely wide enough.

The car behind her laid on its horn as it swerved around her.

"I hate August!" she yelled after it while her vehicle burped out steam into the already-miserable air.

So much for getting to Maddie's surprise baby shower early.

Ali was never going to forgive Greer. Unlike their sister, Maddie, the soul of patience she was not. Just that morning Ali had called to remind Greer of her tasks where the shower was concerned. It had been the fifth such call in as many days.

Marrying Grant hadn't softened Ali's annoying side at all.

Greer wasn't going to chance exiting through the driver's side because of the traffic, so she hitched up her skirt enough to climb over the console and out the passenger-side door.

In just the few minutes it took to get out of the car and open up the hood, Greer's silk blouse was glued to her skin by the perspiration sliding down her spine.

The engine had stopped spewing steam. But despite her father's best efforts to teach the triplets the fundamentals of car care when she and her sisters were growing up, what lived beneath the hood of Greer's car was still a mystery.

She knew from experience there was no point in checking her cell phone for a signal. There were about four points on the thirty-mile stretch where a signal reliably reached, and this spot wasn't one of them. If a Good Samaritan didn't happen to stop, she knew the schedules of both the Braden Police Department and the Weaver Sheriff's Department. Even if her disabled vehicle wasn't reported by someone passing by, officers from one or the other agency routinely traveled the roadway even on a hot August Saturday. She didn't expect it would be too long before she had some help.

She popped the trunk a few inches so the heat wouldn't build up any more than it already had and left the windows down. Then she walked along the shoulder until she reached an outcrop of rock that afforded a little shade from the sun and toed off her shoes, not even caring that she was probably ruining her silk blouse by leaning against the jagged stone.

Sorry, Ali.

Ryder saw the slender figure in white before he saw the car. It almost made him do a double take, the way sailors did when they spotted a mermaid sunning herself on a rock. A second look reassured him that lack of sleep hadn't caused him to start hallucinating.

Not yet, anyway.

She was on the opposite side of the road, and there was no place for him to pull his rig around to get to her. So he kept on driving until he reached his original destination—the turnoff to the Diamond-L. As soon as he did, he turned around and pulled back out onto the highway to head back to her.

It was only a matter of fifteen minutes.

The disabled foreign car was still sitting there, like a strange out-of-place insect among the pickup trucks rumbling by every few minutes. He parked behind it, but let his engine idle and kept the air-conditioning on. He propped his arm over the steering column and thumbed back his hat as he studied the woman.

She'd noticed him and was picking her way through the rough weeds back toward her car.

He'd recognized her easily enough.

Greer Templeton. One of the identical triplets who'd turned his life upside down. Starting with the cop, Ali, who'd come to his door five months ago.

It wasn't entirely their fault.

They weren't responsible for abandoning Layla. That was his late wife.

Now Layla was going through nannies like there was a revolving door on the nursery. Currently, the role was filled by Tina Lewis. She'd lasted two weeks but was already making dissatisfied noises.

He blew out a breath and checked the road before pushing open his door and getting out of the truck. "Looks like you've got a problem."

"Ryder?"

He spread his hands. "'Fraid so." Any minute she'd ask about the baby and he wasn't real sure what he would say.

For nearly five months—ever since Judge Stokes had officially made Layla his responsibility—the Templeton triplets had tiptoed around him. He'd quickly learned how attached they'd become to the baby, caring for her after Daisy dumped her on a "friend's" porch.

Supposedly, his wife hadn't been sleeping with that friend but Ryder still had his doubts. DNA might have ruled out Jaxon Swift as Layla's father, but the man owned Magic Jax, the bar where Daisy had briefly worked as a cocktail waitress before they'd met. He would never understand why she hadn't just come to *him* if she'd needed help. He had been her husband, for God's sake. Not her onetime boss. Unless she'd been more involved with Jax than they all had admitted.

As for the identity of Layla's real father, everyone had been happy as hell to stop wondering as soon as Ryder gave proof that he and Daisy had been married.

Didn't mean Ryder hadn't wondered, though.

But doing a DNA test at this point wouldn't change

anything where he was concerned. It would prove Layla was his by blood. Or it wouldn't.

Either way, he believed she was his wife's child.

Which made Layla his responsibility. Period.

The questions about Daisy, though? Every time he looked at Layla, they bubbled up inside him.

For now, though, he focused on Greer.

It was no particular hardship.

The Templeton triplets scored pretty high in the looks department. He could tell Greer apart from her twins because she always looked a little more sophisticated. Maddie—the social worker who'd been Layla's foster mother—had long hair reaching halfway down her back. Ali—the cop who'd shown up on his doorstep—had blond streaks. And he'd never seen her dressed in anything besides her police uniform.

Greer, though?

Her dark hair barely reached her shoulders and not a single strand was ever out of place. She was a lawyer and dressed the part in skinny skirts with expensive-looking jackets and high heels that looked more big-city than Wyoming dirt. She'd been the one who'd ushered him through all the legalities with the baby. And she was the only one of her sisters who hadn't been openly crying when they'd brought Layla and all of her stuff out to his ranch to turn her over to his care. But there'd been no denying the emotion in her eyes. She just hadn't allowed herself the relief of tears.

For some reason, that had seemed worse.

Ryder had been uncomfortable as hell with so much female emotion. Greer's most of all.

He'd rather have to deal with the general animosity Daisy's brother clearly felt for him. That, at least, was straightforward and simple. Grant's sister was dead. Whether he'd voiced it outright or not, he blamed Ryder.

Since Ryder was already shouldering the blame, it didn't make any difference to him.

Now Greer was shading her eyes with one hand and holding her hair off her neck with the other. Instead of asking about Layla first thing, though, she stopped near the front bumper of her car. "It overheated. I saw steam coming out from the hood and pulled off as soon as I could."

He joined her in front of the car. He knew the basics when it came to engines—enough to keep the machinery on his ranch running without too much outside help—but he was a lot more comfortable with the anatomy of horses and cows. "How long have you been sitting out here?"

"Too long." She plucked the front of her blouse away from her throat and glanced at the watch circling her narrow wrist. "I thought someone would stop sooner than this. Ali'll think I'm deliberately late."

The only heat from the engine came from the sun glaring down on it. He checked a few of the hoses and looked underneath for signs of leaking coolant, but the ground beneath the car was dry. "Why's that?"

"We're throwing a surprise baby shower for Maddie today. I'm supposed to help set up."

"Didn't know she was pregnant." He straightened. It was impossible to miss the sharpness in Greer's brown eyes.

"Why would you, when you've been avoiding all of us since March?"

"Some law that says I needed to do otherwise?" He hadn't been avoiding them entirely. Just…mostly.

It had been easy, considering he had a ranch to run.

She pursed her bow-shaped lips. "You know my family has a vested interest in Layla. At the very least, you could try accepting an invitation or two when they're extended."

"Maybe I'm too busy to accept invitations." He waited a beat. "I am a single father, you know."

If he wasn't mistaken, her eye actually twitched.

She'd always struck him as the one most tightly wound.

It was too bad that he also couldn't look at her without wondering just what it would take to *un*wind her.

He closed the hood of her car with a firm hand. "You want to try starting her up? See what happens with the temperature gauge?"

He thought she might argue—if only for the sake of it—but she opened the passenger door. Then he had to choke back a laugh when she climbed across and into the driver's seat, where she started the engine. Her focus was clearly on her dashboard and he could tell the gauge was rising just by the frown on her face.

She shut off the engine again and looked through the windshield. "Needle went straight to the red." She climbed back out the passenger side.

"Something wrong with the driver's-side door?"

She was looking down at herself as she got out, tweaking that white skirt hugging her slender hips until it hung smooth and straight. "No, but I don't want it getting hit by a passing vehicle if I open it."

He eyed the distance between the edge of the road and where she'd pulled off on the shoulder. "Real cautious of you."

"I'm a lawyer. I'm always cautious."

"Overly so, I'd say." Not that he hadn't enjoyed the show. She was a little skinny for his taste, but he couldn't deny she was a looker. He pulled off his cowboy hat long enough to swipe his arm across his forehead. "I can drive you into town, or I can send a tow out for you." He didn't have time to do both, because he had to be back at the ranch before the nanny left or his housekeeper, Mrs. Pyle, would have kittens. "What's your choice?"

Greer swallowed her frustration. Considering Ryder Wilson's standoffishness since they'd met, she was a little surprised that he'd stopped to assist at all.

As soon as she'd realized who was driving the enormous pickup truck pulling up behind her car, she'd been torn between anticipation and the desire to cry *what next?*

It was entirely annoying that the brawny, blue-eyed rancher was the first man to make her hormones sit up and take notice in too long a while.

Annoying and impossible to act on, considering the strange nature of their acquaintance.

All she wanted to do was ask Ryder how Layla was doing. But Maddie had been insistent that none of them intrude on him too soon.

They'd all been wrapped around Layla's tiny little finger and none more than Maddie, who'd been caring for her nearly the whole while before Ali discovered Ryder's existence. Yet it was Maddie who'd urged them to give Ryder time. To adjust. To adapt. They knew Ryder was taking decent care of the baby he'd claimed, because Maddie's boss, Raymond Marx, checked up on him for a while at first, so he could report back to the courts. Give Ryder time, Maddie insisted, and eventually he would see the benefit of letting them past his walls.

Didn't mean that it had been easy.

Didn't mean it was easy now, not dashing over to the truck to see Layla.

She didn't know if it was that prospect that made her feel so shaky inside, or if it was because of Layla's brown-haired daddy. She wasn't sure she even liked Ryder all that much.

Yes, he'd been legally named Layla's father and yes, he'd taken responsibility for her. But there was an edge to him that had rubbed Greer wrong from the very first time they met. She just hadn't been able to pinpoint why.

"If you don't mind driving me into town," she managed, "I'd be grateful."

The brim of his hat dipped briefly. "Probably should lock her up." He started for his big truck parked behind the car.

She watched him walk away. He was wearing blue jeans and a checked shirt with the sleeves rolled up to his elbows. Except for when he'd briefly swiped an arm over his forehead, he appeared unaffected by the sweltering day.

"Probably should lock her up," she parroted childishly under her breath. As if she didn't have the sense to know that without being told.

She retrieved her purse and briefcase from the back seat, looping the long straps over her shoulder, then warily lifted the trunk lid higher. The shower cake that she'd nestled carefully between two boxes full of work from the office amazingly didn't look too much the worse for wear. It was a delightful amalgam of block and ball shapes, frosted in white, yellow and blue. How Tabby Clay had balanced them all together like that was a mystery to Greer.

She was just glad to see that the creation hadn't

melted into a puddle of goo while she'd waited on the side of the road.

She carefully lifted the white board with the heavy cake on top out of the trunk and gingerly carried it toward Ryder's truck. Her heart was beating so hard, she could hear it inside her head. The last time she'd seen Layla had been at Shop-World in Weaver, when she'd taken a client shopping for an affordable set of clothes to wear for trial, and Ryder had been in the next checkout line over, buying diapers, coffee and whiskey.

Layla had been asleep in the cart. Greer had noticed that her blond curls had gotten a reddish cast, but the stuffed pony she'd clutched was the same one Greer had given her for Valentine's Day.

It had been all she could do not to pluck the baby out of the cart and cuddle her close. Instead, after a stilted exchange with Ryder, she'd hustled her client through the checkout so fast that he'd wondered out loud if she'd slid through without paying for something. *No. That's what* you *like to do*, she'd told him as she'd rushed him out the door.

But now, when she got close enough to Ryder's truck to see inside, her feet dragged to a halt.

There was no car seat.

Definitely no Layla.

The disappointment that swamped her was so searing, it put the hot afternoon sun to shame. Her eyes stung and she blinked hard, quickening her pace once more only to feel her heel slide on the loose gravel. The heavy cake started tipping one way and she leveled the board, even as her shoulder banged against the side of his truck.

She froze, holding her breath as she held the cake board aloft.

"What the hell are you doing over here?"

She was hot. Sweaty. And brokenhearted that she wasn't getting a chance to see sweet Layla.

"What do you care?" she snapped back. She was still holding the cake straight out from her body, and the weight of it was considerable. "Just open the door, would you please? If I don't deliver this thing in one piece, Ali's going to skin me alive."

He gave her a wide berth as he reached around her to open the door of the truck. "Let me take it." His hands covered hers where she held the board, and she jerked as if he'd prodded her with a live wire.

Her face went hot. "I don't need your help."

He let go and held his hands up in the air. "Whatever." He backed away.

Nobody liked to feel self-conscious. Not even her.

She turned away from him to set the cake board inside the truck, but it was too big to fit on the floor, which meant she'd have to hold it on her lap.

Greer heaved out a breath and looked at Ryder. He wordlessly took the cake long enough for her to dump her briefcase and purse on the floor, and climb up on the high seat.

"All settled now?" His voice was mild.

For some reason, it annoyed her more than if he'd made some snarky comment.

Unfortunately, that's when she realized that she'd left her trunk open and the car unlocked.

She slid off the seat again, mentally cursing ranchers and their too-big trucks as she jumped out onto the ground. Ignoring the amused glint in his dark blue eyes, she strode past him, grinding her teeth when her heel again slid on the loose gravel.

She'd have landed on her butt if not for the quick hand he shot out to steady her.

She shrugged off his touch as if she'd been burned but managed a grudging "thank you." It figured that he could manage to hold on to the heavy cake and still keep her from landing on her butt.

She finally made it to her car without further mishap and secured it. The passenger door of his truck was still open and waiting for her when she returned.

She climbed inside and fastened the safety belt. Then he settled the enormous, heavy cake on her lap, taking an inordinate amount of time before sliding his big, warm hands away.

As soon as he did, she yanked the door closed.

The cool air flowed from the air-conditioning vents.

It was the only bright spot, and gave a suitable reason for the shivers that skipped down her spine.

She wrapped her hands firmly around the edge of the cake board to hold it in place while Ryder circled the front of the truck and got in behind the wheel.

His blue eyes skated over and she shivered again. Despite the heat. Despite the perspiration soaking her blouse.

Annoyance swelled inside her.

"I hope you have someone decent watching Layla."

His expression turned chilly. "I've got plenty of things I needed to be doing besides stopping to help you out. You really want to go there?"

She pressed her lips together. If Maddie ever found out she'd been rude to Ryder, her sister would never forgive her.

"Just drive," she said ungraciously.

He lifted an eyebrow slightly.

God. She really hated feeling self-conscious.

"Please," she added.

He waited a beat. "Better." Then he put the truck in gear.

Chapter Two

"I knew you'd be late."

Greer ignored Ali's greeting as she entered the stately old mansion that Maddie shared with her husband, Lincoln Swift. She kicked the heavy front door closed, blocking out the sound of Ryder's departing truck. Passing the round table in the foyer loaded down with fancifully wrapped gifts and the grand wooden staircase, she headed into the dining room with the cake.

The sight of a cheerfully decorated sheet cake already sitting in the middle of the table shredded her last nerve.

She stared over her shoulder at Ali. Her sister looked uncommonly pretty in a bright yellow sundress. More damningly, Ali was as cool and fresh as the daisy she'd stuck in her messy ponytail. "You have a *backup* cake?"

"Of course I have a backup cake." Ali waved her hands, and the big diamond rock that Grant had put on her ring finger a few months earlier glinted in the sunlight shining through the mullioned windows. "Because I knew you would be late! You're always late, because you're always working for that slave driver over at the dark side."

"Well, I wouldn't have *been* late, if I hadn't broken down on the way back from Weaver! Now would you move that stupid cake so I can put this one down where it belongs?"

"Girls!" Their mother, Meredith, dashed into the dining room, accompanied by the usual tinkle of tiny bells on the ankle bracelet she wore. "This is supposed to be a party." She tsked. "You're thirty years old and you still sound as if you're bickering ten-year-olds." She whisked the offending backup cake off the table. "Ali, put this in the kitchen."

Ali took the sheet cake from their mother and crossed her eyes at Greer behind their mother's back while Greer set Tabby's masterpiece in its place.

"It's just beautiful," Meredith exclaimed, clasping her hands together. Despite her chastisement, her eyes were sparkling. "Maddie's going to love it." As she turned away, the dark hair she'd passed on to her daughters danced in corkscrew curls nearly to the small of her back. "It's just too bad that Tabby wasn't able to come to the party."

"If Gracie weren't running a fever, she'd have brought the cake herself." Greer glanced around. "Obviously Ali didn't have a problem decorating without me. It looks like the baby-shower fairy threw up in here." The raindrop theme was in full force. Silver and white balloons hovered above the table in a cluster of "clouds" from which shimmering crystal raindrops hung down,

drifting slightly in the cool room. It was sweet and subtly chic and just like Maddie. Altogether perfect, really.

As usual, Ali hadn't really needed Greer at all.

Meredith squeezed her arm as if she'd read her mind.
"Stop sweating the details, Greer. You had a hand in the
planning of this, whether you were here to help pull it
together this afternoon or not. Now—" she eyed Greer
more closely "—what's this about your car breaking
down?"

It was a timely reminder that she probably looked as
bedraggled as she felt. A glance at her watch told her
the guests would be arriving in a matter of minutes.
Linc was supposed to be delivering Maddie—hopefully
still in the dark about the surprise—shortly after that.

"The car overheated. I left it locked up on the side
of the road."

"How'd you get here?"

She felt reluctant to say, knowing the mention of
Ryder would only remind them all of how much they
missed Layla. "Someone stopped and gave me a ride to
town. I'll arrange a tow after the shower." She dashed
her hand down the front of her outfit and headed for
the stairs. "I need to put on something less wrinkled
and sweaty. Hopefully there's more than just maternity
clothes in Maddie's closet." She hadn't made it halfway
up the staircase before the doorbell rang and she could
hear Ali greeting the new arrivals.

She darted up the rest of the stairs.

Even after more than half a year, it was hard to get
used to the fact that Maddie lived in this grand old
house with Linc. The place had belonged to his and
Jax's grandmother Ernestine. When the triplets were
children, Meredith had cleaned house for Ernestine.

Greer and her sisters had often accompanied her. Now, Jax no longer shared the house with Linc. Maddie did.

She entered the big walk-in closet, mentally sending an apology to her brother-in-law for the intrusion. She knew that Maddie wouldn't mind. Not surprisingly, most of the clothes hanging on the rods were designed for a woman who looked about a hundred months pregnant.

She could hear the doorbell chime again downstairs and quickly flipped through the hangers, finally pulling out a colorful dress she remembered Maddie wearing for Easter, when she'd had just a small baby bump. The dress had a stretchy waist that was a little loose on Greer, but it would do.

She changed and flipped her hair up into a clip. If there'd been blond streaks in her hair, she'd look just like Ali. Tousled and carefree.

But Greer hadn't felt carefree in what was starting to feel like forever.

She stared at her reflection and plucked at the loose waist of the dress. Maddie was pregnant. Now Ali and Grant were married. Considering how the two couldn't keep their hands off each other, it was only a matter of time before they were starting a family, too.

But Greer?

The last date she'd had that had gotten even remotely physical was more than two years ago, so if she wanted a baby, she was going to need either a serious miracle or big-time artificial intervention. As it was, the little birth control implant she had in her arm was pretty much pointless.

From downstairs, she heard a peal of laughter. Turning away from her reflection, she headed down to join them. She might not feel carefree, but she *was* thrilled about Maddie's coming baby. So she would put on a party face for that reason alone.

And she would try to forget that Ali had gotten a damn backup cake.

Ryder stared at Doreen Pyle. "What do you mean, you're quitting?"

"Just that, Ryder." Mrs. Pyle continued scooping mushy green food into Layla's mouth, even though the little girl kept twisting her head away. "When you hired me, it was to be your housekeeper. Not your nanny."

"That's because I *had* a nanny." His voice was tight. "Look, I'm sorry that Tina took a hike this afternoon with no warning." At least the others who'd come before her had given him some notice. "I'll start looking again first thing tomorrow."

"It won't matter, Ryder. Nobody wants to live all the way out here." She finally gave up on the green mush and glanced at him. The look in her lined eyes was more sympathetic than her tone had been. "You need to give up the idea of a live-in nanny, Ryder. Or else give up the idea of a housekeeper. You can't afford both."

He could, if he were willing to dip into his savings. But he wasn't willing. Any more than he was willing to take Adelaide's money. She'd made her way on her own, and he was doing the same. On his own. But if he were going to continue growing this small ranch, he couldn't be carting a growing baby around everywhere while he worked. "I'll give you another raise." He'd already given her one. "Stay on and take care of Layla. You're good with her. I'll hire someone to help with the housekeeping."

"I don't want to live out here, either." She pushed off her chair, wincing a little as she straightened. "The only difference between me and Tina is that I won't take off while your back is turned." She grabbed a cloth and started wiping up Layla's face. The baby squirmed, trying to avoid the cloth just like she'd tried to avoid the green muck. But Mrs. Pyle prevailed and then tossed the cloth aside. "You don't need a nanny around the clock, anyway. You're here at night." She lifted the baby out of the high chair. "You can take care of her yourself. Then just get some help during the day. Preferably someone who doesn't have to drive farther than from Braden, or once the winter comes, you're going to have problems all over again." She plopped Layla into his arms and hustled to the sink where she wet another cloth. "But it won't be me. I have my own family I need to look out for, too. My grandson—" She broke off, grimacing. She squeezed out the moisture and waved the rag at him. "I won't apologize for not wanting to be tied down to a baby all over again. Not at my age." She sounded defensive.

"I don't need an apology, Mrs. Pyle. I need someone to take care of Layla!"

The baby lightly slapped his face with her hands and laughed.

Mrs. Pyle's expression softened. She chucked Layla lightly under the chin. "Maybe instead of looking for a nanny, you should start looking for a mama for this little girl."

Ryder grimaced.

"There are plenty of other fish in the sea. All you need to do is cast your line. You're a good-looking cuss when you clean yourself up. Someone'll come biting before you know it."

"I don't think so." One foray into so-called wedded bliss was one disaster enough.

The look in Doreen's eyes got even more sympathetic. "I know what it's like to lose a spouse, hon. Single parents might be all the rage these days, but I'm here to tell you it's easier when two people are committed to their family. You're still young. You don't want to spend the rest of your life alone. I'm sure your poor wife wouldn't have wanted that, either. She'd surely want this little mite to have a proper mama. Someone who won't toss aside caring for Layla on some flighty whim the way Tina just did."

He managed a tight smile. His "poor wife" had been exactly that. A poor wife. But not in the way Doreen Pyle meant. Abandoning Layla had been a helluva way to show off her maternal nature. Tina's quitting out of the blue was a lot more forgivable. "Would you at least stay until I find someone new?" He had to finish getting the hay in before the weather turned. And then he and his closest neighbor to the east were helping each other through roundup. Then he'd be sorting and shipping and—

"I'll stay another week," she said, interrupting the litany of tasks running through his mind. "But that's it, Ryder."

Layla grinned up at him with her six teeth and smacked his face again with her hand.

He looked back at his housekeeper. "A week."

"That's all the time I can give you, Ryder. I'm sorry."

A week was better than nothing.

And it was damn sure more than Tina had given him.

"I don't suppose you could stay and watch Layla for another few hours or so?" As his housekeeper began shaking her head no, he grabbed the refrigerator door and stuck his head inside, so he could pretend he didn't see. "Got a friend—" big overstatement there "—who needs help towing her car back to town. Broke down up near Devil's Crossing." He grabbed the bottle of ketchup that Layla latched onto and stuck it back on the refrigerator shelf. She immediately reached for something else and he quickly shut the door and gave Mrs. Pyle a hopeful look. The same one he'd mastered by the time he was ten and living with Adelaide.

Instead of looking resigned and accepting, though, Mrs. Pyle was giving him an eyebrows-in-the-hairline look. "*Her* car? Is this female friend single?"

Warning alarms went off inside his head. "Yeah."

She lifted Layla out of his arms. "Well, go rescue your lady friend. And give my suggestion about a wife some thought."

He let her remark slide. "Thank you, Mrs. Pyle."

"Not going to change my leaving in a week," she warned as she carried the baby out of the kitchen. "And you might think about washing some of the day off yourself, as well, before you go out playing Dudley Do-Right."

He hadn't showered, but he *had* washed up and pulled on fresh clothes. And he still felt pretty stupid about it.

It wasn't as if he wanted to impress Greer Templeton. Not with a clean shirt or anything else. And it damn sure wasn't as if he was giving Mrs. Pyle's suggestion any consideration.

Marrying someone just for Layla's sake?

He pushed the idea straight out of his mind and shifted into Park at the top of the hill as he stared out at the worn-looking Victorian house.

The white paint on the fancy trim was peeling and the dove-gray paint on the siding was fading. The shingle roof needed repair, if not replacement, and the brick chimney looked as if it were related to the Leaning Tower of Pisa. But the yard around the house was green and neat.

Not exactly what he would have expected of the lady lawyer. But then again, she worked for the public defender's office, where the pay was reportedly abysmal and most of her clients were supposedly the dregs of society.

He turned off the engine and got out of the truck, walking around to the trailer he'd used to haul Greer's little car. He checked the chains holding it in place and then headed up the front walk to the door.

The street was quiet, and his boots clumped loudly as he went up the steps and crossed the porch to knock on the door. The heavy brass door knocker was shaped like a dragonfly.

If he could ever get Adelaide to come and visit Braden, she'd love the place.

When no one came to the door, he went back down the porch steps. There was an elderly woman across the street making a production of sweeping the sidewalk, though it seemed obvious she was more interested in giving him the once-over.

He tipped the brim of his hat toward her before he started unchaining Greer's car. "Evenin'."

The woman clutched her broom tightly and started across the street. A little black poodle trotted after her. "That's Greer's car," the woman said suspiciously.

He didn't stop what he was doing. "Yes, ma'am."

"What're you doing with it?"

"Unloading it."

She stopped several feet away, still holding the

broom handle as if she was prepared to use it on him if need be. "I don't know you."

"No, ma'am." He fit the wheel ramps in place and hopped up onto the trailer. "I assure you that Greer does." He opened the car door and folded himself down inside it.

Maybe Greer—who was probably all of five two or three without those high heels she was always wearing—could fit comfortably into the car, but he couldn't. Not for any length of time, anyway.

He started the car, backed down the ramp and turned into the driveway. Then he shut off the engine, crawled out from behind the wheel and locked it up again before sticking the key back into the magnetic box he'd found tucked inside the wheel well.

The woman was still standing in the middle of the street.

He secured the ramps back up onto the trailer and gave her another nod. "If you see her, tell her she's got a thermostat problem."

"Tell her yourself." The woman pointed her broom handle at an expensive black SUV that had just crested the top of the hill. "Bet that's her now."

He bit back an oath. He still didn't know what had possessed him to haul Greer's car into town for her, particularly without her knowledge. And his chance of a clean escape had just disappeared.

The SUV pulled to a stop in front of Greer's house. The windows were tinted, so he couldn't see who was behind the wheel, but he definitely could see the shapely leg that emerged when the passenger-side door opened.

It belonged to Greer, looking very un-Greer-like in a flowy sort of dress patterned in vibrant swirls of color that could have rivaled one of his aunt's paintings. Half her hair was untidily pulled up and held by a glittery pink clip.

He still knew it was her, though, and not one of her sisters. No question, considering the sharp look she gave him as she closed the SUV door and approached him. "*You* hauled my car here?"

"I suppose there's no point in denying the obvious." He watched the big SUV pull around in the cul-de-sac and head back down the hill. The identity of the driver was none of his business. He wondered, anyway. "Boyfriend?"

She frowned. "Grant. And why did you haul it?"

No wonder the SUV had turned around and left. "You'd rather have it still sitting out on the side of the highway?"

"Of course not, but—" She broke off, looking consternated, and only then seemed to notice that they had an audience. "How are you doing, Mrs. Gunderson?" She leaned down to pet the little round dog. Ryder wasn't enough of a gentleman to look away when the stretchy, ruffled neckline of Greer's dress revealed more than it should have.

"Just fine, dearie. Oh, Mignon, don't jump!"

Mrs. Gunderson's admonishment was too late, though, because the dog had already bounced up and into Greer's arms.

He was actually a little impressed that the fat Mignon could jump.

But he was more impressed by the way Greer caught him and laughed.

He had never heard her laugh before. Not her or her sisters. Her chocolate-colored eyes sparkled and her face practically glowed.

And damned if he didn't feel something warm streak down his spine.

"You probably need a new thermostat," he said abruptly.

The dog was licking the bottom of her chin even though she was trying to avoid his tongue, but she didn't put Mignon down. "How do you know?"

"Because I checked everything else that would cause your overheating before I towed it back here." He stepped around the two women. "And think about keeping your car key in a less obvious hiding spot," he advised as pulled open the door to climb inside his truck.

Greer's jaw dropped a little, which gave Mignon more chin to lick. She set the dog down and trotted after him, wrapping her fingers over the open window. "You're just going to leave now?"

His fingers closed over the key in the ignition, but didn't turn it. "What else do you figure I should do?"

Her lips parted slightly. "Can I pay you for the tow at least?"

He turned the key. "No need."

"Well, I should do something." She didn't step back from the truck, despite the engine leaping to life. "To thank you at least. Surely there's something I can do."

The "something" that leaped to mind wasn't exactly fit for sharing in polite company. Particularly with her elderly neighbor still watching them as though they were prime-time entertainment.

He said the next best option that came to mind. "Next time I need a lawyer, you can owe me one." He even managed a smile to go with the words.

Fortunately, it seemed like enough. She smiled back and patted the door once. "You'll never collect on that." Her voice was light.

"One thing I've learned in my life is to never say never." He looked away from her ringless ring finger. "Where'd that dog go?"

Greer looked around, giving him a close-up view of the tender skin on the back of her neck. She had a trio of tiny freckles just below the loose strands of hair. Like someone had dashed a few specks of cinnamon across a smooth layer of cream.

He focused on Mrs. Gunderson, who was skirting the back of his trailer, calling the dog's name. "Mignon, get out from under there, right now!"

Greer had joined in, crouching down to look under the vehicle.

He figured if he revved the engine, it might send the fat dog into cardiac arrest. He shut it off again and climbed out. "Where is he?"

"He's lying down right inside the back tire." Mrs. Gunderson looked like she was about to go down on her hands and knees. "Mignon, you naughty little thing. Come out here, right now. Oh, darn it, he seems to have found something he thinks is food."

"Why don't you get one of his usual treats?" Greer suggested.

"Good idea." Mrs. Gunderson set off across the street once more.

If he'd hoped that her departure would spur the dog to follow, he was wrong. He knelt on one knee to look under the trailer. "Come 'ere, pooch."

Mignon paid him no heed at all, except to move even farther beneath the trailer.

Greer crouched next to him. The bottom of her dress puddled around her. "He doesn't like strangers."

Ryder slid his hand out from beneath the soft, colorful fabric that covered it. "He wouldn't like getting flattened by my trailer, either."

"He'll come out for his treats," she assured him.

"Since he looks like he lives on treats, I hope so." It would take the better part of an hour to get home and he'd probably already used up Mrs. Pyle's allotment of patience. If the treat didn't work, he'd have to drag the little bugger out.

"She's actually gotten him to lose a couple pounds."

"He's still wider than he is tall. Reminds me of my aunt's dog, Brutus." He straightened and looked across the street, hoping to see Mrs. Gunderson heading back. Instead, she was just reaching the top of her porch stairs and he could feel the minutes ticking away.

Even though he didn't say anything, Greer could feel the impatience coming off Ryder in waves. She stood, hoping that Mrs. Gunderson moved with more speed than she usually did. It was obvious that he was anxious to be on his way. "Your aunt has an overweight poodle?"

He lifted his hat just long enough to shove his fingers through his thick brown hair. "Overweight pug." His blue gaze slid over her from beneath the hat brim as he pulled it low over his brow. "Adelaide spoils him rotten."

She couldn't help but smile. "A pug named Brutus?"

He shrugged. "She has a particular sense of irony."

"I love your aunt's name," she said. "Adelaide."

A dimple came and went in his lean cheek. "Coming from the woman who lives in that Victorian thing behind us, I'm not real surprised."

She leaned against the side rail of the trailer. "Does she live in New Mexico?" Greer and her sisters didn't know much about Ryder, but had learned that he'd lived in New Mexico before moving to Wyoming.

The brim of his hat dipped slightly. "She has a place near Taos."

"The only place I've ever been in New Mexico was the Albuquerque airport during a layover." She glanced toward her neighbor's house. The front door was still open, but there was no sign of Mrs. Gunderson yet. "Did you grow up there?"

The dimple came again, staying a little longer this time. "In the Albuquerque airport?"

"Ha ha."

His lips actually stretched into a smile. "Yeah. I spent most of my time in Taos."

So she now knew he had an aunt. But she still didn't know if he had parents. Siblings. Other ex-wives. Anybody else at all besides Layla. "What's it like there? It's pretty artsy, isn't it?"

"More so than Braden."

"Does your aunt get to visit you often?"

"She's never been here. She doesn't like to travel much anymore. If I want to see her, I have to go to her." He thumbed up the brim of his hat and squinted at the sky.

"You're anxious to go."

"Yup." He knelt down to look at the dog again. "My housekeeper's gonna be peeved." He gave a coaxing whistle. "Come 'ere, dog."

"Your housekeeper's Doreen Pyle?"

Still down on one knee, he looked up at Greer and something swooped inside her stomach. "Keeping close tabs on me?"

She ignored the strange sensation. "Braden is a small community. And I happen to know her grandson pretty well."

"Dating him, are you?"

She couldn't help the snort of laughter that escaped. "Since he's not legally an adult, hardly. Haven't even had a date in—" She broke off, appalled at herself, embarrassed by the speculative look he was giving her. She pointed, absurdly grateful for Mrs. Gunderson's timely reappearance on her front porch. Her neighbor was holding something in her hand, waving it in the air as she came down the steps. "There's the treat."

And sure enough, before his mistress had even gotten to the street, Mignon was scrabbling out from beneath the trailer, practically rolling over his feet as he bolted.

Ryder straightened and gave her that faint smile again. The one that barely curved his well-shaped lips, but still managed to reveal his dimple. "Never underestimate the power of a good treat."

Then he thumbed the brim of his hat in that way he had of doing. Sort of old-fashioned and, well, *rancherly.* He walked around his truck and climbed inside. A moment later, he'd started the engine and was driving away.

Mrs. Gunderson picked up Mignon, who was happily gnawing on his piece of doggy jerky, and stood next to Greer. "He's a good-looking one, isn't he?"

At least her elderly neighbor could explain away her breathlessness. She'd had to climb her porch stairs to retrieve the dog treats.

Greer, on the other hand, had no such excuse. "He's surprising, anyway." She gave Mignon's head a scratch. "I've got to go call my dad before he drives out to haul my car that no longer needs hauling."

Then she hurried inside, pretending not to hear Mrs. Gunderson's knowing chuckle.

Chapter Three

"Ryder Wilson towed your truck?"

Greer tucked her office phone against her shoulder. "Hey, Maddie. Hold on." She didn't wait for her sister to reply, but clicked over to the other phone call while she scrolled through the emails on her computer. It was Monday morning. She wished she could say it was unusual coming in to find fifty emails all requiring immediate attention. The fact was, coming in to *only* fifty emails was a good start to a week.

"Mrs. Pyle, as I explained to your son last week, Judge Donnelly has refused another continuance in Anthony's case. He's already granted two, which is unusual. Your grandson's trial is going to be on Thursday and my associate Don Chatham will be handling it. He's our senior attorney, as you know, and handles most of the jury trials." After she had handled all the other steps, including negotiating plea deals. Which the prosecutor's office wasn't offering to Anthony this go-round.

Not surprising. It was an election year.

"I know Judge Donnelly." Doreen Pyle sounded tearful. "I can't be in court on Thursday. If I just went to him and asked—"

She shook her head, even though Doreen couldn't see. "I advise you not to speak directly to the judge, Mrs. Pyle."

"Then schedule a different date! You know how unreliable my son is. Anthony needs his family there. If his father would have told me last week, I could have made arrangements. But I have to work!"

Doreen Pyle worked for Ryder Wilson.

Greer pressed her fingertips between her eyes to relieve the pain that had suddenly formed there and sighed. The only adult Anthony truly had in his corner was his grandmother. "I'll see what I can do, Mrs. Pyle. I'll call you later this afternoon. All right?"

"Thank you, Greer. Thank you so much."

She highly doubted that Mrs. Pyle would be thanking her later. "Don't get your hopes up too high," she warned before jabbing the blinking button on her phone to switch back to the other call.

"Sorry about that, Maddie." She sent off a two-line response to the email on her computer screen and started composing a new one to the prosecutor's office. She wouldn't present a motion to the court until the prosecutor agreed to another delay. "You all recovered from the baby shower?"

"The only thing that'll help me recover fully from anything these days will be going into labor. About Ryder—"

"Yes, he towed my truck." She switched the phone to her other shoulder and opened the desk drawer where she kept her active files. "I suppose Ali told you?" She'd caught their father before he'd made a needless trip out to Devil's Crossing but she hadn't told him the finer details of who'd taken care of the chore.

She pulled out the file she was seeking and flipped it open on her desk. Anthony Pyle. Seventeen. Charged with property destruction and defacement. It was his second charge and he was being tried in adult court. Anthony and his grandmother had good cause for worry since he was facing more than six months in jail if convicted.

Greer doubted that his father, Rocky, cared all that much about what happened. He provided for the basic needs of his son, but beyond that, the troubled boy was pretty much on his own. Rocky had told Greer outright that Anthony deserved what he got. Didn't matter to his father at all that the boy had consistently proclaimed his innocence. That the real culprit was his supposed friend—and the son of the man who owned the barn that had nearly burned down.

"Ali? No."

Greer held back a sigh. If Grant had told his wife that he'd seen Ryder with her, there was no way that Ali would have stayed quiet about it. And the fact that Grant hadn't told Ali just meant that he was still conflicted over everything that had happened with his sister.

"You know how news gets around," Maddie said.

In other words, Mrs. Gunderson had told someone she'd seen Ryder towing her car, and that someone had told someone, and so on and so forth.

Greer forestalled her sister's next question, knowing it was coming. "Ryder didn't have Layla with him."

"I heard. Did you know that his latest nanny quit on him?"

Greer's fingers paused on her computer keyboard. Doreen hadn't mentioned *that*. "That's the fourth one."

"Third," Maddie corrected. "Ray has been keeping track."

Greer spotted Keith Gowler in the hallway outside her office and waved to get his attention. He was one of the local private attorneys who took cases on behalf of the public defender's office because they were perpetually overworked and understaffed. "Is Ray concerned?"

"Not that he's said. We have no reason to think Layla's not being properly cared for."

"That's probably why Ryder was anxious to get moving the other evening, then. Doreen must have been watching Layla." And that was why she was upset about not being available for her grandson's trial.

"She's got a lot on her plate, too."

Greer glanced at Anthony's file. Despite the jurisdiction of the case, he was still a minor, which meant the case also involved Maddie's office. "Did you get notice of the trial date?"

"Thursday? Yes. I can't be there, though. Having another ultrasound at the hospital in Weaver and Linc will have kittens if I say I want to reschedule it."

"Everything okay?" she asked, alarm in her voice.

"Everything's fine, except I'm as big as a house and due in two weeks. And don't you start acting as bad as my husband. He's turned into a nervous Nellie these last few weeks. Driving me positively nuts."

"He's concerned. You're having your first baby."

"And I'm already thirty and yada yada. I know."

Keith stuck his head in her doorway. "Got the latest litter?"

She nodded at him and glanced at the round, schoolroom-style clock hanging above the door. It had a loud tick and tended to lose about five minutes every few days, but it had been a gift from one of her favorite law professors what felt like a hundred years ago. "Listen, Maddie, I've got a consult, so I need to go. But I want to know more about the ultrasound. We'll talk—"

"—later," her sister finished and hung up. At least Greer and Maddie were almost always on the same wavelength. It was too bad that Greer couldn't say the same about Ali.

She made a note on her calendar to call her. Maybe if Greer were the one to plan dinner next Monday, she'd get herself back in Ali's good graces. The three of them usually tried to get together for dinner on the first Monday of each month, but their schedules made it difficult. And when it came to canceling, Greer had been the worst offender. The fact that next Monday wasn't the first Monday of the month was immaterial. With Maddie ready to pop with the baby, this might be their only chance for a while.

Keith tossed himself down on the hard chair wedged into Greer's crowded office. "How many assignments this week?"

She closed Anthony's file and plucked a stack from the box on the floor behind her desk. "Too many. Take a look."

"I won't be able to take on as many as usual," he warned as he began flipping through the files. "Lydia and I have set the wedding date next month."

Even though she'd half expected the news, Greer was still surprised. It hadn't been that long since the lawyer was moping around from the supposedly broken heart Ali had caused him when they broke up, before she met Grant. Then he'd met Lydia when he'd taken on the defense case involving her son. "Congratulations. You're really doing it, huh?"

"I'd have married her six months ago, but she wanted to wait until Trevor's case was settled. Now it is and we can get on with our lives." He glanced up for a moment. "How's the Santiago case coming?"

"Pretrial motions after Labor Day. Michael has the investigator working overtime."

"I'll bet he does. Because your boss wants the case dismissed in the worst way."

"We'll see." Stormy Santiago would be the jewel in the prosecutor's reelection crown. She was beautiful. Manipulative. And charged with solicitation of murder. "Don's already prepping to go to trial on it."

"I'll bet he is. He gets her off and he'll be onto bigger pastures, whether he's best buddies with your boss or not. Mark my words."

Greer couldn't imagine Don wanting to leave their department, where he was a big fish in a small pond. "You think?"

Keith shrugged. He slid several folders from the stack toward her. "I can take these."

It was up to her to ensure the assignments were correctly recorded and submitted to the appropriate court clerk. Between municipal, circuit and district courts, it meant even more paperwork for her. "Great. See you in court."

Morning and afternoon sessions were held daily every Monday through Thursday, with Greer running between courtrooms as she handled arraignments and motions and pleadings and the myriad details involved when an individual was charged with a criminal offense. Occasionally, there was a reason for a Friday docket, which was a pain because they all had plenty of non-court details to take care of on Fridays. And increasingly on Saturdays and Sundays, too. Most of those days, Greer was meeting clients—quite often at the various municipal jails scattered around their region.

Such was the life of a public defender. Or in her case, the life of a public defender who got to do all the prep but rarely actually got to *defend*. It was up to Greer to prepare briefs, schedule conferences, take depositions and hunt down reluctant witnesses when she had to. She was the one who negotiated the plea deals that meant Don typically only had to show up in the office on Thursdays, when most of the trials were scheduled. She'd gotten a few bench trials, but thanks to Don and his buddy-buddy relationship with Michael Towers, their boss and the supervising attorney for the region, her experience in front of a jury was limited.

She also photocopied the case files and made the coffee.

But if Don were to ever leave…

She exhaled, pushing the unlikely possibility out of her mind, and sent off her message to the prosecutor. The rest of her email would have to wait. She shoved everything she would likely need into her bulging briefcase, grabbed the blazer that went with her skirt and hurried out of her office.

Michael was sitting behind his desk when she stuck her head in his office. "Any news yet on a new intern?" Their office hadn't had one for three months. Which was one of the reasons Greer had been on coffee and photocopy duty.

He shook his head, looking annoyed. Which for Michael was pretty much the status quo. "I have three other jurisdictions needing interns, too. When there's something you need to know, I'll tell you. Until then, do your job."

She managed not to bare her teeth at him and continued on her way. She didn't stop as she waved at Michael's wife, Bernice, who'd been filling in for the secretary they couldn't afford to hire, even though she hopped up and scurried after her long enough to push a stack of pink message slips into the outer pocket of Greer's briefcase.

"Thanks, Bunny."

Greer left the civic plaza for the short walk to the courthouse. It was handy that the buildings were located within a few blocks of each other. It meant that she could leave her car in the capable hands of her dad for the day. Carter Templeton was retired with too much time on his hands and he'd offered to look at it. He might have spent most of his life in an office as an insurance broker, but there wasn't much that Carter couldn't fix when he wanted to. Which was a good thing for Greer, because she was presently pretty broke.

She was pretty broke almost all of the time.

It was something she'd expected when she'd taken the job with the public defender's office. And money had gotten even tighter when she'd thrown in with her two sisters to buy the fixer-upper Victorian—in which she was the only one still living. She couldn't very well start complaining about it now, though.

The irony was that both Maddie and Ali could now put whatever money they wanted into the house since they'd both married men who could afford to indulge their every little wish.

Now it was just Greer who was holding up the works.

She'd already remodeled her bedroom and bathroom when they'd first moved in. The rest of the house was in a terrible state of disrepair, though. But if she couldn't afford her fair third of the cost, then the work had to wait until she could.

She sidestepped a woman pushing a baby stroller on the sidewalk and jogged up the steps to the courthouse. There were thirty-two of them, in sets of eight. When she'd first started out, running up the steps had left her breathless. Six years later, she barely noticed them.

Inside, she joined the line at security and slid her bare arms into her navy blue blazer. Once through, she jogged up two more full flights of gleaming marble stairs to the third floor.

She slipped into Judge Waters's courtroom with two minutes to spare and was standing at the defendant's table with her files stacked in front of her before the judge entered, wearing his typically dour expression.

He looked over his half glasses. "Oh, goody." His voice was humorless as he took his seat behind the bench. "All of my favorite people are here. Actually on time for once." He poured himself a glass of water and shook out several antacid tablets from the economy-sized bottle sitting beside the water. "All right. As y'all ought to know by now, we'll break at noon and not a minute before. So don't bother asking. If you're not lucky enough to be out of the court's hair by noon, we'll resume at half past one and not one minute after."

He eyed the line of defendants waiting to be arraigned. They sat shoulder to shoulder, crammed into the hardwood bench adjacent to the defendant's table where Greer stood. After this group, there was another waiting, just as large.

Judge Waters shoved the tablets into his mouth. "Let's get started," he said around his crunching.

All in all, it was a pretty normal morning.

* * *

Normal ended at exactly twelve fifty-five.

She knew it, because the big clock on the corner of Braden Bank & Trust was right overhead when she spotted Ryder Wilson walking down the street.

He was carrying Layla.

Greer's heart nearly stopped beating. Heedless of traffic, she bolted across Main Street to intercept him.

A fine idea in theory. But she was wearing high heels and a narrow skirt, and had a ten-pound brief-case banging against her hip with every step she took. Speedy, she was not.

He'd reached the corner and would soon be out of sight.

She'd run track in high school, for God's sake.

She hopped around as she pulled off her pumps, and chased after him barefoot.

The cement was hot under her feet as she rounded the corner and spotted him pulling open the door to Braden Drugs halfway down the block.

"Ryder!"

He hesitated, glancing around over his shoulder, then let go of the door and waited for her.

"Hi!" She was more breathless from the sight of Layla than from the mad dash, and barely looked up at Ryder as she stopped. She knew her smile was too wide but couldn't do a thing about it as she leaned closer to Layla. "Hi, sweetheart. Look at you in your pretty pink sundress. You probably don't even remember me. But I sure remember you."

Layla waved the pink sippy cup by the handle she was clutching and showed off her pearly white teeth as she babbled nonsensically.

Everything inside Greer seized up. She wanted to

take the baby in her arms so badly it hurt. She contented herself with stroking the tot's velvety cheek with her shaking fingertip. "I sure have missed you." The words came out sounding husky, and she cleared her throat before looking up at Ryder.

He was looking back at her warily, which she supposed she deserved, after chasing him down the way she had.

"What brings the two of you to town?"

He looked beyond her to the drugstore. "She's got some special vitamin stuff she's supposed to have. Aren't your feet burning?"

She looked down and felt the searing heat that was only slightly less intense than the heat that filled her cheeks. She quickly leaned over, putting her shoes back on. "Probably looks a little silly."

"Yep."

She huffed. "You didn't have to agree. Do you always say what you're thinking?"

"Not necessarily." His eyebrows quirked. It was her only hint that he was amused. "But I generally say what I mean."

Layla babbled and smacked the sippy cup against Greer's arm. "I think I recognize that cup," Greer said to her.

Layla jabbered back. Her bright green eyes latched onto Greer's.

She felt tears coming on. "I can't believe how much you've grown." The huskiness was back in her voice.

"You want to hold her?"

Now, given the opportunity, Greer was suddenly hesitant. "I don't know if she'll remember me. She might not—"

He dumped the baby in her arms.

Layla smiled brightly. She didn't care in the least that Greer's vision was blurred by tears as she looked down at her.

Greer wrapped her arms around the baby and cuddled her. "I thought she'd be heavier." She closed her eyes and rubbed her cheek against Layla's soft hair. "Nothing smells better," she murmured.

Ryder snorted slightly. "Sure, when she's not fillin' her diaper with something out of a horror flick."

Greer smiled. She caught Layla's fist and kissed it. "What's Daddy talking about, huh, baby? You're too perfect for anything like that."

"Excuse me."

They both looked over to see an elderly woman waiting to enter the door they were blocking.

"Sorry." Greer quickly moved out of the way while Ryder opened the door for her.

The woman beamed at him as she shuffled into the drugstore. "Thank you. It's so nice to see young families spend time together these days."

Greer bit the inside of her cheek, stifling the impulse to correct her. It was the same tactic she'd used many times in the courtroom.

Ryder let the door close after the woman. "Proof that appearances are deceiving."

Greer managed a smile. She was suddenly very aware of the time passing, but she didn't want to look at her watch or give up holding Layla a second sooner than she needed to. "What's special about the vitamins?"

He shrugged. "Something her pediatrician has her taking."

"Do you still take her to my uncle?" David Templeton's pediatrics practice in Braden was older than Greer. He'd been the first one to see Layla when Lincoln had discovered her left on the mansion's doorstep last December.

"You mean he hasn't told you?"

She gave him a look. "Wouldn't be very professional for him to talk about his patients to outsiders. And like it or not, that's what we are these days."

Ryder's lips formed a thin line.

Layla suddenly sighed deeply and plopped her head on Greer's shoulder.

Greer rubbed her back and kissed the top of her head. "I've heard about the nanny problems you've had."

"How?"

She stepped out of the way again when the shop door opened and a woman pushing two toddlers in a stroller came out. "Braden is a small town. Word gets around." She turned slightly so that Layla wasn't positioned directly in the sun. "Nannies don't hold to the same principles of confidentiality that a pediatrician's office does."

His lips twisted. "S'pose not." He reached for Layla, his hands brushing against Greer's bare arms as he lifted the tot away from her.

It was insane to feel suddenly shivery on what was such an infernally hot day.

She adjusted the wide bracelet-style watch on her wrist and wanted to curse. She was late getting back to the courthouse. On foot from here, it would take at least twenty minutes. "I still feel I owe you a favor for helping me this weekend with my car."

"Was it the thermostat?"

"I don't know yet. My dad is looking at it. He's pretty good with cars. I told him what you thought, though." She shifted from one foot to the other and smoothed her hand down the front of her blouse, where it was tucked into the waist of her skirt. He'd taken a step toward the drugstore. "Maybe I could help you on the nanny front," she offered quickly.

"You?" He sounded incredulous. "Kind of a come-down in the world from lawyering to nannying, isn't it?"

"I don't mean *me* personally." She worked hard to keep from sounding as offended as she felt. She might not have a lot of experience with babies, but Layla wasn't just any baby, either. "I mean with advertising for a nanny. I'm on a lot of loops because of my work. I could post ads if you wanted."

His blue eyes gave away none of his thoughts. "I'll think about it."

She took that as a sign he was willing to negotiate. "I've got a lot of connections," she added. "I'd like to help."

Layla's head had found its way to his wide chest and she was contentedly gnawing the handle of her sippy cup.

"I suppose it wouldn't hurt," he said abruptly.

She'd fully expected him to say no. "Great! That's... that's really great." She cringed a little at her overen-thusiasm, not to mention her lack of eloquence. She looked at her watch again and quickly leaned forward to kiss Layla's cheek. Then she started backing down the block. "I'll call you later to get the particulars. Pay range, hours, all that."

He resettled his black cowboy hat on his head, look-ing resigned. "Are you asking or telling?"

She knew her smile was once again too wide, but so what? She'd finally gotten to Layla. And even if she earned Judge Waters's wrath for not making it back to court on time, she couldn't bring herself to care.

Chapter Four

Ryder spotted the little foreign job sitting in front of his house. It looked as out of place there as it had stalled on the side of the road out near Devil's Crossing.

The second thing he noticed was that Doreen Pyle's ancient pickup truck wasn't there.

When he'd set out that morning to get more hay cut, Mrs. Pyle had been sweeping up cereal after Layla over-turned her favorite red bowl.

But now, Mrs. Pyle's truck was gone and the lady lawyer's was parked in its place.

It was too much to hope that she'd come all the way out here to tell him she'd found the perfect nanny candidate. She could've done that over the phone, the same way she'd gotten the particulars from him the other day.

He glanced at the cloudless sky. "What fresh new problem are you giving me now?"

As usual, he got no answer. The air remained hot and heavy, filled with the sound of buzzing insects.

He half expected to find Greer in the kitchen with Layla, but the room was empty when he went in.

He flipped on the faucet and sluiced cold water over his head. Then he grabbed the dish towel hanging off the oven door to mop his face as he went in search of them.

There weren't a lot of rooms in the place, so it didn't take him long. He found both females in the living room, sprawled on his leather couch, sound asleep.

Layla wore a pink sleeveless T-shirt and diaper. She was lying on Greer's chest, who was similarly attired in a sleeveless pink shirt and denim cutoffs.

He looked away from her lightly tanned legs and quietly went up the iron-and-oak staircase. At the top, he crossed the catwalk that bisected the upper back half of the barn. All he had to do was look down and he could see his living area and who was occupying it.

Aside from the failed nannies and Mrs. Pyle, the last woman who'd spent any real time under his roof had been Daisy. When he thought about it, Mrs. Pyle had lasted longest.

He entered his bedroom. He'd put up sliding barn doors in the upper rooms after he'd taken custody of Layla. Before then, the only enclosed spaces had been the bathrooms. Two upstairs. One down.

He went into his bathroom now and flipped on the shower. Dust billowed from his clothes when he stepped out of them. He got into the shower before the water even had a chance to get warm.

He still had goose bumps when he stepped out a few minutes later, but at least he wasn't dripping sweat and covered in hay dust anymore.

He stepped over the dirty clothes, pulled on a pair

of clean jeans and a white T-shirt from his drawer and went back downstairs.

They were still sleeping. He retrieved a bottle of cold water from the fridge in the kitchen, then wearily sat on the only piece of adult-sized furniture in the living room except for the couch. His aunt had designed the armless, triangular-backed chair during her furniture phase, and he had brought it with him along with the couch more for sentimental reasons than because it was comfortable.

He slouched down in the thing as much as he could and propped his bare feet on the arm of the couch by Greer's feet. Instead of opening the water bottle, he pressed it against his head and closed his eyes. Already the relief from the cold shower was waning and he caught himself having fond memories of the three feet of snow piled up against his house last March.

Not two minutes passed before Greer spoke, her voice barely above a whisper. "Do you think the heat's ever going to end?"

He didn't open his eyes. "I spent a summer near Phoenix once." Adelaide had been doing an exhibition there. "I was fifteen." He kept his voice low, too, because he knew what it was like when Layla didn't get in a decent nap. When he'd been rodeoing, he'd drawn broncs that'd been easier to handle. "It was like living inside a pizza oven."

"Descriptive. But you didn't answer my question."

He ignored that. "Where's Mrs. Pyle?"

"Still not answering my question. Obviously, Mrs. Pyle is at her grandson's trial."

He opened his eyes at that. The baby was still sleeping and Greer watched him over her head, eyes as dark and deep as the blackest night.

"What trial?"

"She didn't tell you?"

He spread his hands. "Obviously not."

"You do recall that Doreen Pyle *has* a grandson?"

He gave her a look.

"Anthony's seventeen. And he's being tried for burning down a barn."

Ryder swallowed an oath and pulled his feet off the couch. "She should have told me." He wasn't an ogre. "So why are *you* here?"

"Because I couldn't get the prosecution to agree to another continuance and Judge Donnelly has a stick up his—" Greer broke off with a grimace. "Anthony has a very competent trial lawyer representing him. Today, it's more important for him to have his grandmother there than me."

"Not because you wanted to spend time with Layla?"

"It's the one thing that made today tolerable. I've been working on Anthony's case since his prelim."

"Did he do it?"

"My client is innocent."

"Spoken like a defense lawyer."

"I am a defense lawyer. Just a poorly paid one, thanks to the great state of Wyoming."

"If he's your client, why is someone else handling the trial?"

Her lips twisted. "That, my friend, is the fifty-dollar question." She rolled carefully to one side so that she could deposit Layla on the couch cushion and then slid off the couch to sit on the floor.

It was almost as interesting as watching a circus contortionist.

Once she was on the floor with her back to the couch, she tugged her shirt down over her flat stomach where it had ridden up and blew out a breath. "This place of yours has a lot going for it, I'll grant you, but you need air-conditioning."

"I have a window rattler upstairs in my bedroom." He wondered why he didn't tell her there was another one in Layla's bedroom, too.

She slanted a look toward him from the corner of her eye. "Meaning?"

He smiled slightly. "Meaning I do have air-conditioning. Just not down here. I wish Mrs. Pyle would have told me."

"She must have her reasons. She's known since Monday."

He sat forward and offered her the unopened water bottle. "Why didn't you say something about the trial when you chased us down the street the other day?"

"Because it was Mrs. Pyle's business to tell you." Her fingers grazed his when she leaned over to take the water.

Adelaide had done her best to give him an appreciation of beauty and the visual arts. She'd always been asking him, *But what do you see?* and he never knew exactly what kind of answer she wanted. But he figured he must have learned something from her after all, given his appreciation of the way Greer tilted her head and tipped the bottle back, taking a prolonged drink. Her neck was long and lovely. Her profile pure. Watching her was almost enough to compensate for her and Mrs. Pyle's keeping him in the dark.

Greer handed him back the half-empty bottle.

Her lips were full and damp.

Even though he didn't need the trouble it would likely bring, he didn't look away from her when he took the bottle from her and finished it.

Her gaze flickered and she looked away as she pushed to her feet. She tugged at the hem of her T-shirt as she paced around the couch. "Did she give you any other reason to be quitting?"

"Maybe you should ask Mrs. Pyle."

She gave him a look and he relented, proving that he needed more willpower to resist the women in his life. "She tells me she's a housekeeper. Not a nanny."

"Because scrubbing floors is so much easier than heating a bottle?" Her voice rose a little and she pressed her lips together self-consciously.

"Layla doesn't use a bottle anymore. She only uses her cup. The pink cup. And if the pink cup isn't handy, she screams bloody murder until it is. Trust me, Counselor. Cleaning house is easier than childcare." He waved at Layla, who hadn't budged an inch from where she had rolled onto her side against the back couch cushion. She drooled all the time these days, and now was no exception. But the leather had survived him growing up, so he assumed it would survive a while longer.

"Did she say when she's leaving?"

"She gave me a week's notice."

"Even if we haven't found a nanny by then?" Greer propped her hands on her slender hips. "Did she say anything else?"

"Yeah. That I'd be better off finding a wife than a nanny."

Greer's eyebrows rose halfway up her forehead. Then she scrubbed her hands down her face. "I'm sorry."

"For what?"

She dropped her hands. "That she said something so...so insensitive!" She pressed her lips together again and watched Layla warily, as if expecting her to wake because her voice had risen once more.

"Insensitive how?"

A small line formed between her eyebrows. "Your wife passed away less than a year ago," she said huskily. "I'm sure remarrying is the furthest thing from your mind."

"It was until my housekeeper brought it up. But she had a valid point. Layla deserves a mother." At least he'd had Adelaide when his mother had died. He leaned back in the chair again and propped his feet once more on the couch arm. He linked his fingers across his stomach. "You never knew Daisy, did you?"

The line deepened slightly as she shook her head. "I never met her. But Grant has been talking more about Karen these days."

"The man actually talks?"

She gave him a look. "What she did has been hard on him, too. He was Karen's brother, but even then, the court wasn't ready or willing to hand over Layla to him."

He grunted. "She was never Karen to me. She was Daisy Miranda. That was the name she used when we met, the name she used when we got married and the name she used when she left me. She never said she had a brother at all. Either he didn't matter enough for her to mention, or I didn't matter enough. Considering the way things went down, I'll give you a guess which one I'm more inclined to believe."

Greer tucked her hair behind her ears. Her forehead had a dewy sheen. "Regardless of her name, you loved her enough to marry her. You don't just get over that at the drop of a hat."

"You been married to someone who ran out on you? Ever gone through a bunch of tests just to make sure she didn't leave you with something catching to remember her by?"

"No, but—"

"Ever married at all?"

She needlessly retucked her hair. "No. But that doesn't mean I don't have feelings. That I have no appreciation for the pain involved when you lose someone. Hearts don't heal just because we decide they should."

He couldn't help the amusement that hit him.

And she saw it on his face. The line between her brows deepened even more. "What's so funny?"

He schooled his expression. "Nothing."

She let out a disgusted sound and his lips twitched again. Stopping the smile would've taken more willpower than he possessed.

She glared at him even harder and her eye got that little twitch she was prone to.

"Relax, Counselor. You don't have to worry that I'm withering away with grief or anything else because of my beloved wife. You do recall that *she* ran out on me, right?"

"And no matter what you say now, I'm sure that was very painful for you. But you know—" she waved her hands in invitation "—if you feel the need to pretend otherwise so as to maintain some false manly pride, be my guest."

He watched her for a moment. Then he pulled his feet off the couch again and sat forward. "Want a beer?"

She blinked. "What?"

He stood. Layla was still sound asleep. Snoring even, which meant that although he'd showered off the hay dust, she'd still probably gotten a whiff of it and her nose was getting congested. The pediatrician had warned him that Layla seemed to be developing some allergies. "A beer," he repeated, and headed into the kitchen, where he grabbed two cold bottles from the refrigerator.

Greer was standing in the same spot when he returned and handed her one. "It's five o'clock somewhere." He twisted off the cap and set it on the fireplace mantel.

Still looking suspicious, she slowly did the same.

He lightly tapped his bottle against hers and took a drink.

After some hesitation, she took a tiny sip.

"Let's go out back. It might be cooler."

She looked at Layla. "But—"

He scooped up the baby, who didn't even startle, and transferred her to the playpen. Then he picked up the baby monitor and turned it on, showing Greer the screen where the black-and-white image of his living space, including the playpen, was flickering to life. "Happy?"

Beer and monitor in hand, he headed out through the kitchen door, and Greer followed.

It wasn't any cooler outside. But at least there was a slight breeze and the gambrel roof provided shade from the sun. He gestured with his bottle to the picnic table and benches that he'd found stored in the root cellar when he'd bought the place.

"Wouldn't have expected something so fanciful from you," she said as she straddled one of the benches and set her bottle on the cheerfully painted table. "Flowers?"

He took the opposite bench. "Daisies." He set the baby monitor on the center of the weathered table and took a pull on the cold beer. "Twenty-five cents if you can guess who painted them."

"Ah." She nodded and fell silent.

He exhaled and turned so his back was against the table and he could stretch out his legs. The rolling hillside was his for almost as far as he could see. Beyond that was his by lease. His closest neighbor was ten miles away as the crow flew, and just to get to the highway meant driving down his seventeen-mile driveway, three miles of which were actually paved. Until he'd bought the place, he felt like he'd been looking for it his entire life.

But his housekeeper did have a point about his place being remote. "Mrs. Pyle's grandson going to get off?"

"It's a jury trial, so you never know until the verdict comes in. But I believe the facts are on Anthony's side."

"Doesn't it bug you not being there in court?"

"There are a lot of things about my job that bug me." He took another drink and looked her way.

"Yes. It bugs me. But we've built a solid defense and Don Chatham—much as he annoys me personally—is a fine attorney. I can zealously represent my clients through the fairest plea negotiations to resolve their cases as well as anyone working in the PD's office. But when my client refuses to plea, or when they're truly better served going to trial?" She rolled the bottle between her fingertips. "Anthony *is* in good hands. Better than mine, when it comes down to it, since Don's experience before a jury exceeds mine by about a decade."

"When's the verdict likely to come in?"

"Before six tonight. The judge runs a tight ship and he likes to be home for dinner with his wife every night by seven. If the jury is still deliberating, he'll call a recess and resume tomorrow morning. But he'll be in a bad mood because he doesn't like working on Fridays any more than Don does. Did you move here because of Daisy?"

Her abrupt question was surprising. "No. We didn't meet until after that." He rolled his jaw around. "Not long after," he allowed.

"So why did you buy this place? Did you ranch in New Mexico?"

"I did a lot of ranch work. For other people. Along the way was some rodeoing. A few years in the service. Did you always want to be a lawyer?"

"What branch?"

"Army."

She smiled slightly. "My dad, too. Way before I was born, though." Her smile widened. "And I wanted to be a lawyer from the very first Perry Mason novel I read. My dad has a whole collection of them from when he was a kid and I started reading them one summer when I was grounded. I had romantic visions of defending the rights of the meek and the defenseless. And I also fancied following in Archer's path."

Ryder lifted his eyebrows.

"My older brother. Half brother, to be accurate. On my dad's side. I have a half sister on my mom's side who's also an attorney. But I didn't grow up with Rosalind the way I did with Archer. They're both in private practice."

"Classic yours, mine and ours situation?"

"Sort of. I have another half sister, too, who is a psychologist. Hayley lives in Weaver with her husband, Seth, and their baby. What about you?"

"No sisters. No brothers. Half or otherwise."

"But you have an aunt Adelaide with a pug named Brutus."

"Lawyers and their penchant for details."

"I'd be worried about my memory if I couldn't recall something you mentioned less than a week ago," she said drily. "What about your parents?"

"What about them?"

She waited a beat, and when he said nothing more,

she took a sip of her beer. She squinted and her cheeks looked pinched.

Her face was an open book, which for a lawyer was sort of a surprise. Maybe it was a good thing she didn't face juries very often. "Not your cup of tea?"

"It's fine."

He rolled his eyes and took the beer out of her hands. "I suppose you're a teetotaler."

"Not at all. I just… Well, wine is more my thing."

It was his turn to pull a face. "And not mine. Whiskey?"

"If the occasion calls for it."

"We've at least got that in common." He got up and she looked alarmed. "Don't worry. I'm not bringing out a bottle of the good stuff. A cold beer at three on a hot afternoon is one thing. We'll save the whiskey for cold nights and staying warm. I'll get you a soda."

Greer chewed the inside of her cheek, watching Ryder head inside his house.

She thought she'd done pretty well not falling right off the couch when she'd wakened to find him sitting there. He'd obviously showered. His hair was dark and wet, slicked back from his chiseled features. His T-shirt was clinging to his broad shoulders. His feet sticking out from the bottom of his worn jeans had been bare.

And her mind had gone straight down the no-entry road paved with impossibility.

She hadn't expected to doze off along with Layla. But then again, she hadn't expected to be so pooped out after spending six hours taking care of the baby, either.

When she'd arrived out at the house, it had been early enough to relieve Doreen Pyle so she could get into town before court started. But Ryder hadn't been there, even though Greer had spent most of last night sleeplessly preparing herself for the encounter.

Doreen had told her that he'd headed out more than two hours earlier. "Haying," she'd said, as if that explained everything.

Foolishly, Greer had assumed that Doreen would have told her employer that Greer was pinch-hitting that day. And why.

She turned the baby monitor so she could see it better. Layla had turned around in a full circle inside the playpen, but still looked to be sleeping.

She reluctantly set the monitor on the table when Ryder returned. He set a bottle of cola in front of her. "Better?"

She rarely indulged, but it was still better than beer. And it was wonderfully cold. "Thank you."

His lips stretched into a brief smile. Then he sat down again, but this time he straddled his bench the same as her. "Why choose the public defender's office to zealously defend your clients?"

She'd been asked that question ever since she'd passed the bar. She'd always given the same answer. "Because I wanted to help people who really needed it." Her eyes strayed to the baby monitor. She couldn't help it. That grainy little image fascinated her.

"And do you?" His question dragged at her attention. "Help people who really need it?"

She twisted open the soda and took a long drink. The fact that she wasn't really sure what she was accomplishing anymore wasn't something she intended to share. "Everyone deserves a proper and fair defense," she finally said, which she believed right to her very core. "More than eighty percent of criminal defendants in this state end up in the public defender's office. I do my part as well as I can."

"Just not in front of a jury."

She realized she'd picked up the monitor again and made herself put it down. "Not generally. Although, honestly, I stay busier with my cases than Don does. We have a handful of trials a month. Unless it's something really big like the Santiago thing that's been on the news, Don spends most of his weekends fishing while I'm chasing around between courts and jails and—" She broke off. "I've never had a caseload that drops under one hundred clients at any given time."

The slashing dimple in his cheek appeared for a moment. "Do they all say they're innocent?"

She smiled wryly and let that one pass. "We cover a few counties here. But I know some offices with caseloads that are even heavier. We all make use of interns, but getting them can be sort of cutthroat." She shook her head. "The real problem is there's never enough money in the coffers to equip our office with everything and everyone we need."

"Now you sound like a politician."

On the monitor screen, Layla had turned around and was facing the other corner, her little rump up in the air. "Not in this lifetime," Greer responded. "Though I'd probably make more money if I were. Nobody I know has ever gotten rich working as a PD."

"Do you want to be rich?"

She laughed outright at that. "I'm more about being able to pay all the bills on time."

"What about that house of yours? That's gotta be a money pit."

"I'll take the fifth on that. I love my house. It has character."

"Like your car?"

She gave him her best stern look. The one she'd learned from her father. "Don't be dissing my car."

He lifted his hands in surrender.

"It *was* the thermostat, by the way. So thank you for that heads-up."

"Ever considered private practice?"

"Most lawyers do."

"Well, then? It's not like you don't have an in with people in the business."

"Much as I love Archer, I have no desire to actually *work* with him. Rosalind is with *her* father's practice down in Cheyenne and does mostly tax and corporate law. Bo-ho-ring. So—" She took another drink just so she wouldn't pick up the monitor again.

"So…?"

"Why are you so interested?"

"Shouldn't I know more about the woman who's been watching Layla behind my back?"

"For one day. Don't imply it's been a regular occurrence." She nudged the monitor with her fingertip. "We all fell in love with her, you know." She brushed her thumb across Layla's black-and-white image. "Right from the very beginning when Linc called in Maddie because he'd found a baby on his doorstep. The only identifying clue she had on her was the note Daisy left with her."

"'Jaxie, please take care of Layla for me,'" he recited evenly.

"Right. When Daisy cocktailed for Jax at his bar, she routinely called him that. That's the only reason we ever suspected she was Layla's mother in the first place."

Ryder's expression was inscrutable but she could easily imagine what his suspicions were. She'd had them herself. So had Linc. His brother, Jax, had been on one of his not-infrequent jaunts, which was why Linc hadn't immediately turned over the baby when he first discovered her. But whether or not Jax had been involved with Daisy in a more personal way, they'd nevertheless conclusively ruled him out as the baby's biological father last December.

She set the monitor down again. "By the time we knew about Daisy, though, Layla was already under the court's protection. The judge named Maddie as Layla's emergency foster parent while an investigation began." She was reiterating facts that he'd been told months ago.

"Your sister and Linc wanted to adopt her themselves. Before you ever even knew Daisy's brother existed."

She glanced at him. It wasn't a detail they'd shared when he took custody. "Who told you that?"

He swirled the liquid in his bottle and took a drink, making her wonder if he was stalling or if he was simply thirsty.

Then he turned the bottle upside down and poured out the remaining beer onto the grass beneath their feet. "Not cold enough," he said, and she thought he wasn't going to answer her at all.

But he surprised her.

He laid the empty bottle on its side on the table between them and slowly spun it. "As you've pointed out before, Counselor, word gets around in a small town." He stopped the bottle so it pointed her way. "Isn't it true?"

She was a lawyer. Not a liar. And what was the harm if he knew the truth now? Maybe if he really understood, he wouldn't be so standoffish where her family and Layla was concerned. "They would have, but

Maddie knew she and Linc would never get her. There were too many people in line ahead of them waiting to adopt a baby."

She clasped her hands on the table in front of her before she could pick up the monitor again. Her fascination with it was vaguely alarming. "The search for Daisy was leading nowhere and it was only a matter of time before Judge Stokes made a permanent ruling about placement. Not even the fact that Ali found Daisy's brother and discovered her real name was Karen Cooper changed that. We couldn't prove Layla was Karen's daughter and Grant's niece through his DNA because both he and Karen were adopted. Siblings by law, but not by genetics. Which meant that not even Grant could stop the legal forces at work. The one established fact the court recognized was that Layla had been abandoned and, as such, would benefit from placement in a suitable home through adoption. A family had even been selected." She sneaked a look at Ryder's face but his expression still told her nothing. She spread her fingers slightly, then pressed the tips of her thumbs together. "And then we discovered that your...that Karen had died in a car accident in Minnesota. Thanks to the photo that Grant and Ali found in her effects, we learned about you. Until then, we had no idea that Daisy Miranda or Karen Cooper had acquired a husband."

"The presumptive father, you mean."

She studied him. He'd had an opportunity to disprove it simply by requesting a paternity test.

But he hadn't.

Instead, he'd admitted—under oath—that he'd known about his absent wife's pregnancy. Combined with all their other information about Karen Cooper, it was enough for Judge Stokes to determine that Layla was legally Ryder's child. She'd been born during their marriage. No further questions asked. Certainly not about why Karen hadn't left their child with Ryder when she'd apparently decided parenthood wasn't for her.

The case may have been closed, but that didn't mean there weren't still questions.

"You didn't have to do it, you know," she said after a moment. "Claim Layla as your child. Not when we'd already failed so spectacularly to prove maternity." She didn't want to know if he'd lied under oath. It was hard enough suspecting that he had.

"It was the right thing to do."

"Even though *we* didn't know for certain that Daisy is…was Layla's mother." She could think of a dozen clients who wouldn't have done what he'd done. He'd told Ali when they'd first notified him that his wife hadn't been pregnant when she'd left him. Yet when he'd appeared before Judge Stokes, he'd attested that Daisy *had* notified him.

"How often do you run into someone named Layla?" He didn't wait for an answer as he spun the bottle again. "It was my mother's name. Daisy knew it. And I know Daisy liked it, because she told me once—in the beginning when I thought we actually had something—that if we ever had a baby girl, she wanted to name her Layla. Daisy *was* Layla's mother." He dropped his hand onto the bottle again, stopping its spinning once more. "It was the right thing to do," he repeated after a moment.

Greer's chest squeezed. He believed Daisy was Layla's real mother. But did he believe that Layla was his biological daughter?

She reached across the table and covered both his hand and the bottle with hers. "I'm sorry, Ryder. I really am." That he lost his wife. That he'd become a father in such an unconventional way. If she had questions, he surely had many more.

His jaw canted to one side. Then his blue eyes met hers and for some reason, an oil slick of panic formed inside her. She started to pull her hand back, but he turned his palm upward and caught hers.

"Sorry enough to marry me?"

Chapter Five

"*Marry you?*"

Greer yanked on her hand and nearly fell off the bench when he let go of it. She caught herself, only to knock over the bottle of soda, which gushed out in a stream of bubbly foam, splashing over the front of her T-shirt and shorts. "Now look what you've done!"

It was obvious he was having a hard time not laughing. "Gonna sue me over it? You know, for a woman who looks like she can run the world, you're kind of a klutz. Did you really think I was serious?"

She plucked her wet shirt away from her belly. Now she wasn't just sweaty, she'd be sticky, too. And she'd never been klutzy. Until she was around him. "Of course not," she lied. "You're just full of funny things to say this after—" She broke off when he suddenly stood and went inside the house.

She muttered an oath after his departing backside and swiped her hand down her wet thighs.

He returned a moment later, holding a sleepy-looking Layla and a checkered dish towel that he tossed Greer's way. "She needs a fresh diaper."

"Am I supposed to take out an announcement in the newspaper?" She swiped the towel over her legs. She could feel the damn soda right through to the crotch of her cutoffs.

"You're pretty snarky when you're caught off guard, aren't you?" He went back inside.

Then she realized the baby monitor had gotten doused with soda, too. She snatched it off the table and started drying it with the towel.

The screen had gone black.

She carried it inside. Ryder was bending over Layla on the couch, changing the diaper. "Do you have any dried rice?" She didn't wait for an answer, but started opening cupboard doors. "Ali got her cell phone wet last year and kept it inside a container of rice for a day to dry. I had my doubts, but the thing worked afterward." Greer found plates. Drinking glasses. At least a dozen boxes of dry cereal. Only half of it was suitable for Layla, which gave her quite the insight into his preference for Froot Loops.

She moved on to the lower cabinets and drawers.

"No, I do not have rice."

He spoke from right behind her and she straightened like he'd poked her with an electric prod. "Oh." She slammed the drawer she'd just opened shut. "Well, then I don't know what you'll want to do about this." She set the monitor on the butcher-block counter. "More soda got on it than me."

He lifted an eyebrow as he settled Layla into the high chair and managed to fasten the little belt thing around her wriggling body. "You look pretty soaked."

It was all she could do not to pluck at the hem of her shorts. "Yeah, well, you shouldn't joke like that."

He slid the molded tray onto the high chair and grabbed one of the boxes of cereal. He dumped a healthy helping onto Layla's tray and she dived into it like she hadn't eaten in days.

There was no question that Layla liked her food. Greer had fed her both jars of the food that Doreen had left out, plus a cubed banana and a teething biscuit, right before her nap.

"Yeah, well, maybe I shouldn't be joking. Mrs. Pyle's the one who reminded me Layla'd be better off with a mama than a nanny. Not that I've had any luck keeping either one around," he added darkly.

She felt that slick panic again and opened her mouth to say something, but nothing came. Which was such an unfamiliar occurrence that she felt even more panicky. "You can't judge everyone based on Daisy and a flighty nanny," she finally managed to say.

"Three nannies," he reminded her. "Easier to discount one two-week wife than three nannies. Mrs. Pyle had a point."

She wasn't sure her eyebrows were ever going to come back down to their normal spot over her eyes. "On what planet?"

He slid a look her way. "I know I'm not Wyoming's biggest catch, but you really think I can't find a wife if I set my mind on it? At least this time, I'd be choosing with my head instead of my—"

"Heart?"

His lips twisted. "That wasn't exactly the body part I was thinking about."

She felt her cheeks heat, which was just ridiculous. It wasn't as though she was some innocent virgin. She was well versed in the facts of life, whether or not she'd acted on any of those facts lately.

"Anyway," he went on, "it wouldn't be a one-way deal." He'd pulled a covered bowl from the refrigerator and dumped the contents in a saucepan that he set over a flame on the stove. "I realize that she'd need to get something out of it, too. It'd be a business deal." He bent over, picking up the sippy cup that Layla had pitched to the floor. "Both parties benefit."

Greer nearly choked, looking away from the sight of his very, very fine jean-clad backside.

He set the cup back on the tray. "If you throw it, I'm going to take it away," he warned.

The baby laughed and swept her hands back and forth against the cereal, sending pieces shooting off the tray.

"Yeah, you laugh, you little terror," he muttered. "You know better." He went back to the stove to poke a fork at the concoction he was heating.

It all felt strangely surreal.

"I've always been better in business than relationships. So go with your strengths, right?" He glanced at her again.

"Marriage isn't a business deal."

He snorted. "Better a business deal than the real deal. As they say, Counselor, been there, done that. Not really a fan. You've been a lawyer for a while now. Haven't you seen the value of pragmatism over idealism?"

She wanted to deny it, but couldn't. "I don't think pragmatism is a basis for marriage, either."

"But it's a good basis for good business. At least that's been my experience. So—" he tested the temperature of the contents in his saucepan with his finger and pulled the pan off the flame "—like I said, Mrs.

Pyle has a point. Two parents are supposed to be better than one. Didn't have two, myself, so I don't know about that. Maybe if I had—" He broke off, shaking his head and leaving Greer wondering.

He tipped the saucepan over a small bowl and grabbed a child-sized spoon from a drawer before flipping one of the table chairs around to face the high chair. "Every kid deserves a mother. Don't you agree?"

"Yes, but that doesn't mean I agree with this method of acquiring one!"

"People have been marrying for practical reasons a lot longer than they've been marrying for romantic ones. I could advertise for a wife just as easily as I can a nanny."

"You know what this sounds like to me? Like you've put all of five minutes of thought into it."

"And you'd be wrong. What happens to Layla if something happens to me?"

Her lips parted. "You… Well, Grant—"

"Daisy didn't dump Layla on Grant's doorstep. You think that was just an oversight? She didn't want him to have her!"

"You can't blame him for that! She didn't leave Layla with you, either!"

"Yeah, and that's something I get to live with. Daisy still named her after *my* mother. She was as unpredictable as the wind, but that means something to me."

She exhaled, feeling a pang inside. "Ryder. We'll find you a nanny. One who'll stay."

"If you were a kid, would you rather have a mom or a paid babysitter?" He didn't wait for her to answer. "Putting that aside for the moment, I'd rather have another plan in place for Layla if I get stomped out by a pissed-off bull one day."

"I've got to sit down." She grabbed one of the wood chairs from the table and sank down onto it. "I'm a lawyer. I appreciate your wisdom in planning for disasters, but I don't particularly want that vision in my head."

"You've heard worse in court, I'm sure."

She had, but that was different. "You can name anyone you want as a guardian for Layla if something were to happen to you. For heaven's sake, if you want to write up a will right now, I can help you. It doesn't mean you have to have a business-deal wife."

"Fine." He gestured with the spoon. "There's paper in that drawer. Get out a piece."

She slid open the drawer in question and pulled out the notepad and a short stub of a pencil. "You don't have to do it this very second."

"No time like the present." He scooped food into Layla's mouth.

"Maybe you should give it more thought," she suggested. "Deciding who would best—"

"I, Ryder Wilson, being of sound mind and body, yada yada. I assume you can fill in the blanks."

She exhaled noisily. "I'm not so sure about the soundness," she muttered. "But yes. So who do you want to name as guardian? Your aunt Adelaide?"

"She's already done her time raising me. You."

"Me, what?"

"You. Put your name down."

She dropped the pencil back into the drawer and shut it with a snap. "I don't find this funny."

"I don't find it funny, either, Counselor. There's no denying you've got a strong concern for Layla. But if your concern isn't that strong, no sweat." He scooped up another spoonful of the unidentifiable substance and evaded Layla's grasping hands to shovel it into her greedy mouth.

Something about his actions made Greer's insides feel wobbly. So she focused instead on the goopy little chunks on the spoon. "What *is* that?"

"Sweet potatoes, beets and ground chicken."

"Good grief."

"Don't knock it. I call it CPS."

"What?"

"Cow Pie Surprise."

She grimaced. "You just said it was chicken."

"It is. But doesn't matter what meat I add, it all looks the same. Like Cow Pie Surprise. But Layla loves it and she's sleeping better at night since I started spiking her food with meat." He gave Greer a sideways look. "You're not vegetarian or something, are you?"

She shook her head, keeping silent about her brief stint with the practice during her college years.

"Good." He focused back on Layla, slipping in a couple more bites before she managed to commandeer the spoon and whack it against the side of the tray. She chattered indecipherably, occasionally stopping long enough to focus on drumming her spoon or carefully choosing a round piece of cereal.

He tossed the bowl in the sink and wet a cloth to start wiping up the mess that was all over Layla's face and hands and hair and tray and clothes.

"Don't you have a bib?"

"Couple dozen of 'em. All came in the boxes of stuff your sister sent. Short-Stuff here doesn't like 'em." He freed the baby and set her down on the floor, and she immediately started crawling out of the room. "Decided a while ago that it wasn't worth the battle."

Having spent much of the day keeping up with Layla,

Greer was less surprised by the rapid crawl than she was by Ryder's ease with Layla. She'd pictured him as struggling a bit more with the day-to-day needs of a baby.

"Do you have other children?"

His eyes narrowed and Greer knew she'd annoyed him. "D'you see any other kids here?"

She scooped up Layla before the baby could get too far. "Don't be so touchy." She much preferred taking the offensive tack to being on the defensive. "Nanny problems or not, you've obviously settled into the routine."

"Better than you expected."

"Not at all." *Liar, liar, pants on fire.*

"I've got roundup facing me whether this heat breaks soon or not, and it'll mean being gone a couple days. No matter what you think it looks like, I still need help. Nanny, wife or otherwise."

"And I'll remind you yet again that I have an entire family willing to help you out where Layla is concerned."

"Like Maddie? Your sister who is so pregnant she looks like she's about ready to explode?"

"How do you know what she looks like?"

"She was in Josephine's diner the other day."

"She didn't mention seeing you."

"She didn't."

He didn't elaborate, and Greer stomped on her impatience as though she were putting out a fire.

"I've already made some job postings for another nanny. It's only a matter of time before you find the right person. Here." She handed Layla to him. "I have briefs I need to prepare." She'd even brought her case files with her, thinking she might have time to make some notes while Layla napped. But since Greer had napped right along with her, clearly *that* had been a silly notion. And even though she did have work to do, it was the sudden need to escape from Ryder that was driving her now.

"Briefs for a job that's not everything you'd hoped for."

"I didn't say that."

"You didn't have to." His gaze pinned hers and she felt uncomfortably like a witness about to perjure herself before the court.

She dragged her soda-moist shirt down around her soda-moist shorts. "I'll let you know when there are a few candidates—*nanny* candidates—for you to interview." She waved her hand carelessly. "But by all means, don't let that stop you from putting out word that you're wife-hunting if you're actually serious about that."

"Maybe I'll do that."

"If you do, I hope you'll look beyond the pool of cocktail waitresses at Magic Jax." The second she said it, she felt terrible. "I'm sorry. That was in poor taste."

"At least it was honest. You can let me know if you want to toss your name in the pool, after all."

She wasn't falling for that again. She snatched up her purse and her briefcase where she'd stashed them out of Layla's reach and hurried to the front door. "I'll be in touch about your will." She didn't wait for a response as she stepped outside and yanked the door closed.

She stood still for a moment and exhaled shakily. It was that time of day when the sun cast its rays beneath the covered front porch. It shone over her shoes. Her legs.

Marry Ryder.

She blinked several times, trying to ignore the words whispering through her mind.

Marry Ryder.

Try as she might, the thought would not be ignored.

"Get real," she whispered. He'd been no more serious about that than he had about naming her as Layla's guardian in his will. She stepped off the porch and strode decisively toward the car.

Marry.

Ryder.

Greer heard the front door open. "In the kitchen," she yelled, where she was putting the final touches on the tray of cold veggies and fruit. The heavens had finally smiled on her and her sisters' calendars, and Monday dinner was actually under way. She picked up the tray and carried it into the living room, where Maddie was struggling to lower herself onto the couch.

"Hold on. I'll help you." She set the tray on the coffee table, but Maddie waved her off.

"It's so hot," she grumbled, pushing her dark hair off her forehead.

"I've got lemonade or iced tea ready."

"Can you throw in some vodka?" Maddie made a face when Greer hesitated. "I'm joking." Even though she'd just sat, she pushed to her feet again and rubbed the small of her back. "Maybe."

The door opened and Ali blew in. "Have you heard Vivian's latest?"

Greer met Maddie's gaze before they both warily looked toward their sister. Where their paternal grandmother was concerned, anything was possible. Vivian Archer Templeton was nothing if not eccentric. And the fact that she was enormously wealthy thanks to Pennsylvania steel and several dead husbands meant she usually had no obstacles standing in the way of exercising those eccentricities.

"No," Maddie said cautiously. "What's she done now?"

"She went out on a *date* with Tom Hook!"

Greer stared. Tom Hook was an attorney. And a rancher. And a good twenty years younger than their eighty-ish grandmother. "Are you sure it was a date?"

Maddie let out a wry laugh. "Better a date than a marriage."

True enough. Their grandmother had already buried four husbands. "Vivian's always saying she has no interest in another husband because she's already had the love of her life in dear Arthur," Greer needlessly reminded them. He'd been the fourth of their grandmother's husbands. The only one who hadn't been rich. And Vivian made no secret of the fact that she would be happy to join him whenever the good Lord saw fit. After a life riddled with mistakes for which she'd been trying to make amends during the last few years, she maintained that Arthur was the one thing she ever did completely right.

"I'm guessing she's not looking for the love of her life," Ali said drily as she dropped her keys on the little table by the stairs. "Maybe she just wants some male companionship." She wiggled her eyebrows, looking devilish.

Greer made a face. "Don't be gross, baby sister."

Instead of getting Ali's goat, the reminder that she was the youngest of the triplets just made her laugh. "I'm a married woman now," she retorted, waggling her wedding rings. "Maybe I *like* thinking that I'll still be interested in that sort of thing when I'm Vivian's age."

"I'm even less eager to hear about your sex life than Vivian's."

Ali's eyes were merry. "Admit it, Greer. You're jealous. You need a date way worse than Vivian."

She rolled her eyes, ignoring the accusation that was too close to the truth. "So we can suspect why Vivian's dating Tom, but what's Tom up to?"

"Greer," Maddie chided. "Vivian's an intelligent, stylish woman."

"She's loaded," Ali said, ever blunt.

"Tom's not seeing her for her money," Maddie argued. "It doesn't jibe with his personality at all. He's a good guy. Tell her I'm right, Greer."

"He's a good attorney," Greer allowed. "I always thought he had a lot of common sense. But to date Vivian? I don't know about that." She was as fond of their eccentric grandmother as her sisters were, but Tom and Vivian dating? "What if he's after her money?"

"You think if he were that she's too feeble to know?" Ali smiled wryly. "Fact is, *he's* the one we should probably be worried about. Vivian's pretty wily."

"It's just a date!" Maddie objected. "It's certainly not the craziest thing that's ever happened around here. And it doesn't have to mean marriage is afoot." She was still rubbing her back as she waddled into the kitchen. "Even for Vivian."

"Watch out for the two loose floorboards," Greer called out to her. What would her sisters say if she told them about Ryder's ridiculous wife idea? "I put a chair over them."

Maddie reappeared in the doorway. She was carrying a second tray and her cheek bulged out like a chipmunk's. "I wondered why it was sitting in the middle of the room," she said around her mouthful of food.

She bent her knees enough so that she could slide the tray of cheese and crackers onto the coffee table without spilling the contents, then worked her way back down onto the couch. "When did we start having loose floorboards?"

"When did we not have them?" Ali responded. She sat down in the chair across from Maddie and pulled the trays closer, selecting a cluster of fat red grapes. "Are we having anything hot, or just cold stuff?"

"Just cold." Greer grabbed a fresh strawberry from the tray. "I have cold cuts and rolls, too, if you're interested."

"Much as I love sandwiches, it's too dang hot." Ali propped her sandaled feet on the edge of the couch. "Heard your esteemed colleague got Anthony Pyle off in court last week." She dangled her grapes in the air before plucking one from the stem. "Must feel good to know your department has put another little punk back on the streets."

Greer's nerves tightened. Anthony's verdict hadn't come in until evening on the day that she'd babysat Layla. But instead of being in the courthouse as she should have been, she'd been pacing around her house trying to forget everything that Ryder had said. "It does feel good. Particularly since your department neglected to arrest the right person in the first place."

"Come on," Maddie said tiredly. "No arguments about work, okay?" She winced a little and rubbed her hand over her massive belly.

Greer peered at her. "When are you going to start your maternity leave from Family Services?"

"End of the week. I'm not due until next week, of course, but it's just starting to be too hard to get through—"

"—the doorways?"

Maddie elbowed Ali. "Ha ha. Soon enough you'll be in the same fix." She looked back at Greer. "The days," she finished. "Linc's been on my case to stop working for the past month, and my obstetrician for the past two weeks. Arguing with them both is too much work when—" She winced again and blew out a long breath.

"When you're this close to popping," Ali interjected. She closed her hand over Maddie's and squeezed. "You know you don't have to justify anything to us."

"Ali's right." Greer sat on the arm of the couch next to their pregnant sister. She rubbed Maddie's shoulder, left bare by the loose, sleeveless sundress she wore. "I'm just looking forward to meeting our new niece or nephew."

Maddie's lips stretched into a smile.

"Speaking of nieces and nephews…" Ali looked at Greer over Maddie's head. "Grant wants to know if there's anything we can do legally to ensure access to Layla. Are there visitation rights for uncles or something?"

Maddie made a sound. "Surely that's not necessary."

"It's been nearly six months," Ali said quietly. "Ryder hasn't made any attempts—"

"Has Grant?" Greer asked. She read the answer in Ali's expression. "Nothing will be accomplished if you and Grant take what Ryder will see as an adversarial angle."

Ali's chin came up. "And you know so much about Ryder's mind-set, do you?"

"I know that unless there's a custodial issue, a parent pretty much has the right to determine who has access to their own child!"

Ali looked annoyed.

"Remember that if it weren't for Ryder, Layla would have been adopted by now and off living in Florida where there would be *no* possibility at all for any of us to have some part in her life."

"That's right." Maddie was nodding. "Everyone just needs time. Things will work out for everyone. I know it will. We just have to have a little more patience. Meanwhile, I know there've been some problems with keeping a nanny, but Ray's last report to the court was positively glowing where Ryder's care of her is concerned."

"That's because Ryder *is* good with her. I've seen it for myself."

Both her sisters looked at her.

"I babysat for him last week. I filled in for Mrs. Pyle so she could be at court with her grandson."

Maddie's mouth formed an O. Ali looked annoyed.

"It was a last-minute decision," she added.

Ali held up her hand. "Thursday, Friday, Saturday." She ticked off on her fingers. "Sunday. Monday." She held up her hand. "Five days, Greer. It took you five days to tell us? What other secrets are you keeping?"

Greer pushed off the couch arm. "I'm not keeping secrets."

"What would you call it then?"

"Okay, fine." Ali had a point. "So I've…I've had a few encounters with Ryder lately."

Maddie's eyebrows rose. "A few?"

"How few?" Ali demanded. "And when?"

"Last week!" Greer hated feeling put on the hot seat, but knew she had only herself to blame for not telling them sooner. "I ran into him and Layla when I was on a break during court on Monday. It was just a coincidence." Though her chasing him right down the street hadn't been.

"So you think there's no reason to mention it?"

"No! I just—" She broke off. "I offered to help him find a nanny."

Maddie had closed her eyes and was breathing evenly. Ali, on the other hand, was watching Greer as though she'd committed a federal offense. "Why?"

"Because I wanted to help! You know that he was the one who got me to Maddie's shower."

"And why *did* he do that? He showed up just like that?" Ali snapped her fingers. "Out of the clear blue sky?"

"For God's sake, Ali. You're always suspicious. Yes, out of the clear blue sky! Maddie's been coaching us since you found Ryder not to push ourselves into his life until he gave some hint he'd welcome it. Well, he gave a hint! I didn't deliberately flag him down when I was stuck out by Devil's Crossing. But he helped and so I offered to help him in return. I'm not going to apologize for it. In fact, I would think you'd be glad for it!"

"Glad that you've been seeing my husband's *niece* without telling us a word about it? You *know* how important that is to Grant! Considering how estranged he'd been from Karen?"

Greer propped her fists on her hips. "I'm telling you now! Look, I know your husband is still dealing with his grief where his sister is concerned. But if he's been so concerned about Layla, why *hasn't he* gone banging on Ryder's door demanding to see her?" She waved at Maddie, who was looking pale. She'd always hated it when Greer and Ali went at it when they were kids, and things hadn't changed much since then. "Don't pretend that a man like your husband will follow *anyone's* advice if he doesn't agree with it! He blames Ryder and we all know it!"

"He *doesn't* blame Ryder! He blames himself!" Ali's raised voice echoed around the room. She was breathing hard. "And judging by Ryder's attitude these past months, he blames Grant, too."

The wind oozed out of Greer's sails. "Of course Grant's not responsible for what his sister did. Any more than Ryder is."

"I know that. And you know that. And my husband knows that, too. In here." Ali touched her forehead. "But in here," she said, tapping her chest, "it's still killing him."

Greer pushed aside the fruit and veggie tray and sat on the coffee table in front of her sisters. She grabbed Ali's hands and squeezed them. "It's not just hot monkey sex, right? The two of you are okay all the way around?"

Ali smiled slightly. She squeezed Greer's hands in return. "All the way around," she said huskily. "Grant is everything to me. I just want to be able to make this better for him."

"You will," Maddie murmured. "Just tell him about the baby."

"The baby," Greer echoed. "You think having another niece or nephew will make him less concerned with Layla?"

"Of course not," Maddie replied.

"She's talking about my baby."

Greer startled, looking at Ali. But Ali was looking at Maddie. "What I'd like to know is how *you* knew? I haven't told anyone yet that I'm pregnant!"

"I could just tell." Maddie blew out another audible breath as she scooted herself forward enough to push off the couch. "Now do me a favor, would you?" She pressed her hands against the small of her back and worked her way around the two of them. "Call *my* husband and tell him it's time."

Alarm slid through Greer's veins. "Time?"

"What d'you mean, *time*?" Ali looked even more alarmed.

"I mean baby time," Maddie exclaimed, thoroughly un-Maddie-like. "Now *move*!"

Archer was on his way from the...

Chapter Six

The hands of the clock on the hospital waiting room wall seemed like they had stopped moving.

No matter how urgently Maddie had entered the hospital six hours earlier, time seemed to be crawling now.

Greer's dad was pacing the perimeter of the room, his steps measured and deliberate. Her mom, Meredith, was curled up in one of the chairs, her long hair spread over her updrawn knees. Vivian was sitting next to her, dozing lightly over the *Chronicle of Philanthropy* magazine on her lap. Archer was on his way from Denver, where he'd been consulting on a case, and Hayley and Seth had left only an hour ago, because it was long past time to put baby Keely to bed. Then there were Ali and Grant. Greer's brother-in-law wore the broody sort of expression that never really left his darkly handsome face. But there was still tenderness in his face as he looked down at Ali's tousled head on his shoulder. She was asleep.

"How much longer d'you think it will take?" Carter finally stopped in front of Meredith.

"I left my crystal ball at home." She looked amused. "It's a baby. It'll take as long as it takes."

Her dad made a face. "What if something's gone wrong?"

Meredith smiled gently and took his hand. "Nothing's gone wrong," she assured him.

"You don't know that. Things go wrong all the time."

"Carter." She stood, wrapping her arms around his waist and looking up at him. "It was only a few months ago that Hayley had Keely. That all went perfectly. And things are going to go perfectly with Maddie, too."

He pressed his cheek to the top of her head.

Frankly, Greer sympathized more with her dad. Things did go wrong all the time. Her career proved that on a daily basis.

What's happens to Layla if something happens to me?

"I'm going down to the cafeteria," she said, pushing away the thought. "Get myself a coffee. Can I bring back anything?"

Grant raised his hand. "Coffee here. I'll go, though."

Greer waved away his offer. "And wake Sleeping Beauty?" In the commotion of getting everyone to the hospital, Greer couldn't help but wonder if Ali had told him yet that they were expecting. She suspected not.

"Your dad'll take some coffee, too, sweetheart."

"I don't suppose there's a chance for a cocktail here?" Vivian commented, opening her eyes.

Carter grimaced. He didn't have a lot of affection for his mother, but since she'd moved to Wyoming in hopes of making amends with him after years of estrangement, he'd at least gotten to the point where it wasn't always open warfare with her whenever they were in the same room. "It's a hospital, Mother, not a bar."

"You never did have a sense of humor." Vivian looked at Greer with a twinkle in her eye as she patted her handbag sitting on the chair beside her. "I have my own flask with me for emergencies just like this. Just enough to make a cup of the dreadful coffee they have here a little more palatable."

Greer smiled, though it was anyone's guess whether or not Vivian was being serious. Not that it mattered to her if her grandmother wanted to spike her coffee while they waited for the baby to arrive. As far as she was concerned, nearly anything that got them through was fine. "I'll be back in a few."

She left the waiting room and started toward the elevator, but then aimed for the stairs instead to prolong her journey. As she passed the window of the nursery, she slowed to look inside. A dozen transparent bassinets were lined up, four of them holding tiny occupants, wrapped so snugly in white blankets that they looked more like burritos than miniature human beings.

A blonde nurse wearing rubber-ducky-patterned scrubs walked into view and picked up one of the baby burritos, affording Greer a brief view of a scrunched-up red face and a shock of dark hair before the nurse carried the baby out of sight again.

Greer lifted her hand and lightly touched the glass pane with her fingertips as she lingered there.

When Daisy had left Layla on Linc's doorstep, they'd estimated she was about two or three months old.

Looking at the babies inside the nursery, Greer still found it unfathomable how Daisy could have done such a thing. If she had lived, if she'd been charged with child endangerment, if her case had managed to land on Greer's desk like so many others, would she have been able to do her client justice?

The blonde nurse returned to the area with the bassinets. She didn't even glance toward the window, which made Greer wonder if the view was one-way. She plucked another baby from its bassinet, but instead of carrying the infant out of sight, she sat down in one of the rocking chairs situated around the nursery and cradled the baby to her shoulder as she began rocking.

Greer finally turned away, but the hollowness that had opened inside her wouldn't go away.

It was still there when she went down the cement-walled staircase, footsteps echoing loudly on the metal stairs. At the bottom, she pushed through the door, and realized that the staircase hadn't let her out in the lobby like the elevator would have, but in the emergency room.

Since there had been plenty of times when she'd had to visit a new client in Weaver's ER, she knew most of the shortcuts. She headed past the empty waiting area and the registration desk, aiming for the hallway on the other side that would take her back into the main part of the hospital.

"Hey, Greer. Heard that Maddie came in earlier. How's she doing?" the nurse behind the desk asked.

Greer slowed. "Six hours and still at it." She smiled at Courtney Hyde, who'd been an ER nurse since well before Greer had learned that they were cousins a few years ago. "Thought you didn't work nights anymore?"

Courtney tucked her long gold hair behind her ear. "Don't usually. But we're shorthanded at the moment, so." She shrugged. "We're all doing our part." Then she smiled a little impishly. "And it gives Sadie an opportunity to have her daddy all to herself at bedtime. Yesterday when I got home, she'd convinced Mason to build her an 'ice palace'—" she air-quoted the term "—to sleep in, using every pillow and furniture cushion we have in the house. Sadie slept the divine sleep that only a three-year-old can sleep."

"And Mason?"

Courtney grinned. "My big tough husband had me schedule him for a massage just so he could work out the kinks from a night spent on the floor crammed inside an igloo of pillows."

Considering the fact that Mason Hyde was about six and a half feet tall, Greer could well believe it.

"I swear I'll never stop melting inside whenever I see the way he is with her, though," Courtney added, sighing a little. "Just wait. Someday you'll see what I mean."

Greer kept her smile in place, even though the image inside her head wasn't one of Mason Hyde and his little girl. It was of Ryder, scooping Cow Pie Surprise into Layla's greedy mouth.

"You going to be at the picnic?"

"Sorry?"

"Gloria and Squire are hosting a big ol' picnic next week out at the Double C. To celebrate Labor Day. Whole family will be there." Courtney's eyes twinkled. "That includes all of you Templetons now, too."

Greer chuckled wryly. "I kind of need to show my face at the county employee picnic that weekend. My boss's wife organizes it. Besides which, just because the Clay family lines have expanded our way doesn't necessarily mean we're welcome. If *my* grandmother finds out we're consorting with *your* grandfather, who knows how bad the fireworks will be."

"Old wounds," Courtney said dismissively. "Vivian might have shunned Squire's first wife sixty years ago, but she's apologized. It's high time he let it go. At least think about the picnic." She reached out an arm and picked up the phone when it started ringing. "Emergency," she answered. "Think about it," she mouthed silently to Greer.

Nodding, Greer left the other woman to her duties and continued on her way, only to stop short again when the double doors leading to the exam rooms swung open and Ryder appeared. He was holding Layla, wrapped in a blanket.

Alarm exploded inside her.

When he spotted her, his dark brows pulled together over his bloodshot blue eyes. He stopped several feet away. "What're you doing here?"

"What are *you* doing here?" Without thought, she closed the distance between them and put her hand on Layla's back through the blanket. The toddler's head was resting on his shoulder. Her eyes were closed, her cheeks flushed. "What's wrong?"

"Nothing."

The comment came from Caleb Buchanan, and Greer realized the pediatrician had followed Ryder through the double doors. "However, if she hasn't improved in the next twenty-four hours, give me or her regular pediatrician a call."

"Thanks." Ryder's jaw was dark with stubble and he looked like he hadn't slept in a couple days.

"And don't worry too much," Caleb added. "Kids run fevers. As long as it doesn't get too high, her body's just doing what it's supposed to do."

When Ryder nodded, Caleb transferred his focus to Greer. "Heard Maddie was here. How's everyone doing?" Thanks to the prolificacy of Squire Clay's side of the family, Caleb was also a cousin. His pale blue scrubs did nothing to disguise his Superman-like physique. But Greer knew from experience that the doctor was singularly unconcerned with his looks.

"Fine. Anxious for the baby to get here. We've been waiting hours."

"Want me to check in on them?"

"That'd be great, if you've got the time. Everyone's up in the waiting room. I was just gonna grab some coffees from the cafeteria."

He smiled and patted her shoulder. "I'll see what I can find out." Then he retreated through the double doors.

Greer immediately focused on Ryder again. "How long has she been sick?"

"She didn't eat much of her dinner, but she seemed okay until she woke up crying a couple hours ago." He shifted the baby to his other shoulder. Layla didn't stir. "She threw up all over her crib, then threw up all over me and was hot as a pistol."

Greer couldn't help herself. She rubbed her hand soothingly over the thin blanket and the warm little body beneath. "Poor baby."

"Speaking of. Your sister's having hers?"

She nodded. "Whole family's been here at some point tonight."

"Hope everything goes okay." He took a step toward the sliding glass entrance doors.

"Ryder—"

He hesitated, waiting.

She wasn't sure why her mouth felt dry all of a sudden, but it did. "I...I haven't heard anything on the job postings yet. Have you?"

He shook his head. "Mrs. Pyle said she'd give me the rest of this week, after all." He shifted from one cowboy boot to the other. "Think she's feeling in a good mood after her grandson's acquittal last week."

"But not good enough to stay on indefinitely."

"She's a housekeeper. Not—"

"—a nanny," Greer finished along with him. "Well, I should get back up to the waiting room. They're probably wondering what's keeping me." She chewed the inside of her cheek. "I don't suppose you want to come..."

He was shaking his head even before her words trailed off. "Need to get her back in her own bed." He grimaced a little. "After I've gotten it all restored to rights, at least."

"Of course." She pushed her hands down into the back pockets of her lightweight cotton pants. It was silly of her to even have the notion. "Well." She edged toward the elevator. "Fingers crossed someone nibbles at one of the job posts."

The corner of his mouth lifted slightly and she felt certain he was thinking more about his wife idea than the nanny. "Yeah."

She took two more steps toward the elevator and jabbed her finger against the call button.

"Don't forget the cafeteria."

"What?" Her face warmed. "Oh. Right." The elevator doors slid open but she ignored them.

He smiled faintly. "G'night, Counselor."

She managed a faint smile, too, though it felt unsteady. "Good night, Ryder."

He carried Layla through the sliding door and disappeared into the darkness.

Greer swallowed and moistened her lips, then nearly jumped out of her skin when Courtney walked up and stopped next to her. She was carrying a stack of medical charts. "If I weren't already head over heels for my husband," she whispered conspiratorially, "I'd probably be sighing a little myself over that one."

"I'm not *sighing* over him."

Courtney grinned. "Sure you're not." With a quick wink, she backed her way through the double doors.

Left alone in the tiled room, Greer pressed her palms against her warm cheeks. She shook her head, trying to shake it off.

But it was no use.

And then her cell phone buzzed with a text from Ali. Where are u?! Baby here!

Forget the coffee.

She pushed the phone back into her pocket and darted for the elevator.

"If we're keeping you awake, Ms. Templeton, maybe you should consider another line of work."

Greer stared guiltily up at Judge Manetti as she tried to stop her yawn. It was a futile effort, though.

Just because she'd been at the hospital until three this morning celebrating the birth of her new nephew didn't mean she'd been allowed a respite from her duties at work.

"I'm sorry, Your Honor," she said once she could speak clearly. In the year since Steve Manetti had gone from being a fellow attorney to being a municipal court judge appointed by the mayor, she had almost gotten used to addressing him as such. But it had been hard, considering they'd been in elementary school together.

She glanced down at her copy of the day's docket before slipping the correct case file to the top of her pile. "My client, Mr. Jameson, wishes to enter a plea of not guilty."

Manetti looked resigned. "Of course he does." He

looked over his steepled fingers at the skinny man standing hunched beside her. "Is that correct, Mr. Jameson?"

Johnny Jameson nodded jerkily. Every motion since he'd entered the courtroom betrayed the fact that he was high on something. Undoubtedly meth, which was what he was charged with possessing. Again. "Yessir."

Manetti looked at Greer, then down at his court calendar. "First available looks like the second Thursday of December."

She made a note. "Thank you, Your Honor."

Judge Manetti looked at the clock on the wall, then at the bailiff. "We'll break for lunch now."

"All rise," the bailiff intoned, and the small municipal courtroom filled with the rustling sounds of people standing. Manetti disappeared through his door and the courtroom started emptying.

Greer closed her case file and fixed her gaze on her client. "Johnny, the judge just gave you four months. I advise you to clean up your act before trial. Understand me?"

Johnny shrugged and twitched and avoided meeting her eyes. She shifted focus to Johnny's wife behind him. "Katie? Do you want another copy of the list of programs I gave you before?"

"No, ma'am." Katie Jameson was petite and polite and as clean as her husband was not. "Johnny's gonna be just fine by then. I promise you."

Greer dearly wished she could believe it. "All right, then." She pushed her files into her briefcase and shouldered the strap. "You know how to reach me if you need me. Mr. Chatham will be in touch with you to go through your testimony before December."

Johnny grunted a reply and shuffled his way out of the courtroom.

"You're a lot nicer than Mr. Chatham," Katie said, watching her husband go. "I wish you could handle Johnny's trial."

Greer smiled. "Don't worry. You and Johnny will be in good hands."

"Well, thank you for everything you've done so far."

It was a rare day when Greer received thanks for her service. More often than not, she busted her butt negotiating a deal for her client only to have him or her walk away without a single word of appreciation. She shook Katie's hand. "You're welcome, Katie. Take care of yourself, okay? I meant it when I said you can call if you need me."

The young woman nodded, ducking her chin a little, then hurried after her husband.

Greer stifled another yawn as she walked out of the courtroom. She had two hours before her next appearance. If she'd had more than a few dollars left in her bank account after spending most of her paycheck on bills, she would have gone down to Josephine's for a sandwich. Instead, she walked back to her office, where she closed the door and kicked off her pumps. Then she sat down at her desk, and with a good old peanut-butter-and-jelly sandwich in one hand and a pencil in the other, she started in on the messages she hadn't been able to respond to before morning court.

She'd been at it for barely an hour when her office door opened and her boss tossed another stack of papers on her desk. "We're not getting an intern this round. There were only two available and the other offices needed them more." He pointed at the papers he'd left. "Plead all those out."

She swallowed the bite of sandwich that had momentarily stuck to the roof of her mouth and thumbed the latest pile. "What if they don't all want to plead?" She knew the futility of the question, but asked out of habit.

"Talk them into it," he said, and then left as unceremoniously as he'd entered. He always said that. Even though he knew some cases and some defendants never would plead.

Or should.

She glanced at the clock above the door. She started to lift her sandwich to her mouth, but her phone rang and she answered it. "Public defender's office."

There was a faint hesitation before a female spoke. "I'm calling about the job posting? The one for a nanny?"

Greer sat up straighter.

"This is the right number, isn't it?" The woman had a faint accent that Greer couldn't place. "You said public defender's office?"

"Yes, yes, it's the right number." She set her sandwich down on the plastic wrap. "I'm Greer Templeton. I represent—" She cringed, realizing how that might sound. "I'm *assisting* a friend with his search for a nanny."

"He's not in trouble with the law?"

"No, not at all."

"That's a relief," the woman said with a little laugh. "The last thing I desire is another job that leaves me wanting. I prefer something that will be steady. And lasting. Your post said you're—he, your friend—is looking for a live-in? Is that written in stone?"

"It's probably negotiable. Why don't you give me your contact information and you can discuss it with him directly."

"Very good. My name is Eliane Dupre."

"Would you mind spelling—"

The caller laughed lightly. "Like Elaine but reverse the *i* and *a*. It's French."

Greer immediately imagined a beautiful, chic Parisian singing French lullabies to Layla while Ryder looked on. She cleared her throat, and her head of the image. "Is that where you're from? France?"

"Switzerland, actually. I moved to the States a few years ago with my husband. Alas, that didn't work out, but here I am. I'm a citizen," she said quickly, "in case that is a concern."

Her right to work should have been more of a concern to Greer, but her imagination was still going bananas. Swiss? Had Maria in *The Sound of Music* been Swiss? She sure got her man. No, that was Austria.

Still, the loving governess had captured the heart of the children and their father.

She shook her head at her own nonsense, making notes as Eliane provided her phone number and an address in Weaver in her musical, accented voice.

"You understand that the location where you'd be working is fairly remote?"

"Yes. Quite to my liking."

"How long have you lived in Weaver?"

"I've only been here a few weeks. I'm staying with an acquaintance while I look for employment. Shall I expect a call from your friend, then?"

There was no reason to hesitate, but Greer still felt like she had to push her way through the conversation. "Yes, I'll get your information to him as soon as I can."

"Thank you so much. Have a lovely day."

"You, too," Greer said faintly. But she said it to the dial tone, because Eliane had already ended the call.

She dropped the receiver back on the cradle and stared blindly at her notes. Then she snatched up the phone again and punched out Ryder's phone number.

Neither Mrs. Pyle, Ryder nor the machine picked up.

Was Layla still sick? Maybe Ryder had caught whatever bug she'd had. Or maybe her fever had gotten worse.

Greer rubbed at the pain between her eyebrows. "Stop imagining things," she muttered, "and be logical here."

She pulled up the information she had on record for Anthony Pyle. But when she called that number, there was no answer.

She hung up and looked at the time. She couldn't very well drive Eliane's information out to the Diamond-L and check on Ryder and Layla herself. Not when she was supposed to be back in court in less than an hour.

She looked at the docket she'd printed that morning. Hearing conferences and motions.

She reached for the phone again and dialed. This time, she received an answer. "Keith? It's Greer. Can you pinch-hit for me this afternoon? I know it's short notice, but I have a personal matter that's come up."

"Personal matter!" He sounded surprised. "You're joking, right?"

She made a face at the wall. "Does it sound like I'm joking?"

He chuckled. "I'm just yanking your chain. Nice to know that you're human like the rest of us. So, yeah. Sure. Just for today?"

"Just for today. I'll leave my files at the front desk with Bunny. Court's back in session at two."

"I'll be there," he promised. "Everything all right? I heard Maddie had the baby last night—"

"They're all fine," she assured him. It never failed to

surprise her how quickly news spread in this town. "It's nothing to do with that. I really appreciate the favor. I'll owe you one."

"And I plan on collecting," he said with a laugh before hanging up.

Now that she'd made the decision, she tossed the rest of her sandwich in the trash. The bread was already getting stale, anyway. She bundled up everything that Keith might need for the afternoon and left it with Bunny Towers. Then she went back to retrieve her shoes and purse and left the office.

Not even Michael noticed, which had her wondering why she'd never tried taking off an afternoon before. No matter what she did, her boss seemed to remain unimpressed.

It took nearly an hour to get to Ryder's place. There were no vehicles parked on the gravel outside the house. Even though she'd seen it more than once now, the sight of the converted barn was still arresting. The only barn conversions she'd ever seen before were in magazines and on home decorating shows.

No doubt, Eliane-of-the-beautiful-accent would only add another layer of interest to the surroundings.

"Get your brain out of high school," she muttered, and snatched up her purse before marching to the front door. There was no answer when she knocked, but the door was unlocked when she tried it. She cautiously pushed it open. "Hello? Mrs. Pyle?" She stepped inside. "Ryder?"

The last time she'd been there, the house had been as tidy as a pin.

Now it looked like a tornado had hit.

Layla's toys were everywhere. Laundry was piled on the armless chair, overflowing onto the floor. The couch was nearly hidden beneath a plastic bin that she felt certain contained the baby gear that Maddie and Linc had given Ryder when they'd turned Layla over to him.

She dropped her purse on top of it and walked into the kitchen. Cereal crunched under her shoes. The sink was filled halfway to the top with dirty dishes.

She crunched her way to the back door and looked out at the picnic table with its painted daisies. It hadn't even been a week since she'd been there, but the grass was already overgrown.

Weren't Swiss people notoriously tidy? Maybe Eliane would take one look and run for the hills.

The thought should have been worrying.

The fact that it was not was an entirely different cause for concern.

She left the door open slightly to allow for some fresh air—hot as it was—and went upstairs.

Layla's nursery was empty. The mattress had been stripped of bedding. It was probably sitting in the pile of laundry downstairs.

The air was stuffy here, too. One window held a boxy air conditioner. It wasn't running, and Greer left it off. She went to the second window and opened it; the hot breeze fluttered at the simple white curtains.

She left Layla's room, intending to go back downstairs, but she hesitated, looking down the hall toward the other open door. She could see the foot of a bed where a navy blue quilt was piled half on and half off the mattress. A pair of cowboy boots were lying haphazardly on the wood floor.

Unquestionably, the room was Ryder's.

When she'd babysat Layla, the sliding door to the room had been closed.

She knew the house was empty.

Still, Greer's heart beat a little faster as she stepped closer to the room. She peered around the edge of the doorway. The dresser was wide, with six drawers. One framed picture sat on top, but otherwise it was bare.

His bed was big with an iron-railed headboard. Three white pillows were bunched messily at the head of the mattress. Instead of a nightstand next to the bed, there was a saddletree complete with a fancy-looking tooled leather saddle. An industrial sort of lamp was attached directly to the wall. There was an enormous unadorned window next to the bed, and before she knew it, she'd walked across the room to look out.

Directly below was the picnic table.

She wondered how often he looked out and thought about his late wife.

She wondered if he'd look out and still think about her when he had a delectable Swiss confection under his roof tending to his child.

Disgusted with herself, she turned away from the window. She bent down slightly to look at the framed photograph on his dresser. It was an old-fashioned black-and-white wedding photo. Maybe his parents? Or the aunt named Adelaide? Then she heard a faint sound and her nervousness ratcheted up.

She darted out of the bedroom and was heading to the staircase when Ryder—looking entirely incongruous in cowboy hat and boots with a pink-patterned baby carrier strapped across his chest—appeared.

Even before he saw her, his eyes were narrowed. "What're you doing here?"

Chapter Seven

What're you doing here?

Ryder's question seemed to echo around her.

He looked hot and sweaty, as did Layla in the carrier, and Greer's mouth went dry.

Not only from nearly being caught out snooping in his bedroom, but from the strange swooping feeling in her stomach caused by the sight of him.

"Greer?"

She felt like her brains were scrambled and gestured vaguely toward Layla's bedroom. "I was…ah—"

"Never mind." In a move that she knew from personal experience was more difficult than he made it look, he unfastened Layla from the carrier and handed her to Greer. "Take her for a few minutes while I clean up."

Layla's green eyes were bright and merry as she looked at Greer. She was wearing a yellow T-shirt that felt damp and a pair of yellow shorts with a ruffle across her butt. Her reddish-blond curls were spiked with perspiration. "Is she still running a fever?"

"Nah. Even on a cold day the carrier gets hot." He pulled off his hat as he brushed past Greer, smelling like sunshine and fresh hay. He continued along the hallway, pulling off not only the carrier, but his T-shirt, as well. "She popped out two more teeth this morning, though. I don't care what that doc said last night about teething not causing a fever. Soon as those teeth showed up, she was right as rain, just like my aunt Adelaide predicted." He stepped inside his bedroom and looked at Greer. "Be down in a few." Then he pulled on the rustic metal handle and slid the door closed.

She closed her eyes. But the image of his bare chest remained.

Heaven help her.

She opened them again to find Layla smiling brightly at her, displaying the new additions to her bottom row of teeth. She jabbered and patted Greer's face.

Greer caught the baby's hand and kissed it. "Hello to you, too, sweetheart."

She heard a couple thuds from behind Ryder's bedroom door. It was much too easy imagining him sitting on the foot of that messy, wide bed, pulling off his boots and tossing them aside.

After the boots would come the jeans—

"Let's go downstairs," she whispered quickly to Layla, who laughed as if Greer had said something wonderfully funny.

"At least *you* think it's funny." Greer hurried to the staircase. "You have a lot in common with your aunt Ali, that's for sure."

Once downstairs, she settled Layla into her high

chair. It was much cleaner than the kitchen counters were, so she had to give Ryder points for that.

She opened the back door wider so there was more air flowing, then found a clean cloth in a drawer. She wet it down with cool water and worked it over Layla's face and head. Layla took it as a game, of course, and slyly evaded most of Greer's swipes before gaining control of the cloth, which she proceeded to shove into her mouth.

Chewing on a wet washcloth wasn't the worst thing Greer could think of, so she let the baby have it and turned her attention to the dishes in the sink. They weren't quite as dirty as she'd first thought. At least they'd been rinsed.

Loading the dishwasher didn't take much time. She found the soap and started it. But the sound of the dishwasher wasn't enough to block the sound of water running overhead, and Greer's imagination ran amok again.

To combat it, she found another cloth and furiously began wiping down the counters. When she was done with that, she found the broom and swept up the scattered cereal crumbs. And when she was done with *that*, she grabbed an armful of clothes from the pile on the chair and blindly shoved it into the washing machine located in a sunny room right off the kitchen.

The cheeriness of the room was almost enough to make up for the laundry drudgery, and she wondered if he'd made it that way for Daisy.

With the washing machine now running, too, she went back into the kitchen, lifted Layla out of the high chair and took her outside.

"You like this soft grass as much as I do?" Greer unfastened the narrow straps around her ankles and kicked off her high-heeled shoes, curling her toes in the tall grass. She bent over Layla, holding her hands as the baby pushed up and down on her bent knees, chortling.

"Wait until next year. You're going to be running all over the grass on your own." They slowly aimed toward the picnic table. But they made it only partway before Layla plopped down on her diaper-padded, ruffle-covered butt. She grabbed at the grass undulating around her and yanked, then looked surprised when the soft blades tore free.

Greer tugged her skirt above her knees so she could sit in the grass with her. She mimicked Layla's grass grab and then held open her hands so the pieces of green blew away on the breeze.

Layla opened her palms and her grass blew away, too. Instead of laughing, though, her brows pulled together and her face scrunched.

Greer laughed. "Silly girl." She tore off another handful of grass and let it go again. "See it blow away?" She leaned over and nuzzled her nose against Layla's palms. "Smells so good." Then she rubbed her nose against Layla's and plucked a single blade of grass and tickled her cheek with the end of it. "Smells kind of like your daddy, doesn't it?"

"Mama mamamama!" Layla laughed and grabbed the grass, but missed and rolled onto her side. She immediately popped up and crawled over to Greer, clambering onto her lap.

Knowing Layla hadn't really said *mama* didn't stop Greer's heart from lurching. She wrapped her arm around Layla's warm body and kissed the top of her head.

Then they both yanked hunks of grass free and tossed them into the air.

He had a perfect view of them from his bedroom window.

Ryder dragged the towel over his head and down his

chest. The water in the shower hadn't been much above tepid to begin with, but it had turned altogether cold after only a few minutes.

Probably a good thing.

Below, Layla had crawled onto Greer's lap. As he watched, Greer rolled onto her back, heedless of her silk blouse and her hair that today had been pulled back into a smooth knot behind her head. She pushed Layla up into the air above her, and even through his closed window, he could hear her peals of laughter.

He'd been cursing Mrs. Pyle's absence after she'd promised him another week of work. With no alternative, it had meant hauling a baby around with him on a tractor for half the day. Which meant he still wasn't finished haying. He was falling behind on everything.

But right now, looking down at Greer and the baby, he almost didn't care.

Almost.

As if she sensed him watching, Greer suddenly looked up at his window. It was too far for him to see her exact expression, but he had no trouble imagining her dark brown eyes.

They were mesmerizing, those eyes of hers. They kept entering his thoughts at all hours of the day.

And the night.

The air-conditioner kicked on, blowing cold air over him and drowning out the sound of Layla's high-pitched squeals.

He took a step back and blew out a long breath, not even aware that he'd been holding it.

"You're losing it, man," he muttered to himself, roughly dragging the towel over his head once more before tossing it aside. It knocked over his grandparents' picture and he automatically set it to rights while he pulled out the last clean shirt he possessed, plus a pair of jeans that weren't so clean. He quickly got dressed and went downstairs.

As soon as he walked through the kitchen, he understood why his shower water had been cold. Both the washing machine and the dishwasher were going.

It wasn't Mrs. Pyle's doing, that was for certain.

The mug tree sitting on one corner of the butcher-block island had three clean mugs still hanging from the metal branches. He took two, filled them with water and pushed open the wooden screen door.

When it slammed shut behind him, Greer froze and looked his way. Her face was as flushed as Layla's and dark strands of hair had worked loose to cling to her neck.

The ivory blouse she wore had come partially free from the waist of her light gray skirt. As if she were following the progression of his gaze, she suddenly pushed the hem of her skirt down her thighs and swept her legs to one side as she set Layla down on the grass. "It's still crazy hot," she commented, not exactly looking his way. "What happened to Mrs. Pyle?"

"Her grandson." He was as barefoot as the two females, and the earth beneath his feet felt cooler than anything else as he walked toward them. It was no wonder Greer had chosen to sit in the grass rather than at the picnic table. He extended one of the mugs to her. "It's just water."

She smiled a little as she took it from him. "Thank you." Before she could get the cup to her mouth, though, Layla launched herself at it, and Greer wasn't quite quick enough to avoid her. Half the water sloshed out of the cup and onto her blouse, rendering several inches of silky fabric nearly transparent.

Ryder was polite enough not to comment, but too male to look away. He could see the scrolling lacework of blue thread beneath the wet patch and had no trouble at all imagining the soft flesh beneath that.

Greer plucked at the fabric, though as far as he could tell, she only succeeded in pulling the rest of the blouse loose from the skirt. She took a sip of what was left of the water, then held it to Layla's mouth. "What's going on with Anthony? He was just acquitted last week."

"And he turned around and got picked up on drunk driving last night."

She jerked, giving him a sharp look that was echoed somewhat by the sharp look that Layla gave *her*. "What? Where? I haven't heard about it."

"I don't know where." He sat on the grass, leaning his back against the picnic table. "I just know she dropped everything and immediately took off to rescue him." Mrs. Pyle had given him the courtesy of a rushed phone call, but that was it.

Greer frowned, then focused once more on Layla, who'd started fussing for the mug of water. "I'm sorry, sweetheart. It's empty now. See?" She turned the mug upside down and glanced back at Ryder. "You make that sound like a bad thing."

"I don't have a lot of sympathy for people who drink and drive."

"Because of what happened to Layla's mother."

"Because of what happened to my mother." The second the words were out, he regretted them. "Here." He leaned forward and poured half his water into her mug, then sat back again. "You obviously didn't come out here because Mrs. Pyle asked you to sub for her." He repeated what he'd asked when he walked into his house and found her there. "So what *are* you doing here?"

"Someone called me about the nanny position."

"You must be pretty excited about the prospect to drive out here to tell me. I do have a phone, you know."

"Which nobody answered when I called. And then after last night... Layla's fever and all." She lifted one shoulder, watching Layla, who'd lost interest in the mug and had started crawling toward the far side of the picnic table. "I was concerned. So I drove out."

"And found the place looking like a bomb had hit."

"You want me to say it wasn't that bad?"

"I have a feeling you're not much for lies, even the polite ones."

She got on her hands and knees and crawled after Layla. "I did watch her for the better part of a day," she reminded him. "I can appreciate that she's kind of a force of nature." She looked over her shoulder at him for a moment. "Toss in last night's trip to the hospital, and a messy house doesn't seem so strange."

The afternoon was admittedly hot. But that wasn't the cause for the furnace suddenly cranking up inside him. He looked away from the shapely butt closely outlined by pale gray fabric. "What did she sound like?"

"Who? Oh, right." Greer pushed herself up to sit on the bench. "Her name's Eliane. Eliane Dupre."

"French."

She gave him a surprised look.

"I knew an Eliane once."

Surprise slid into something else. Something on the verge of pinched and suspicious. "Oh?"

"She was a model for Adelaide during her nudes phase."

"Excuse me?"

"My aunt's an artist." And Eliane had been an incredible tutor for a horny seventeen-year-old. He didn't share that part, though, much as he was coming to enjoy the game of keeping the lady lawyer a little off-balance. It was his one way of feeling like things were sort of even between them. "What else did you learn besides her name?"

Greer was still giving him a measuring look.

Or maybe she was just trying to keep her eye from twitching.

"She's currently staying in Weaver. She did ask if the live-in part was negotiable. So when you talk with her, be prepared."

"What else?"

"She's from Switzerland. Divorced, it sounds like. And looking for a steady job. I have her phone number in my purse."

He pushed to his feet. "Let's do it, then."

Greer's expression didn't change as she lifted Layla and stood. But he still had the sense that he'd surprised her. And not necessarily in a good way.

They went inside and she handed him a slip of paper from her purse. Then she carried Layla back outside.

To give him privacy? Or because she wasn't interested in the conversation in the first place?

Even wondering was stupid. Pointless.

Maybe he needed more sleep.

He snatched the phone off the hook and looked at the paper.

Greer's handwriting was slightly slanted and neat. *Spare*, as Adelaide would say. There were no curlicues. No extra tails or circles. While he dialed the number, his mind's eye imagined her hand quickly recording the information on the paper.

Daisy's handwriting had been all over the place. All loopy letters and heart-dotted *i*'s.

He pushed away the thought. He definitely needed more sleep.

The phone rang four times before it went to voice mail. He wasn't sure if he was disappointed or not. He left his name and number and hung up, then went back outside. It was hotter outside than in, but at least the air was moving.

This time Greer was sitting at the table bouncing Layla on her lap.

"No answer. I left a message."

"I'm sure she'll call you back. She sounded pretty interested to me."

The wet patch on her blouse had dried. No more intriguing glimpses of white lace with blue threads. But there was a smudge of green on her thigh. "You have grass stains."

Her eyebrows rose, then she quickly looked down at herself. She swiped her hand at the mark. "Dry cleaners will get it out. Hopefully." Her shoulders rose and fell as she took a deep breath. "I should be going."

"Back to the office, I suppose."

She glanced at the narrow watch on her wrist. "Court should be finished for the day, but yes, I probably should go back. Start reviewing everything for tomorrow's docket."

"Probably." He waited a beat, but she didn't move an inch. "Or—"

Her gaze slid toward him.

"Or I could pull out a couple steaks." He jerked his thumb toward the covered grill. "Throw 'em on the grill after I give Short-Stuff a badly needed bath."

Greer's lips parted slightly. The top one was a little fuller than the bottom, he realized.

"Or you could give her a bath," he said casually. "If you wanted."

Her lips twitched. "I do like steak. Medium rare."

"I wouldn't do well-done even if you asked."

She ran her fingers over Layla's curls. "You feed her *after* her bath?"

"Counselor, sometimes I'm feeding her ten times a day. I learned real quick there's no point in sweating about the order of things when it comes to her."

"My mother would love you," she murmured. She stood with Layla. "And I'm clearly not above a bribe, whether there's dinner payment or not." She marched past him into the house.

He scrubbed his hand down his face and followed her inside. She was fastening Layla into the high chair.

"Have any of your cow pie stuff?"

"Not today." He took the last banana from the holder and started peeling it. "Personally, I hate bananas, but she loves 'em." He tossed the browning peel in the trash, then cut the fruit into small chunks and dropped them into a shallow plastic bowl that he set in front of Layla.

She was already starting to look heavy-lidded, but she dived into the bowl with both hands. "Greedy girl." He plucked a mushy piece of banana from her cheek and fed it to her.

Greer was watching him when he turned away. "What?"

She just shook her head slightly and cleared her throat. "What else besides overripe banana? Does she still have a bottle?"

"Formula, but she wants it in her cup." He looked in the sink.

"I loaded everything in the dishwasher."

He pulled it open and steam spewed out. He plucked

out the cup and lid, then closed the door and started it up again. He rinsed both pieces under cold water, then filled it with premixed formula. "There's a container in the fridge with some cooked vegetables. She didn't eat 'em last night."

Greer went to the refrigerator and opened it.

He glanced over. "Top shelf. Red lid."

She pulled out the glass container and peeled off the lid. "Yum. Carrots and peas."

"Don't knock it." He gave Layla her sippy cup, then took the container from Greer, dumped the vegetables in a pan and set it on the stove.

"Wouldn't the microwave be faster?"

"Yep." He made a face as he lit the flame under the pan. "Adelaide'll lecture me for a week about the dangers."

"There are dangers?"

"Probably not as many as my aunt can name." He jabbed a spoon at the vegetables. "It's one of those lose-the-battle-win-the-war things, I think."

"You're in a war with the microwave?"

He chuckled. "More like a war with my aunt over the microwave. You might say she's a little—" He broke off when the phone rang. "Eccentric," he finished. "Watch these, would you?"

"An eccentric aunt who paints nudes and names her dog Brutus. She sounds like quite a woman. You mention her a lot." Greer's fingers brushed his as she took over the spoon. "Afraid I'm not much of a cook."

"She photographs nudes," he corrected. "Among other things. And I'm afraid I'm not much of a cook, either. But I like to eat, so—" He picked up the ringing phone. "Diamond-L."

"Is this Mr. Wilson?" The voice was female. Accented. "I'm Eliane Dupre."

"Eliane," he repeated, watching Greer turn toward the stove so that her slender back was to him.

Her shoulders were noticeably tight beneath the thin, silky blouse.

Interesting.

The conversation was brief.

Greer's back was still to him when he hung up. She was stirring the vegetables so diligently, he figured they'd end up mushier than the banana. He moved next to her and turned off the heat beneath the pan.

"I'm meeting her tomorrow over lunch at Josephine's," he said.

She gave him an overbright smile. "Great." She brushed her hands down the sides of her skirt. "You know, I just remembered I *do* have to go back to the office before tomorrow morning. So I'm going to have to pass on the bribery, after all." As she spoke, she was backing out of the kitchen, stopping only long enough to lean over and kiss Layla's head as she passed.

"You sure?" He tested the vegetables. Definitely mushy. But at least not too hot. He dumped some into Layla's now-empty banana bowl.

Greer's head bobbed. "I'm sure. Let me know how it, uh, how it goes tomorrow." She grabbed her purse that was sitting on the couch and clutched it to her waist with both hands.

"Will do."

"Great." Her head bobbed a few more times. "Well, good…good luck." She quickly turned on her bare feet and hurried to the front door.

"By the way, what did she have?"

She'd made it to the vestibule and she gave him a startled look. "Excuse me?"

"Your sister."

She looked even more deer-in-the-headlights. "Maddie! She had a boy. Seven pounds, thirteen ounces. Twenty-one inches long. They named him Liam Gustav after Linc's grandfather. Mommy and son are doing well." She smiled quickly and yanked open the front door. "Daddy is, reportedly, a basket case." She lifted her hand in a quick wave and darted out the door, closing it behind her.

He waited.

But she didn't come back.

Even though her feet were bare, since her high-heeled pumps were still out back, lying in the grass.

He looked at Layla.

She was plucking a pea out of the carrots with one hand and clutching her pink cup with the other.

"Interesting, indeed," he told her.

She smacked her cup against the high chair tray and gave him a beatific smile. "Bye bye bye bye!"

"You got that right, Short-Stuff. She sure did go bye-bye." He chucked her lightly under the chin. "But I'm betting she'll be back."

Chapter Eight

"What the hell did you do to your feet?"

Greer looked up to see Ali standing in the doorway to her office and yanked her feet down from where they were propped on the corner of her desk. "Nothing." She tugged her black skirt down around her knees.

"You have bandage strips all over the soles of your feet."

"I know you're in uniform, but you can stop the interrogation. Bandage strips aren't a criminal offense." Greer slid her feet into the shoes under her desk. She was still embarrassed over the way she'd raced out of Ryder's place the evening before. She didn't particularly want to explain why to her sister. "What brings you to the dark side?"

"Glad you're finally ready to admit the truth about your work." Ali grinned and threw herself down on the chair inside the doorway. She leaned back and propped her heavy department-issue boots on the corner of the desk.

"Hey!" Greer shoved at them. "Just because I did, doesn't mean you can. Have a little respect, please."

"For the dark side? Never." She put her feet on the floor, still smiling.

"You're in an awfully good mood," Greer complained. "If you've come to brag about the latest night or morning or afternoon of hot sex you've had with your new husband, spare me."

Ali looked at her fingernails. "Well, it is pretty bragworthy," she drawled.

"Save me."

"You don't need saving. You need sexing."

"Ali, for God's sake."

Her sister laughed silently. "Your chain is so easy to yank these days."

"And if you weren't pregnant, I'd yank yours but good. Speaking of." She pinned her sister with her fiercest lawyer look. "Have you told Grant?"

"Yes."

"And?"

"Between looking like he wanted to pass out and suddenly treating me like I'm made of Dresden Porcelain, I think he's pretty much okay with it." Her expression sobered. "He still needs to create some kind of relationship with Layla, though. He's not going to let it go, Greer. He can't."

"Nor should he even think he has to." She dropped her head onto her hands, pressing her fingertips into her scalp. She exhaled and lifted her head. "Ryder's coming along, Ali." She hoped. "Is that what you came here to find out?"

"Actually, I came here to invite you to lunch. Josephine's. On me."

"Oh, that's right. You're not living only on a public

servant's salary anymore. You have a bestselling thriller writer as a husband now."

"Poke as much as you want. Do you care for a free lunch or don't you?"

"I do." She glanced at her watch. "It'll have to be quick, though. I have less than an hour before I need to be over at the courthouse."

"Yeah, yeah." Ali pushed to her feet. "I know the drill. Josephine's pretty much makes a living off the police department and the courthouse. It's always quick." She waited while Greer collected her purse and they left her office. "Seriously." Ali gave her a sidelong look. "What is going on with your feet? You're limping. You didn't actually fall through one of the floorboards in the kitchen, did you?"

"Of course not. I just, uh, just broke a glass."

Ali pushed through the entrance door first. "You never could lie for squat." She stopped short. "Hello, Mr. Towers. Out enjoying the weather?" She smiled the same sweet smile she'd used all her life when she didn't particularly like someone. "I've heard you like things hot."

Michael looked right through Ali to focus on Greer. "I learned that you didn't take the plea on Dilley."

"The client refused."

Her boss looked particularly annoyed. "I told you to plead them all."

"I cannot force a client to accept a deal! Particularly one that isn't even a good deal. Come on, Michael. We're better than that, aren't we?"

His jaw flexed. His gaze slid to Ali, then back to Greer. "We'll talk about it later," he said brusquely and pushed past them, going inside.

"How do you stand working for him?" Her sister made no effort to lower her voice.

Greer closed her hand around Ali's arm, squeezing as she pulled her farther away from the office. "Michael has a lot on his plate."

"Yeah, Stormy Santiago, from what I hear."

"It's a big case."

"Considering he's sleeping with her, yeah."

Greer dropped her hand from her sister's arm. "What?"

Ali gave her an incredulous look. "Don't tell me you haven't heard the rumors."

"Michael Towers is not sleeping with Stormy Santiago," Greer said under her breath. "He could get disbarred!"

"And maybe he should." Ali's voice was flat. Disregarding the fact that she was jaywalking, Ali set off across the street, leaving Greer to catch up.

"He's also happily married," Greer said when they reached the sidewalk on the other side.

Ali just shook her head. "And I thought Maddie was the naive one. Maybe you're just so busy with your clients that you can't notice what's going on right in your own office." She pulled open the door to Josephine's and gestured. "Age before beauty, dear sister."

Greer went inside, only to stop short at the sight of Ryder sitting in a booth across from a very attractive blonde.

Ali practically bumped into her. But she couldn't fail to notice, either. "*Who* is that?"

"Eliane Dupre," she said in a low voice, steering her sister toward an empty booth on the opposite side of the nearly full restaurant.

"And who is Eliane Dupre?" Ali asked with an exaggerated accent once they were seated. She looked over her shoulder in Ryder's direction.

Maybe the next Mrs. Ryder Wilson.

Greer kept the thought to herself. "Don't stare. They might notice you."

Ali looked back at her and spread her hands. "So?"

"Eliane is interested in the nanny position. She responded to one of the notices I placed for Ryder."

"Ah."

"Mrs. Pyle must be back. Otherwise he'd have Layla with him."

"Too bad. *I* would've loved a chance to see her."

Greer snatched one of the laminated menus out from where they were tucked against the sugar shaker and the bottles of ketchup and hot sauce. It didn't matter that she knew the contents by heart. She still made a point of reading it. Or pretending to read it.

"How's that new baby doing?" Josephine herself said, stopping at the table and without asking, setting glasses of water in front of them before flipping over both of their mugs to slosh steaming coffee into them.

"Liam's perfect," Ali said. Her gaze slid over Greer. "Went over to see them at the hospital yesterday evening. Maddie's supposed to be released today sometime."

"Give her and Linc my best when you see them. You two know what you'd like today?"

"French dip," Ali said immediately. It was pretty much what she always ordered.

"Chef's salad." It was pretty much what Greer always ordered, too. She slid the menu back where it belonged.

"Coming up." Josephine headed back toward the kitchen.

"I suppose that was a dig about me not going to the hospital last night."

"It wasn't a dig. More like a...curiosity. I was there for a few hours. Mom and Dad came by. Vivian. Squire and Gloria Clay. Fortunately, Vivian had already left before they got there. We all sort of just assumed you'd show up after court was through for the day."

Greer grimaced. "I wasn't in court yesterday afternoon. Keith Gowler stepped in for me. Did I tell you that he and Lydia Oakes are getting married?"

Ali wasn't sidetracked. "You took off work? That's the second time this month. You never do that."

"Well, I did. I'll go see Maddie and the baby tonight when they're home." From across the busy diner, she heard a laugh and looked over toward Ryder's booth. His back was to her. But that only meant she had a perfect view of the fair Eliane.

Despite Greer's ripe imagination where the nanny applicant had been concerned, she'd nevertheless pictured someone older. Someone old enough to have left her own country for another. Someone old enough to have a failed marriage under her belt.

But Eliane—with her long, shiny, corn silk–colored hair and perfectly proportioned features—looked no older than Greer.

Younger, even.

"Because of Ryder?"

She belatedly tuned back into Ali. "What?"

Ali turned sideways in the booth. A move clearly designed so that she could look at the man in question without craning her head around.

Greer's lagging brain caught up. "I took off work because of *Layla*," she corrected.

Ali unrolled her knife and fork from the paper napkin. "Sure you did."

"Ali—" She broke off when another musical laugh filtered through the general noisiness of the diner. She exhaled and rubbed her fingertips against her scalp again.

"Having headaches a lot these days?"

"No," she lied.

Ali just watched her.

Greer dropped her hands. The sight of Ryder's booth in her peripheral vision was maddening. "Change seats with me."

Ali's brows disappeared beneath her bangs. But she slid out of the booth and they traded places. Greer pushed Ali's coffee mug over to her and wrapped her fingers around her own. She swallowed. "What if I told you I might have the solution to all of our problems where Layla is concerned?"

Ali mirrored her position: arms resting on the Formica tabletop, hands cupped around her mug. Her voice was just as low as Greer's. "The only problem we have with Layla is Ryder refusing all the offers of help he's gotten from us these past months. The fact that he's still keeping us all at a distance."

"Particularly your husband."

"He *is* her uncle. So what's the solution? Did you find some legal loophole?"

"It's something legal," Greer allowed. "But not a loophole." And she was insane to even be mentioning it to Ali. Much less to think that somewhere along the line, she'd even been giving it the slightest consideration.

"Just cut the mystery, Greer. What?"

Greer exhaled. "Ryder mentioned finding a wife instead of a nanny. You know. For Layla's sake." She took a quick, nervous sip of coffee.

Ali immediately looked toward his booth. "Are you kid—" She broke off when Josephine appeared, carrying their lunch plates.

She started to set down the meals, but stopped. "You switched places. I remember when you used to do that when you were girls, trying to pass for one another."

Ali flicked her streaky hair. "Don't think we'd have much luck on that anymore," she said lightly. "Don't s'pose you have any of that chocolate cream pie left, do you? I thought I'd take a slice home to Grant."

"I'll package one up for you," Josephine promised, and headed off.

"He's buried himself in a new manuscript he started," Ali confided.

"I thought he never intended to write another T. C. Grant book."

"I don't know if it will be another CCT Rules military thriller or not." Ali picked up half of her sandwich. "For all I know, it might be a children's book. I'm just thrilled that he's feeling an urge to write again. As for Ryder—" She broke off, glancing around and lowering her voice. "You think he's going to marry the nanny?"

Greer pressed the tip of her tongue against the back of her teeth for a moment. "Or…someone else," she said huskily. "Me, for instance."

The sandwich dropped right out of Ali's hand, landing on the little cup of au jus and sending it splashing across the table toward Greer.

Greer barely noticed until Ali slapped a napkin over the spill before it dripped onto Greer's lap.

Then her sister sat back on her side of the booth and

stared at her with wide eyes. "How long have you two been..." She trailed off and waved her hand.

"We haven't been." Greer mimicked the wave. She didn't mention the fact that she'd thought about it often enough.

Ali leaned closer. "Yet he *proposed* to you."

"N-not really." He'd been joking. Hadn't he? "But the subject has come up. It would just be a business arrangement," she clarified. "Not a romantic one."

Ali sat back again. She picked up a french fry and pointed it at Greer. "Are you crazy?" She shoved the fry in her mouth.

"Nobody thought the idea was more insane than me." Greer forced herself to pick up her fork and at least look like she was eating. "At first."

"When did all this come up?" Ali waved another fry.

"Last week."

Ali suddenly dropped her french fry and assumed an overly casual smile.

And the back of Greer's neck prickled.

A second later, Ryder was passing their table. He was following Eliane, his hand lightly touching her arm as they progressed through the busy diner. They made a striking couple. Both tall. Both perfect specimens of their gender.

His blue eyes moved over Greer's face and he gave a faint nod.

Heaven help me.

Then he was reaching around Eliane to open the door for her, and they were gone.

Greer's breath leaked out of her. She actually felt shaky.

"Here." Ali pushed a water glass into Greer's hand. "Drink. You look like you're going to pass out."

"I've never passed out and I'm not going to start now." Still, she sucked down half the contents. Then she picked up her fork and jabbed it into her salad, even though the thought of food was vaguely nauseating.

She was well aware of Ali's concern, which was the only reason she was able to swallow the chunk of ham and lettuce. But as soon as had, she set her fork down again. "Layla deserves a mother," she said huskily.

Ali's eyes immediately glistened. "You can't marry someone just because you love a little girl," she said softly.

"Want to bet?" Greer cleared her throat, but it still felt tight. "I also love my sisters. And if I did this, Layla *would* be part of our family. For real. For good. You know I would be able to make certain of it."

"And you? What about you?"

"What about me? I'd be getting the best part of the deal. Layla."

"You know that's not what I mean."

Greer swallowed. "You know I've never thought about the whole marriage thing. My career's been everything."

"Are you sure this isn't *about* your career?" Ali pushed aside her plate of food and leaned her arms on the table again. "Six months ago you told me you were thinking about quitting. Remember that?"

"Trust you to throw a moment of weakness in my face."

But Ali didn't bite. She just sat there, watching Greer, eyes more knowing than Greer wanted them to be.

"It's not about my career," she finally said. "At least I don't think it is. Entirely, anyway."

"Gotta say, Greer. I'm feeling a little freaked out at this indecisive version of you."

"Yeah, well, I'm a little freaked out by the settled-and-married-gonna-have-a-baby version of you. Maddie was one thing. She's had *mama* written all over her since she was playing with dolls. You used to cut off the heads of your dolls and shoot them out of your slingshot."

Ali snorted softly. "I did not."

"Just about. You were both the ultimate tomboy and the ultimate flirt. Everything you want to try your hand at, you succeed at. I'm sure you'll be the same way with motherhood."

"So says Madame Lawyer," Ali said drily. "Maybe I had to try so hard because you've always been the brilliant one. Well. Until now." She spread her palms. "You cannot marry a man you don't love, Greer. Not even for Layla."

"Even if it means solving this problem between Grant and Ryder? I'm at a crossroads here. All I have to do is turn the right way! Maddie's a mom. You're going to be a mom. Well, maybe I want to be one, too!" So what if he'd been joking? He'd been serious enough about the will. She could do a business deal just as well as *Eliane.*

"What happens if you meet someone you really *do* love?"

"I'm thirty years old. It hasn't happened yet."

"You're already talking yourself into it. I can tell."

Maybe she was.

"If you do this, what're you going to tell Mom and Dad? The truth? Or are you going to try making up some story about a sudden romance between the two of you? Because we all know what a rotten liar you are. They'll see right through it. And Mom'll be brokenhearted at the thought of you locked in a loveless marriage."

Greer exhaled. "It wouldn't be like her history with Rosalind's dad."

"She stayed married to Martin Pastore for years because of Rosalind. How's it different?"

"Well, for one thing, Ryder isn't like Martin!" Her encounters with their mother's first husband were mercifully few and far between. "He's not cold and controlling."

"Could've fooled me by the way he's acted for the last six months."

"You don't know him. He's...warm and...and loyal."

"Sounds like a lapdog."

Greer glared.

"Oh, come on. You left yourself wide open for that one."

"You're impossible."

"Admittedly, he's an awful good-looking lapdog. We've grown up around guys in boots and cowboy hats. He does the whole rancher look better than most."

"He does the entire *male* look better than most." She dropped her head into her hands again and massaged her temples. Then she raised her head again and looked at her watch. "I have to get to court."

"You didn't eat anything."

"Trust me. Judge Waters isn't going to care about that." She slid out of the booth. "I appreciate the thought, though." She headed for the door.

Ali followed her, calling out to Josephine that she'd be right back. Then she pursued Greer right out onto the sidewalk. "Promise me you'll think about this a little longer."

A gust of hot wind buffeted the striped awning

over the door and she glanced up, absently noticing the clouds gathering overhead. Maybe the weatherman was finally going to get a prediction right.

"All I've been doing is thinking. Maybe it's time I stopped and just—" She broke off. Shook her head.

"Tossed a coin?"

She managed a faint smile. "Maybe."

Ali grabbed her hands and squeezed them. "Greer, I know what marriage is really supposed to be. I want that for you."

Her throat tightened. "Baby sister, I'll never forgive you if you make me cry now."

Ali made a face.

Greer kissed her cheek and pulled away, checked the street for traffic, and started across.

Ali's voice followed her. "What *did* you do to your feet?"

Greer waved her arm without answering and quickened her pace, trying harder to ignore the tiny cuts she'd gotten from the gravel outside Ryder's house.

She was breathless when she rushed past Bunny Towers sitting at the reception desk and headed straight for her office.

"Oh, Greer. You have some—"

Greer nearly skidded to a halt at the sight of Ryder leaning against her desk. His arms were crossed over his wide chest. He'd set his cowboy hat on the desk beside him.

She swiped her palms down the sides of her black skirt and briskly entered her office, moving around to the opposite side of her desk. "I have to be in court in a few minutes." She started shoving files into her briefcase, heedless of whether or not they were the right ones. "The interview with Eliane went well?"

"She's ready to start tomorrow if I say the word. Didn't even ask about the live-in part. She also agreed to sign an agreement that she'd stay at least six months."

Greer felt a pang in her chest. Who was it that said timing was everything? "I see. Did you tell her about your other idea?"

His eyes narrowed slightly. "You haven't tossed your name in the pool. Does it matter to you?"

She pulled out the will she'd drafted for him and handed it to him. "Not as long as you sign that." Not as long as he didn't decide the lovely Eliane would make a lovely mama and there was no need to plan for disasters.

He tossed the document down onto her desk. "No. I didn't tell her. Yet."

She shoved in a few more files, then hefted the strap over her shoulder. "A live-in nanny's a lot easier to manage than a wife." She edged out from behind her desk again and scooted past him to the door. "I'll cancel the job postings when I finish with court today. Thanks for coming by to tell me."

"I came to bring those, too." He nodded toward the chair sitting inside her doorway and she felt her cheeks turn hot.

Her high-heeled shoes were sitting there.

The same pale gray high-heeled shoes that she'd left in the grass at his place the night before when she'd run out on him like the devil was at her heels.

"Right," she said in a clipped tone. "Thank you. I'm sorry if that took you out of your way."

"Not out of my way. I was in town, anyway."

The clock on the wall above her head seemed to be ticking more loudly than usual. "Did Eliane, uh, remind you of your aunt's model?"

His lips twitched slightly and she wished the floor would open up and swallow her.

"Hey. Didn't expect to catch you."

She whirled to see Ali striding up the hall carrying two plastic bags containing takeout.

"Figured you might as well have your uneaten lunch for—" Ali obviously noticed Ryder then. "Dinner, instead," she finished more slowly. "I'll just stash it in the break room fridge for you. Leave you two to...talk... or whatever."

"No need." Ryder straightened away from the desk and slid his hat in place with a smooth motion. "I was just dropping off those." He pointed at the shoes. "Your sister left 'em behind last night."

Greer cringed even as she saw her sister's gaze drop to the chair.

Ryder's chin dipped a fraction as he thumbed the brim of his hat and turned sideways to go past Greer through the doorway. His arm still managed to brush against hers and she felt hotter inside than ever.

Tick.

Tick.

The clock above Greer sounded louder and louder as Ali slowly looked from the shoes back to Greer.

Her mouth felt dry, which was ridiculous. Ali was her sister. Together with Maddie, they were triplets, for God's sake. "It's not what you're thinking."

Tick.

"Sure," Ali finally said. "Circumstantial evidence, right?"

"Exactly!"

"I think I'm worrying about the wrong thing."

"You don't have to worry about anything, period."

Ali pointed. "You can tell yourself this is about

Layla. And you can tell yourself this is about your job. About being at a crossroads. And I get that it's all true. But if you think you're considering marrying Ryder only because of all that, you're dreaming, big sister. So what happens if you end up actually going through with this, only to realize you're not on the business track at all, but *he* is?"

"That's not going to happen," Greer said flatly. "And it's all semantics, anyway. He's set to offer the job to Eliane."

"The job of wife?"

"Nanny!"

"Are you sure about that?"

Tick.

Chapter Nine

"Templeton! Get your rear end in here."

Greer's shoulders slumped at the command.

She dumped her overstuffed briefcase on her desk and backtracked to Michael Towers's office. *You bellowed?* "Yes?"

"Shut the door."

After her encounters with Ryder and Ali, she'd had a crappy afternoon in court. She'd been late getting to two different arraignments. One of her clients already facing a misdemeanor drug charge got popped with a second offense, meaning she'd lost all the ground she'd made on negotiating a fair plea deal. And she'd gotten into an entirely uncharacteristic argument with Steve Manetti about Anthony Pyle's DUI charge, nearly earning herself a contempt charge.

She closed the door uneasily.

"Sit."

Michael's office was twice the size of hers. Which still meant that there was only room for two chairs. She nudged the one on the right slightly and sat. "If this is about Manetti, I can expl—"

"I warned you to plead out Dilley."

Her lips parted. She swallowed what she'd been going to say about Judge Manetti.

"I tried," she said. "Mr. Dilley refused. He's insistent on having his day in court."

"You have more clients going to trial than any other attorney in my jurisdictions." He was drumming the end of his pencil against his ink blotter. "I think you'd be more effective in Hale's office."

"Hale!" She popped to her feet and the chair wobbled behind her. "He's eighty-five miles away!"

"He's getting ready to retire. You'd be the senior attorney on staff. You could take as many cases as you want to trial."

"Sure. In municipal court." It was the only one located in Lillyette, Wyoming. "Which is in session maybe three times a week. On a busy week. You're punishing me for something. What?"

"I'm not punishing you. I'm trying to promote you."

"By sending me to Lillyette." Braden was a booming metropolis in comparison to the tiny town. "What if I turn down this…kind…promotion?"

Michael stared back at her, unmoving.

Her jaw was so tight it ached. "I see." She aligned the chair neatly where it belonged. She felt blindsided. She'd never lost a job in her life. But she knew that if she didn't accept the reassignment, that was what would happen. "When do you need my decision?"

"End of the week."

She supposed it was better than at the end of this little tête-à-tête. Unable to get out a polite response, she nodded and left his office.

She returned to her own. It was a closet of a space. But whether she'd been feeling frustrated there or not, it had been hers.

Her eyes suddenly burned. Blinking hard, she emptied her briefcase of files and loaded it up for the following day. She scrolled through her email and sent a few brief replies.

Then she shut down the computer, shouldered her briefcase once more and looked up at the clock above the door. As usual, it was a few minutes behind.

She set down her briefcase and moved the chair so she could stand on it to reach the clock. She pulled it off the wall and adjusted the time.

She started to hang it back in place but hesitated. It would just continue to tick along, losing time along the way.

She inhaled deeply and held the clock against her chest as she exhaled.

Tick. Tick.

She climbed off the chair. Moved it back against the wall.

Then she tucked the clock inside her briefcase and left.

Ryder barely heard the knock on his front door above the sound of thunder. The clouds had been building all afternoon. But it hadn't helped with the heat. And aside from the noise, there hadn't been any rain.

The knock sounded again. He closed the logbook he kept on his livestock and went to the door.

Greer stood on his front step.

Her windblown hair gleamed in the porch light. She was still wearing the closely fitted white blouse and black skirt from this afternoon. But she'd unbuttoned a couple of the buttons and rolled up the sleeves. She had bright orange flip-flops on her feet.

And a bottle of whiskey in her hand.

She held it up for his inspection. He looked from the familiar label to her face. It wasn't the finest whiskey on the planet. But in his experience, it did the job pretty well. "Does the occasion call for it?"

"You tell me. I think I quit my job today."

Without asking, she stepped inside, brushing past him.

Another low rumble of thunder rolled through the night. Greer's car, parked on the gravel, was little more than a shadow.

Layla had been asleep for the last few hours. Hopefully she would sleep all the way through to morning, though with the thunder he wasn't going to hold his breath.

He closed the door.

Greer had sat down on one side of his leather couch and propped her feet on the coffee table. The fluorescent orange flip-flops looked more like they belonged on a teenager. But the slender ankles and long calves belonged to a grown woman.

He sat down on the other side of the couch—one full cushion between them—and took the bottle from her. He, too, propped a bare foot on the coffee table. He peeled off the seal on the bottle and pulled out the cork. "Ladies first."

Her dark eyes slid over him as she took the bottle. She lifted it to her lips and took a sip.

He expected a cough. A sputter. Something.

She merely squinted a little, obviously savoring the taste as she swallowed.

When he'd ridden rodeo, the girls had tended toward beer. Daisy had liked a strawberry daiquiri, sweet as hell and topped with hefty swirls of whipped cream. Eliane—the model, not the nanny—had given him his first taste of red wine before Adelaide caught them. Instead of firing Eliane, his aunt had sat down and poured herself a glass, too. Then made him finish the bottle.

To this day, he couldn't drink wine without thinking about that.

It occurred to him now that there was something a little dangerous about being turned on by the way Greer drank a shot of whiskey straight from the bottle.

She handed it to him.

Their fingers brushed. Him, taking. Her, not yet releasing.

"When Daisy first left, I spent a fair amount of time in Jax's company."

Her fingers slid away from his. Away from the bottle. "You must have loved her very much."

"I thought I did. Enough to give her a wedding ring." Just not *the* ring. His grandmother's ring. The one his aunt had kept in safekeeping for him since he'd been a kid. Since she'd taken him in when there was no one else to do so.

He took a drink, squinting a little at the familiar burn and savoring the warmth as it slid down his throat. "Adelaide says I've got a hero complex. That marrying Daisy was more about trying to save her than loving her."

"What do you think?"

He thought about his mother, who'd been just as troubled as his erstwhile bride. He took another drink and handed Greer the bottle.

She cradled it, running her thumb slowly over the

black label. Her nails were short. Neat. No-nonsense. "I've never loved anyone like that," she murmured. "I think it might not be in my makeup."

"Just don't tell me you're a virgin," he muttered.

If he'd thought he would set her off guard, he was mistaken.

She made a dismissive sound. "Sex and love don't have to be the same thing."

"Adelaide would agree."

"I think I'd like your aunt. You talk about her, but you don't talk about anyone else in your family."

"There wasn't anyone else."

Greer studied him for a moment, then looked away. She took another sip. A longer one this time. She tilted her head back a little and her eyelids drifted closed.

He got up and opened the kitchen door. The breeze was finally cooler. He stood in the doorway for a long minute and felt the base of his spine prickle when she came up to stand beside him in her silly orange flip-flops.

"D'you think it'll actually rain?" Her voice was little more than a whisper.

"Finished haying this morning. It can rain for a week straight, as far as I'm concerned."

She pressed her fingertips against the wooden frame of the simple screen door. "Layla?"

"Asleep."

She pushed open the screen door and went outside, taking the whiskey bottle with her. Ryder hadn't turned on the back porch light. Her blouse showed white in the light coming from the kitchen, but the rest of her melted into the darkness.

He caught the door before it could snap shut and followed her out, holding the screen until it sighed silently closed.

He sat on the end of the picnic table, watching the gleam of her blouse moving around as she swished her feet through the grass. Her restlessness was as palpable as the weight of thunder overhead.

"How old are you, Ryder?" Her voice sounded farther away than she appeared.

"Thirty-four." He cupped his hands around the edge of the table. The wood felt rough. It would be full of splinters if he didn't sand it down sometime soon. While he was at it, he could slop a coat of barn-red paint over the whole thing. Cover up all the flowery stuff.

"I'm thirty."

"Are we trading statistics? Want to know my boot size?" He listened to the grass swishing and wasn't sure if it was from her feet or from the breeze. But the gleam of her blouse was getting closer and then she stopped a few feet away from him. "Thirteen."

"Did you give Eliane the word?"

"No."

She took another sip from the bottle, then stepped close enough to set it next to his hip. "Why?"

He moved it down to the bench seat. "Why do you think you quit your job today?"

She started to move again, but he reached out and caught her hands and she went still. Her palms were small. Her long fingers curled down over his. He could see the faint sheen of moisture on her lips.

"Because I don't want to drive eighty-five miles to work every day. Or move eighty-five miles away from my home. Because." She took a step closer. She exhaled a shaky-sounding sigh. "Because."

He let go of her hands and slid his palm behind her neck. Her skin was warm. Silkier even than his imagination had promised. But that was as far as he went.

He didn't pull her forward. Didn't make another single move.

It was one of the hardest attempts at self-control he'd ever made.

"Were you really joking the other day?"

He didn't have to ask what she meant. He didn't have to think about the answer. "No. Are you tossing your name in the pool?"

After a moment she took another step forward and stopped against the edge of the table, between his thighs. When she drew breath, he could feel the press of her breasts against his chest.

"If we do this—" his voice felt like it was coming from somewhere way down inside "—I know what I get out of it. What do you get out of it?"

"Are we talking about marriage?" Her fingertips drifted over his knees, slowly grazing their way higher up his thighs, leaving heat in their wake even through his denim jeans. "Or this?"

He pressed his hands over hers, flattening them. Stilling their progress. "Counselor, I know what you'll get out of *this*."

She leaned closer, bringing with her the seductive scents of warmth and whiskey and woman. The breeze blew over them, and her hair danced against his neck. Her lips brushed against his jaw, slid delicately across his chin. Then she found his mouth for a moment that was strangely endless but much too brief. Her fingers pressed into his thighs. "I get the assurance that Layla will be part of our lives. Permanently. If you want to marry to give her a mother, then I want to *be* her mother. Legally."

He caught her behind the neck again, pulling back so he could see her face. But it was too dark. The sky too black with clouds. Her cheekbones were a faint high-light. Her lips a dark invitation. And her thickly lashed, deep brown eyes...they were the most mysterious abyss of all. "You want to adopt Layla."

"Is that so strange?"

He wasn't sure what it was, except that it made something inside his chest feel strange. "I'll consider it. What else?"

"Our wills. Anything happens to us both, then Layla goes to Grant and Ali. Those are my terms."

"What about starting your own legal firm?"

"Maybe someday when I've won the lottery and can afford it, I'll have one."

He moved his hand along her neck and over her shoulder. The gleam of white fabric looked crisp but did a poor job of hiding the heat radiating from her. "I could stake you."

"It's not just money. An office. Equipment. All that sort of thing. It's time. Time I won't have much of, if I'm out here taking care of Layla."

"You're a lawyer. Your greatest equipment is your brain. And you can turn that fancy-ass Victorian house you're supposedly renovating into an office."

Her hands slid out from beneath his as she stepped back from him. Cool air seemed to flow between them. "You're full of ideas all of a sudden."

"I've given it a thought or two."

"Why does it matter to you? I've already said that Layla is what's important."

"Because I'm never going to be the cause of a woman giving up her dream." He reached for the bottle of whiskey and cradled it in his hand.

She was silent for a moment while the thunder rumbled. "Is this about Daisy?"

"The only dream that Daisy claimed to have was being married to me." He scratched at the edge of the bottle label with his fingernail. "Whatever her real dreams were, she obviously never shared them with me." He figured it was progress that he could make the observation without feeling much of anything.

"What's your dream?"

He spread his arms. "This place."

"The Diamond-L."

"Named for my mother. The original Layla. You want me to talk about her?" He felt the label tear. "She was born here. In Wyoming."

He felt her surprise.

"Her dad—my grandfather—was a minister. Moving his family from one small town to another every few years. They died before I was born. But my mom dreamed of adventure. Of seeing more of the world than a string of tiny towns needing a preacher. Finding the end of the rainbow. And she gave it all up because she got pregnant with a baby she wasn't at all equipped to handle." He took a last burning sip of whiskey before tossing the bottle away into the dark, even though it meant a waste of perfectly good liquor. "She was an alcoholic. One night, she got behind the wheel of a car, drunk, and killed herself as well as two other people."

"Oh, Ryder." Greer's sigh was louder than her words. "How old were you?"

"Eight."

"Your father?"

"She never said who he was."

"And your aunt?"

"Adelaide didn't know who he was, either. She was the only one left to take me in. She's not my real aunt. She was my grandmother's best friend. She was there when my mother lost her mother. And she was there when I lost mine. Adelaide gave me a home." He felt a raindrop on his hand. "I asked her why once. She said it was the right thing to do."

Greer stepped close again and slid her arms around his shoulders. "The Victorian would make a good office," she whispered. "I'll consider it. Put your arms around me."

He didn't need to be told, though it was a novel enough occurrence that it appealed to him. Her waist was so slender, his fingers could span it. But as he slowly ran his hands down over the flare of her hips, he discarded the notion that he'd ever considered her too skinny for his tastes.

"If we do this, it doesn't change anything." She arched slightly when his hands drifted down over her rear. "Layla will have two parents. We'll raise her together. But the deal between us stays—"

"—business." He'd discovered the zipper on the back of her skirt and slowly drew it down. The skirt came loose and slid down her thighs. All she wore beneath was a scrap of lace.

"That's right." She angled her head and brushed her lips against his ear. "Business," she breathed.

He slid his fingers along her slender neck. Felt the pulse throbbing at the base. The way she swallowed when his fingers curled beneath her chin. He nudged at it slightly, lifting it. "You saying this is a one-and-done, Counselor?"

"I'm saying let's not call this marriage something it's not. It'll be a marriage of convenience. Pure and simple."

He lowered his head and slowly rubbed his lips across hers. Felt the softening. The parting. The invitation.

He lifted his head again. Eased his fingers behind the nape of her neck once more. "I'm not thinking too many pure thoughts at the moment."

Her breasts rose and fell, pressing against him. Retreating. "Neither am I. As long as we don't confuse this with something it's not, I don't see the problem. Just because marrying would be convenient doesn't mean it has to be sterile. It'd be a different matter if we weren't attracted to each other. But we are." Her lips were close to his, her whisper soft yet clear. "So we might as well be realistic from the start."

"Realistic. Works for me."

She took a deep breath again. Her breasts pressed against his chest and stayed there. "And…and if…*when* it stops working, when Layla's older, we'll end the deal. No fuss. No muss." She waited a beat. "As long as I'm just as much her legal parent as you. My family—*all* of my family—becomes her family. That means Grant, too."

He felt another plop of warm rain. This time on his arm. "If I agree to you adopting her, you have to agree about your own practice."

"Negotiation?"

"You told me you were good at it."

"Okay. Agreed."

The second she said the words, he closed his hands around her hips again, pulling her in tighter. She was warm. Soft. "It's going to rain."

"As far as I'm concerned, it can rain for a week." He felt her words against his lips.

He smiled slightly and pushed her away. Only a few inches. "Take off your shirt, Counselor."

She made a soft sound. He sensed more than saw her dark eyes on him. "I'd rather you take it off me."

There were invitations to ignore.

There were ones he couldn't.

His fingers brushed against her skin as he found the tiny buttons on her shirt. Impatience raged inside him, but he took his time. One button. Two. All the way down, until it took only a nudge of his fingers and the shirt fell away, too. The bra and panties she wore were as white as the shirt had been. But lacy. Stretchy. No protection at all when he tugged them off.

And then she took a full step backward, giving him enough room to push off the table and pull his shirt over his head. He unfastened his belt and jeans and shoved them down his legs.

Then she crowded close again, slipping her hand under his boxer briefs. She inhaled audibly when she closed her fingers around him. "Perfect," she breathed.

He looked up at the sky, dragging in an audible breath of his own. Another raindrop hit him square on the face. His shoulder. His back. "I should take you inside."

"I'm not sugar." She dragged his briefs down, bending her knees, going down with them, setting them aside when he stepped out of them. But she didn't stand back up. "I'm not the Wicked Witch. I won't melt from some water." Her hair brushed his knee. His thigh. And her lips...

"Maybe not," he said. Her mouth closed over him and he exhaled roughly. He slid his fingers through her hair. He couldn't help himself. She had a lot of hair. The strands were silky. Slippery. He wanted to wrap his fingers in it and hold her. His hands were actually shaking from resisting the urge. "But what you're doing feels damn—" another oath slid through his teeth "—wicked."

The air suddenly felt electric and thunder cracked.

She made a sound. Sexy. Greedy. And took him even deeper.

He let her go. Let her do as she pleased. And oh, how it pleased. For as long as he could hold out. Then a flash of soft light flickered in the distance, giving shape to the canopy of clouds. Giving shape to the woman kneeling before him.

"Enough." It was a rough order. A rough plea. He pulled away. Pulled her up. Maybe it wasn't going to be one-and-done. Maybe they'd manage a year. Two. Before convenience didn't matter to her so much and she'd want more out of life than a business deal of a marriage.

But he wanted more this time—this first time—than just *this*.

Another fat raindrop splashed on his shoulder as he drew her up to him and found her mouth with his. Found her breasts with his hands. And she was right there with him. Pressing herself against him, her nipples tight points against his palms. Her tongue mingling with his, her hands dragging up and down his spine before closing over his head.

He could feel her heart pounding as hard as his own as he lifted her against him. Her legs slid along his thighs and wrapped around his hips. And then she cried out when he slid inside her, and he froze. Because she was so tight. So small in comparison to him, and he was suddenly afraid of hurting her.

Thunder cracked overhead and the clouds finally opened up, drenching them in seconds.

Holding her ought to have been impossible. Water rained down on them, making her flesh slick. But she simply twined herself around him, holding him tightly gloved within. "Don't stop now." She sounded exultant as she dragged his mouth back to hers.

And then everything that was perfect overrode his fear.

Wet inside.

Wet outside.

And she wanted him as much as he wanted her. He backed up until he felt the table. There'd be time for bed later. Time for every other thing he could possibly imagine. He ignored the rough, splintering wood as he leaned against it and took her slight weight in his hands and thrust.

"Yes." She arched in perfect counterpoint.

Again. And again. And again. He wanted to go on and on and on, but he knew he wouldn't last. Not with the way he could feel her quickening. Tightening. Shuddering.

Lightning flashed.

Her head dropped back but she clung to him. "Yes!"

The rain fell and the world shrank down to this one woman in his arms.

And he let himself go.

"Yessssss."

Chapter Ten

"Yes. I do."

Judge Stokes smiled at Ryder and turned to Greer to repeat the vow. "And will you, Greer Templeton, take this man, Ryder Wilson, to be your lawfully wedded husband? To have and to hold, in sickness and in health, for richer or for poorer? Forsaking all others and keeping only to him?"

It was vaguely surreal, standing there in Judge Stokes's chambers.

But there was nothing surreal about Greer's answer. Since she'd made the decision to marry Ryder, she hadn't suffered any second thoughts. "Yes," she said just as clearly as he had. "I do."

The judge smiled benevolently at them. With his white hair and beard, and his tendency toward wearing red shirts, he looked a bit like Santa Claus. Even though it was only the end of August. "Then—" he closed his small black book "—by the authority vested in me by the State of Wyoming, and with a great deal of personal delight I might add, I declare you to be husband and wife." He spread his hands. "Congratulations. You may kiss your bride."

Ryder, looking uncommonly urbane in a dark gray suit with a lighter gray striped tie knotted around his neck, turned to her. He took her hands and his thumb brushed over the narrow platinum band he'd given her. His thick hair was brushed back from his face. There was no hatband mark in evidence. His jaw was clean-shaven and his blue eyes were brilliant. When he leaned down, instead of his usual scent of hay or grass or fresh open air, he smelled faintly woodsy. Exotic.

He was entirely *un*-rancherly.

And for the first time in thirty-six hours—since the night she'd gone to his house and she'd thrown herself, mind and body, into his marriage plan—she felt a wrinkle of unease.

How well did she really know this man to whom she'd just promised herself? This rancher who had a beautiful gray suit that looked as if it had been custom tailored just sitting around in his closet?

Was it a leftover from his Vegas wedding to Daisy?

It was just a suit, she reminded herself. She'd pulled her dress from her closet, too.

Then his eyes met hers, and it felt as though he knew exactly how she was feeling.

"We can do this," he murmured. Low. For her ears only.

She gave a tiny nod.

The faint lines beside his eyes crinkled slightly and his dimple appeared. Then his lips brushed slowly, lightly across hers.

It was barely a kiss. Yet it was still enough to make her feel warm way down inside.

But there was no time to dwell on it, because the judge's wife and his usual clerk, Sue, who were acting as their witnesses, had started clapping. Layla, dressed in a ruffled yellow jumper, jabbered and clapped her hands, too. Sue had insisted on holding her during the ceremony.

"Just lovely," Mrs. Stokes said. "So romantic."

Greer bit back a spurt of amusement that she knew Ryder felt, as well, and relaxed even more.

They were of one mind when it came to that particular element of marriage. They could rock each other's socks off in the bedroom while Layla slept. Or on a picnic table in the rain. Or in his shower that ought to have been too cramped, but wasn't. All of which they'd done in the span of a mere day.

But this legal union of theirs wasn't about romance. It was because of Layla, and for no other reason.

"If I could get your signatures here?" Sue pointed to the marriage license they'd obtained just that morning from the county clerk's office. She evaded Layla's grab for the pen and handed it to Ryder.

He signed the document and handed the pen to Greer before lifting Layla out of Sue's arms. "Thanks."

"My pleasure. It's just so exciting to see a happy ending for all of you."

Greer finished signing her name next to Ryder's and she capped the pen before handing it back. "Thanks, Sue."

"I still can't believe you did this without your family, though. They're going to be so surprised."

"We didn't want anything or anyone—not even family—delaying it," Greer explained smoothly.

"That's how it is, isn't it?" Sue's eyes sparkled. "When you know you absolutely can't spend one more minute without committing to the person you love?"

"It was like that for us, wasn't it, Horvald?" Mrs. Stokes commented as she signed the witness line.

It was easier to let them think that than to tell them the truth. That Greer hadn't wanted to give her family a chance to talk her out of it. Which they would surely have done, no matter how much they, too, loved Layla.

Ryder had disagreed with her. Said they should wait, at least long enough to tell her family. It wasn't about seeking approval or blessings. It was about respecting them enough to give them the truth.

Greer had prevailed, though. They'd made the decision. If they'd waited, they'd have had to wait through Labor Day holiday weekend to be married. Meaning she'd also have to wait four more days to file the petition to adopt Layla.

Sue took up the pen and signed after Mrs. Stokes. Then the court clerk set the document on the judge's desk. "Congratulations again." Sue linked her arm through Mrs. Stokes's and the two of them left the judge's chambers.

"All right." The judge signed the license with a flourish after they'd gone. "I guess I can trust you to turn that in to the recorder's office." He slid the paperwork into its envelope and handed it to Greer. "And now for your next item of business."

He moved another document to the center of his desk. "I've reviewed your petition for Layla's adoption and everything is in order." As he spoke, he signed his name and then he flipped open an enormous date book in which, Greer knew, he kept all of his case schedules. It didn't matter that Sue managed his official calendar by more efficient—namely computerized—methods. Horvald Stokes still liked his old-fashioned calendar. And it was legend how he'd never once made a scheduling mistake.

He flipped through it, studying and muttering to himself under his breath. Then he went back a few pages. Then forward again. And finally he stopped. "Hearing will be November 19." He made the notation in his book and then on the petition. "That's before Thanksgiving."

For the first time that day, Greer's smile felt shaky. Becoming Layla's mother was the crux of the matter, the reason they were there at all. When they were done, Layla would have a father and a mother. The hearing in November would be little more than a formality before Judge Stokes could sign the final decree. "Sounds perfect to me, Your Honor."

"It really is my genuine pleasure." He stood and pulled one of the black robes off the coat stand behind his desk and slipped his arms into the voluminous sleeves. "Layla had a rocky start through no fault of her own. I'm more than pleased that things have resolved themselves in this manner."

A manner that Greer never would have imagined six months ago.

Her throat felt tight. "Thank you again for fitting us into your schedule today."

He winked. "Fifteen minutes for a good cause."

Sue returned then and gathered up both the thick, stapled document that he'd signed and his oversize date book. "Both parties for your next case are present, Judge Stokes, whenever you're ready."

He nodded and she went through the doorway that Greer knew led directly from his chambers into his courtroom. The fact that he zipped up his robe before he headed toward the door meant he was prepared to get straight to business. "Will we be seeing you at the county picnic this weekend?"

Greer moistened her lips and adjusted the band of black velvet fabric around her waist. By itself, her knee-length ivory cotton sundress had seemed a little too casual to wear to her own wedding. Marriage of convenience or not. After seeing Ryder's suit, she was glad she'd made her outfit a bit more formal by adding the wide black belt. The black touches were repeated in the jet clip she'd pinned into her chignon and her black suede pumps.

"I'm afraid not. I've left the public defender's office." She'd turned in her notice to Michael the day before. He'd been livid and told her she needn't serve out the two weeks. Considering the choice he'd given her, she felt like she was the one who had a right to be livid. "I'm cleaning out my desk when we're finished here, actually."

The judge was clearly surprised. "You're not leaving the practice of law, I hope. You're an incredibly valuable part of the legal community, Greer."

The praise was as unexpected as it was touching and she didn't know quite what to say.

"She's opening her own firm," Ryder said.

Greer understood why it was so important to Ryder, even though, in her own mind, it was a much hazier proposition.

The judge's expression cleared. "Good for you! I look forward to you really spreading your wings." His smile broadened. "And one day, Mrs. Wilson," he said, winking, "I'll expect to see you on the bench." He pulled open the door and went into his courtroom.

Which left Greer alone with Ryder.

Her husband.

They'd married so quickly she hadn't even thought whether she was going to take his name. Mrs. Wilson...

Layla was yanking on his tie, jabbering away in her sweet little-girl babble, and Greer pushed away the thought.

"That went smoothly," she said. "Don't you think?"

"It was smooth enough." He tugged at his tie, but Layla looked ready to do battle over it. "I should have said before—you look real pretty."

She dashed her hand quickly down the skirt of her dress, suddenly feeling self-conscious. "I guess the dress did the job. It's ancient. Back from law school days. You...you look very nice, too." She snatched up the small black clutch she'd brought with her, along with the entirely unexpected nosegay of fresh lavender stalks wrapped in gray ribbon that he'd given her. "I guess you must subscribe to the theory that every man should have a decent suit in his closet."

His dimple appeared. "I was afraid it would be a little tight. Last time I put it on was at least five years ago." He looked at Layla, chuckling. "Gonna need a new tie now, though."

So. *Not* the suit from his Vegas wedding.

She lifted the bouquet and inhaled the soothing fragrance. "Looks like it fits you just fine," she managed, and led the way out of the judge's office.

As she clutched the lavender, she noticed how foreign the shining ring felt on her wedding finger. It was a little too loose.

She honestly wasn't sure what had surprised her more.

The flowers or the ring.

He'd chosen both. She couldn't imagine when he'd had the time.

She reminded herself that the ring would simply take some getting used to. As would chasing after Layla instead of chasing clients right here among these courtrooms every day.

Simple enough.

They'd reached the wide central staircase. Her high heels clicked on the marble as she started down. It was only ten in the morning. But it was a Friday, which meant that most of the courtrooms weren't in use and the building was pretty empty.

The recorder's office on the first floor was open every weekday, though, and they stopped there to turn in their signed wedding license.

"Don't forget this." The girl working behind the counter was new. She didn't know Greer. She was holding out the certificate portion of the wedding license. Though it was nothing more than a souvenir, the reality suddenly sank in.

Greer's head swam. She took the certificate, feeling embarrassed by the way her fingers visibly trembled. "Thank you." She went to tuck the folded paper in her clutch, but the thick parchment slid out of her grasp. She knelt down to grab it.

When she rose, she swayed.

Ryder's hand closed over her elbow, steadying her. "When's the last time you ate?"

"Yesterday evening." She'd spent the night before at home, wrapping up the details of her resignation. Contacting her former clients and letting them know that she wasn't abandoning them, even though it felt like it. That someone else from her office would be taking good care of them.

She'd fallen asleep in the middle of making case file notes for the attorney who would come after her.

When she'd woken up, she had a crease in her cheek from the folders and a stiff neck from sleeping with her head on her desk. She still felt a little stiff now.

"Let's get you fed, then," he said, caressing her neck, his fingertips somehow magically discerning the tight spots.

"After I clean out my office."

His hand closed around her shoulders. "Your office can wait." Holding her in one arm and Layla in the other, he headed toward the courthouse exit.

"But—"

He didn't slow his long, measured strides. "What's left that matters, Greer? You told me about the clock."

"I don't know," she admitted. "I have stuff there still."

"Paper clips?" They'd reached the courthouse doors and he let go of her to hold one open. "Face it, Counselor. If anything else had truly mattered, you'd have taken it the same time you took the clock."

She hated to admit he was right. "I need to at least drop off the box of files I still have."

"Fine." When they stepped outside, they were greeted by clear blue skies. The heat had broken a little. "*After* you've eaten."

"Is this what being married to you is going to be like? You telling me what's what?" She stopped on the courthouse steps, tucking her clutch beneath her arm and pointing her lavender bouquet at him. Layla was playing with his ear and yanking on his tie as though it was a rein.

"It is when I know I'm right." He tried to smooth his

tie; the attempt seemed futile. He took Greer's hand in his and they began to descend the courthouse steps.

That's when she saw them.

Her parents. Vivian. Her brother and sisters. Their husbands. All of them were there. Even Rosalind, who hadn't visited Braden in years.

Greer yanked her hand from Ryder's. "What did you do?"

"You want Layla to be part of your family. So." He took her hand again, firmly, and nodded toward the not-so-small crowd assembled at the bottom of the stairs. "I called them. Last time I got married it was supposedly for the right reasons. We eloped. Never told a soul until after the fact. And you know how that turned out. So I'm doing things differently this time. I'm not going to pretend we're living in a vacuum. We can't shut out the people who care about us the most." He looked into her eyes, his expression intense. "They're gonna say we didn't marry for the right reasons but I don't care. Our reasons are our own. As long as you and I are on the same page, we're good." He squeezed her hand. "We are good," he repeated. "*Showing* them is the only way they'll get on board."

She moistened her lips. "I'm not so sure I like it when you're right."

He smiled faintly. "You'll get used to it in time."

A fine idea in theory. So why did it make her feel increasingly disconcerted?

Adjustments, Greer.

She tugged his tie away from Layla and smoothed it down the front of his hard chest. Her fingers wanted to linger. Her common sense insisted otherwise. "I guess now I don't have to keep running scenarios in my mind about how to tell my parents."

His dimple appeared. "There you go."

"Have you told Adelaide?"

He smiled slightly. "Who do you think reminded me that a bride should have flowers on her wedding day?"

And just like that, her chest felt tight all over again. "You called my family, but will she come, too?"

He shook his head. "She doesn't travel anymore, remember?"

"Has she met Layla?"

"I had sort of figured I'd visit for Christmas. A few days. Can't spare a lot of time away from the ranch." He was silent for a moment. "We could go. You know. As a family."

"That sounds nice." She lifted her small bouquet and inhaled the lovely, calming scent, though it wasn't quite enough to soothe away the disconcerting butterflies flitting around inside her. "Did she tell you to choose fresh lavender, too?"

"Didn't need to. They were the only flowers that seemed fitting for a woman who lives in a house like yours."

"Lived," she corrected, and looked down at her family. "Well. We can't stand here forever, I suppose. At least they're smiling."

"Yep." He muttered an oath when Layla yanked his tie again. "You're gonna strangle me with it, aren't you, Short-Stuff?"

"I'll take her." Greer handed him her clutch and bouquet, lifted Layla out of his arms and propped her on her hip. Then she took back her bouquet.

He gave her clutch a wry look, then slid it into his pocket. "Ready?"

She nodded.

And they continued down the stairs.

They'd barely made it to the bottom before a collective command came for them to stop where they were. Out came a half dozen cell phones to take their pictures. But then, clearly too excited to wait a second longer, Meredith darted up to greet them, throwing her arms around Greer and Layla, engulfing them in her familiar, uniquely Meredith fragrance.

"Oh, my darlings," she cried, and somehow Greer managed to lose Layla to Meredith in the embrace. But then her mom always had been sly that way. She kissed the baby's face. "You've grown so much! And you!" Meredith dragged Ryder's head down and gave him a smacking kiss on the cheek before he had a hope in heaven of avoiding it. He gave Greer a vaguely startled look. "I knew you were a special man," Meredith was saying, "and when you called us last night, I—"

"Last night!" Greer gave him a look.

"You were home doing your thing. I was doing mine."

Meredith laced her free arm through Ryder's and pulled him the rest of the way down the steps. Since his hand was locked onto Greer's, that meant she went, too, and they didn't stop until they came up against her father's stalwart body. Carter's service in the military might have ended decades earlier, before Greer, Ali and Maddie were even an idea, but he still carried himself as though he wore a uniform and a chest full of medals.

He and Ryder were about the same height. But Ryder's brawny build, hidden so spectacularly beneath his tailored suit, made him seem even larger than her dad.

The men were eyeing each other. Taking measure.

Predictably, her dad went on the offensive. "Guess you didn't figure you needed to call and get permission to marry my daughter before you just did it."

"Dad! I don't need—" Greer broke off when he lifted his hand. She looked to her mother. "Mom."

Meredith just gave her an amused look. She was as unconventional as her husband was conventional, and yet together, they were the perfect couple.

"If I'd done that, and Greer had found out, I'm pretty sure she wouldn't be standing here this morning with my ring on her finger," Ryder replied easily.

"Darn right," Greer started, only to break off again when her dad gave her the same silencing look he'd given all of them growing up.

"The fact that you didn't call for permission makes me feel you know my girl pretty well. The fact that you let us know so we could be here this morning makes me think you've got a few good brain cells."

"Dad!"

"But the fact that my girl chose you, well, that says a lot, too." He looked over at Greer's sisters. "I didn't raise any of my daughters to choose badly. So." He stuck out his hand. "Welcome to the family, son."

It was ridiculous, but Greer's eyes stung a little as her father shook Ryder's hand.

After that, it was pretty much a free-for-all. She wasn't sure if they would have made it from the court-house steps to Josephine's diner if Ryder hadn't taken charge and made it happen. There was a general jostling for seats and the usual chaos of menus and ordering for such a large party, but the diner was half-empty and nobody else there seemed to mind.

Greer now had stiff competition for Layla's attention. Between Ali and Maddie and her mother fawning, Layla was wholly and delightedly occupied. Linc, with tiny Liam sleeping against his shoulder, was holding his own in a debate about politics with Vivian and Hayley's husband, Seth, who had tiny Keely sleeping against his shoulder. Hayley was trying in vain to change the subject before Carter blew a gasket and jumped into the lively exchange. At the other end of the tables, Rosalind and Archer were giving each other the same fulminating glares they'd always exchanged growing up. Which left Grant. Sitting on the other side of Ryder.

Greer considered offering to switch seats with Ryder, but decided not to. Instead, she just stood up from her own chair and crouched a little, wedging herself in the narrow space between them. A human buffer between her new husband and his former brother-in-law.

The looks she earned from both of them were nearly identical.

She wanted to point that out but knew better. Among her relatives, there was already the likely explosion over politics before too long. She didn't want to chance adding more combustible material because of Ryder's and Grant's mutual grudges.

The fact that Grant had accompanied Ali was promising as far as Greer was concerned, and she gave him a bright smile. "Ali tells me you're working on something new. I think that's great. How's it coming?"

"Fair."

She looked from him to Ryder. Grant's hair was blacker than Ryder's, his blue eyes lighter. Grant had a swimmer's build. Ryder, a linebacker's. Grant was an author who'd already made a fortune several times over with his military thrillers. Ryder was a rancher, whose resources were considerably more modest. They couldn't be more different.

Their only common ground was Layla and the mother who'd abandoned her.

"Ryder was in the army," she said brightly. She rested her hand on his shoulder. "How long were you in?"

He knew what she was trying to do. She could tell. "Four years. Right outta high school."

"And you, Grant?" She glanced at Ryder again. "He served in the air force. That's how he started writing the CCT Rules series. From his experiences there." She looked from Ryder's face to Grant's. "You put in a fair amount of time, didn't—"

"Yoohoo!" The loud greeting came from across the diner and Greer automatically glanced over. Ryder, on the other hand, shoved back his seat with an exclamation and strode toward the tall, gangly woman who'd entered the restaurant.

She had hair dyed black, and turquoise dripping from her ears and her neck and surrounding nearly every finger. A designer dog carrier hung from one skinny shoulder and Greer could hear the yapping of a dog.

There was no question in Greer's mind who the woman was when Ryder swung her right off her feet in a boisterous hug.

No matter what he'd said, Adelaide had still come.

Across the table, Vivian suddenly stood. She was staring at the woman, too. "Oh, my word! That's Adelaide Arians."

"Who the hell's Adelaide Arians?" Grant asked.

"She raised Ryder." Greer had to push the words through the ache in her throat. Across the restaurant, Ryder had set Adelaide back on her feet and she'd handed him something. As Greer watched, he shook his head as if refusing, but then he looked her way and seemed to still.

"She's only considered one of the seminal artists of our age," Vivian was saying as if it were a fact any person should know. "Her work hangs in the Museum of Modern Art! Wyoming and *culture* are simply two different universes," she huffed. "Sometimes I wonder why I bothered coming here." She tugged at the sleeves of her Chanel suit, and the diamonds on her fingers winked.

"Spoken like the snob you are," Carter observed acidly.

"Dad," Hayley started to caution. She was always trying to be the peacemaker between their father and his mother.

"The apple doesn't fall far from the tree, son." Vivian spoke right over her. "You just save your judgment for *me*."

"You are *impossible*!" At the other end of the table, Rosalind had risen from her seat and was glaring at Archer. In turn, he wore the goading expression he always had around her. "Just crawl back under your rock!" Rosalind was practically shrieking.

Liam and Keely were no longer sleeping like little angels against their daddies' shoulders. They both were crying. Which had their mamas jostling to get out of their chairs to resolve the situation.

Layla was banging her sippy cup against the table and joyfully knocking down the towers of plastic creamer containers that Meredith built for her.

And there was Ryder, drawing his aunt up to their table, which had suddenly lost its collective mind. Whatever his aunt had given him was no longer in evidence.

"And this must be her." Adelaide had an unexpectedly booming voice that carried over the bedlam. She gave Greer an appraising look, but there was a glint of humor in her heavily made-up eyes and a smile on her deeply red lips that helped calm the sudden butterflies inside Greer's stomach. "I've got to say, Ryder my boy, your taste has sure improved since that last one."

Grant shoved his chair back and stood. He tossed down his napkin and walked out of the restaurant.

"Oh, dear." Adelaide's voice could have filled an auditorium without need for a microphone. She set the dog carrier on the chair he'd abandoned. "Did I say something wrong?"

Ryder looked at Greer.

She exhaled. "So. Not everything can go as smoothly as it did with the judge."

He frowned. But the lines beside his eyes crinkled slightly and his dimple came out of hiding.

Greer held out her hand toward his aunt. "I'm very pleased to meet you, Ms. Arians. I'm Greer."

"Call me Adelaide," she boomed, and jerked Greer into a nearly bone-crushing hug. "Oh, yes, indeed, the next few months are going to be *great fun*!"

She let go of Greer so suddenly, she had to catch her balance. "You're going to stay for a while, then?"

"Right through Christmas, sugar pie." Adelaide adjusted the eye-popping tie-dyed scarf she wore around her wrinkled neck. "Now where's the little peanut at the center of all these goings-on? Oh, there you are." She strode around the table. "Cute little thing!"

Layla's eyes went round as saucers as she stared warily up at the tall, loud Adelaide. She banged her cup a few times, but without her usual emphatic enthusiasm. Then she opened her mouth and wailed.

Adelaide whipped one of her chunky rings off a finger and waved it in front of Layla. The distraction worked enough to have Layla grabbing the bauble, but not enough to silence her plaintive howling. Adelaide laughed delightedly. "Little thing already knows what she likes and doesn't like!"

"She's gonna put that ring in her mouth," Ryder warned.

"And why not? You used to do that when you were a little mite, too. Stone's the size of a golf ball. She's not gonna choke on it!" She stood there, hands on her skinny hips, and grinned down at Layla.

Greer's arm brushed Ryder's. She was curious about what Adelaide had given him, but figured if he wanted to mention it, he would. Meanwhile, the cacophony around them was only increasing, made worse by the dog's shrill yipping from inside the carrier. She had to raise her voice. "Still think the one-big-family thing is going to be all it's cracked up to be?"

He dropped his arm around her shoulder. "Time'll tell, Counselor. Time'll tell."

Chapter Eleven

". . . Happy birthday, dear Layla, happy birthday to you!"

While their party guests finished singing, Greer set the cake she'd gotten from Tabby Clay in front of Layla. It was shaped like an enormous white cupcake with huge swirls of pink frosting on top, and had a single oversize white candle.

"No, no, no," Layla chanted as she looked at the confection facing her. It had become her favorite word of late. Along with "Dadda" and "bye-bye" and "sus-suh," which Greer had figured out was her version of "Short-Stuff." She even had a name for Brutus and Adelaide.

But there had been no more instances of "mama," inadvertent or otherwise.

"Yes, yes, yes," Greer told her, and shooed Brutus away so she could scoot Layla's chair with its booster seat closer to the table. "It's the prettiest cake for the prettiest girl."

"You guys need to sit next to her," Maddie ordered, gesturing at Ryder. "I want a picture of the three of you together." She had Liam strapped to her chest in a fabric carrier and a camera in her hand.

It was October 27.

And though they'd planned to have Layla's first birthday party outdoors, an early snow had put paid to the notion. Which was why the family was instead crowding around the dinner table inside.

"So we don't really know for sure this is her birthday?" Even after two months with them, Adelaide's voice could still reach the back row of an auditorium.

Greer, sitting down on one side of Layla, looked over at Ryder, who'd pulled out the chair on the other side.

He returned her wry look. "No, we don't know for sure," he told his aunt, not for the first time, "but since we could never find out exactly where or when she was born, it's as close as we can determine. So this is what we've chosen."

"You know it was your grandmother's birthday, too!" Adelaide now had her camera out. But since she was just as likely to take a photo of a dust mote that caught her interest as she was to capture Layla's expression when she smashed her hands into the cake, Greer was glad Maddie was there with the fancy digital camera that Linc had gotten after Liam's birth.

Ryder caught Greer's eye above Layla and winked. He hadn't shaved in the last few days, and Greer hadn't quite decided whether she liked the stubbled look or not. "I know it was, Adelaide," he said patiently.

"Don't you think it'll be confusing if you ever find out where and when she really *was* born?"

"It won't really matter," Meredith answered before they could. She slipped closer to the table, snapping off pictures with her cell phone while skillfully managing not to trip over Brutus. "Layla's going to have a brand-new birth certificate once the adoption's final."

Ryder's hand went to the back of Layla's chair, and his fingers came close to touching Greer's.

But didn't.

"You going to let my niece demolish that cake, or what?" That came from Grant, who was leaning against the couch with Ali beside him.

It might have been two months since he'd walked out on Greer and Ryder's wedding breakfast, but there had been little sign of softening between Ryder and him. The two men were grudgingly polite whenever there was a family event, like today, but that was as far as it went.

Frankly, it made Greer want to smack their two stubborn heads together. But generally, she didn't have time to worry about it too much. Not with taking care of Layla, who was walking now and getting into everything. It was almost impossible to take the toddler with her to the Victorian, where she was trying to supervise the work of the two-man crew Ryder had found. Luckily, Meredith had come to the rescue. She never missed an opportunity to babysit. She'd started on the day of the wedding, insisting that Ryder and Greer should have a proper wedding night.

What Ryder and Greer had had was an awkward wedding night spent sleeping on opposite sides of his wide bed. As if their marathon of lovemaking the night of the rainstorm had never occurred.

She'd never believed that night would be a one-and-done, as he put it. Yet it basically was. Sure, they'd indulged themselves several times that night. So was it a one-and-done or three-and-done? What was the difference?

There had been no repeat performance.

"Of course she's going to demolish her cake," she assured Grant, blocking the memories as she drew it a little closer to Layla. "This is all yours, sweetie." She pulled one of Layla's fingers through the icing and caught it in her mouth, sucking it off noisily. It was more whipped cream than frosting. "Yum yum."

"Num!" Layla lovingly patted Greer's face. Her green eyes were full of devotion. "Nummy."

Feeling like her heart would burst, Greer pressed a kiss to their toddler's palm. She couldn't keep herself from looking up at Ryder.

He was grinning; he looked dark and piratical with his short, stubbly beard. "Nummy, indeed."

She tried to ignore the heat shimmering through her, but it was futile.

Instead, she turned her focus back to Layla. Camera shutters clicked all around them as she suddenly launched herself toward her cake, squealing with pure, excited delight, sending Brutus into a frenzy of yipping.

It was, Greer decided, a very perfect first birthday for their little girl.

Eventually, though, it was time to clean up the mess.

Not surprisingly, at that exact moment, everyone conveniently found something else to do.

Vivian and Meredith took off in Vivian's ostentatious Rolls-Royce; heaven only knew where or for what purpose. Her grandmother was a terrible driver, but as long as Vivian didn't run her car over something or someone, Greer wasn't going to worry about it. Maddie and Ali were upstairs, giving Layla and Liam a bath. And all of the men, along with Adelaide and the dog, were out checking the cows Ryder had gathered in the big pasture over the last few weeks.

With the dishwasher already full, Greer set herself to the enormous stack of dishes still waiting on the counter and in the sink. She moved them aside, fit the stopper in the drain, squirted dish soap under the running water and got to work.

Overhead, she could hear laughter from the bath and she smiled to herself.

It hadn't been a bad two months since she and Ryder signed their name on that marriage certificate. Moments like this—even elbow-deep in dish water and dirty dishes—were pretty sweet. Ryder had been able to catch up on his nonstop chores and Greer hadn't even missed the PD's office too badly. Particularly once the scandal broke that Michael Towers really was sleeping with their most notorious client, Stormy Santiago. From what Greer had been hearing, nobody from the office was escaping entirely unscathed. There were rumors that a new supervising attorney was going to be brought in from Cheyenne.

Most important of all, though, Layla was thriving.

Greer let out a long breath and turned on the tap to rinse the stockpot she'd just washed.

"That's a big sigh."

She startled, looking over to see Grant closing the kitchen door. "Decide one cow looks pretty much like the next?" she asked.

A smile touched his aquamarine-colored eyes. "Something like that."

She hesitated, wanting to say something, but not knowing what. Instead, she turned back to the stockpot and tipped it upside down on the towel she'd spread on the counter for the clean dishes. "Ali's upstairs. I'm sure Layla and Liam have both had plenty of time in the tub by now."

He didn't head upstairs to retrieve his wife, though. He stopped next to Greer, picked up one of the towels from the pile she'd pulled from the drawer and lifted the stockpot.

"Thanks."

"That was good chili you made. Reminded me of my mom's cooking."

She shoved her hands back into the water. The suds were all but gone. "Thank Adelaide. She supervised. On top of all the other stuff she's done, she wrote a cookbook more than twenty years ago. There are a few used copies still out there. Selling for a ridiculous amount of money online."

"She's something, that aunt of his." He didn't look at her as he ran the towel over the pot. "Whatever comes into her head seems to go right out her mouth."

"At broadcast decibels," Greer added wryly. "I thought at first that maybe she was hard of hearing, but she's not. I think she could hear a pin drop from a mile away. It's just her way."

"Ali says you must be pretty cozy here, all three of you. There are only two bedrooms?"

"Yeah." She rinsed the last pot and handed it to him, then let out the water so she could start with fresh. She had all of the glassware yet to wash. "We've got Layla's crib in with us." More often than not, the toddler ended up in bed with them, usually sprawled sideways and somehow taking up the lion's share of the mattress. Fortunately, Ryder had drawn the line at Brutus coming into the room. Adelaide's rotund pug seemed to think he owned the place now and he'd have been up with them for sure.

"I'm surprised Adelaide didn't take up Vivian's offer to stay with her in Weaver. She's got a lot more space."

"Ryder would sleep on the floor before he'd let Adelaide stay somewhere else. I know she's a bit of a character, but she means a great deal to him. Her coming here at all is major. She doesn't travel." She chanced a quick glance at Grant's profile as she stoppered the sink again and waited for it to fill once more. She knew he'd had a troubled early childhood until he'd been adopted as an adolescent by the same family who'd adopted his sister. "He lost his mother when he was young, too."

"Ali told me."

She turned off the faucet and set a few glasses in the water. "Oh, stuff it," she said under her breath, and angled sideways to look straight at him. "He blames himself, too, Grant. For what happened. Daisy, Karen, whatever name she went by, she was his *wife*. She didn't turn to him any more than she turned to you when she chose to leave her baby with someone else."

He cleared his throat. His jaw looked tight. "I was her big brother a lot longer than she was his wife," he said in a low voice.

"So that means his self-blame is misdemeanor level but yours is felony grade?" She shook her head. "It doesn't work that way, Grant. You must know that. Time is not the measure. You've been married less than a year to my sister. If—God forbid—something happened to her, would your loss be less devastating than mine or Maddie's? We shared our mother's womb."

Heedless of the water still on her hands, she closed her fingers over his arm. "You and Ryder knew your sister in different ways. She didn't tell you everything. She certainly didn't tell him everything. She married him entirely under false pretenses. Whatever your childhoods were like, as an adult, Daisy did some things that were terribly wrong. I get that she was troubled. I do. But she abandoned her child when she had other options she could have taken! Maybe she regretted it but didn't know how to make it right before it was too late. I know that's what Ali says you believe. And maybe she didn't regret what she'd done at all. Regardless, what she did was what *she* did. What she did not do, *she* did not do. Neither you nor Ryder was her keeper. And you're both losing out, because out of all the people Layla has in her life, the two of you were the ones closest to her real mother!"

Greer's eyes were suddenly burning. "I'm adopting your niece. I don't see how I can possibly love her more than I already do. We can give her an official birthday and a new birth certificate. But one day Layla is going to want to know about her biological mother. Who else is going to be able to give her the answers she needs besides you and Ryder? Seems to me that would be a lot easier if the two of you would stop acting like adversaries and start acting like what you are! Two men who cared deeply for the same woman who deeply hurt you both!"

She huffed out a breath and turned to plunge her hands back in the suds. "I'm sorry." The glasses clinked as she grabbed one and started scrubbing it with her dishrag. "I'm sure Ali won't appreciate me sticking my nose into your business."

"As you've just eloquently put it, Karen wasn't only my business." He gently pulled the glass away from her furious scrubbing. "That's quite a closing argument you give." His hand lingered on the glistening glass after he'd rinsed it and turned it upside down onto the cloth. "I just wish things had been different," he said after a moment.

"I'm sure you do." Her eyes were still burning. She couldn't bring herself to say that she wished things had been different, too.

Because if they were different, she believed Ryder would still be with Daisy. Because that was the kind of man he was.

The kind of man who did what was right.

Her stomach suddenly churning, she pulled her hands from the water and hastily dried them. "I'm just going to run up and see what's going on with bath time. The babies must be prunes by now." She hurried out of the kitchen, but instead of heading up the stairs, she bolted for the bathroom behind them and slammed the door shut. She barely made it to the commode in time to lose all of the dinner she'd eaten.

Afterward, feeling breathless and weak, she just sat there on the wood-tiled floor, her head resting against the wall.

It had been two months since she and Ryder had stood in front of Judge Stokes and repeated those simple vows.

It had also been two months since she'd had a period. And this was the fourth time in as many days that she'd lost her cookies after supper.

That little implant in her arm had proven itself to truly be pointless.

She hadn't taken a test. But she knew the truth, anyway.

She was pregnant.

* * *

The house had been quiet for hours since the party when Ryder quietly stepped into the dark bedroom and slid the heavy door shut.

He didn't need a light to see. The moonlight shining through the windows gave him plenty.

He expected to see Layla's crib empty. But there was a bump in one corner: her diapered fanny sticking up in the air.

There was also a bump visible on the far edge of the bed. The sheet and blanket were pulled up high, only leaving visible Greer's gleaming brown hair spread out against the stark white pillow.

He turned away from the sight and exchanged his flannel shirt and jeans for the ragged sweatpants that he'd taken to wearing to bed ever since he'd gotten himself a wife.

The irony wasn't lost on him.

He could say he'd gotten into the habit because his aunt was right there under their roof, snoring away in the second bedroom. He could say it was because they had a toddler in the room.

He could say it.

Couldn't make himself believe it.

He went into the bathroom and quietly closed the door before turning on the light. He brushed his teeth and when he was finished, rubbed his hand down his unshaven jaw. The beard was part laziness, part convenience. It helped keep his face warmer when he was out on horseback gathering cows and the wind was cold and whipping over him.

Mostly, though, it was just his way of being able to face himself in the mirror every morning.

He tossed the soft, plush hand towel over the hook

next to the sink. Somewhere along the way since he'd married Greer, things like threadbare towels and wrinkled bedding had been replaced by thick terry cloth and smooth, crisp sheets. There were clean clothes in his drawers and sprigs of fresh flowers stuck inside glass jars on the dinner table. And though Greer claimed not to be much of a cook, Layla had learned there were good things to eat besides Cow Pie Surprise. Greer hadn't just kept to the inside of the house, either. The picnic table he'd intended to sand and repaint had gotten sanded, all right. Just not by him. And the daisies he'd thought to cover with red paint, she'd sealed with shellac instead.

Greer's mark was everywhere. Even when it meant preserving something he hadn't really cared to preserve.

He went back into the bedroom and lowered himself to his edge of the bed.

It had been two months of nights lying on his side, one pillow jammed under his neck. Watching her in the moonlight as she slept on the other edge.

As always, she wore striped pajamas. The kind with the buttoned top and the pull-on pants. She had them in yellow. And blue. And red and purple and pink.

The few months that Daisy had been there, she'd worn slippery satiny lace things or nothing at all. The bed he'd had then had been smaller. There hadn't been so much space between them.

He'd gotten rid of the bed.

Gotten rid of the slippery satiny lace things, along with every other item she'd left behind, except the picnic table. And he'd only kept that because it was practical.

He'd never figured striped two-piece pajamas were a particularly sexy thing to wear to bed.

Until he'd spent two months of nights thinking about

reaching across the great divide to unbutton that buttoned top. To slide those pull-on pants off.

Thoughts like that tended to make a long night even longer. So he'd started earlier in the morning with chores. Gone later at night before finishing.

Every square foot of his ranch was benefiting from the extra hours of attention.

Except for the 150 square feet right here in his own bedroom.

He could have made things easier on himself. Could have refrained from insisting Adelaide stay with them even though she'd clearly been interested in taking Vivian up on her offer to stay at her place. The two women couldn't be more different; the one thing they had in common was that they both were uniquely eccentric. Yet they'd hit it off. Ryder knew that big house Vivian had built on the edge of Weaver had more than enough space for a half dozen Adelaides and their pain-in-the-butt pugs.

Yeah, Ryder could have let Adelaide accept Vivian's invitation. If he had, Layla's crib wouldn't be blocking half his dresser drawers. He wouldn't be waking up six nights out of seven to her toddler feet kicking him as she rolled around in her sleep, unfettered in the space between Ryder's edge of the bed and Greer's because she wasn't even sleeping in her crib.

It was his own fault.

The night of their courtroom wedding, he should have pulled Greer across the mattress. Should have met her halfway.

He should have started as he meant to continue. Should have given her his grandmother's wedding ring that Adelaide had produced when she'd shown up so unexpectedly on their wedding day. Should have made love with her on their wedding night.

But he hadn't. And he was damned if he knew why.

The ring was sitting in its box inside the dresser half-blocked by Layla's crib.

And here they were.

As far apart as humanly possible on a king-size bed.

He lifted his head, rebunched the pillow and turned to face the saddle propped on the saddletree. If he moved the damn thing to the tack room where it belonged, there'd be room for the crib there instead.

But he was proud of that saddle. He'd won it at the National Finals the last year he'd competed. The same year he'd won the money that he'd kept so carefully in savings because ranching was never a sure thing and he'd wanted to be certain he had enough to carry him when times were lean.

The money that he was dipping into now just to make sure his wife from the other edge of the bed had a place to hang her legal shingle that didn't have rotting floorboards and dicey electrical wiring.

Two minutes later, cursing inside his head, he turned over again to stare at his sleeping wife's back.

Only she'd turned, too.

And she wasn't asleep.

And so there they lay. Facing each other across the great divide. Her eyes were dark pools of mystery.

Finally, she whispered, "What are you thinking?"

He cast around for something to say. "It was a nice party."

"Mm." She shifted a little. "Even after Brutus jumped on the counter to eat the leftover cake." She tucked her hands beneath her cheek in the same manner as Adelaide's angels from her ceramic phase. "Can I ask you a question?"

She was still whispering. Probably didn't need to. At least not for Layla's sake. Lately, the baby had been able to sleep through anything. Not even Adelaide's booming voice disturbed her anymore.

"What?"

"Why didn't you want to do the paternity test?"

Of all the things she might have asked, that was the last thing he expected.

She shifted again, and for half a moment, he thought maybe she was shifting closer. An inch. Even two.

But no. Nearly an entire mattress still lay between them.

"What purpose would it have served? Soon as I learned her name, I knew I was going to take her."

"But don't you want to *know*?"

"Have it confirmed that on top of everything, she cheated on me?"

"It might confirm that she didn't."

"And which is worse?"

Greer didn't respond to that. She turned her head slightly and he knew she was looking toward the crib. At Layla inside it. "Are you afraid it will change how you feel about her?"

"No."

"Are you lying?"

He thought about not answering. But there was enough distance between them just from the gulf of mattress. "Maybe." He wasn't proud of it. "She's mine. *Ours*," he corrected before she could. The adoption wasn't yet final, but it might as well have been. "I don't want what the DNA test says to matter, and that is more about Layla's mother than it is about Layla."

Greer was silent for so long, he thought maybe she was simply going to turn over once more. Turn her back to him. But she didn't. "Do you still love her?" she finally asked in her hushed voice.

"No. And you don't have to ask if I'm lying. The answer's no." On that his head was clear. He wished it were as clear when it came to the woman lying across from him.

"There might come a day when Layla wants to know."

He knew she meant about the DNA. "That's another matter." He'd given it some thought. "I already have a DNA profile. If it ever comes time to use it, it'll be waiting."

She pushed up onto her elbow, obviously surprised. Her hair had grown since they'd said "I do." It curled around her shoulders now. Softer. Lusher. It was almost as unfamiliar as his beard. "You do?"

"That last year I was bronc bustin'." He pushed up onto his elbow, too, and nodded his head toward the saddle behind him. "When I won that. I was served with a paternity suit. The girl was looking for a piece of my winnings. She thought I'd just let her take it. But I knew it was bull. I'd slept with her, but that baby wasn't mine. Test proved it."

"But Layla's different?"

"Layla had no one else. She was my wife's child."

She lowered herself back down off her elbow with her hands tucked beneath her chin. "So it was the right thing to do," she whispered.

He lay back down, too. Bunched the pillow beneath his neck. There was no need to answer, but he did. "Yes."

She exhaled softly. Leaving him wondering what she was thinking.

All he had to do was ask.

All he had to do was stretch his arm toward her. Offer his hand.

It wasn't too late to break the habit of two months of long nights. The great divide could be breached. Could be destroyed.

All it would take was a step.

He shifted and in the moonlight he could see the way she tensed.

He lifted his head, rebunched his pillow and closed his eyes.

Chapter Twelve

"Happy Thanksgiving!"

Greer smiled at her mom as she walked into the house where she'd grown up. Layla was walking at her side. Her steps were the sweet, plopping sort of steps that all toddlers took at first. She had one hand clasped in Greer's, the other in Ryder's. "Happy Thanksgiving. Smells great in here."

Despite the bare, frozen ground outside, the house was warm. Greer noticed Meredith's feet were typically bare as she hurried out of the kitchen and across the foyer to give them a hug. The tiny bells around her ankle jingled and Layla immediately crouched down, trying to catch them. "Bell," she said clearly.

"That's right, darling. Grandma's bells." Meredith scooped up the baby and nuzzled her nose. Layla's rosy-gold hair would probably never be as thick as Greer's mom's, but it might turn out to be just as curly. "Did you get it?"

Greer held up the envelope she was carrying. "It's official. I picked up our copy of the final adoption decree yesterday just before the recorder's office closed for the holiday." She pulled out the document and handed to her mother.

"Well." Meredith was teary as she paged through it before setting it on the entryway table. Her gaze shifted from Ryder to Greer. "Congratulations, Mommy."

If they only knew.

Greer blinked back the moisture in her own eyes. She glanced at Ryder and quickly looked away. She still hadn't told him that she was pregnant. She hadn't told anyone, except her doctor.

"It's a fabulous day," Adelaide practically shouted in greeting, coming inside behind them. She was carrying Brutus inside his expensive leather transport. "Meredith, I've decided I need to photograph you."

Her mom's eyebrows flew up. "Whatever for, Adelaide?"

"Just be glad she's out of her nude phase," Ryder commented drily.

He was still wearing the closely cut beard he'd started before Layla's birthday. Now the stubble was full-on beard. Still short. Still groomed. But his dimple was hidden.

"She'd still be a fine-looking nude," Carter said as he walked past. He was carrying two bottles of beer and handed one to Ryder.

"Dad!"

Meredith was smiling, though, and the look that passed between her parents was almost too intimate to bear.

"Pardon me while I go throw up," she muttered for effect as she walked around them and headed into the kitchen. Her mother's laughter followed her.

Fortunately, Greer's after-dinner morning sickness had faded. Unfortunately, she knew she was going to have to fess up sooner rather than later to everyone— her husband most particularly. So far, she hadn't even let her belt out a notch; her stomach was as flat as ever. The obstetrician she'd sneaked over to Weaver to see had needlessly reminded her it wasn't going to be long, though. When Maddie was carrying Liam, she'd been visibly pregnant at four months. Same with Ali, who was now six months along.

Greer could either admit the truth in the next few weeks, or she'd be showing it, if her sisters were anything to go by.

But that didn't mean she was going to worry about the fallout today.

Not when it was Thanksgiving. Not when she felt positively ravenous and there was a veritable feast for the taking.

Every inch of kitchen counter was covered with trays of food. She grazed along, plucking olives and candied pecans with equal enthusiasm. Within minutes, she could hear more people arriving. More family members. More friends. Even Vivian, despite the ongoing animosity between her and Greer's dad and uncle. And soon the house was bulging at the seams.

There was laughter and squabbling and it was all dear and familiar. And despite the secret she harbored, Greer felt herself relax. Even when she and Ryder were sitting so close to each other at the crowded table that the length of his strong thigh burned against hers, and they couldn't lift their forks without brushing against each other.

After the glorious feast, it was football. The options were to watch it on television or play it on the winter-dead front yard, where Archer was warming up, tossing the football around with their cousins and their brothers-in-law.

Ali intercepted the ball and looked toward her sisters and their cousins. "Guys against the girls? Cousins against cousins? What'd we do last year?"

"Cousins," Maddie reminded her with a laugh. "And it was a slaughter."

"Only because Seth turned out to be a ringer." Quinn was the eldest of their cousins and, like Archer, had only sisters. "I say Templetons against the spouses!"

His wife, Penny, rubbed her hands together and laughed. "I'm game for that. Means I've got nearly all the guys on my side!"

Ali looked toward Greer where she stood on the sidelines.

"Count me out," Greer said hastily. She had her hands tucked into her armpits and was stomping her feet to keep them warm. The snow in October had been a onetime occurrence and melted away, but the temperatures had hovered around freezing ever since. "It's too cold!"

"What a wuss you've become," Ali chided with a laugh. "Go find Maddie, then. And Ryder. It's his first Thanksgiving game, same as Grant and Linc." Her smile was devilish. "Gotta initiate these men of ours into the family just right." She tossed the ball from one bare hand to her other. "Rules are same as always. No tackle. Just touch."

"Think you've been touched enough," Archer called

to her. "Don't know what's bigger, that football or your belly."

Ali preened, tucking the ball under her arm as she framed her bulging bump against the Green Bay sweatshirt she wore in honor of their father's favorite team.

Then Grant, the guy responsible for her baby bump, came up behind her, poked the ball free, and the game was on in earnest even though the teams weren't entirely present and accounted for.

But that was always how it went.

The most basic rule of Templeton Family Football was for everyone to have fun. The second basic rule was for everyone to stay out of the hospital.

Greer was smiling as she went back inside. She found Maddie in the study, nursing Liam while she ate another piece of pumpkin pie with her fingers. Greer let her be and went to find Ryder. He wasn't in the family room, where her dad and uncle were sprawled out in front of the large-screen television. Nor in the kitchen, where her mom and aunt were still cleaning up the dishes.

"Have you seen Ryder?"

Meredith pointed toward the screened sunporch off the kitchen. Beyond that, Greer could see him and Adelaide sitting outside on the park-style bench in the middle of the flower garden. Right now, the only flowers in view were the brightly painted metal ones that were planted in the ground on long metal spikes. Layla was chasing after Brutus as he ran around the yard sniffing every blade of dead grass.

Greer smiled at the picture they all made and opened the kitchen door, going out to the sunporch. She peeled back a corner of the thick clear plastic that her dad hung up in the screened openings so that Meredith could enjoy the space whether it was cold or not. "Ry—"

"Why haven't you?" From all the way across the yard, Adelaide's voice wasn't quite megaphone-ish, but it was still audible.

Something about the tone made Greer swallow the rest of her husband's name.

"It's my decision, Adelaide." Ryder's voice was much quieter. Underlaid with steel.

Disquiet slithered down her spine. One part of her urged retreat. The other part refused. Morbid curiosity kept her pinned to the spot, prepared to witness disaster.

"If I wanted to give her the ring, I would have."

"It's a mistake, Ryder."

Oblivious to their audience, Ryder shoved off the filigreed bench. "Consider it one more mistake I've made when it comes to marriage." He whistled sharply. "Brutus. No." The dog had started digging near the base of a tree. His words had no effect on the little dog. "Adelaide—"

"Brutus, come." At least the pug sometimes listened to his mistress. The dog retreated and hopped up onto Adelaide's lap.

Ryder swung Layla up high and she laughed merrily, sinking her hands into his hair when he put her on his shoulders as he headed in Greer's direction.

Closer. Closer.

She exhaled, finally managing to drag her mired feet free as she hurried back into the house before he could see her.

She caught the glance her mother gave her as she scurried through the kitchen. "Cold out there," she said a little too loudly.

"Your dad's got a fire going—"

Greer waved her hand in acknowledgment as she

fairly skidded around the corner and escaped into the hallway by the front door.

She sucked in a breath, pressing her palm against her belly, knowing she had to keep it together even though inside she felt like she was unraveling.

Ryder never said what he didn't mean.

No matter what he'd said the day they got married, he obviously considered the business of *their* marriage as one more mistake.

"There you are." The man in her thoughts rounded the corner of the hallway and she froze. Layla was no longer on his shoulders. "Adelaide's getting pretty tired. I thought I'd run her back to the ranch."

"I can do it," she heard herself offer. "Layla's going to need her bath and bed soon, anyway. Your...your presence is wanted on the football field."

Even as she said the words, the front door flew open and Grant rushed in. His hair was windblown, his cheeks ruddy. "Tell me you played football."

Ryder's eyes narrowed slightly. "Running back, but not since high school. Helluva while ago."

Grant beckoned. "Better'n nothing." He looked at Greer. "I'm pretty sure we've been sandbagged. Archer—"

Any other day, Greer would have enjoyed the moment. "All-state quarterback."

"And my wife? What was she? All-state sneak?"

"Track. All three of us." She spread her hands, managing a smile even though it felt as brittle as her insides. "We grew up on football. Dad didn't care whether we were girls and more interested in horses and ballet or not."

"Should've known." Grant turned to Ryder. "We spouses lose this game and you know it's gonna follow us the rest of our married lives." He clapped his hand over Ryder's shoulder. "It's a matter of pride."

Ryder looked her way.

"It's a matter of pride," she parroted. "Vivian'll give you a ride home. I'm sure she'd be happy to detour to the ranch on her way back to Weaver."

"She'd be happy, but I've seen her drive." Still, he was smiling a little as he went out the door with Grant.

As if all was right.

As if it mattered to him that losing this first game might seal his fate for all their Thanksgiving football games to come.

She looked out at the two of them jogging out to join the scrimmage. She called after them. "Just remember, no tackling!" If her voice sounded thick, it didn't matter.

She was the only one who noticed.

She closed the door.

The adoption decree was sitting on the table against the opposite wall. She picked it up and slid it carefully back into its envelope.

Then she went to retrieve her daughter and Adelaide and her yapping dog, and they went home.

She was glad that all of her passengers fell asleep on the way.

It meant that they never saw the tears sliding silently down her cheeks.

"Here." Ali handed Greer a hanger. "Try that one."

Greer slid the red tunic off the hanger and pulled it over her head. It hung past her hips over her long black palazzo pants She turned sideways to view herself in the full-length mirror.

The small bulge of her abdomen was disguised among the ridges of the cable knit.

She exhaled. "Okay. This one'll work." She dashed her fingers through her hair. She hadn't had it cut in months. Not since she'd left the PD's office. With the help of her prenatal vitamins, it was growing even faster than usual. It was already down to her shoulder blades.

Unfortunately, her good hair days weren't making up for all that was wrong.

Ali just shook her head, looking decidedly Buddha-like as she sat cross-legged on the counter in Greer's bathroom at the Victorian. "You should've told him by now, Greer."

"I will." She lifted her chin as she peered into the mirror and applied some blush so that her face wouldn't look quite so washed out against the brilliant vermilion tunic. "Adelaide is leaving the day after Christmas. I'll tell him about the baby after she's gone. That's only four days from now."

Ali folded her hands atop her round belly. While Greer was hiding the changes in her body, her sister was delighting in showing off hers. At that moment, she wore a clingy white sweater and burgundy leggings that outlined every lush curve she'd developed.

And why not?

Ali and Grant were besotted with each other. She had no reason whatsoever to want to hide what that love had produced.

It was Greer's bad luck that she'd somehow fallen in love with her own husband. She knew when he learned about the baby, she wouldn't be just another mark in his column of marital mistakes. She—and their baby—would become his next "right thing to do."

And it was almost more than she could bear.

She didn't want to be his responsibility. And she

didn't want to be his business partner in this sterile marriage.

"I still can't believe Ryder hasn't noticed," Ali was saying. "Maybe you can hide that bump under thick sweaters and shapeless pajamas, but your boobs are another story. Is the guy blind?"

Greer tossed the blush in the vanity drawer and pulled out the mascara. They'd met at the Victorian—which was still undergoing renovations—to finish wrapping the Christmas gifts they'd been stashing away there, before heading over to Maddie and Linc's place. They were hosting a party for his employees at Swift Oil.

Grant was waiting downstairs in what was originally the living room, but was now a framework for a reception area and two offices.

Ryder hadn't come at all. He'd been moving the bulls to their new pasture that day and the task was taking longer than he'd planned.

Greer suspected he was just as relieved as she was that he had a valid reason to miss the party.

"He doesn't have to be blind when he doesn't look to begin with." Her voice was flat.

"I don't know." Her sister was unconvinced. "You guys still share a bed."

Greer cursed softly when she smudged her mascara. "A bed where he stays on his side and I stay on mine. And never the twain shall meet."

"Seems to me you could twain your way over to him if you wanted to. You did it before. That's how you got yourself in the family way."

Greer ignored that as she snatched a tissue from the box next to Ali's knee and dabbed away the mess she'd made.

It was too bad she couldn't dab away the mess of her marriage with a simple swipe.

"I should have never confided in you in the first place," she told her. Not about the rainstorm. Definitely not about the great divide that existed between her side of the bed and his.

"I think you needed to tell somebody," Ali said quietly. Her eyes were sympathetic. Ali was always easier to take when she was full of sass and vinegar than when she wasn't.

Greer cleared her throat as she balled up the tissue and tossed it in the trash. "You just happened to catch me in a bad moment."

"Sure. Sitting on the side of the road near Devil's Crossing bawling your eyes out. A little more than a bad moment in my view, but if that's what you want to call it."

She'd been on her way back from an appointment with her obstetrician in Weaver. She'd started blubbering near the spot where Ryder had rescued her that day in August, which now felt so long ago. She had pulled off the road before she ran off it. Ali, in her patrol car, had spotted her. And the entire story had come pouring out of Greer, along with her hiccupping sobs.

"Hormones." Finished with the mascara, Greer capped the tube and tossed it next to the blush, then shut the drawer with a slap. "I'm ready." She tugged her pants hem from beneath her high heel where it had caught.

"More like a broken heart," her sister was muttering under her breath as she unfolded her legs and slid off the counter. "I warned you that something like this would happen." She followed Greer through the bedroom and downstairs.

While Greer didn't appreciate the "I told you so," she did appreciate Ali's return to form.

"Finally," Grant said when he spotted them. "Sooner we get to this deal, sooner we can leave. We're already going to be late."

"Party animal," Ali joked. She lifted her hair when he helped her on with her coat.

Grant's smile was slanted. "I'll party your socks off when we get home."

"Well, now, that *is* a good reason to get moving along."

Greer grabbed her coat and headed out the door. She didn't begrudge her sister's happiness. Truly, she didn't. But her hormones were at work again, and she really didn't want to have to go back upstairs and redo her mascara again.

She paused on the front porch as she pulled on her coat. Every house down the hill from the Victorian was outlined in bright Christmas lights. There still hadn't been any snow since October, but it was pretty all the same.

At the ranch, Ryder had put up the Christmas tree he'd cut down himself. He'd left the decorating of it to Greer and Adelaide, though. The results had been interesting, to say the least. Adelaide's unusual eye might be highly regarded at MoMA, but Greer was probably a little too traditional to fully appreciate the strange paper clip–shaped objects juxtaposed with the popcorn garland she was used to.

She stifled a sigh, climbed behind the wheel of her car and pulled away from the curb. Ali and Grant were in their SUV behind her. She'd become accustomed to using Ryder's truck, because Layla's car seat fit so much better into it. But Layla was back at the ranch with Adelaide. Ryder's aunt had declined the invitation, saying that two parties within just a few days of each other were more than she was used to. And Vivian's annual fete was the night after next on Christmas Eve.

Greer wondered if Ryder would find an excuse to miss that party, too. If he did, it was going to be a little harder for her to explain away his absence. Her brother-in-law's company party was one thing. Vivian's, quite another.

As Grant had predicted, the party was in full swing when they arrived at the Swift mansion.

Greer left her coat in the foyer with the teenager who'd been hired to handle them and aimed straight for the bar. She longed for a cocktail, but made do with cranberry juice and lime. Then she filled a small plate with brownies that she knew Maddie had made from scratch and a half dozen other little morsels.

If anyone did notice her bump, they'd just figure it was from gorging herself.

Christmas music was playing in the background, loud enough to cover awkward silences as employees settled in but not so loud that it was annoying. If Vivian held true to form for *her* party, she'd have a live quartet. When it came to her grandmother, expense was no object. She imported the musicians from wherever she needed to.

Greer wandered through the house, smiling and greeting those she knew as if she wouldn't want to be anywhere else. There wasn't a corner or a banister that hadn't been decked with garland and holly, and the tree that stood in the curve of the staircase was covered in pretty red-and-gold ornaments. She stood admiring it, sipping her juice.

"Looks a little more like a normal tree than ours."

Greer jerked, splashing cranberry juice against her sweater. She blotted the spot with her cocktail napkin and stared at Ryder. "I thought you weren't coming." He was wearing an off-white henley with his jeans, and it just wasn't fair that he should look so good when she felt so bad.

"I thought I wasn't." He shrugged. "But I got the bulls settled finally and decided to come." His blue eyes roved over her face, but they didn't give a clue to what he was thinking. They might be married, but she felt like she knew him no better than she had when they'd first met.

He took the napkin from her, folded it over and pressed it against her sweater. "Would you have preferred I hadn't?"

Her heart felt like it was beating unevenly and she hoped he couldn't feel it, too. "Of course not," she managed smoothly. "You just surprised me, that's all." She tugged the napkin away from him and crumpled it. "There's a bar and an entire spread." She gestured with the hand holding her plate of food. "You should go help yourself. Maddie's brownies will go fast."

His gaze seemed to rest on her face again for a moment too long before he headed off.

She blamed the impression on her guilty conscience.

No matter how strained things were between them, she knew she needed to tell him about the baby.

This time, there'd be no room for him to doubt the paternity. It was the only positive note that she could think of in what felt like an intolerable situation.

"That you, Greer?"

She looked away from watching Ryder to see a familiar face. "Judge Manetti!"

He smiled. "It used to be Steve, remember? We're

not in my courtroom now." He leaned over and kissed her cheek. "When I saw you at first, I thought you were Maddie." He waved his fingers. "The hair's longer. You're looking good. Heard you got married. It must suit you."

She kept her smile in place. It took an effort, but she'd had a lot of practice. "I didn't know you were part of Swift Oil."

"My wife started there a few months ago." He looked around the room. "Always wondered what it was like inside this old mansion. Pretty impressive."

It was a little easier to smile at that. "I think so, too. How're things over at civic plaza?"

"Crazy. You know about—" He broke off and nodded. "Of course you know about it. Heard they've got a short list for the top spot in your old office."

From the corner of her eye, she saw Ryder returning. "Oh? Someone from Cheyenne, I suppose."

He shook his head. "You really don't know?"

"I really don't—ah. Keith Gowler? He's got the trial experience. I think he's pretty happy being in private practice, though. Means he can take cases for PD when he chooses."

"Not Keith. You."

She blinked, then shook her head. "No. Not possible. There're too many other attorneys in line ahead of me. And I quit, remember?"

Ryder stopped next to her and set his hand against the small of her back. She nearly spilled her drink again. "Friend of yours?"

She turned and set the cranberry juice on the edge of a stair tread at the level of her head, along with her still-full plate. "This is Judge Steve Manetti," she introduced. "Steve, my...my—"

"Ryder Wilson." He stuck out his hand. In comparison to Steve's, his was large. Square. A working man's hand.

She moistened her lips, reminding herself to keep a friendly smile in place. "Steve and I have known each other since elementary school."

"I was just telling your wife that she's on the short list for replacing Towers."

Ryder's brow furrowed. "She's opening her own practice."

"No kidding!" Steve gave her a surprised look. "I hadn't heard that. Not that you wouldn't be great at it, but I always thought you had the public defender's office running in your veins."

"Guess not," Ryder answered before she could. His fingers curled against her spine. "If you'll excuse us, there's someone we need to see."

The judge smiled as Ryder ushered her away, but Greer recognized the speculation in his gaze. As soon as they were out of earshot, though, she jerked away from Ryder. "I didn't know caveman was your style. What was that all about?"

"You're not going to work for the PD office again."

She felt her eyebrows shoot up her forehead. "First of all, I haven't heard this short-list rumor. And second of all, even if I had, I would think that's my decision, wouldn't you?"

"Working in that office ran you ragged. And that's when you were an expendable peon."

She stiffened. "Good to know you had such respect for the work I did there!"

His lips tightened. "That's not what I meant and you know it."

She propped her hands on her hips and angled her

head, looking up at him. "No, I don't know it. Why don't you explain it to me?"

"You really want to run that place? What about Layla? Months ago, you told me she was what was important and I believed you. Who's going to take care of *our daughter* when you're spending eighty hours a week defending drunk drivers and shoplifters?"

She gaped. "If that's the way you feel, why on earth did you ever insist on my opening my own practice? And don't go on about it being my *dream*! You think I'd be able to grow a practice from scratch with Layla on my hip 24/7?"

"You'd be calling your own shots," he said through his teeth. "Controlling your own schedule. You'd still have time to be a mother. Or now that you've finally got that right legally, has it lost the luster? You want to dump her off on someone else while you go off to do your own thing?"

She could barely form words for the fury building in her. She was literally seeing red. "You can regret marrying me." Her fingers curled into fists as she pushed past him. "But don't you *ever* compare me to Daisy."

He caught her arm. "Where are you going?"

She yanked free. "Away from you."

The foyer had become a traffic jam of people arriving at the party. Greer veered away and started up the staircase instead.

"Dammit, Greer." He was on her heel. As unconcerned as she was that they'd begun drawing attention. He closed his hand over her shoulder and she lost it.

Quite. Simply. Lost it.

She whirled on him. *"Don't touch me!"*

He swore and started to reach for her again.

That he kept doing so now infuriated her, when he

hadn't reached for her at all in the way that mattered most ever since they'd been married. She swatted his hands away, taking another step. But her heel caught again in the long hem of her pants and she stumbled. She steadied herself, though, grabbing the banister, and blindly took another step.

Right into the plate that she'd set on one of the treads. Her shoe slid through brownies and ranch dressing and she felt herself falling backward, arms flailing. Some part of her mind heard someone gasp. Another part saw Ryder's blue eyes as he tried to catch her.

And then she landed on her back and bounced against the banister so hard the Christmas tree next to the staircase rocked.

And then she saw no more.

Chapter Thirteen

"How is she?"

From the hard plastic chair he'd been camped in, Ryder lifted his head and looked from Meredith and Carter to Greer. She was lying asleep in the hospital bed. The white bandage on her forehead was partially hidden by her hair. The rest of the damage from her fall was harder to see. Harder to predict.

Which was why she was still lying in the hospital bed at all thirty-six hours later.

His jaw ached. "She hasn't lost the baby." *Yet.* He didn't say that part. But it felt like the word echoed around the small curtained-off area all the same.

He still was trying to resolve the fact that he'd learned she was carrying his child at the same time he'd learned she was very much in danger of losing it.

Now his wife was being carefully sedated while they waited.

Meredith's hand shook as she pressed it to her mouth.

"She's going to be all right," Carter told her, kissing her forehead. His arm was around her shoulder. "Nothing is going to happen to our girl on Christmas Eve."

Ryder wished he were so convinced.

Meredith finally lowered her hand. "Where's Layla?"

"Ali picked her up this morning." Much as he loved Adelaide, she wasn't up to the task of keeping up with an active one-year-old for more than a few hours at a time.

"That's good." Meredith nodded. She scooted past Ryder's legs until she reached the head of the bed, and then dropped a tender kiss on her daughter's forehead.

Ryder looked away, pinching the bridge of his nose.

"Have you gotten any sleep?" That was from Carter.

He shook his head. How could he sleep? Every time he closed his eyes, he saw Greer tumbling backward down those stairs.

"Maybe you should."

He shook his head.

"At least take a break."

He shook his head.

Carter stopped making suggestions. He sighed and squeezed Ryder's shoulder. "She's going to be all right, son. If the baby—" He broke off and cleared his throat. "I know you don't want to hear it. But there can be other babies."

But Ryder knew otherwise. This baby was their only chance. Greer was never going to forgive him no matter what happened. He was never going to forgive himself.

He propped his elbows on his knees again and stared at the floor.

Eventually, Meredith and Carter left with promises to

return later. They'd bring him something to eat. They'd bring him something to drink.

It didn't really matter to him.

The only thing that did was lying in a hospital bed.

Inevitably, more family members visited. Hayley. Archer. Cousins he knew. Cousins he didn't.

Nobody stayed long. There wasn't space for more than the one chair Ryder was occupying. And he was too selfish to give up his spot by Greer's bed, even to all the other people who loved her, too. Finally, he must have dozed off. But he jerked awake when he heard a baby cry.

But when he opened his eyes, there was no baby. Only his wife. Eyes still closed. Breath so faint that he had to stare hard at the pale blue–dotted gown covering her chest to be certain that it was moving.

"How is she?"

How many times had he heard the question? A dozen? Two? He focused on the petite woman standing inside the curtain. "Vivian? What're you doing here?"

"Checking on my granddaughter, of course." She slipped past him to peer closely at Greer. "You're a Templeton," she told her. "We're many things, but we're not weak." She kissed Greer's forehead, much like Meredith had, and straightened.

Her face seemed more lined. Wearier. He offered her the chair.

She took it and held her pocketbook on her lap with both hands. "I've spent so many days in my life at a hospital." She shook her head slightly and reached out to squeeze his hand. "It's Christmas Eve. Nothing's going to happen to our girl on Christmas Eve."

"That's what Carter said."

Her lips curved in a smile. Bittersweet. "He's like his father," she murmured.

Then it occurred to him. "Your party is tonight."

"It's on hold."

"Greer said you invited a hundred people."

She waved her fingers dismissively. "And they'll likely come when I reschedule. When you and Greer can both be there."

"I don't know if that's gonna happen," he admitted in a low voice.

She smiled gently. "I do." Then she pushed to her feet. "I've picked up Adelaide. She wanted me to see Greer first, but she's in the waiting room."

"That was nice of you, Vivian. Thank you."

"Don't get too sentimental on me. I have a selfish motivation, as well. She and Brutus will be coming home to stay with me. I convinced her to stay awhile." She reached up and patted his cheek. "And that's final, dear boy." Then she tugged on the hem of her nubby-looking pink suit and left.

Ryder moved back next to the bed. Greer's hand was cool when he picked it up. He pressed it to his mouth, warming it. He was still like that when he heard the curtain swish again.

Adelaide stood there.

He exhaled and lowered Greer's hand to the bed. Then he stood and let his aunt wrap her skinny, surprisingly strong arms around him. "You love her," she said in a whisper. He hadn't ever heard her speak so softly. "You need to tell her."

"How do you know I haven't?"

She pulled back and gave him a look out of those crazy made-up eyes of hers. "I've been living in the same house as the two of you for four months. How do you think I know?" Then she set a familiar-looking ring box in his hand.

He slid his jaw to one side. Then the other. "How'd you find it?"

Now she just looked droll. "You've always hidden your treasures in your sock drawer. Not very imaginative if I must say, and it was quite the nuisance getting past Layla's crib to get the drawer all the way open."

There was nothing to be amused about. Yet he still felt a faint smile lift his lips. Then he looked back at his wife. Lying in that bed.

And he closed his eyes.

"Ryder," Adelaide whispered. "Have faith."

"Faith hasn't gotten me very far before, Adelaide. You know that."

"You just weren't looking." She gestured toward the bed with her turquoise-laden hand. "What do you see when you look at her?"

My life.

"Tell her you love her. Give her your granny's ring. I know you said before that you were afraid to. Afraid she wouldn't want it. Wouldn't understand the treasure you were trying to give. This last thing that remains from your family." She squeezed his hand around the ring box. "And I'm telling you that she will." She went from squeezing his fingers to squeezing his jaw. "What do you *see* when you look at her, Ryder?"

His eyes burned. "My life."

She gave a great sigh and smiled. She pulled on his jaw until he lowered his head and she kissed his forehead, like she'd done about a million times before.

Then she, too, went back outside the curtain.

Ryder pushed open the ring box. The box alone was ancient. The filigreed diamond ring inside was from the

1920s. He slid it free from the fading blue velvet. It was so small it didn't fit over the tip of his finger.

He sat down beside the bed again. Slowly picked up Greer's hand. It was still cool. Too cool.

When they'd brought her to the hospital, they'd taken her jewelry. Her wedding band. Her earrings. Placed them in a plastic bag that they'd given to him. He wasn't sure where he'd even put it.

He slowly slid his grandmother's ring over Greer's wedding finger. He didn't expect it to fit. But it did. "With this ring," he whispered huskily.

"I thee wed." Her words were faint, her touch lighter than a whisper as she curled her fingers down over his.

His heart charged into his throat and he looked up at her face. Her eyes were barely open but a tear slid from the corner of her eye. "The baby..." Her lashes closed.

He leaned close and smoothed away that tear. "The baby's okay." His voice was rough. "You're okay. All you have to do is rest."

Her lashes lifted again. A little more this time. Her hand slowly rose. The back of her knuckles grazed his cheek. "You're crying. Just tell me the truth. The baby—"

"Is going to be okay."

Her eyes drifted closed again. "I should've told you." Another tear slid from her eye. "I'm so sorry I didn't tell you the truth."

"I should've seen." He cupped her head in his hand. "I should have seen all along. And you are the truth." He pressed his mouth against hers. "You're my truth. I just didn't let myself see it. You're my wife, Greer. For all the right reasons, you're my wife." He pulled in a shaky breath. "So just get better and come home with me and Layla. You can work any damn job you want. Just…don't give up on me. Don't give up on our family."

Her eyes opened again and she stared up at him. "I thought you gave up on me," she whispered.

"Not in this lifetime," he promised thickly. He pressed another shaking kiss to her lips, and her hand lifted, closing around his neck.

"Don't leave me."

He shook his head, but her eyes had closed again. He lowered the rail on the side of the bed. Carefully, gingerly, with the same caution he'd felt when he'd first taken Layla all those months ago, he moved her an inch. Two. Just enough that he could slide onto the edge of the hospital bed with her. It was crowded. He had to curl one arm awkwardly above her just to be sure that he wouldn't jostle her. Jostle their baby. But he managed.

"I love you, Greer."

She exhaled. Turned her head toward him. "Love… you…" Her fingers brushed his cheek. "No more great…divide."

A soft sound escaped him. "No more great divide," he promised. "Never again."

And then he closed his eyes, cradling his life against him.

And they both slept.

Epilogue

"Welcome home, Mrs. Wilson."

Greer smiled up at Ryder as he carried her across the threshold of their house. It was an interesting experience. He carried her. She carried Layla. "We could've walked, you know. The doctors said the baby was okay. So long as I don't try running a marathon, we're all good."

"I know." He shouldered the door closed behind him. "But then I wouldn't have this opportunity to impress my ladies with my manliness as we made the trek through the deep, freezing snow."

Greer pressed her cheek against his chest and looked at their daughter. "Daddy's very silly today. Two snowflakes. That's what we trekked through."

Layla's green eyes were bright. "Dadda!"

Ryder's dimple appeared. "Daddy's very happy today," he corrected. He carried the two of them right through the house and deposited them carefully on the couch. He peeled off his coat and pitched it aside, then sat down beside them, his fingers twining through Greer's. "It's Christmas Day and I've got the very best presents. Because Mommy's home."

"Mama!"

Greer went still. "Did she just—"

"She did. Who's Mama, Short-Stuff?"

"Mama." Layla patted Greer's cheek and pressed a wet kiss on it. Then she patted Ryder's face, kissing his clean-shaven jaw. "Dadda."

She clambered off Greer's lap and ran over to the oddly decorated Christmas tree. She started tearing into the wrapped presents beneath it. "Sus-suhs," she chanted.

"She's gonna demolish them all," Ryder commented.

"Probably." Greer slid her fingers through his and pulled his hand over the baby nestled inside her. "I wouldn't be too concerned. Most of them are hers, anyway. Between you and me and Adelaide, we might have gone a little overboard with the gifts."

"It's our first Christmas together. Overboard is expected."

"Now you sound like Vivian."

He grinned. "She rescheduled that party of hers for tomorrow night, you know. Just like that." He snapped his fingers.

"The advantages of outrageous wealth."

"Mama." Layla toddled back to the couch, her fists filled with the shreds of Christmas wrapping paper. She dropped it on Greer's lap.

"For me?"

Bright-eyed, Layla returned to the tree and started back in on the presents.

"We could go over to your parents', you know. Everyone's there. Hoping to see you."

She shook her head and wrapped her arms around his neck. "Maybe later. Right now…right now, everything I never even knew I wanted is right here."

His eyes smiled into hers. "Merry Christmas, Layla's mommy."

She smiled back. He thought he'd gotten the best gift. But she knew better. They'd all gotten the best gift. And she was going to treasure it for now and for always.

"Merry Christmas, Layla's daddy."

* * * * *

MILLS & BOON

Coming next month

THEIR CHRISTMAS MIRACLE
Barbara Wallace

'Can I get you lads something to drink?'

Thomas's breath caught. It happened every so often. He'd catch the hint of an inflection or the turn of the head, and his mind would trip up. This time, it was the waitress's sharp northern twang that sounded uncannily familiar. He looked up, expecting reality to slap him back to his senses the way it had with his cottage memories. Instead...

He dropped the phone.

What the...?

His eyes darted to Linus. His brother's pale expression mirrored how Thomas felt. Mouth agape, eyes wide. If Thomas had gone mad, then his brother had plunged down the rabbit hole with him. And, mad he had to be, he thought, looking back at the waitress.

How else to explain why he was staring at the face of his dead wife?

'Rosie?' The word came out a hoarse whisper; he could barely speak. Six months. Praying and searching. Mourning.

It couldn't be her.

Who else would have those brown eyes? Dark and rich, like liquid gemstones. Bee-stung lips. And there was the scar on the bridge of her nose. The one she always hated, and that he loved because it connected the smattering of freckles.

How….? When? A million questions swirled in his head, none of which mattered. Not when a miracle was standing in front of him.

'Rosie,' he said, wrapping her in his arms.

He moved to pull her closer, only for her to push him away.

He found himself staring into eyes full of confusion.

'Do I know you?' she asked.

Continue reading
THEIR CHRISTMAS MIRACLE
Barbara Wallace

Available next month
www.millsandboon.co.uk

COMING SOON!

We really hope you enjoyed reading this book. If you're looking for more romance, be sure to head to the shops when new books are available on

Thursday
1st November

To see which titles are coming soon, please visit
millsandboon.co.uk

LET'S TALK
Romance

For exclusive extracts, competitions
and special offers, find us online:

Want even more
ROMANCE?

Join our bookclub today!

**Visit millsandbook.co.uk/Bookclub
and save on brand new books.**

MILLS & BOON